HOW EVAN BROKE HIS HEAD AND OTHER SECRETS

ALSO BY GARTH STEIN

Raven Stole the Moon

HOW EVAN BROKE HIS HEAD AND OTHER SECRETS

a novel

GARTH STEIN

SOHO

Published by

Soho Press, Inc.

853 Broadway

New York, N.Y. 10003

Library of Congress Cataloging-in-Publication Data

Stein, Garth

How Evan broke his head and other secrets / Garth Stein.

p. cm.

ISBN 1-56947-390-0 (alk. paper)

1. Rock musicians—Fiction. 2. Fathers and sons—Fiction.

3. Teenage boys—Fiction. 4. Birthfathers—Fiction. 5. Epileptics—Fiction.

I. Title.

PS3569.T3655H69 2005

813'.54—dc22

2004059127

10 9 8 7 6 5 4 3 2 1

In Memory
Jeanette Saget
1919–2004

MAYBE A LITTLE reflection at this point in Evan's life isn't a bad thing. A gathering of mourners on a hill at a cemetery outside Walla Walla, a good five-hour drive from Seattle. A hot morning under an intense and brilliant sky. A dead girl in a box, suspended over a hole dug in the fertile soil. And Evan, watching from a distance like a father gazing through a nursery window at his newly born son, whose cries go unheard, untended, a helpless flail of tiny arms and legs and a little mouth that is open in silent scream, all of it safe from Evan's unsanitary touch.

He hikes up the hill and takes his place among the circle of attendees. They are all the same: pale complexions, downcast eyes; a wash of chalky faces. There are fewer than he'd hoped. Twenty at most. He'd been warned that the burial service would be small, reserved for family and the closest of friends. Still, he'd envisioned a pack into which he could fade. After all, Mormons tend to stick together; they like to travel in groups.

He shifts uncomfortably. He has nowhere to hide. They are looking at him. Not directly, not staring. They are sneaking peeks, stealing sideways glances from behind flapping paper fans. They have no idea who he is; they don't seem to care. A man speaks a few elegiac words that are swallowed by the breeze, tossed around and thrown over his shoulder for no one to hear.

Evan recognizes Tracy's mother and father. He remembers her brother, Brad, one of those high school peers who fell somewhere between friend and acquaintance. Around them stand several of Tracy's older siblings. He doesn't know them, couldn't recall their names if called upon to do so. Three or four or five brothers and sisters who were already grown and were never around when Tracy was a teenager; shards of a fractured family. And there is another important family member present: Tracy's son.

Evan doesn't recognize Dean, but he knows well enough who he is. A young man, fourteen-years-old, who, like Evan, stands out from the crowd, his dark hair hacked short, his face alert and defensive.

Dean looks up and meets Evan's eyes. He looks at Evan without suspicion. But why would he suspect? What could he think, other than that Evan was another from Grandpa's congregation, come late for the passing of Tracy Smith? But he is curious about something, for he doesn't look away.

Tracy's father places his arm around Dean's shoulders, a gesture of comfort. Dean shifts slightly, stiffens a little bit, not dramatically, but enough to indicate that the gesture is not welcome. Enough so that Tracy's father withdraws his arm.

And in an instant, Evan knows Dean. He knows what is going on. For Dean to have to witness his mother's burial is bad enough, but for him to be so uncomfortable with his fellow grievers that he cannot grieve himself is crushing. Evan remembers his own grandfather's funeral, watching the people cry. He felt so separate from them. They may have been friends with his grandfather for a long time, but they didn't really know him. Not like Evan did. And so he couldn't join them. He could only get through it and then grieve later, when he was alone, when it really mattered, as, he knows, Dean will grieve for his mother later. Until then, Dean stands, stoically, guarded, comforting no one, allowing no one to comfort him.

Evan's mind drifts from the scene; the tentacles of his attention are caught by the breeze and gently sway toward the land around him. He hears the combines grinding away in the distance, whirling their razor-sharp blades as fast as they can, slicing at the dry stalks of winter wheat. It is mid-July and the harvest season is upon Walla Walla. He can feel the trucks, heavy on the highway; he can envision the people in town walking with a bounce to their step. He knows that this is what they wait for every year, to gather up the fruit of the earth and revel in its bounty. We are in the days of plenty. The fruits and vegetables and grains allow us to grow and prosper. All partake of the cornucopia. Save for Tracy Smith, whose body, now released from its earthly commitment, is being returned to the soil from which it sprang.

Evan snaps himself back into the frame; he attends to what is before him, the burial of his ex-girlfriend. He scrapes his teeth against his lower lip, scratching an itch that is not really there but somewhere in his brain. A seizure? Is one coming? No, no. The heat, the long drive. It's fatigue, not a seizure. It had better not be a seizure. Not here. It would be too ironic for him to come down with a case of the falling sickness at Tracy's funeral when he was trying to be as inconspicuous as possible. It would be almost funny to have twenty or more Mormons stand over his convulsing limbs, questioning in breathless voices: *Who is he? What is he doing? Why is he here?*

The service ends. Mourners amble back to their cars. Evan wonders what is next for him. He has seen the remains of Tracy properly attended to, and he has seen Dean, his child, now grown. What else is there to do but to return to his car and make the five-hour drive back to Seattle, take his place again in his life and wonder, as he always has, what was to become of Dean, the Boy Wonder, whom Evan has never met.

"You came. I'm shocked."

Evan turns. Tracy's brother, Brad, stands directly in front of him, not more than two feet away.

"You're the one who—" Evan starts.

"Called you," Brad finishes for him. "I know I did. My father would kill me if he knew. Don't tell him."

"I won't."

"You must feel guilty as hell," Brad says, and as he says it, he sticks out a long finger and tries to jab Evan in the chest; Evan, quickness being one of his assets, takes a step back and out of range.

"Where's Dean's father?" Evan asks.

"I'm looking at him, stupid," Brad replies.

"His *step*father," Evan clarifies.

Brad laughs a quick snort. "How have you been, Evan?"

Evan shrugs. He was kind of hoping for a real answer.

"I heard that song of yours on the radio," Brad continues. "About ten years ago."

"Eleven."

"I never could find the album, though. It must not have been that big."

"It was big enough," Evan says, an edge creeping into his voice.

"Really? Ever think of sharing any of the money you made with Tracy and Dean?"

But she was the one who abandoned him, remember. He had wanted to keep the baby. She was the one who left Seattle. She was the one who stole away in the middle of the night.

"I gotta go, man," Brad says, "my diplomatic immunity is about to wear off."

"What does that mean?"

"It means what it means. What do *you* think it means. I'll see you, man. Good luck."

Brad starts to leave.

"Give me your number," Evan says quickly. "I'll give you a call. I want to know what's going on with you."

"Nah," Brad grins, "you know everything you need to know about me, Evan. I'm just like you, man, still fighting the good fight, you know?"

And he's gone. All around, black-clad bodies murmur down the hill toward their cars.

Evan spies Tracy's mother, Ellen, who is being consoled by another woman. His first impression is that she looks old. When Evan first met her, he was only fourteen and she—but a child herself when

Tracy was born—was thirty-six. That was seventeen years ago. Evan is now thirty-one, Ellen fifty-three. And while the seventeen years has hardly changed Evan—he is still boyish and almost beardless—those same years have taken a different toll on Ellen Smith. Her face is etched with deep wrinkles. Her hair is dull brown with streaks of gray. Her blue eyes are pale.

"Hello, Mrs. Smith," he calls out, approaching the women. Ellen's friend excuses herself; Ellen looks toward Evan blankly. "It's Evan," he says. "Wallace."

She doesn't respond. Why would she? She hated him, back when he and Tracy were high school sweethearts. She and her thickly muscled husband, Frank. They both hated him. So what should he say to her now? Should he accuse her, and by accusing her make it clear that he feels the magnitude of her actions?

"Evan?" she asks, the mist clearing.

"I'm so sorry about Tracy."

"Yes."

"How is Dean?" he asks.

"Oh! Dean's fine."

Evan nods. "He looks good. Healthy."

"He is," Ellen smiles painfully. "What are you doing here?"

Evan shifts his weight from one foot to the other.

"I'd like to meet him," he says.

Ellen looks quickly over her shoulder and down the hill to where people are climbing into their hot cars and driving off. A small group lingers near two black limousines. Frank is among them.

"I don't believe that would be in his best interest. Not now, anyway."

Evan cocks his head, unsure how to take her response. But it doesn't matter. Before he can think about it long, his request is granted. Without warning, Dean is standing beside Ellen as if Evan had made a wish.

Dean. The Boy Wonder. So close now, so near, Evan feels his pulse quicken. What is it about Dean? His presence is almost intoxicating. His long, thin limbs draped in a black suit, his collar too large for his neck, his navy-blue tie knotted in an old-fashioned style quite beyond Evan's sartorial expertise. So casually he hangs his arm around Ellen's neck and rests his head on her shoulder, turning slightly toward Evan, his green eyes blaring out from their sockets, screaming at Evan that I am yours, yes, I am *of* you, yes I am.

"I'm hot, Grandma," the young man complains.

"This is an old friend of your mother's," Ellen says deliberately, almost forcing herself to say it, pushing through her misgivings. "He's come from Seattle to pay his respects."

Dean unhooks his arm and offers his hand to Evan, which Evan takes, awed, in a way, by such self-control, such a display of courtesy in the face of such real grief.

"I'm terribly sorry about your mother," Evan mumbles. He's caught off guard. The new sensation of Dean's hand in his own, the feelings rushing through his body, his nerves sending confused signals to his brain, that not only is he holding a hand, shaking a hand, but that it is a hand that belongs to his own flesh and blood, his own son.

"Thank you," Dean responds evenly.

Evan doesn't let go; he holds on and they stay like that, hand-in-hand, for several moments.

"We have to go, Evan," Ellen breaks in. "The reception."

Again she looks down toward Frank, who is in the parking lot staring up at them with piercing eyes. Evan has always been afraid of Frank Smith, a stocky man who wears his gray hair tightly shorn. His neck is thick with ropes of muscles that disappear into the collar of his shirt. His nose was flattened—Tracy once told Evan—from years of boxing while in the Marines. He has little hands that he clenches into fists of calloused and scarred flesh that appear to be made of clay. He speaks not like an average man, but like a little Moses, a man of God, a man who carries lightning in his arms and breathes the flames of Righteousness. He is not one to be challenged.

Evan releases Dean's hand; Ellen nudges Dean to start down the hill, which he does. She does not immediately follow.

"Please don't interfere," she whispers at Evan. "Not after all this time."

"But—"

"Please, Evan. I don't know why you're here. But please don't interfere. Not after all this time."

She turns and hurries after Dean, catches him, and then ushers him to the bottom of the hill. When they arrive, Frank directs them into one of the limousines, waves his arm to those still standing by, who obediently climb into their vehicles, and they all drive off, leaving Evan alone at Tracy's grave.

Evan cannot move. He stands silent for several minutes, long after the last black car has left. What happened? He was so young when it all occurred. A sperm and an egg met, cells began to multiply and divide, and a child was born. But then what? What became of Evan? What became of his son? It's all so murky, the circumstances so obscure that he doesn't even remember how the story goes, or whose story he really believes. The truth belongs to he who tells it, so what good is it, anyway?

He starts back down the hill toward his car. His steps fall heavily against the hard-packed dirt path, and he raises his eyes to the surrounding land; the harvesting machines continue to work over the amber hills, threshing the wheat that has grown all spring, plowing an ever-widening swath of brown through the endless golden fields.

E VAN CRUISES SLOWLY by Frank Smith's house, which he finds on an annoyingly pleasant, shady block among other modest houses with perfectly pruned lawns, about a half mile off of Main Street, Walla Walla. The house is a characterless late-fifties ranch-style, most likely outfitted with all the conveniences one would expect of generic Middle America: cable TV, a dishwasher, a microwave oven, and a basement full of canned goods in the event the civilized world were to end tomorrow and they were forced to fend for themselves for a year until the Lord came down to save them.

The street is lined with cars, evidence that the reception is at the Smith house and not at some undisclosed neutral location. He circles around and drives by again. He can see people inside, standing by the window, drinking punch and holding plates of food. Proof positive. *Now* what is he supposed to do? Crash the party? Not likely. As much as he would love a crustless egg-salad sandwich and a warm bottle of Perrier, he generally draws the line at crashing funeral banquets.

He pulls around the corner and parks. He'll wait it out. He rolls down the windows, hoping to catch a breeze, reclines his seat, and closes his eyes. He'll rest a while, then try again.

THEY USUALLY SPENT part of the night together. He preferred going to her house, based on some youthful notion that it would be better to be caught by her father and die a quick death from a bullet wound than it would to be caught by his own parents and die a slow death by guilt. He also preferred her house because it was darker and thicker, almost warrenlike in its depth, and completely different from his parents' sterile, brittle, strained home.

He sneaked out of his house when all was dark and walked fifteen minutes down unlit streets until he got to hers. He climbed in her window. They fooled around, fumbled with each other, quick sessions that were silent and largely unappreciated. Sex for sex's sake. Sex because they could. They could, and they did. *Fucking for sport*, she told him. Funny.

Afterwards, Tracy indulged in contraband. A pint of Seagram's perhaps. Some Marlboros. Maybe some pot. Evan never joined in. He knew what it was like to be out of control, and didn't seek it out voluntarily. It would be many years before he would realize the medicinal qualities of marijuana and look back on that time as a missed opportunity. But there had been so many missed opportunities; what was one more?

She told him things. She told him what she wanted out of life. He learned that her dream house was one with a white picket fence and a green, green lawn. Her dream vocation was to be a writer. Her dream family was two boys, a girl, and a dog. Her dream man was—

I'm late.

She was a half a head shorter than he was. Her hair was long, curly, thick and ash-blond. She sometimes referred to herself as Cousin It.

How late?

Late enough.

A full year older, she was a senior, he a junior. She was one of the smartest people he knew. Intuitively smart, not like his father or his brother, who were book-smart. He once overheard a teacher call her "gifted," and it surprised him—not that she would be gifted, but that she had never mentioned it to him.

Are you sure? Mr. Hill in Health said that some girls are too thin— girls who do gymnastics—

I took a test.

She told him once—her dream man was tall. He kept his hair cut short. It was black hair, very neat. She watched him shave every morning; his face was soft. His breath smelled like autumn leaves. He stood very straight, but not stiffly, and he wore dark suits. When he came home from work he opened the white gate and stepped sweetly up the flagstones to the stoop. He played with his children, fed the dog, drove the car, fixed the sink, and mowed the lawn. Evan was disappointed; her dream man wasn't him. He wondered why she told him this, but he knew it was to keep him honest, to make sure he understood that his was a temporary harbor.

I'm pregnant.

They were an old couple at age seventeen, having dated since his freshman year. He loved Tracy. But he knew that he loved her more than she loved him.

Marry me.

Very funny, Evan.

Marry me.

Evan, seriously—

Yes, seriously. There was a child involved now. They could raise a child together. And that would be some great kid. Some great family, a family of love, Evan's music and Tracy's gift and the baby. He would be a cool kid, asking questions about everything he saw, playing ball, learning to read, to climb trees. Evan suddenly felt so tremendously happy thinking about the future. They would live in a little house, they would raise their kids, and most of all, they would be happy. They would be so happy.

Evan, Tracy said forcefully, *I got accepted to Reed.*

Reed College. That's where the gifted people go.

I got accepted.

Of course she did. They would be fools not to accept her.

That's great.

A long pause.

I'm not going to college with a baby.

He studied her face at length and knew that she was right. She couldn't go to college with a baby. Of course not. And how would it work, anyway? How could Evan make *his* end of it work? He would go to his parents, lay himself at their feet, confess his sins, more sins than they could possibly have guessed. They would be disappointed in him. They would feel let down by him again. His father would accuse him of having done it on purpose. He would say something like, *You sure know how to stick it to us, don't you, Evan?* Or he would look out at Evan from under his dark brow and say, *I suppose when you don't have to clean up after yourself, you don't care how big a mess you make, isn't that right, Evan?*

How could Evan disappoint them again? First the accident, a family-shattering event. Now this. A child at seventeen? How could he let them down again?

I have money, he said. *I can give you money.*

She didn't answer.

It's the best thing, right?

Again, she didn't respond.

It's the best thing, he said again, trying to convince himself that it was.

Is it what you want? she asked.

It wasn't what he wanted, no. Not at all.

Yes.

Are you sure?

Yes, he said. *I'll pay for it. It's what I want.*

A LASER BURNS his eyes. He brings a hand to his face and squints through his fingers. The reflection of the late afternoon sun off a car mirror. A burgundy minivan pulls out from a driveway. What time is it? His watch says five. That was some nap. He's starving, but otherwise he feels good, refreshed.

He pulls around the corner and finds the street almost completely deserted. That's good. That means the party's over. He parks across the street and surveils the house for a few minutes. It's quiet.

Finally, after what he thinks is long enough, and eager to get on with it, Evan pops open the door to his car and steps out into the newly energized air around Walla Walla.

Yes, that's right. Something electric. About the situation and about the air. Ionized. Tingly. For the instant Evan climbs out of his car, the front door of the Smith house opens and out comes Dean. He's changed out of his black suit and into something a little less formal. He's carrying an old push broom, and he begins to sweep the porch. Doing chores, even on the day of his mother's funeral. Give the kid a break already. Still, it offers Evan the perfect opportunity.

Without thinking he swoops across the street and up the walk, hops the two steps onto the porch. He doesn't want to think too much about it, about what he will say or how he will act. He just wants to do it. He has his feeling he can rely on. The electric feeling, the tingling, like something good is bound to come of it all. It quashes all of his natural inhibitions. It allows him to bound into a stranger's life. Bound right in and change it all around.

"Dean," Evan says, arriving on the porch, looking at the thin boy, fourteen, but boyish, his chopped-salad hair, his pimples, his magnetic eyes that are like emeralds, glowing across the porch at Evan. His small hands and pink fingers, chewed fingernails, gripping the old shop broom. Feeling comfortable in his old clothes, ripped jeans cut off just above the knee, washed out black T-shirt with a Nine Inch Nails logo on it, skateboard sneakers without socks, chicken legs, knobby knees, not really comfortable in his body yet. It occurs to Evan that when he was this boy's age, he was having sex. He was putting his erect penis into a girl. But, oh, how he would try to prevent this boy from doing the same, if he were this boy's father. Do what I say, not what I do. Be what I should have been, not what I am.

Dean looks up at Evan, waiting for an introduction of some kind. Any kind. And Evan starts to give it. But it never finds its way out of Evan's mouth. God damn. This isn't stage fright. This isn't being overcome with emotions. This is a seizure.

Makes sense. The sense it makes is too clear now. A little baby seizure, a so-called simple partial, is flipping its way though the railway that is Evan's brain, hitting switches in the wrong direction, firing synapses out of turn and, all-in-all, causing a veritable cacophony of electrical impulses that freezes Evan in his tracks, nails his tongue to the roof of his mouth, and prevents him from speaking to his son. His own son, now not more than ten feet away.

"You're a friend of my mother's," Dean says, puzzled by Evan's lack of presentation.

Evan stands before Dean, shaking his head. The only thing he can do. Shake his head, frustrated, angry at the implacable little fucker of a seizure rendering him mute.

"I met you at my mom's funeral."

The crying shame of it all. Being where you want to be and not being able to take advantage of it. Evan holds his finger to his lips. *Shhh.* A gesture of quiet. *Shhh.* It will all pass. He holds his finger to his lips and hopes that Dean will understand. No questions now. No talking. It will pass. It's a baby. A simple partial seizure. Really very elementary when you understand the pathology of it. It begins with a misfire.

"Why are you here?" Dean asks. Evan shakes his head. "What do you want?" *Shhh.* "Who are you?" *No.* "Grandma."

No. Not grandma. *No.* It's going. The electrical firestorm. The giddy feeling that Evan had attributed to the excitement of the moment had actually been an aura preceding a seizure. He should have known. He should have sensed it. So easy. A lab rat would have known. *There will be no cheese for you!*

"Grandma!"

Ellen appears. It's almost gone. Bad timing.

"Go inside, Dean," Ellen says sharply. She walks toward Evan. "What are you doing here?"

Finger to the lips. *Shhh.* It's okay. Really. It isn't contagious. It's called epilepsy.

"Frank's sleeping," Ellen says. "You don't have to worry about him waking up, he took a pill."

That's not it.

"How did you know?" she demands. "Was it Brad?"

Evan nods. Yes, yes, it was Brad. Brad told him everything.

She allows herself a burst of rueful laughter, which seems to expel some of the anger from her system and soften her demeanor a bit. She runs her hand up her forehead. It brushes against her stiff hair. It's been styled. Not like when she was young and Evan would see her around Tracy's house, back in high school. She smoked back then for one thing, and drank. White-trash Mormon. Now she's reformed.

"He looks like you," she says rather sadly.

The words are almost free, almost turned loose by the brain. Evan strains. He tries to speak. *"Gaaa,"* is all that comes out.

Ellen looks at Evan strangely, but she ignores his sound. She's obviously wrestling with demons of her own. Her glance darts from Evan to the door and back.

"I think you—" She stops, squeezes her eyes closed, composes herself. "You haven't come to take him away, have you?"

He shakes his head. No, no. Not that.

"Because I don't know what I'd do if . . . I can't lose him again."

Again? Lose him again? What does *that* mean?

She takes a deep breath and resigns herself to something.

"Please don't make trouble, Evan," she says. "Tell him you're a friend of Tracy's, all right? Tell him you and she were very close. But—Please. Don't take him away from me."

She disappears into the house. A moment, then Dean emerges.

"Who are you?" Dean asks.

Evan's ready. It's gone. He knows he can talk if he wants to. But his confidence is understandably low. He needs a few more seconds to get things together. He motions for Dean to follow. Dean does. Evan leads him to his car, a place where he feels safe, where they are both protected. He gestures for Dean to get in; he does. They sit for a moment.

"Who are you?" Dean asks again.

Evan turns to him. The tip of his tongue.

"I'm getting out if you don't tell me who you are."

Evan closes his eyes. It's right there. The tip of his tongue.

"I'm your father," he says softly, amazed, himself, that anything came out.

A moment of shock flashes across Dean's face. But only a moment. Then a half-smile.

"Where are we going?" he asks.

Where are they going? He hadn't thought they were going anywhere.

Dean snaps on his seat belt and looks forward.

Evan, startled, mimics Dean's movements. He starts the car. Evidently they're going somewhere. He shifts into first and pulls away from the curb. But *where*? He laughs to himself. He doesn't know.

H E HAS HALF a mind to keep on driving. Just go, man. Drive all the way home to Seattle. Beyond Seattle. To Canada. To Japan. China. Get a rice paddy and live off the earth for the rest of his life. Raise his son to be a peaceable man, a leader of the free world, a respectable man whom people will want to follow.

They don't speak as they leave town. Evan takes quick stock of his brain state and determines that he's okay. Having a small seizure doesn't mean a big one is coming, though it doesn't entirely preclude the possibility. The good news is that a big one is always preceded by an aura—a bit of a warning sign—so he'd have time to pull over. It's all about risk management.

Evan glances over at Dean and wonders what he's thinking. What on earth could be going through this boy's mind? He has just met his absentee father. Is there resentment? Hatred? Or just relief that he has a father at all and that he wasn't spawned from some kind of weird laboratory experiment, a fatherless child, the cloned replica of FDR or something, merely DNA scraped from the polio-withered big toe of the great orator, injected into an unsuspecting egg and implanted into the waiting wall of his mother's womb.

And still they don't speak.

Evan doesn't know where he's going, so he heads west. He saw a sign for the Whitman Memorial on his way into town, and thinks that might be the ticket. He vaguely remembers the Whitmans from his ninth-grade history class. Missionary martyrs. Maybe if he takes Dean to the Whitman Memorial, they will find some kind of greater truth. Maybe they will both be better able to understand their unique situation.

They drive into the parking lot and Evan stops the car. He glances at Dean who seems unimpressed by the location. Like he was expecting a water-slide park or something. Evan opens his door. When he sees that Dean isn't getting out with him, he sits back in his seat. This wasn't a good idea, he thinks. Say something. Do something.

He's still feeling sluggish from the seizure. He can talk okay. It's just that the link between his brain and his tongue is a little scrambled. He may think to say one thing, but something else might come out of his mouth. It happens. Best to avoid dialogue at this point. He reaches over and touches the scruff of Dean's neck. A fatherly gesture. Dean pulls away instinctively, but tries not to make it look obvious.

"I thought we could take a walk together," Evan says. It works. That was just what he was thinking and then he said it.

Dean doesn't move. He has no intention of taking a walk.

"Got a cigarette?" he asks.

"You shouldn't smoke," Evan responds without thinking. Ah. Unconscious speech. Everything is in order.

"You're a natural."

"A natural what?"

"A natural father."

Evan nods. They sit silently for a minute, neither of them budging. And then Dean evidently decides something.

"Okay," he says with a snort. "I'll play."

He climbs out of the car and walks toward the park entrance. Evan follows. He pays their admission and they enter the Visitor Center, a dark room boasting intricate dioramas under plastic domes, vast wall hangings detailing the history of Marcus and Narcissa Whitman and their tribe of Presbyterian missionaries, and a massive HVAC system blasting visitors with about a million BTUs of frigid air.

Evan is amazed at how easy it all is. They stroll through the exhibit at a leisurely pace, pausing at each display to read the information cards. They take their cues from each other silently, exchanging glances, moving when the other moves, pausing when the other pauses.

They learn things together. Things like that the Whitmans arrived at this very site in 1836 and built their mission. That they made friends with the Indians in the area. That they called for more missionaries. That they converted the Indians, and that the Indians took to conversion for a time, until the measles nearly killed them off. When the Whitmans' God failed to end the plague, the Indians decided enough was enough and massacred all the missionaries, including poor Narcissa Whitman, who was with child.

"Know your audience," Evan says. "With some Indians it's put up or shut up."

"Huh," Dean says, with a hint of irony. "Interesting."

They continue their game out the rear door of the building and along the path that leads to the hill atop which the Whitman Memorial obelisk stands. Silently, easily, they hike the steep hill together, reaching the summit as if it is some symbolic hurdle they have vaulted together. The light from the sun is golden. The shadows of the wheat are long, and large-winged black birds hover over the fields, searching for prey. Evan feels that he has chosen a magical moment to reunite with his son. He feels the energy of the spirits around him.

"This hill is where the Whitman missionaries were killed," Evan says.

"No," Dean scoffs, "actually, this hill is where the memorial is. They thought it would look nicer if they put the memorial on a hill. The missionaries were killed down there."

He points to a small pond to the southwest.

"You've been here before?" Evan asks.

"Yeah. My mom used to bring me."

My mom . . .

Suddenly the magic is lost. Suddenly Evan feels like he's in over his head. They're playing father-and-son like they've done it before. They're playing make-believe. But none of it is true. The truth is that they are total strangers with no shared experiences, no mutual references, and only one thing in common—Tracy—and she's dead.

He knows he's supposed to say things, but he doesn't know what. Desperately, he looks out to the land, hoping for something to divert Dean's attention. He could continue his conversational evasion, create more distractions, talk about the birds, for instance—hawks, or whatever they are—he could ask Dean what he thinks they're eating—shrews? gophers? voles?

"Okay," Dean says, finally. "We're here. Let's hear it."

"Well, uh . . ." Evan stumbles. He tacks on a chuckle. "Boy, this is awkward."

Dean refuses to acknowledge the awkwardness of it.

"Yeah?" he asks dispassionately. "You said you wanted to talk to me. So talk."

"Well, let's see. I'm not sure how to start," Evan admits.

"Are you kidding?" Dean laughs bitterly. "I'll tell you how to start. Start by telling me you love me. Tell me you missed me all these years. Tell me it's good to see me, that I look just like my mother. Give me a hug and tell me it's good to hold me. Come on, *Dad.* You know the routine. You've seen it on TV. You want to try this again in a couple of days? You could watch some Oprah tapes, study up. She does this kind of thing all the time. You'll pick it up fast."

Evan is rattled by this speech. It sounds remarkably practiced, like Dean's been waiting for this very moment his entire life, rehearsing in front of a mirror for the day he will see his father for the first time.

"That's not what I—" he starts. That's not what he . . . *what?* That's not what he wants to say? That's not true. It *is* what he wants to say. It's not what he expected Dean to act like? What *did* he expect? He must have expected something. After all, he drove all the way across the state for this very moment. It certainly would have been easier to not show up at Tracy's funeral, avoid this scene entirely, treat it like a surgeon might treat a bullet that is lodged next to the heart. Leave it alone. But on some level he knows the simple ineluctability of it: *this trip includes this conversation.* At some point he had to have acknowledged the truth to himself. So why, then, is he unprepared for it?

"I want to start by apologizing," he says.

"Apologizing? For what?"

For all of it. For everything since the beginning of time.

"For everything."

"For everything," Dean repeats. "You're sorry for everything."

"I am."

"You didn't mean any harm?"

No, but—it occurs to him that he and Dean are talking about two different things. Evan's sorry that Tracy ran off; Dean thinks he's sorry because *he* ran off. What does Dean actually know? What did Tracy tell him? What does he think?

"Okay, *Dad*," Dean says. "You're sorry. Sure. I'll buy that. Apology accepted. You're forgiven. Water under the bridge. You're free and clear. Feel better?"

No. He doesn't want to be forgiven. He's sorry that it happened; he's not sorry that he did something wrong.

"So if that's all you came for," Dean continues, "maybe you should take me home. I mean, I understand that when my mom died you probably figured I needed a parent figure, so you felt some kind of obligation to come here, but I'm okay, really. I'll be fine. Don't worry yourself."

"But I want to—"

"Well then you should have a long time ago, right?"

Evan doesn't answer. *But I want to explain—*

"Then you should have a long time ago, right, *Dad*?"

"I wish you'd stop calling me that. My name is Evan."

"Okay, *Evan*, where have you been all my life?"

Evan shakes his head. These are questions that can't be answered so easily.

"Naaaaaa!" Dean makes the sound of a game-show horn blaring. "Sorry, *Evan,* that's not a good enough answer! But we have some nice consolation prizes so you won't go home empty-handed."

Dean turns to go.

"I know I deserve all of this," Evan says as Dean walks away.

Dean suddenly stops.

"All of what?"

"Everything. Your anger. Your frustration."

"My anger? No, Evan, wrong again. You know what you deserve? You deserve to be locked in a room with Frank, that's what you deserve. Frank would teach you a thing or two about forgiveness. I'd pay money to see that."

"I'm sorry," Evan says. "I wish I had time to explain it all, to make you see . . ."

"Great."

"I wish I could tell you all the things I know. I'm sorry."

"Big deal!" Dean shouts, his face tight, shaking with rage. "You're sorry. Big deal! I think it's real nice that you came to see me. You brought me to this nice scenic place, we said hello. You got some things off your chest. You got to apologize to me. I accepted your apology. And maybe all this made you feel better, Evan. But you know how much it means to me?"

Evan doesn't answer.

"It means exactly dick shit."

Dean stalks away.

BY THE TIME Evan reaches the bottom of the hill, he feels like there's an emergency. His brain is firing like crazy. He'd had that seizure earlier, on the porch. A little one, but a seizure nonetheless. And now. A space oddity. Strange sounds in his head, strange feelings. He doesn't like it. He needs some pot.

Dean is in the car already, in the passenger seat, staring straight ahead. Evan opens the driver's side door.

"I need to go to the men's room, then I'll take you home," he says. He feels like his words are slurring. A telltale sign. Tongue thickness is always a precursor.

He grabs his bag and closes the door. The restroom is in the main building, but, thankfully, it's not really inside. The door is on an outer wall. Evan goes in. It's a park bathroom. Cinder block walls, electric hand-dryers. Evan stuffs himself into a stall. He sits. He takes out his pipe—the one-hitter, designed for times like this—and his weed. At this point there's a certain urgency to it all. He feels things that he doesn't want to feel. Twitches. He's having trouble swallowing. His tongue won't move on its own. He's got a big one coming. If only he's in time.

He smokes. Immediately he feels it. Smoke. Hot, sweet-tasting, it creeps down his throat like the fingers of some insidious monster, thin, wispy tendrils that reach into his chest, a forked tongue licking inside his bronchial tubes, depositing its medicine deep into the recesses of his lungs.

He feels the relief. The grip loosens. In a minute there is time. He takes another hit. Much better. He feels glazed now. Protected from the seizure by a coating of hard sugar.

He hears the door to the bathroom open, close. Shit. Busted by the park ranger. It must reek like pot in here. He scrambles to stow his pot and pipe. He flushes the toilet, like anyone would believe he was just going to the bathroom. He opens the stall door. It's not a ranger. It's Dean.

"Dean, I—"

Dean turns to go.

"Dean. I use it as medicine."

Dean stops and turns, his face blank.

"Right," he says. "Me, too."

He leaves.

Evan gathers his bag, flushes again. Like it matters. Like any of the details matter.

• • •

THEY DRIVE THROUGH town in silence. Evan isn't thrilled that he got busted by Dean for smoking pot, but it's better than the other scenario. If Evan had been too late to stave off the seizure and Dean had found him crammed into a stall, his shoes sticking out under the door, jerking and dancing to a rhythm that only Evan could hear, what would Dean have said? Would he have called an ambulance, held Evan's hand through it all? Doubtful. More likely, he would have been afraid of what he was seeing, unsure of what Evan was doing, wanting to keep as far away as possible.

And so Evan is stuck again. Hiding his horrible secret from the world. Trying to live a life without a sign around his neck that says KICK ME, I'M A CRIPPLE. Sneaking around in dark corners, taking the only drug that really helps him, the only drug that helps him without killing him, he affects the attitude of someone who smokes as a lifestyle choice: musicians and drugs were bedfellows thousands of years before Evan came along. But for Evan it isn't a choice. It's survival. It is who he is.

He stops his car across from Frank and Ellen's house.

"Listen, Dean," he says, "when I was seventeen, I got a girl pregnant and she had a baby—you—and I never saw you. It wasn't my fault, Dean, but I can't say I'm not guilty. And I—"

He looks over at Dean, who is sneering at him, and stops. It's no use. He can't stuff his life into a nutshell and make a child see. He can't reverse the past: fourteen years of Dean going to the annual father-and-son picnic with his mother—he can't change that. He can't explain it away; he can't mitigate it in any way: Dean grew up without a father, and it's impossible for Evan to erase that reality while sitting on the sticky vinyl seats of his car, a car that is older than Dean himself.

"Are you done?" Dean asks after a moment.

"Yeah, I guess I'm done."

"Good. Maybe we'll see each other again some day. Like at *your* funeral. I'd like that. Be sure to put me on the invitation list."

He climbs out and walks around the front of the car. As he passes Evan, he calmly reaches out his hand and gives Evan the

finger. The finger. Evan has to laugh. The kid just makes you want
to smack him.

Dean walks across the street and up onto the front porch of
Frank's house. But instead of continuing into the house, Dean
slows to a stop. Evan follows Dean's eyes to the front door. It opens
suddenly and Ellen flies out of the house. She rushes to Dean,
turns him around and herds him off the porch. What the hell is
going on?

Frantic, Ellen prods Dean down the walk toward the street. Evan
rolls down his window.

"Take him," she calls out in hushed hysteria. "Take him away,
please!"

By now they're crossing the street and Dean has pulled away
from her. He stands in the middle of the road, looking at her with
disbelief. She rushes to Evan's car.

"You have to leave here," she pleads. "*Please!*"

It is then, with Ellen practically pushing her way through Evan's
window, that Evan realizes something is terribly wrong. Her cheek
is scarlet and swollen. She's holding a damp washcloth to the corner of her mouth. The towel is dark, but he thinks he sees blood
on it.

"What happened?" he asks. "Are you all right?"

She calms herself, musters her energies, looks Evan directly in
the eyes.

"You have to take him away from here," she says as steadily as
she can. "Take him away, Evan. I'll call you when you can bring
him back. Please, just—"

Bang!

They both jump. Dean spins toward the sound. A door slamming violently, a house shaken. A bear wakened from its slumber.
Frank.

He storms out of the house with a great roar, which might have
been funny if it weren't so fucking scary. He's still wearing his suit.
No tie. He is barefoot.

"Get your ass in this house!" he yells.

A dog down the street barks violently at Frank, charging and hurling itself against a chain link fence with a *CHING-ing-ing!* Bark, bark, shuffle, *CHING-ing-ing!*

Evan, Ellen, and Dean are all frozen. A living tableau.

What has Evan gotten himself into? What's going on?

There's no time to wonder. Frank has been loosed, and he's on his way, a human cannonball, a projectile ready to explode on impact. Evan doesn't know what the story is, but there's time for that later. Right now, he wants to take Ellen's advice and get out. He looks at Dean, who still hasn't moved though Frank is closing in, off the porch, onto the walk, fifteen yards at most and closing fast—

"Please!"

"Get in the car, Dean!"

"Wha?—"

"Get in the fucking car!"

Dean hesitates. Ten yards from being smashed to oblivion.

"NOW!" Evan screams.

And this time Dean moves, bolts from his position on the broken yellow line, shoots around the car and into the passenger seat. Frank is at full speed, running at them. Ellen quickly backs away, and for a moment, Evan wonders what will happen to her. But he can't worry about that now. He revs the engine and drops the clutch, leaving squealing tires and a cloud of acrid smoke in his wake. They fly down the idyllic residential street, posted speed limit twenty-five (the old Saab still can get off the line pretty good, Evan notes with a grimace), and away from some crazy scene. Dean twists himself around and looks out the rear window.

"We should go back."

"She told me to get you out of there, Dean. She knows what she's doing. She said she'd call."

"But—"

"Sit down!"

Dean reluctantly resumes his seat, snaps on his seat belt.

"Grandpa's scary," he says.

"To you and me both."

• • •

THEY STOP FOR gas about an hour out of Walla Walla. Dean has sucked himself into his shell. He isn't Dean; he is a husk, a hollow casing. The real Dean is somewhere else, far, far away.

Evan gets himself a bottle of water; Dean doesn't want anything. While he's in the mini-mart, Evan takes out his cell phone and gets Ellen's number from information.

"Hello?" she answers with false brightness.

"It's Evan."

"I said you could talk to him," she says, dropping her voice to a whisper. "I said you—"

"What's going on there, Mrs. Smith?"

"I said you could *talk* to him, not *take* him."

"I thought you meant—"

"Frank was very angry."

"Did he hit you? Is that what happened?"

"No, Evan."

"Is he abusing you? Should I call the police?"

"No, Evan, don't be so melodramatic. We had an argument and I bumped into the freezer door, if you can believe that. The door was open and I turned."

She abruptly stops; a moment of silence; then she says cheerfully, "I'll call you in a few days and we'll get together."

What? She's either lost her mind or Frank has walked into the room.

"What am I supposed to do with him?" Evan asks.

"Thank you so much for calling. I'll be sure to pass along your thoughts to Frank, of course."

"What am I supposed to *do* with him?"

"We'll be fine. It's difficult, yes, but we'll get through. I'll call you in a few days and we'll get together for a nice lunch, okay? Okay, talk to you soon, Sally."

She hangs up. Wonderful.

Evan could have anticipated almost all of this: seeing Dean, having Dean yell at him, even having a barefooted Frank chase him down the street. But bringing Dean home with him? No. Not in a million years.

He goes outside and climbs back into the hot car. Dean doesn't acknowledge him; he stares out the window as they pull onto the road.

"Can you turn on the air conditioner?" Dean asks.

"It's on."

"Can you turn it up?"

"It's up."

Dean closes his eyes and leans back in his seat.

"I wish my mom were here," he says quietly to himself, his last words until they arrive in Seattle, almost four hours later.

T RACY CALLED FROM the hospital to tell him.

"I didn't do it," she said.

"Didn't do what?"

"I mean I *did* it."

"You *did* what?" Evan asked, feeling his pulse quicken.

"I had it. Him."

Evan's head spun once around, a perfect three-sixty, and stopped. It. Him. She had it. Him.

"Are you all right?" he asked, not knowing what else to ask.

"I'm fine. I just wanted you to know that I didn't have the abortion. I had the baby. It's a boy. I named him Dean."

Evan stood, dumbfounded, for several seconds before he hung up.

I had him. There were implications to that statement. There were strings attached. Lots of strings. He'd given her money to have an abortion and she didn't do it. But she'd taken the money, didn't that make it a contract? He definitely wanted the abortion done. She'd convinced him of it. Didn't she? He wanted the baby killed. He really did. (Didn't he?) He was seventeen years old. He wasn't supposed to want a child. He wasn't supposed to want to worry about another life. So he paid Tracy to kill the baby.

I had him. Dean.

What a great name. That's the name I would have picked, Evan thought to himself. And suddenly everything made sense. He and Tracy had steered clear of each other at school after he gave her the money, and he only saw her once after she graduated in June. It was then that she told him she didn't want to see him any more. It made her too sad, she said. And, besides, she had to start thinking about college. So he left her alone. She lived a mile away from him and had his son right under his nose.

His son. What should he do? Didn't he have some kind of an obligation? And even if he didn't have a *legal* obligation, didn't he have a *moral* one? Wasn't there some code of honor that he had to abide by? Didn't he have to pick up his son and say, *I am your father and I will not allow anyone in this world or any other world to hurt you? I am your father and I will lay down my life so that you can live?* Didn't he have an obligation to pick up his son and say *I AM YOUR FATHER?*

So that afternoon he went to Swedish Hospital. He strode into the maternity ward and demanded to see his son.

"Baby Smith," the nurse said, scanning a list.

"Dean Smith."

"We call them all 'Baby,' in case the parents change their minds."

"Well, I'm his father, and I won't change my mind."

The woman raised her eyebrows and continued scanning.

"Your wife is in her room. *Dean* is in the nursery. I'm sorry for the formality, but if you want to see Dean, you'll have to show me some I.D. You're not wearing a bracelet."

Evan pulled his driver's license out of his wallet and handed it to the woman. She studied it for a moment.

"Your name isn't Smith."

"No."

"Do you have a marriage license or a health insurance card?"

"No."

"I'm afraid I can't let you hold the baby, then. Only immediate family."

"I'm his father."

"You'll have to offer proof of that."

Evan smiled. It was all he could do, considering that he wanted to throttle this officious little nurse with her white hat and white uniform, white stockings and white crepe-soled shoes.

"Can I at least look at him?"

The nurse nodded.

"You can see him through the nursery window, but you can't hold him."

But I need to tell him. I need him to know. I am your father. I am. Your father. Me.

"Where is it?"

She pointed down the hall and Evan wandered off in a daze.

"Young man?" the nurse called out.

Evan turned.

"Your girlfriend is in room 236. If she asks to have the baby brought in, you could hold him there. I'm sorry."

Evan nodded. He didn't really care about her rules. He had to tell Dean something.

He found the nursery window, behind which were half a dozen bassinets, two with pink cards and four with blue. Blue for boy. One blue card read: SMITH, B.B. Inside that bassinet was a tiny baby who'd already managed to undo his swaddle, and who flailed with purple fingers, closed eyes, and cupped mouth in search of food.

Evan pressed his face against the window.

I am your father. I am your father and I will protect you.

Evan watched little Dean with a complex mix of emotions coursing through his body. Guilt, shame, love. Helplessness. Evan felt as helpless as this child who couldn't yet see or feed himself or survive without the intervention of others. That was Evan. He survived, but not without the help of others, and if he assumed responsibility for a baby, he would need those who helped him to help the baby as well, which would then make him nothing more than a middle man. Completely dispensable.

Evan left Dean alone in the nursery and went to find room 236. He would talk to Tracy about it. She had called him, maybe she had a grand plan. She usually thought things out pretty well. She was sharp. Together. She wouldn't be taken unawares by something like this.

He paused outside her door. He could hear conversation inside. A man, a woman, another man, Tracy. Her family was there. They were all there. He peered around the corner of the doorway. Tracy was lying in the bed. Frank was standing over her, his back to Evan. Ellen was sitting, facing the bed. Brad was saying something. It sounded like he was behind the door. None of them but Tracy could see Evan.

She looked up. He caught her eye. Frank was talking now. Softly, tenderly. Tracy looked right at Evan. Evan smiled at her. She shook her head almost imperceptibly. Evan didn't move. Had she waved him off? He waited. She did it again. Ever so slightly. A shake of the head.

No. She's saying no. She's saying don't come in here.

Evan backed away from the door and leaned against the wall. He held his head in his hands, dejected. *I am your father.*

True. But what good is that? Who really cares? *I am your father and I paid money to have you killed. Now that you are alive, I love you.*

No. It doesn't hold water. It doesn't wash. If you pay to have someone killed, you can't repair that. You can't then go back and say I was just kidding. Once you pay to have someone killed, it's over. Finito. The man with fire in his belly will come after you and crush your skull with his clay hands.

Evan went home and waited, thinking that perhaps Tracy would call later that day, or maybe the next. She would call and reveal her plan, tell him that he was a part of it, and the two of them would go off with their child and raise him to be smart and kind and well-rounded. But Tracy didn't call again.

Several days later, he called her house and she answered the phone. She told him her parents had both taken off from work to care for her, so it wouldn't be a good idea for Evan to visit now. But they were returning to work the following week and he could see Dean then as long as he came during the day and only if he didn't see any cars in the driveway. So he waited. The following week he went to Tracy's house with some flowers and a little stuffed bear that played a squeaky computer-chip song when you squeezed its foot. When he knocked on the door, there was no answer. He looked in the window; the house was empty.

Not just empty of people. Empty of everything. Furniture, rugs, wall-hangings. Everything.

Stunned, Evan turned and walked back toward the street.

"You missed them," an elderly neighbor called out as he carried boxes of Christmas lights out of his garage and lined them up neatly on the walk next to an aluminum extension ladder. "Moved out over the weekend."

They'd moved out with Dean.

"You're a friend of hers?" the man asked.

"Yes."

"I can see that she gets those," the man said, approaching. "The flowers won't last, of course, but the doll—I can see that the boy gets the doll."

"Yes." Evan nodded blankly, handing the things over. "Thank you."

"A fine-looking baby," the man said. "And the little mother is doing well, also. Kind of you to stop by."

"Where did they go?" Evan asked.

"They're making a fresh start, son. I have to respect their privacy."

Of course. Of course you do.

Evan quietly asked around school; he didn't want to draw too much attention to himself. But no one knew where Tracy's family had gone.

He was angry with her at first. But over several months, his anger faded into acceptance; if he assumed Tracy knew what she was doing in telling him about Dean, wouldn't she also know what she was doing by excluding him from her family?

So, he carried with him some resentment. But he also carried the belief that Tracy and Dean had found some kind of promised land somewhere; that they had gotten their fresh start, their picket fence, that they were doing well, and that they were better off without him.

QUIETLY, GENTLY, HE picks his way through the dark edges of Seattle's midnight, slips down onto Westlake, up and around to Dexter, where he finds his apartment building just where he left it. He pulls into his stall in the garage.

It was originally his grandfather's apartment. Evan would never have chosen it, nor would he have been able to afford it, a small one bedroom with spectacular city-lake-mountain views and considerable value on the open market. When his grandfather died, he left it to Evan. And for eight years it collected enough rent to cover Evan's living expenses when he finally moved out of his parents' house.

It's a sad low-slung building with damp brown carpeting in the hallways, inhabited mostly by old people and recent business school grads, the equally pungent smells of mothballs and sandalwood incense intermingling hideously in the halls. Still, it's the perfect place to hide. No one would ever think to look here. No one ever has.

He hesitates. Dean is sleeping soundly in the passenger seat, and has been for the past hour, since somewhere near North Bend.

Evan briefly considers carrying Dean upstairs. A fatherly thing to do. Carry your sleeping kid. And if Dean were ten years younger, Evan would do just that. But the image he has of himself—by no means a hulking brute—struggling up the steps while cradling a fully-grown fourteen-year-old in his arms, stumbling into walls, trying to protect Dean's head from smacking into doorjambs and corners, is almost laughable. Fantasy, after all, is just that. It allows you to see what could never really happen. Indulge in it, but do not cling to it.

"Dean."

Crouched next to the open passenger door, he pokes Dean's arm. "Deano."

Dean awakens.

"We're here."

EVAN'S PAD IS a bachelor pad, plain and simple, not a place for kids. The kitchen cupboards are grossly understocked. The living room (now the guest room), has a hide-a-bed sofa and a TV and is decorated pragmatically for a musician—a couple of amplifiers and a few guitars on stands—but for no one else. The bedroom is small and messy. The only bathroom is accessed through the bedroom, portending privacy issues. Good for a couple of nights at best. Certainly not for a long-term relationship, which, thankfully, this isn't.

Dean props himself against a wall, drunk with sleep, while Evan makes the bed. It hasn't been slept on in years; it smells musty. Evan hopes Dean doesn't have any environmental allergies which are so common in today's youth, due largely to trigger-happy doctors and their misguided policies of over-vaccination.

"Maybe we can find a mattress cover for this thing, but I doubt it," Evan says. "We'll go out tomorrow and get you a toothbrush."

Dean mumbles a response.

"Your grandmother's going to call once the coast is clear," Evan says, though he isn't really sure what a clear coast might look like. "I'll drive you back."

More mumbling.

"Right. Here you go." He picks up the living room phone and turns off the ringer.

Dean falls face first onto the bed, tries briefly to straighten himself out, but gives up, his legs dangling toward the floor. Evan looks down at him, unsure of what to do. He can't very well undress Dean; there would be something creepy and inappropriate about that. But he can help him onto the bed. And he can throw a blanket over him. He can watch over him for a second or two. And he can say, "Good night, son," as he retreats from the room.

IT'S PAST MIDNIGHT when Evan lies back on his own bed, exhausted. Out of habit he opens *The Stranger* and glances at the listings. He pages through the tabloid for a few minutes, not really paying attention to the words, until he finally gives up and sets the paper down. It's no good. He isn't going anywhere. Not with Dean in the next room. And it's just as well. There's nothing quite like ending up on the sticky beer-glazed floor of a bar with some idiot trying to shove a spoon down your throat.

He takes off his shoes and closes his eyes. He's beat. Beat down, beat up, beat in. Driving a ten-hour round trip in one day to attend the funeral of the mother of your estranged child is not something your neurologist would recommend. Nor would he recommend confronting the aforementioned child's violent grandfather and then fleeing with said child. Too much stress, and you know what stress does to your blood levels. Is that an aura I'm feeling, or are you just glad to see me?

He reaches for his stash, which he keeps not-very-discreetly hidden in an old Dunhill cigar box next to his bed. He slips across the floor to the window, opens it a crack and lights his pipe. A gram of prevention. He closes his eyes and exhales the sickly sweet smoke.

He hears Dean snore softly. What a world. He was seventeen when Dean was born. Three years later, he was the lead guitar player for a hot new band with a single climbing the charts and a platinum future ahead. A week after that, he was an out-of-work slacker with decent chops and a pleasant-enough demeanor to teach middle-aged rich guys how to coax music from a Fender Strat. And now, fourteen years after Dean was born, Evan is just fourteen years further down the line, and nothing more. He's grown out, not up.

He's grown tired. He slides back onto his bed and lies down. The ceiling is doing a dance for him. A stoned eurythmics. Ten hours of driving. If that isn't stupid, what is? He's lucky he's still alive. He could have had a seizure, rolled his car into the median, become partially ejected and then cut in half by the door as the weight of the car settled on top of him. That would have been nice. Maybe they would have buried him next to Tracy. HERE LIE THE MOTHER AND FATHER OF DEAN, the marker would read. THEY MISSED THEIR CHANCE.

EVAN WAKES UP in the middle of the night in a sweat. His mouth is parched. His sheets are cold and damp. He feels sick.

Water. He needs a glass of water.

He starts to get out of bed, when he realizes that his left leg feels strange. It must have fallen asleep. From the middle of his thigh on down, he feels nothing; it's just numb. Above the numbness, he feels a peculiar pins-and-needles sensation.

He shakes his leg sharply to jolt it back to life, but it doesn't respond. So he starts to massage his thigh to get the circulation going again, coax the blood to flow. He kneads at his quadriceps, working his way down his thigh toward his knee.

But as he gets closer to his knee, his leg seems to change consistency. It doesn't really feel like his leg any more. It feels more like modeling clay. His fingers press into the flesh, but the flesh doesn't spring back, it retains the finger and thumb impressions he's just left.

He continues kneading his leg above his knee until it's become quite narrow. Actually—and he's not even sure how he can be so calm at a time like this, so clinical about what's going on—it would be very easy for him to detach his leg at this point, simply by pulling it free, which he does with a quick twist, and as soon as he does he realizes he's just pulled off his own leg and he panics, dropping the lower part of his leg in shock. He forces himself to lift the sheets and look down, and he sees that what's left is the round stump of his thigh and nothing below. What has he done?

Frantically, he reaches for the rest of his leg—it must still be there—maybe it's not too late to reattach it, maybe he can knead the clay and stick it back on. His hands fly through the blankets, feeling for the amputated foot and shin. He'll call the hospital. He'll put the leg in a garbage bag full of ice and go there and they'll sew it back on.

Ah. He finds it. But suddenly the leg jerks away from him and scurries off, burying itself at the bottom of the bed.

Evan screams in shock. It moved! It moved on its own! Holy shit. The hair rises on the back of his neck. His leg is moving by itself. He can see it shifting around under the sheets; his leg is crawling on its own.

Desperate, panicked, his heart thudding in his chest, he throws back all the sheets and blankets, exposing the entire mattress, and he dives for his leg, which he sees huddled in the corner, suddenly naked and exposed to the cold air in the room. He dives for it and grabs it, but it isn't trying to escape any more. It's frozen in fear, shivering, scared half to death. It doesn't know who Evan is. The poor thing is petrified. Evan lifts it out of the sheets. It's not his leg. It's a baby. Such a pretty baby boy.

Carefully, Evan holds him up. He looks fine. Healthy and fine. He's got a head of raging black hair. His eyes are squinty, his mouth opens and closes like he's an alien, an appropriate image considering he was born from Evan's leg. Evan wraps the tadpole in a blanket so he'll stop shivering. And then he brings the little monster close to him, his tiny hands gripping the air as if he needs something to hold onto, some mama's fur to grasp, a strange anachronistic instinct harkening back to when we were all simple apes swinging from the branches with our pups clinging to our breasts, desperate not to be dropped to the jungle floor.

Evan kisses the munchkin on the forehead. And the funny Turkish Delight looks up at his father and says, quite simply and quite clearly, "Da."

Da.

I'm your Da.

So Evan hugs junior, and the clammy goober hugs back, and Evan closes his eyes because he's so happy, so overjoyed to be the proud father of a freak of nature. And Evan closes his eyes and sings a quiet lullaby for his babe, sleepy-time music to send the booger off to meet the Sandman for some well-deserved rest before the little tyke has to wake up and face the rest of what will turn out to be his sad and miserable life.

L ONG AGO, WHEN he was still a child, Evan learned that if something seems good, it can actually be bad, and that if something seems bad, it might actually be worse. He learned that there is danger lurking behind every corner, that in the darkness of every closet hides a monster. Evan knew. He'd been ambushed by the monster before. He'd felt the creepiness, the cold clammy hands on the back of his neck. He'd felt the fear that rises up in his body so fast it makes his gums tingle. He had known the monster, had intimate dealings with it, as it crept out of its closet and attacked.

So when he wakes at six in the morning with that familiar queasy feeling—familiar not because it was so frequently felt but because it was so distinctive—and with the memory of his odd but extremely vivid dream fresh in his mind, he knows what has happened. In the night, the monster came out of the closet and set upon Evan, shaking him about in his bed, leaving him groggy and spent. Evan has had a seizure.

He pushes off his bedspread and sits up. Where was Dean for all this? Was he awake? Had he heard anything, any strange gurglings or thrashings about? No. All kids sleep hard and long. That much about adolescence he knows. He swings his aching legs over the side of the bed and places his feet on the floor. The carpeting has an uncomfortable feel to it. An itchiness he doesn't usually notice. He stands up. A little spin to his vision. And strips off his clothes; he had fallen asleep fully dressed. He plods into the bathroom and checks himself in the mirror. A crusty trail of drool runs from the corner of his mouth across his cheek. His eyes are baggy and dark. He opens his mouth. The inside of his cheeks are bloody. At least his tongue was spared. You can't swallow your tongue, but you sure can chew the hell out of it. He turns on the water in the shower and stands under the burning hot ribbons, hoping to wash away the crawly sensation on his skin.

A seizure. He hasn't had a big one in quite a while. The little ones don't really count. He has those more often, like on the porch of the Smith house. Little ones are annoyances, mosquito bites on the arm of life. Big ones are to be feared. He felt this one coming, even though he pretended he didn't. He felt it at the Whitman Memorial, and again when he got home. He tried to fool himself and he succeeded, so who's the idiot? Stress, fatigue, not eating properly. He thought maybe if he ignored it, it would go away. He smoked his pot, usually a cure-all. But this one got through the defense grid. Dilantin, Tegretol, marijuana—it doesn't matter. Sometimes the fuse just blows and nothing can stop it. Kind of inconvenient, when you think about it. Kind of a nuisance to carry around the knowledge that at any moment your brain could rage out of control and you could wake up anywhere. And you wouldn't know what was going on until it was too late. As if there were anything you could do to stop it. No. You would see the monster, you would feel its clammy palms, and then darkness. And if you were lucky, you'd wake up where you started, or even—not so good— you'd wake up in a hospital with tubes in your arms. Or, worst case scenario, you just wouldn't wake up at all. Pack up your troubles in a Glad trash bag and smile, smile, smile.

He shuts off the water, still itchy so he doesn't put on any clothes. The smoothest satin feels like wool after a seizure. He tiptoes through the living room and into the kitchen, where he scoops coffee into the coffee maker and turns it on, something to shake the quease, then he stands at his window in all his glory, observing the morning dawn over Lake Union.

The water is quiet and the sky is dull as the morning clouds, portending rain, hunker down over Seattle. A lonely seaplane circles over Fremont and prepares for landing. It looks like a toy plane landing on a toy lake. Everything looks fake to Evan. Plasticky. Like two-dimensional cut-outs pasted on invisible wires, worked by elves from behind a cardboard photo of the city.

The coffee machine heaves its steamy sighs, the seaplane buzzes over the lake. And all is more or less the way it should be.

"You're completely naked."

Evan jumps. His heart nearly stops. He spins around. Dean is standing in the doorway.

"Why aren't you asleep?" Evan asks, brushing by him. Not only was Dean not asleep, he wasn't even rumpled.

"I'm not tired," Dean says.

Evan darts into his room, throws on jeans and a T-shirt, and returns to the kitchen.

"Don't they sleep where you're from?" he asks.

"Not at this hour," Dean replies.

"What, you're usually out picking apples by now?"

Dean doesn't respond. Probably because it was such an asinine comment.

"Sorry," Evan mutters, pouring himself coffee. "I didn't mean to—" He hears a phone ring quietly, distantly, unreally.

Suddenly Evan is very afraid. Dean awake and fully dressed shortly after dawn is strange, but the distant ringing in his ears simply isn't right. His skin crawls as he realizes that maybe he hasn't awakened after all. Maybe the shower and the coffee and the plane are all part of a dream in which he is still trapped. It is perfectly conceivable that he is in a coma this very second, having seizure after seizure in some hospital while doctors pump gallons of sedatives into his veins in their attempts to stay the evil affliction.

Ring. Ring.

Wait—that's a real ring. A phone. From his bedroom. Right. He'd shut off the living-room ringer. The bedroom phone is ringing. Mystery solved.

But there's another mystery. He glances at the kitchen clock. Six o'clock. That doesn't make sense. He woke up after having a seizure while he had slept. That would make this six A.M. Right? Or not? He looks out the window again. Jesus, it isn't six A.M. It's six P.M. Six P.M. and Evan can't tell the difference!

He can tell now, though. He hadn't noticed before because the clouds were so thick and diffused that he couldn't see where the sun was. But the traffic on the street below, the cars on the freeway across the water, Dean: all clues that now tell Evan that it is evening, not morning.

Ring, ring, ring, goes the phone. Then the machine in the bedroom picks up and his mother's voice calls to him. "Evan? Evan? Evan?" Now Evan *really* feels sick.

"You gonna get it?" Dean asks. "Some guy named Lars called earlier."

Lars? He picks up the phone.

"Evan? Are you all right?"

Mom? No, Mom, I'm not. Not really. I'm scared. I just lost an entire day and I have no idea where it went, and there's this kid here who says he's my son, and I'm having seizures and I'm really scared. Can you come and hold me?

"Yeah, Mom, I'm fine."

"You were screening?"

"Yeah, Mom, I was screening. What's up?"

"We were worried."

Evan feels her worry unload through the phone line. Just hearing his voice is enough to satisfy his mother, who is forever worried about him. As she probably has a right to be. Even though Evan is thirty-one, to his parents he is still a kid with epilepsy. They call him twice a day without fail. If he isn't home for a few hours and they don't know where he's gone, they panic and call the local hospitals. They treat him as if he were still in high school, still living at home.

Evan used to feel weird about his parents' concern. Then he got used to it. He even felt at times that if he were suddenly to be rid of his epilepsy and his parents stopped worrying about him all the time, he might actually miss it. It was kind of like a permanent hall pass or diplomatic license plates on your car. Evan was allowed much greater latitude than he would have had if he weren't afflicted.

"But you're okay?"

"Yeah, Mom, I just was out yesterday. No big deal."

"Good. Well, your father wants to know if you're free for dinner soon. He's buying."

Yeah. Like Evan has ever offered to buy.

"I'm pretty busy."

"We haven't seen you in a while."

"A while" in Louise-speak means about two weeks.

"Maybe I'll drop by," Evan says, and almost laughs at his own joke. He could drop by with his teenage son and blow his parents' minds. That would be a good one. He knew he was in their will. Murder by shock. Who would suspect?

"That would be nice," Louise coos. "Oh, Charlie said he was trying to reach you," she adds casually.

"Really? I didn't get any messages."

"He said he's left a few, but you never call back."

"Huh," Evan replies, "maybe my machine is broken."

"Maybe it is. Could you call him?"

His little brother Charlie had, in fact, left five messages, each one ignored. Why? Because whenever Charlie called five times in four days, and Louise called to tell Evan that Charlie had called five times in four days, that meant something good had happened to Charlie—possibly something great—and Evan was supposed to jump up and down with joy and say encouraging and enthusiastic things and proclaim his love and unconditional support. And he was supposed to do it without gagging. *I passed the bar. I'm getting married. I got a raise. I bought a house. I screwed my wife. My wife is pregnant. It's a boy.* Come on, doesn't anyone else get tired of it?

"What is it this time, Mom, they name a street after him?"

Louise takes Evan's crack silently for a moment—but only a moment.

"I don't understand, Evan," she says regretfully. "Why can't you be happy for Charlie? What did he ever do to you that was so bad?"

Evan smiles. Now *that's* a complicated question. What did Charlie do? How about this: he cried. One soggy evening, many, many years ago, Charlie stood there crying and Evan had to act like an older brother, and because of that Evan's life was changed forever. That's what Charlie did that was so bad.

"I'm happy for him, Mom," Evan says. "I really am."

"Then why do you seem so sad?"

Evan glances at Dean, who looks back expectantly, as if he's waiting to be introduced. *Because my son is standing next to me but I'm afraid to tell you about him.*

"Evan?"

He could do it. He could tell her. *Which son?* she would ask. *My fourteen-year-old son,* he would answer. It would be easy, actually. Like jumping out of an airplane. Starting is the hard part. Once you get going, you kind of fall by yourself.

"Hey, Mom? . . ."

Tell her.

"Yes, honey?"

Jump. Jump. Jump.

"Never felt better, Mom."

"Oh," she says, not believing him for a second. "Okay. Well. When do you think you might stop by?"

"Soon, Mom. Real soon."

"Okay. Well, we love you, Evan."

"I love you, too."

We love you. Of course they love him. They have to. He's their son, after all. But Evan knows it's a disappointed love. They love him like they love their retarded dog who eats rocks. They feel bad his teeth get broken, but the dog is happy, isn't he? They love that dog, but they won't think twice about putting him down for his own good as soon as he becomes incontinent. No "Doggie Depends" in

Ralphy's future. Just you wait and see. One puddle on the kitchen floor and Ralphy's gig is up.

Ah.

When Evan announced to his parents that he wasn't taking the SAT because he wasn't going to college, they tried to keep straight faces. They didn't want to fight him any more. They knew he had no place in college, so why should he bother? Evan left them in the kitchen and went to his room to play his guitar.

They thought he couldn't hear them. They had to think that. There was no way they would have said what they did if they knew he was listening.

"Poor Evan," Louise said as she cleared the dinner table.

"What a waste," Carl answered her. "What a waste."

HE FEELS BAD that he didn't tell his mother about Dean, but he just couldn't do it. There's too much going on, his head is swimming and he feels uneasy and confused. He and Dean both fidget uncomfortably.

Evan can see where Dean dragged the easy chair over to the window so he could sit and look out at Lake Union. Dean had probably spent the entire day staring out the window without uttering a word; he probably hadn't even rummaged through the refrigerator for food because he felt so out of place that he didn't know what was acceptable behavior in Evan's world. Who was to say that Evan didn't have a violent temper, and that one of his quirks was to sleep until six P.M. every night, and that even the slightest sound could result in corporal punishment? It wasn't out of the question. So he sat there, all day, not making a sound, not breathing too loudly, for fear of disturbing his new host.

Evan wants to explain why he was so late in rising, he wants to apologize for not being up earlier to tend to Dean, but that would mean he'd have to admit his flaw—a truly tragic one—and he isn't sure he can do that yet.

"You must be hungry," Evan says. "Did you get yourself any food?"

Dean shrugs.

"You want something? I've got cereal, but that's about it."

"A guy named Lars called," Dean reminds him.

"Oh, yeah? What did Lars say?"

"He wondered if you were still going to the show tonight."

Oh, shit. The show. Lucky Strike is playing in Belltown. Evan forgot all about it.

Dean digs a crumpled piece of paper out of his pocket.

"He made me write it down," he says. "He said he assumes you'll be there unless you're a 'total fucking douche-bag fuck,' in which case he'll have to 'rip your balls off and stuff them down your tear ducts' the next time he sees you."

Evan laughs.

"Is he your friend?" Dean asks. Evan can't tell if he's serious.

"Yeah, pretty much," he says.

He scratches his cheek. Damn. He loves Lucky Strike. They're more jazz than rock, and Evan isn't a big jazz guy. But they're a New York band well known for their exceptional chops, and Evan is a fan of their leader, Theo Moody, a saxophonist who has a reputation for mixing it up with record labels.

"Did your mother ever take you to see music?" Evan asks.

"No."

Can he take Dean to see Lucky Strike? Is it something parents do? Or is it the ultimate mistake, the first step down a path that leads to drug addiction and deviant behavior?

"I think they let kids in, but you couldn't sit at the bar or anything. I don't drink, so it wouldn't matter anyway."

Dean hesitates.

"So you want to go?"

"Um, okay," Dean shrugs even though Evan can see the excitement in his eyes. "If there's nothing else to do."

HE GATHERS HIMSELF together and gets dressed in what he deems appropriate musician's garb for a Lucky Strike show: normal-guy look with a touch of cool. He doesn't want to stand out, just come across as a little bit hipper than the rest of the audience so as to be identifiable as part of the musician's tribe. So, in addition to his basic uniform of jeans and T-shirt, he selects a loose-fitting sharkskin shirt he picked up at a vintage clothing store in the Market. Shiny, but not too. Noticeable, but not ostentatious. It shows that he cares about his image, but only casually. He's a guitarist, after all, not a lead singer. His music tells more about him than his image.

He checks himself in the mirror. He's slightly taller than average. His blue-gray eyes are in contrast to his dark hair, which he wears short since, despite his best intentions, his hair does what it wants and sticks together in strange clumps that he has never come to understand. He's thinner than his mother would like. He's less muscular than he would like. He's been told that he was built for fame—the wiry body of a rock star. He never put much store in the idea, but, deep down, he hopes it's true.

They wait for the cab in the drizzle outside Evan's building. They're cabbing it because, for one, it's generally easier than looking for a parking spot, and, two, Evan's seizure activity is something of a concern. He knows he should call his neurologist, Dr. Melon, but he really doesn't want to. Dr. Melon is cool and all, but he's still a neurologist. And, though he's a proponent of alternative therapies (the use of marijuana was *his* idea, not Evan's), when push comes to shove, he still writes a prescription or ups a dosage or calls Evan in for a quick EEG just to "check under the hood." And Evan doesn't need any of that right now. He needs to be cool and calm, cut out the dairy and the wheat—which act as triggers for seizures in rough times, something to do with toxic load, Dr. Melon maintains—and keep a joint with him at all times. Easy enough.

"How about Chinese?" Evan asks. Steamed chicken and rice.

"I hate Chinese."

"What do you want, then?"

Dean shrugs, his trademark nonverbal reply.

"Anything but Chinese, then," Evan says.

"Yeah, anything but Chinese."

"How about Greek?" Grilled fish and rice.

"How about American or Italian?"

American or Italian. Great. Evan's trying to tame his seizures by staying away from wheat and dairy, and his kid only wants to eat hamburgers and pizza.

"Okay," Evan says with a smile, "you got it."

IF THEY'RE GOING to do it, they're going to do it right. Evan takes Dean to Dick's Drive-In up on Capitol Hill. He chooses Dick's because Dick's is a part of the Seattle experience, but also because Evan knows they don't dust their fries with wheat to make them crunchy, like every other burger joint in the world does. And while he eats his three bags of limp fries and drinks his water, he envies Dean who is in the middle of inhaling two Deluxe burgers and sucking down a giant milkshake. The sacrifices we make for our children.

It's crowded at Dick's, as it always is, but the evening is too young for it to be really raucous. The hardcore drunken and stoned Dick's eaters won't arrive until much later. Evan and Dean stand at the outdoor counter eating and watching the people pass by on Broadway. Their conversation is almost nonexistent, but they are spending *time* together, which Evan figures is just as good. People talk too much anyway. Sometimes just standing next to a person is better than making a contrived effort to communicate with him through language.

After they finish dinner, they walk around a while, stopping long enough to watch a guy get his lip pierced in the window of a tattoo shop. Evan, clever father that he is, remembers that there's an Urban Outfitters in the mall on the north end of Broadway, so they go and buy some clothes. Dean changes out of his uniform of protest and paradox and into something more appropriate for a contemporary Seattle teenager.

They hop another cab and head down to Belltown. When they arrive at Jefferson Bank, an old bank building converted to a night club, Lars is waiting on the street. Lars Hero, a six-foot-four Swede, is the drummer of Evan's band, The Last. Amazingly dexterous with drumsticks but almost comically clumsy without, he is a very large, thickly built, platinum-blond man, who, it's been said, is slightly retarded due to a childhood blow to the head he received courtesy of his hammer-wielding brother, Berg. Evan suspects that Lars was slightly retarded long before the blow to his head, since the blow occurred thusly:

Lars and Berg, fifteen and thirteen respectively, were working in the yard, breaking rocks for the Japanese garden their father was building, which, when completed, would boast a twelve-foot waterfall and an impressive collection of immaculately groomed bonsai trees. Lars and Berg argued. Berg, the younger, threatened Lars: "I'm gonna knock your head off with this hammer." Berg gestured with the heavy clawed chipping hammer in his hand.

Lars, not to be intimidated by his little brother, responded: "You're gonna have to pull it out of your ass first."

Then, Berg, being a man of his word and a bit quicker than the hulking Lars, swung the hammer and connected with Lars's head just above his ear. The sound was similar to the sound made when uncorking a bottle of wine. Pock. Not loud, but disturbing nonetheless.

There was blood, screaming, a trip to the hospital, a skull repaired with a hard plastic disk and some baling wire. But no lasting damage, thank God, except that Lars had problems comprehending his math homework after the incident. But, apparently Lars had problems comprehending his math homework before the incident, too. That the incident occurred at all suggested to Evan that there was a certain chemical deficiency in the Hero family.

"Hey, Ev," Lars calls out, waving frantically, as if a giant albino with a dent in his head is hard to pick out of a crowd.

Evan and Dean make their way toward him. There's a larger than normal mob of young Bohemians gathered on the sidewalk. Evan never would have thought Lucky Strike was that big a draw.

"Hey, Lars."

"What's with the kid?"

"This is my son, Dean. Dean, this is Lars."

A look of panic sweeps over Lars's face. His hand instinctively goes to his mouth, he chews at the tender flesh around his thumbnail, a nasty habit.

"I didn't know you had a kid," he whispers to Evan through his thumb.

"I do, his name is Dean. This is him."

"You didn't have a kid last week."

"Well, I do now," Evan confirms.

While Lars digests this new information, he tears a piece of flesh off of his thumb and chews on it with his front teeth, grinding it up, gnashing it, pulverizing it. When it's gone, he licks at the bloody wound he has just created.

"They're sold out," he says. "Do you have a ticket for him?"

"What?"

"The show is sold out."

"You're kidding me!" Evan cries.

"Nope." Lars stuffs his hand in his pocket, apparently overcome by a sudden feeling of guilt at the profuse amount of blood flowing from his thumb wound.

"How could they be sold out?" Evan asks, dismayed.

"Someone posted on the Internet that Tom Waits was showing up. I guess they all figure if Tom Waits shows, Jim Jarmusch might show because he's shooting a film in Portland, and they figure if Jim Jarmusch shows, Johnny Depp can't be too far behind. So, therefore, you get all these loser artfags going to a see a band they've never heard of before tonight."

"Oh, that makes sense."

"So what do you want to do? I mean, I can go inside with him—what was your name again?"

"Dean."

"I can go inside with Dean and you can try to worm your way past the bouncer, I guess. Because you know I'm not giving up *my* ticket and I know you don't want Dean standing out here alone all night. If you don't make it in, I'll just take him to your place after the show, right?"

"Right," Evan sighs.

"See you, sucker," Lars chuckles. "Come on, Dean."

Evan watches them walk away together.

"What happened?" he hears Lars ask Dean as they head toward the entrance. "Your old lady get sick of you and tell you to go stay with Dad for a while?"

"No, my old lady got killed in a head-on collision with someone driving the wrong way on the freeway."

Lars doesn't respond for a moment. Then, "Really?"

"Yeah."

"That fucking sucks, man."

"Yeah."

"Fuck that."

And then they are too far away for Evan to hear.

NO ONE IS scalping on the street, and the doorman won't budge. It's nine forty-five, almost fifteen minutes past the scheduled start time, and, though he doesn't hear any music from inside, he knows it's too late for him. He's about to pack it in when he hears a familiar voice: "Yo, Evbee!"

Evbee? Evan turns around quickly to see who it is. Walking toward him is a stocky black man with close-cropped hair and a broad face, wearing black leather pants and a black leather motorcycle jacket.

"Yo, Evbee. Wassup?"

It's Billy Marx, one of the founding partners of The Sound Factory, the hottest recording studio on the West Coast.

"Hey, Billy."

Billy strides up to Evan and shakes his hand in the cool hip-hop way, a handshake with which Evan was never quite comfortable but always felt he could bluff his way through: slap hands, slide into a thumb-wrestling grip, then, palms together, lean in and give a poundy with the left hand—a quick thump to the hollow of the back of your co-greeter with the flat of your fist.

"What's happening, brother? You here for the gig?"

Evan nods.

"Yeah, but it's sold out. I can't get in."

"There's always room for one more," Billy says. "Come on, I got a table."

Evan follows him to the door and they walk right past the doorman without a pause or word of explanation. The same doorman who had so rudely rejected Evan minutes earlier. Evan smiles. Billy Marx is the one guy Evan knows who actually has enough juice to walk past any bouncer in Seattle.

While Billy and Evan aren't exactly close friends, they see each other around occasionally, and they're always friendly, since they have a mutual bond that goes way back. Billy was the drummer in Evan's first real band, Free Radicals, a band that was full of good musicians, but was ultimately doomed because they were too diverse in styles and interests to really click. After the band broke up, Evan asked Billy what was next.

"Start a rehearsal studio, make a paycheck," Billy said.

"Sounds boring," Evan said.

"You know how much money is in drumming?" Billy asked in response. "Ten bucks a gig. I'm serious. You either write the songs or you produce them. That's the money. Good studio musicians get by all right, if they live in L.A. But a mediocre drummer in a rock and roll band? Screw that. I got a kid, man. I need health insurance."

The prophecy. And now he has health insurance and more. A dental plan, even.

Inside Jefferson Bank is a long, dark bar that is separated from the rest of the large room by a four-foot-high wooden divider. The main area is filled with small tables, all of which are full. At the front of the room is a stage with amps and musical instruments, but no musicians. Evan scans the room for Lars and Dean, but he doesn't see them. "You looking for someone?" Billy asks, noticing Evan's search.

"Yeah."

"Well, come up front for a minute. I want you to meet someone."

Evan really wants to find Dean, but he doesn't want to be rude to Billy, who, after all, was the one who got him inside. He glances around one more time, but the room is packed. He might never find them. So he follows Billy.

They pick their way through a tangle of tables until they reach a long table near the front where about ten people sit. Billy indicates an open chair, then moves around and sits across from Evan, next to an incredibly beautiful woman.

Shockingly beautiful. Indeterminate age, maybe thirty or so, Asian-looking, with milky brown skin and long frizzy hair that is pulled behind her into a low ponytail. She's wearing a little black dress. Her eyes are vast reflection pools, her cheeks are high and defined, her lips are full and pouty. Evan almost can't breathe, he's so taken with her.

She's probably Billy's girlfriend. Evan knew that Billy had a kid, but he also knew that the mother took the kid and left. This girl is a pretty fair consolation prize.

She catches Evan staring. She smiles a little, dips her head modestly, and looks away toward the stage, stretching her long, slender neck into a wonderful arc—not reprimanding Evan for his stare, but encouraging him to look more.

Which he does. Billy doesn't care. He's already deep in conversation with someone else. With extreme effort, Evan takes his eyes off the girl and looks around the table. He doesn't recognize any faces, but he knows he's sitting with the band. They're all dressed in ultra-cool fashion, way beyond Evan's look—charcoal lounge suits with thin ties and French-cuff shirts proclaiming that they are definitely from a different tribe than Evan. Just when you thought you were cool enough. . . He lets his gaze drift back to the girl. She's saying something to the guy seated next to Evan. Evan tunes in.

"—I just think it's inappropriate. I'm not commenting on the value of your music, Theo."

Theo? Evan looks over. Next to him is a tall, gaunt white guy with thinning hair in a floppy drab suit. He's smoking a cigarette. Theo Moody, the leader of Lucky Strike.

"Music doesn't have a bedtime," Theo says. He has a gravelly deep voice. His nose is large and it angles slightly down, as do his eyes, giving him a perpetually sad look. "If there were some rare lunar eclipse and you could only see it at two in the morning, wouldn't you wake your kids up?"

"I think it's sweet that you equate yourself with a rare lunar eclipse, Theo."

"You know what I mean."

"What do you think?" the girl asks.

Theo doesn't answer.

"Yeah," Theo says, "what do you think?"

Again, no response. Who are they asking?

Evan suddenly panics. They're asking *him?* The girl is looking right at him. So is Theo Moody.

"What was the question?" Evan asks sheepishly, feeling like he's back in high school and has failed the pop quiz again.

"There are some kids over there," the girl says, indicating a table. "I think it's inappropriate, Theo doesn't. What do you think?"

Evan looks over. It's a family with two kids, who look to be about eight and ten. What does Evan think?

"*My* kid's here," he says.

They look surprised.

"He's older than they are, though."

"How old?" the girl asks.

"Fourteen. I think *those* kids are too young."

The girl raises her eyebrows at Evan and looks impressed, like somehow he's gained status in her eyes, like he didn't look like the kind of guy who would have a fourteen-year-old son and now that she knows he does, she has to reassess the situation.

"Theo!" Billy shouts from across the table—Billy sitting next to his beautiful girlfriend. "You met Evan?"

"Kind of."

Evan and Theo shake hands, completing the more formal introduction.

"Evan played guitar for Dog Run," Billy says. "Remember them?"

"Should I?" Theo asks.

"One hit wonder," the girl says, staring at Evan now. Evan, father of a fourteen-year-old and former lead guitar for a one hit wonder. What would be revealed next?

"They had a top ten single a bunch of years ago," Billy explains to Theo. "But their lead singer committed suicide—the guy was a total drug addict—and the album bombed anyway."

"Cool." Theo nods, morbidly impressed.

"Evbee's a great guitarist, Theo," Billy says. "You should hear him play."

"Cool." Theo smiles.

"You guys should have him sit in," Billy's girl suggests helpfully.

"Yeah?" Theo wonders aloud.

"I always love a good jam," the girl confirms.

"Okay," Theo agrees. "Our set starts in five."

He looks expectantly at Evan, and Evan suddenly realizes he means they should play now.

"*Now?*" Evan asks.

The girl nods at Evan.

"Why not?" Theo replies.

"I don't have my guitar."

"I've got a guitar for you."

"In front of an audience?"

"You're telling me the lead guitarist of Dog Run is afraid of audiences? Come on, man."

Theo tells his band to start getting ready, and then he leads Evan up to the stage, which is no more than a raised area, two steps above the rest of the room. It was probably where the lending officers originally sat when the venue was still a bank. Theo finds his guitar set up next to two saxophones.

"We'll just stretch a little," he says to Evan. "Don't sweat it. And then you can sit down and we'll play the set. It's cool, man."

He looks at Evan, who doesn't appear totally convinced it is cool. Usually, he loves being on stage. In fact, he feels more comfortable in front of an audience than in one. But now, he's so nervous he's shaking.

"You got chops?" Theo asks.

Evan nods.

"Then don't sweat it, man."

"I play rock, not jazz."

"You play what you play, man. Play what you feel. I don't give a shit. Just play it in key and step back when I say step back. Cool?"

"Cool." Evan nods, still feeling doubtful.

Of all the bands he likes, how many times has he imagined just this situation? How many times has he pictured himself on stage as a guest star? But never with Lucky Strike. He listens to them for pleasure; he doesn't try to figure them out, doesn't try to imitate. Sometimes, in music, *not* imitating is the sincerest form of flattery.

The rest of the musicians assemble. There are seven or eight other guys. A trumpet, a cello, a pedal steel guitar, a bass. So many. How do you communicate with so many players?

Evan introduces himself around. He's nervous, but strangely clear-headed—strange considering his mental state before getting on stage. There's no way he would have a seizure on stage. It's never happened before. And even with some recent seizure instability and the idea that Dean is out in the audience and is about to hear him play, Evan feels totally safe. There is one thing Evan can count on: on stage with a guitar, he is always safe.

"Watch me for the changes," the bass player tells him. "Theo will point to you when you're up, otherwise just play rhythm."

"Cool."

Evan tunes the guitar. It's a Rickenbacker, not Evan's first choice in guitars. He's a Fender man through and through, and isn't used to the sound and feel of a hollow-body. But that's no excuse. A poor artist blames his tools.

While the musicians fiddle around and warm up, Evan glances out into the audience. Way in the back, standing by the bar, he sees Lars with Dean in tow. Lars is holding his arms out wide in disbelief, shaking his head, shouting something—or mouthing it, Evan can't hear him—wondering what the hell Evan is doing on stage.

It's pretty funny and cool. Almost a fantasy for Evan to be play-ing for Dean. It's like he can finally show off. Music, the one thing he can do well, is the one thing his family never sees him do. Oh, his brother used to come to gigs, but then his wife, Allison, stopped coming because she developed an allergy to smoke (aren't we *all* allergic to smoke?), and he doesn't go anywhere without her. His parents went to a gig once, when Evan was just out of high school, and they told him how proud they were of him, but, without excuse or explanation, they never came again. So, to go from being left out on the street to being on stage in front of Dean is kind of a dream come true.

"Hey, everybody," Theo says into the microphone, "A surprise guest dropped in tonight—"

"Tom Waits!" someone shouts out. The crowd cheers.

"If you came for Tom, you came to the wrong place. This here's Evan, formerly of Dog Run. He's supposed to be pretty hot, so we're gonna jam a little. Cool?"

He turns to the band and counts off a quick one, two, three—

And they spring to life. The entire band suddenly jerks into motion and shoots forward and Evan feels like he's barely hanging on. They've all been playing together for who knows how long. They all know each other. And Evan is supposed to play with them? The key changes are abrupt and sometimes discordant. Evan is flailing, not in a groove at all. He's desperately looking at the bass player to see what key they're in, but it's a six string bass and he's all over the fret board.

But then Theo solos on the tenor sax and things settle down. The bass player smiles at Evan and leans in.

"Just chill, man," he shouts. *"Chill."*

Evan calms down and starts comping underneath the sax— ching-a-ching-ching-a-ching—until he gets the changes down.

Again, he looks for Lars and Dean. They're still there, Lars bobbing his big white head to the music and Dean smiling, bobbing along, too. Smiling.

Billy and his girlfriend are still at their table; the seats vacated by the band are filled with new friends. The girl glances up at Evan and smiles. He smiles back. Everyone is smiling. God, he loves music!

They cycle through the solos. Cello, trumpet, pedal steel, and then Theo turns to Evan, holds his hand like a gun, and pulls the trigger.

Bang.

Good musicians have a vocabulary of riffs and phrases and segues they can put together to make musical sense. The better the musician, the bigger the vocabulary, the more dynamic the performance. Evan, who's been playing the guitar seriously for twenty years and has the gift of remembering almost everything he hears, has an Oxford English Dictionary of riffs in his head. And, using as much of his vocabulary as he can, he puts together a solo that starts funky, dips into blues, touches on jazz and wails in rock. The other musicians nod in time, smile at his playing, until Theo points again and mouths "Step back," and Evan steps back. The tune continues a dozen more bars and then peaks with a cacophony of howls from the horns before it crashes to the floor.

"Dead," Theo says into the microphone.

The crowd cheers.

"Let's hear it for Evan, people."

More applause.

The musicians slap at Evan's hands, slap him on the back and then Theo steps up to Evan.

"Billy was right, you're good, man," he says into Evan's ear. "Next time you're in New York, gimme a call, we'll hang out."

"What the fuck were you doing up there?" Lars yells as soon as Evan arrives at the bar. The crowd shushes them. The band is playing.

"What the *fuck?*" Lars repeats in a whisper. He's shaking his head and grinning, his pale blue eyes open wide.

"You were fucking *jamming* with *Lucky Strike!*"

Shh! Shhh!

"This fucking guy," Lars laughs. He reaches out and punches Dean's arm. Dean laughs, too.

Evan tries to find Billy and Theo after the gig, but it's useless; they're gone. Lars offers Dean and him a lift home, and then, once they commit, announces to them that he can't sleep after a show so they all have to go to Denny's for ice cream. Lars and Dean have banana splits. Evan has a fruit salad.

After they indulge, Lars hands Dean a five-dollar bill.

"Go play a video game for a few minutes," he says, referring to the half dozen games in the front of the restaurant. "I need to talk to your dad. Then I'm gonna come and kick your ass."

"You wish," Dean says, scooping up the bill.

"You're gonna wish you hadn't just said 'you wish' by the time I'm done with you."

"I have no idea what that means," Dean says with a devilish grin as he walks away.

When he's safely out of earshot, Lars focuses on Evan.

"So," he says, "his mother died."

"Yes."

"And now you have custody."

"Custody?" Evan asks, startled. "No, not custody. He's just staying with me for a few days. He's living with his grandparents."

"His grandparents."

"Yes."

"His *maternal* grandparents."

"Right."

"And they live? . . ."

"Walla Walla."

"Walla Walla. Nice. And how much time, exactly, have you spent with him before this time?"

Evan doesn't like being questioned like this. He fiddles with his fork and squirms in his seat.

"None," he confesses.

"None. None at all. So you'd have to say you've never seen him before."

Evan thinks about telling Lars that he *has* seen Dean before, back when he was just a day old, but he knows it would make him sound even worse: if you're going to abandon your kid, do it as an act of passion; stand behind it; don't do it half-assed.

"So let me get this straight," Lars says. "You've never met this kid before. You find out his mother dies. You go to her funeral and end up taking the kid home with you—but you don't want custody of the kid or anything, he's just *visiting for a few days*. Is that about right?"

"I don't really feel comfortable discussing this at the present time," Evan says.

"Really. Well, then let me ask you this: why the hell did you go to her funeral in the first place if you didn't want the kid?"

Evan nervously looks around the restaurant. It's almost empty. Leave it to Lars to stick it to him in an empty Denny's.

"I mean, seriously, Ev," Lars continues. "You had to know that the second he saw you he'd want to be with you."

"He doesn't want to be with me. He hates me. He told me—"

"Really? He'd rather hang with his loser grandparents in Walla Walla than his cooler-than-life musician dad who jams with Lucky Strike on any given night and takes him out late for banana splits?"

Evan checks his watch. It's almost midnight.

"I should get him home."

Lars nods. "It's past his bedtime."

"Yeah."

Lars slides over on the banquette and rises.

"Let me play a couple of games with him first, okay? I promised him."

"Okay," Evan says.

Lars starts to go, then stops, "You know, Ev . . ."

But he doesn't say anything else. He just walks away. And Evan knows what Lars was going to say. He knows. So he waits a significant amount of time—more than he normally would have waited—and then he pays the bill and goes to collect Dean.

DEAN STANDS OVER the unblinking answering machine on the floor next to Evan's bed.

"Grandma didn't call."

Evan locks the door and heads toward the sound of Dean's voice.

"I'm sure she'll call tomorrow," he says.

Dean shrugs, pulls off his shirt. "Do you have a washing machine in here?"

"In the basement. Why?"

"I should wash this stuff before I wear it."

"You're already wearing it."

"My mom always said to wash clothes before you wear them," Dean says. "To take off the chemicals in the dye and pesticides they spray on the cotton plants."

Evan's never heard of such a clean concept. But it sounds like something a well-read, concerned mother would say, so he doesn't doubt its validity. Besides, he knows you should never argue with a kid's dead mom.

"I'll take you down tomorrow and show you how it works."

"Okay."

"Good night."

"Night."

AFTER HE BRUSHES his teeth, Evan opens the medicine cabinet and takes out three pill bottles. He spills little white pills from one of them onto the palm of his hand. How easy it would be to kill himself this second. A handful of phenobarbital and a fifth of vodka and he'd be beyond the reach of stomach pumping, that's for sure. It is Evan's ongoing struggle. If some people feel a compelling urge to jump, then he has a compelling urge to swallow every pill in the container every time he opens it. Every single time he has to say to himself calmly, "Only two, Evan. Only two."

Only two.

"I've really gotta—"

"What?" Evan jumps. He's so startled that he drops the bottle; the pills scatter in a million powdery-white directions. Pills, pills everywhere. He scrambles to scoop them up before they get wet.

"Sorry," Dean says as he pees noisily into the toilet. "I really had to go."

Shit. Several have slipped down the drain. A few are soaking up puddled water on the counter. And these are serious drugs, too. You can't just go back to the pharmacy and ask for a refill of barbiturates because you dropped the bottle. They'll want to know what happened to the pills. These pills actually have value on the black market. Some people take them for fun.

"Can I help?" Dean asks.

"No, no, I got it."

Dean watches Evan for a moment. "What are they?" he asks.

"Allergy pills."

"Oh. Sorry."

"No biggie. I have to get used to your being in the house. You startled me."

"Sorry."

Evan waves him off, and Dean goes back to the living room. Evan hears the springs of the bedframe flex as Dean climbs on. He looks down at the pills that are gathered near the drain stopper. Allergy pills. Jesus. What a stupid lie. What a stupid, pathetic lie.

H E WAS STILL in the hospital after the accident when he first
learned he had epilepsy. He was lying in bed watching
Magnum, P.I. with the sound off. His parents were there.

"How are you feeling?" the doctor asked.

"Fine."

"Good, good. Evan . . ." the doctor said, hiking up his hospital
scrubs as he sat at the end of the bed.

Evan waited for the doctor to speak. He was a hawklike man,
long teeth, a hook nose, beady gray eyes behind thick glasses.
Rough cheeks, oversized ears.

"While you were asleep, we had to perform surgery."

Evan stiffened. Asleep?

"You may not remember much of what happened before you
got here. Do you remember?"

Evan thought hard. He remembered things.

"It's very common," the doctor went on, "after a person has
been in a coma for a time, for that person not to remember the
events prior to the coma. Understand?"

Evan nodded. But he remembered things.

"It's the body's way of protecting you from trauma. Your body is censoring its own thoughts. Kind of nice, right?"

Right. But he remembered a lot of it. He remembered a car. He remembered the street.

"There was some bleeding in the membrane that surrounds your brain, and we had to relieve some of the pressure. You probably don't remember. And that's just fine. It was a relatively simple procedure."

A procedure. At twelve, Evan, a doctor's son, already knew most of the medical jargon. A procedure is an operation.

"There was also a small bone fragment we had to dig around a bit to find. We found it, but it seems that there is still some activity in that brain of yours."

With this, the doctor pointed to Evan's head and grinned a long, toothy grin.

"The EEG—the machine we use to monitor your brain waves—shows that your brain is sometimes working even when you think it isn't."

The doctor glanced back at Carl and Louise, who stood underneath Tom Selleck, staring intently at Evan.

But he remembered more. He remembered looking out from the body he was driving (driving, he thought, like driving a large construction crane, because at the time he felt a genuine separation of mind and body, dualism confirmed, *cogito, ergo sum*), looking out of those eyes and wondering at the dark stain on the road that grew and at the effect of parallax, which made the pool look large through his left eye but not so large through his right.

"It's called epilepsy," the doctor explained. "Epilepsy is a generic term for a neurological disorder that is characterized by seizures. Do you know what a seizure is?"

Evan nodded.

"We don't exactly know what causes epilepsy," the doctor continued. "Most epileptics are born with it. Some develop it later in life. Some develop a seizure disorder after a bad sickness. Some after a head trauma."

He remembered a woman asking him a question, and he remembered crinkling his brow. What had he done? He had done something. Something bad. And his actions had produced immediate results. There was blood. There was a taste of powder in his mouth. There was a darkling sky. There was a numbness in his body. He blinked, but he realized it was only a half-blink, really, because his eyes didn't open again. Not until he was safe and warm and dry in a hospital bed.

"We don't know how long you'll have this condition. It could go away tomorrow, or it could never go away. The epilepsy could manifest itself in seizures, or it could simply be a few spikes on our machines and nothing more. We don't know. There's no way to know."

There's no way to know. Evan branded that phrase into his mind. A doctor saying that. *There's no way to know.* That wasn't how Evan was raised. Evan was raised to believe that doctors knew everything. That was their job. To know things. To save lives. To fix problems.

"You'll have to stick close to your parents for a while," the doctor went on. "In case you have a seizure. You won't know about it, most likely, but someone will need to be there who can help you. Don't get down on yourself about it. A lot of people have epilepsy. Many people who have epilepsy lead full and productive lives. Some of them are teachers, for instance. Carpenters."

Evan tried hard to remember everything. He didn't want his body to protect him from anything. He wanted the truth.

"We'll give you some medication," the doctor said. "It may make you feel funny. It may take you a while to get used to. Some of the medication has side effects which you'll learn about. But the side effects are better, generally, than epilepsy. Side effects are predictable, epilepsy is not."

Evan must have had a strange look on his face, because the doctor held his gaze, then appealed to Carl, who said, "Do you understand what the doctor is saying, Evan?"

"Yes."

The doctor nodded approvingly at Carl.

"It's important to remember one thing, Evan," the doctor said. "It's a condition, not a disease. People can't catch it from you. Many great men have had epilepsy. It's nothing to be ashamed of."

Evan remembered the doctor saying that. *It's nothing to be ashamed of.*

Ashamed? The thought hadn't entered Evan's mind. But when he went home two days later and his parents said again, it's nothing to be ashamed of, he began to suspect. And then when they told him not to tell his friends he had epilepsy, not to tell his teachers, even not to tell his cousins, Evan understood what was going on: epilepsy *was* something to be ashamed of. But if anyone asked, he was supposed to say that he didn't feel ashamed.

THE PHONE RINGS late the next morning and it's Lars.

"Listen, Ev," he says, "I hope I didn't bum you out last night, man."

"No."

"I wasn't trying to give you a hard time. Everyone's got to do his own thing, right? I mean, I don't even know the whole situation, so I'm not trying to judge or anything."

"Yeah, sure," Evan says.

"But I've been thinking," Lars plows ahead, "since you're jamming with Lucky Strike and hanging with Billy Marx, I think maybe it's time for us to cut our demo."

Whoa, quick switch. Cut a demo? Their band, The Last, had been gigging for a few months, but they were still a little nervous about cutting a demo and trying to get a record deal. They knew they were good and they didn't want to screw it up.

"Talk to Rod and Tony about it," Evan says.

Rod and Tony were the *de facto* leaders of the band. They started it, found Lars, and then brought in Evan as a ringer. Sure, Evan was

good, but he also had experience and credibility, which he figured
they needed more than a good guitarist.

"I already did," Lars says. "They're cool with it."

"They are?"

"They're up for laying down a couple of tracks and seeing how
it sounds. If it's good enough, we'll mix it and shop it around.
They're cool with it."

But Evan isn't totally cool with it; he thinks they need more
work. Time to mature. Rod doesn't listen to Lars's drumming, and
Tony sounds too much like Kurt Cobain. But if everyone else
wants to . . .

"All right," Evan says. "I'll call Billy and book some time."

"I already did," Lars says proudly.

"Oh?"

"Tomorrow night, seven o'clock, The Sound Factory. Don't forget your guitar."

WELL, THAT CHANGES things. Here he is, expecting to give Dean
back at a moment's notice, and now he can't. He's willing to give
up a lot, but when it comes to his music, Evan does not compro-
mise. There's no way he's going to drive to Walla Walla and back
before a recording session. No way. It would take too much out of
him. Even if Ellen called that minute, he would tell her she had to
wait. So, he's stuck with Dean for a couple of days; at least until
after the session, the day after tomorrow if it doesn't go too late,
probably the day after that. So.

So they head up to Northgate Mall to buy things Dean will need
in the next few days, underwear and socks mostly. They prowl the
cavernous, taupe-colored mall, scavenging for sale items; and they
find stuff. Evan isn't sure how he'll afford it, but his credit card takes
hit after hit without barfing on the counter, so something's going
right for him. All the time they're shopping, young men and
women insistently pop in front of them with offers of a better deal
on a cell phone than the deal they are currently getting. Twenty-five

hundred free—twenty-five *thousand* free—no, no!—twenty-five *million* free minutes—anywhere, anytime, in perpetuity! Evan is afraid of these child-salesmen. They're like twelve-year-old hookers: accepting or declining their offer feels equally horrible. And, on top of that, Evan is mortified that he can't discern the ages of these people. Are they fresh out of high school, or fresh out of college? They're so clean. Haziness about age is not usually a problem Evan has to confront, especially considering that he spends a lot of time in bars playing gigs for these same kids—albeit these same kids in wilder clothes and spikier hair. He has always relied on his ability to divide people into Those Under and Those Over, a simple survival tactic. And he's good at it: he's never gotten into trouble for buying a sixteen-year-old vixen an amaretto sour, for instance. That's why these cell phone warriors confuse and concern him.

"What grade are you in?" Evan asks as he and Dean sit in the food court eating lunch, suddenly fearful that Dean will become a cell phone automaton when he grows up.

"I'm going into ninth."

Ninth? Jesus. It's August first. The new school year is a month away. That leaves only four years before Dean will be wearing a suit, hair neatly combed, hawking cell phone accessories at the local mall.

"Are you doing well?"

"Pretty well, I guess."

Who the hell cares? All you have to do is teach people how to tuck that earpiece thing behind their lobes. Big deal.

"Have you spent much time in Seattle?" Evan asks cheerfully, trying to block out the images he has of *himself*—a worse nightmare, if there could be one—impressed into employment and standing in a ridiculous booth with a handful of literature on roaming plans and calling features. "Do you want to do some sightseeing?"

Dean answers with a Dean-shrug.

"You must want to see *something* in Seattle. The Space Needle? We just have to watch out for earthquakes and terrorist attacks."

"How do you watch out for an earthquake?"

Did Evan detect a half-smile? A snide remark? Sarcasm? Something to build on?

"I don't know. If the monkeys start going crazy, I think. Don't monkeys sense earthquakes?"

"Do they keep earthquake monkeys at the Space Needle? What do they feed them? Popcorn and hot dogs?"

Humor. Excellent. Fantastic.

"Okay, forget it. It was just an idea."

They eat: Evan, his steamed vegetables and rice; Dean, fried clams and French fries and lemonade. When they are finished, they gather their garbage, bus their table, take up their bags and leave the mall.

"Where did my mom live?" Dean asks as they cross the parking lot toward Evan's car.

"When she was growing up?"

"Yeah."

"You want me to show you?"

Shrug. "I don't care."

Sure you do.

MAGNOLIA IS ALMOST an island; a hilly peninsula only accessible by bridge, just north of downtown, just south of Ballard, and just above Puget Sound. Its housing options are highly stratified. Basically, there are those houses with views, and those without, the ones "with" being much more expensive. Evan grew up with a view, Tracy without.

Evan takes Dean to Tracy's childhood house and stops across the street. The house has changed in the fifteen years since Evan last visited. Gone is the dark brown clapboard. Gone is the flat roof with the white rocks on it. (Truly a mystery: why did they put rocks on those roofs?) Gone are the large, unbroken expanses of glass, the aluminum screen doors, the cheap brass-plated door knobs, the uneven slate entryway, the strange ceramic wind chime that hung from the front eaves and played a deep, rich, melancholy tune on breezy nights. Tracy's house is not Tracy's house anymore.

Now it is a low, mission-style remodel, all natural cherry and faux limestone. A new shallow-peaked roof with cedar shakes. Sensible double-glazed windows with real wooden frames. It is a travesty of a renovation carried out by people who had enough money to do whatever they wanted with a house, but not nearly enough to buy a small container of good taste that they could keep in the back of their Sub-Zero and dip into on those rare occasions they might need it to save their aesthetic souls. Evan isn't sure if he feels worse for the people who live there or for Dean, who will never fully understand that his mother grew up in a completely run-of-the-mill Seattle-style, middle-income house, the kind that nobody ever thought twice about until some dweeb invented Windows and changed the world.

"It didn't look like that when she lived there."

The house is on the town side of the bluff, tucked into a winding road toward the south, near the Magnolia Bridge, formerly an undesirable location, but possibly now a New Hot Spot, since it provides a quicker escape at the expense of seclusion.

"It's nice," Dean says.

Is it nice? Maybe. If Evan could face the source of his own resentment, get over himself for a minute and confront his own prejudices, maybe it is nice. Sure. It's nice. But it isn't *Tracy's* house. That's what bugs him. It doesn't reflect her childhood at all. It doesn't hold a single memory for him. It has been gutted, stripped to the studs and rebuilt, and any echo of previous lives still held by the bones of the house are muffled beyond the range of human hearing by sturdy new 5/8" Imperial Sheetrock and skim coating.

"Where did *you* live?"

"Me? On the other side of the hill."

Dean waits. Not with a look of expectation, Evan thinks, but a look of naive assumption: obviously the Wallace house will be the next stop on The Tour. It's on the schedule. So Evan starts up the car and goes along with it.

They drive up through the ravine and around to the edge of the bluff where the madrona trees rustle their leaves at the wind. Here, the houses are bigger in size and stature. The yards are neater. The paint is fresher. Seeing that his mother's car isn't parked in the turning circle where she always parks it, Evan pulls in.

The Wallace house is a grand two-story Colonial, white, and clean, clean, clean. It's so clean, Evan's mother can't even keep a cleaning lady. They invariably quit on her when they realize how much will be asked of them, or they are fired when, after the third week of service, Louise discovers a picture frame that hasn't been moved for dusting. (Nothing bothers Louise more than a dusty spot under a picture frame.) After years of futility, Louise has given up and she cleans the house herself.

"Wow," Dean says, sizing up the place, "you're rich."

"*I'm* not rich, my father is."

"What's he do?"

"He's a heart surgeon—or, he used to be. He doesn't operate anymore. He's too famous. Now he runs the hospital."

"Cool," Dean says.

"Not really."

Evan feels a strange kind of pride, though, having brought Dean to the place he was raised. A sense of authorship over his life, or something. Thus emboldened, he gets out of the car.

"Where are we going?" Dean asks.

"Inside."

Dean hesitates.

"Don't worry," Evan says. "Nobody's home."

The house is, indeed, quite empty. The alarm warning goes off when Evan opens the door, and he feeds it the code to shut it up.

"Shoes," Evan says, slipping his off as an example. You always take off your shoes when you go to Carl and Louise's house. Dean complies.

They hear a weak woof from the kitchen. Evan leads Dean back through the marble hallway. A dog gate is braced between the doorjambs. Behind it is Ralphy.

Ralphy is Carl and Louise's sad old retriever that they got when Evan moved out on his own and Charlie went away to college. At the time they said their house felt so empty that they needed to fill it. So they saved Ralphy from Death Row at the animal shelter and brought him home. Little did they know he would be a major problem. Cute. Scruffy. But totally retarded and untrainable, able to eat entire pillows without so much as a burp, skilled at chewing the most expensive shoes into rawhide and at crapping in the worst possible places. And he eats rocks. Nobody knows why. Veterinarians are mystified. But Ralphy actually eats rocks.

Upon seeing Evan, Ralphy pants and wags his tail so hard he almost knocks himself down (he has arthritic hips, and balance isn't something he's especially good at). He barks once, happily, and then pees on the floor.

"That's why he's locked in the kitchen," Evan explains to Dean. "Easier to clean."

He steps over the gate, takes a mop out of the broom closet and quickly cleans up.

"He smells," Dean says.

Evan opens the back door and lets Ralphy outside, where he begins chasing imaginary flies, another of his quirks. Evan sighs. His parents stick by Ralphy, he has to give them that. They could have dispatched him a decade ago and saved themselves a lot of heartache and who knows how much money. But they wanted to see their project through. Ralphy is living proof that love can persevere through any hardship.

They go on a quick tour of the house, which basically means they walk through the rooms without pause. Upstairs, Evan opens one of the doors.

"This is my old bedroom."

Dean peers in.

"It's an office," he says.

"True. This is my brother's old bedroom."

"Wow."

Evan knew that would get a reaction. It shocks everyone. Evan's old bedroom is a generic and disused office space housing a desk and an outdated computer and not much else, while Charlie's old bedroom is more like a shrine. Every single thing that Charlie ever did is on display. Every poster or photo that he pinned to his walls twenty years ago is still there. The bedspread is the same one he used as a child. The trophies he won for the debate society and school newspaper competitions are brightly polished and prominently displayed. The only recent items are his college and law school diplomas and his *New York Times* wedding announcement, all of which are elegantly framed and hung. It's almost like the Whitman Mission. Evan wonders if his parents ever considered adding an audio element to the display. You know, put on headphones, press play and James Earl Jones tells the story of Charlie's life.

Mention any of this to Evan's mother, and you will get many easy explanations: Charlie has a son, and little Eric needs to see his father's history; your room looks out over the street so I can see when the UPS man is making a delivery; the afternoon sun is too bright in Charlie's room; you don't really care about things like that anyway, but Charlie does—he's so sensitive. Mention it a second time, and you'll get a cold look. Mention it a third time, and she'll stop talking to you for the rest of dinner. A fourth, and you'll get a call from your father late one night asking you to please knock it the hell off, stop badgering your mother, with the bitter tag line: "Stop being such a shit."

Dean, thankfully, doesn't dwell on Charlie's accomplishments, but, instead, ventures into Louise's office. There, Evan's clever child quickly finds the sole artifact of Evan's existence. Neatly framed and hanging on the wall is an album cover.

"What's Dog Run?" Dean asks.

"My band. It's what I'm famous for."

"You don't look famous."

"*Almost* famous. That's an album my old band put out eleven years ago. It had a really good song on it that turned into kind of an overnight grunge hit. The rest of the album sucked. It's not like it mattered. Our lead singer killed himself before anything good could happen. You can't tour without a lead singer."

"How did he do it?"

"What?"

"Kill himself."

Evan hesitates, but he's in too deep. "He crashed his motorcycle."

"Into another car?"

"No, off the Alaska Way Viaduct. He just drove off and died. He was probably on drugs. He usually was."

"Oh."

"You want some juice or something?"

"Okay."

They go downstairs and sit at the kitchen table drinking orange juice. They say nothing, and Evan regrets mentioning the suicide of Jeff Beasley, the ill-fated lead singer of Dog Run. It's clearly not appropriate conversation for a kid whose mom has just died in a car crash.

After a few silent minutes of sipping and gazing out at the Sound, which sparkles beautifully in the afternoon sun, Ralphy scratches at the back door. Evan lets him in and gives him a dog biscuit. He rinses out his glass and puts it on the dish rack, then meanders over to the telephone desk and pokes around. His mother's calendar book is there. He pages through it, finds today's date, looks. *Marty, 1:30–3:00.* Hmm. Marty. Her golf instructor. Until three. Hmm. What time is it now? Three-fifteen.

Holy shit. Suddenly the magnitude of the stupidity of what he is doing crashes down upon him. His mother is on her way home. What the hell is he thinking? They have to get out of there, and fast!

"We should go," he says, scrawling a note: *Stopped by to say hello. No one home. Call me. E.*

He slips the note onto the kitchen table and snatches Dean's half-filled glass away from him.

"Hey, I'm still thirsty."

"We'll stop at the Circle K."

He quickly rinses the glass and sets it on the rack, then catches himself. That's a clue for a good detective, which his mother is. He dries one of the glasses with a paper towel and puts it back in the cupboard. He pats Ralphy on the head and grabs Dean. He sets the alarm and hustles Dean outside to the car. She isn't home yet, thank God. He pulls out of the driveway. At the end of the block he glances into the rearview mirror. Jesus. There she is in her silver Mercedes. What timing. Pulling into one end of the street just as he pulls out of the other. She'll be able to feel the breeze of their leaving in the hallway. She'll be able to smell them in the kitchen. It's like going home and sensing that a burglar was just there, the cord on the window shade still swinging back and forth. Dangerous. What the hell was he thinking?

LATER THAT AFTERNOON, Ellen calls.

"Everything's fine," she says. "You can bring Dean home."

Home? Evan finds her use of the word slightly amusing. Where is his home? His home is in Yakima, not Walla Walla and not Seattle. So when she says to bring him "home," what does she mean?

"You have to understand that Tracy's death took us both very hard," she says in response to his silence. "We were both very upset, Frank and I. He hadn't slept in days, and the doctor gave him some medication which was supposed to help him sleep but just made him irritable and angry, and then he woke up and saw that Dean wasn't there. . . ." she trails off. "Everything's fine," she reassures both Evan and herself. "You can bring him back."

He wants to be snide and tell her to fuck off, but then what would he do with Dean? He needs everything to be fine with Ellen and Frank. So, unfortunately, he has to root for her.

"I can't bring him back right now," Evan says. "I have an important session at the recording studio tomorrow night that's going to go late, and I can't drive to Walla Walla and back tomorrow."

"You could put him on a bus," she suggests.

"I could FedEx him, too, but I won't."

"Oh. Of course not. I didn't mean . . . Well, you two can spend some more time together then. Are you enjoying it?"

"Yes."

"Good. So when *will* you be able to bring him home?"

"Probably Sunday."

"Oh. Sunday would be fine. You can stay for dinner."

Evan doesn't respond.

"We really miss him terribly, Evan," Ellen goes on. "Frank's been painting his room for him. We have an old pool table—oh, it must be thirty years old—that we used to have for the kids, you must remember it."

"I don't recall—"

"We got it when the kids were young. It was in the basement."

"I don't recall ever being made welcome in your house, Mrs. Smith."

"It's in terrible shape now, of course. We're thinking of having it re-felted. And the garage is a workshop—very nice, Frank did all the work himself—we'll clean it out and set up the pool table and Dean will have his own rec room so he can invite his friends over. It would bring us a tremendous amount of joy to have him here, especially after Tracy's death. You understand. And you can visit whenever you like. You can stay with us, or there's an inn down the street, a bed and breakfast, you know, for the parents of the college kids, when they come for commencement. We have a very festive spring here in Walla Walla, I'm sure you didn't know."

"I'm sure."

"So, what time can we expect you?"

He stews. He doesn't like Frank and he doesn't like Ellen. And he doesn't like how this whole thing went down, how they took Dean away as a baby and excluded Evan. But he has no choice really—*realistically*—he has no alternative.

"Around three," he says.

"Wonderful," Ellen beams. "We'll be expecting you."

THEY DRIVE ON a thin strip of pavement that is balanced high in the air between the impassive buildings of downtown and the hustle of the waterfront; past the way-too-cute stadiums—and calling anything that size "cute" has got to be a compliment; past rows and rows of revitalized warehouses; past the old Sears building—the new Starbucks headquarters; past the galleries and espresso shops and cleverly designed logos on neatly painted offices for Information Age technologies already obsolete; into the heart of SoDo, South of Downtown, an area that twenty years ago was a dangerous place to go after dark, where companies preferred razor ribbon over welcome mats, but has since become home of the hipsters and shakers, and home to Billy Marx's recording studio, which is the ultimate badge of cool.

The Sound Factory. The place where any movie, commercial, music video, or album worth a damn is recorded. It's a massive, squat three-story building filled to the brim with rehearsal spaces, Foley rooms, and high-tech studios jammed with millions of dollars worth of the latest digital gear that can handle just about anything anyone can think of.

Billy, the consummate nice guy, knows how the balance of power and money works in the recording industry: the labels have all the power and the money, the musicians don't. So he has a floating rate scale. Hollywood pays a million dollars an hour, anyone who was cool enough to be with The Sound Factory guys when they started, over a dozen years earlier in a little building in Pioneer Square, pays a dollar. A modern-day socialism. To each according to his needs, from each according to his familiarity.

As soon as they enter the building, Evan relaxes. The lobby itself isn't very inviting. It's a hollow, stark-white room with high ceilings of exposed I-beams, industrial lighting with a purplish glow, and poured concrete floors. But everything else about the room is welcoming. It's the perfect temperature. Not too hot, not too cold. The air circulates enough to keep everything fresh, but not so much as to create a breeze. There are no windows, no clocks, no indication of time whatsoever. Once inside, one loses all temporal reference; literally, one loses one's ability to discern day from night. Like a casino, The Sound Factory is a biorhythmic obfuscation chamber. Time is not the issue at The Sound Factory. It's never late at The Sound Factory. Work through the night. Work through the next day. Our staff is happy to serve you, and we have comfortable couches for you to nap on. Work forever. And please pay your bill within thirty days. Thank you.

Evan notices Dean's mouth, which is agape at the spectacle.

"Pretty nice," Evan says.

Dean closes his mouth and shrugs like it's an everyday thing in Yakima. *We've got places like this on every corner.* He coolly plants himself in one of the arm chairs and picks up a magazine.

Evan is too high to sit. He's charged up and ready to go. He's cleared the weekend out. (Evan, one of the best commissioned salesmen on the floor at Fremont Guitar, always gets the prime hours: Thursday through Sunday afternoons and evenings; times when guitar buyers are at their peak. So Angel, the new kid, was happy to take Evan's spot in exchange for Evan working Angel's graveyard days: Monday through Wednesday.) And Dean, who's turning out to be a pretty cool, self-reliant kid—probably the result of growing up without a father—has been great. Evan told him he needed to practice for the session, and Dean, without so much as an eye roll, hopped a bus and spent the day at some upscale video arcade in a new shopping center downtown. He had a blast, and it only cost Evan forty bucks. Parenting ain't that hard, but it can be expensive.

A doorbell rings, a pleasant electric chime. The receptionist, a pretty young blonde, glances at a video monitor set into her desk, and then presses a button. The lock clicks, and in comes Lars, toting his stick bag and cymbal case. Right behind Lars is Billy Marx.

Billy notices Evan, stops and smiles.

"Evbee." He strides over and greets Evan with the obligatory hip-hop embrace. "I ran into Lars in the parking lot. I didn't know you guys were coming in tonight. Why didn't you call me?"

"He did the calling," Evan says, gesturing to Lars.

"I called," Lars says, "but I just talked to whoever was in scheduling."

"You know better than that, Lars. If you want a first-class upgrade, you gotta talk to me, brother."

"My bad," Lars says with a sheepish grin. "Next time."

"Lars is all hot to make a demo," Evan says.

"Oh, yeah? You guys ready to break out?"

"Looks like."

"Theo's still talking about you, man," Billy says. "He said he wanted to lift one of your riffs, but he couldn't figure it out. He said you have thumbs like Jimi Hendrix. Hendrix had the longest motherfucking thumbs!"

They all laugh, including Dean, who's sitting in his chair paging through a copy of *Billboard*.

Billy points at him with his chin.

"Who's that?"

"My son," Evan says. "Dean, come here and meet the smartest guy I ever met who I wasn't related to."

Dean jumps up and comes over, offering his hand, which Billy takes.

"Your son?" Billy shakes his head. "Fucking Evbee." Then to Dean, "Nice to meet you," along with a regular white person's handshake.

"Hold on." Billy suddenly breaks off and crosses the lobby to the receptionist.

"Where are they, Sybil?"

"Studio E. All night."

"Lemme see the schedule."

Sybil, the receptionist, hands over a large ledger sheet, which Billy studies.

"Who's free?"

"Mica is."

"Mica? Why?"

"Pepsi canceled," Sybil says.

"Those crackheads. When are they gonna get their shit together?"

Sybil shrugs and smiles, as if to say "I just work here."

"So Mica's just sitting around eating carrot sticks and doing sit-ups all night?"

Sybil nods.

"The Van Sant movie's in C. So put these guys in B, and give them Mica."

He hands the ledger back to Sybil and looks over to Evan.

"Anybody paying for this, Evbee?"

"Just us," Evan says.

Billy turns back to Sybil.

"Straight up, then. No room charge and bill them at rate on Mica, no premium. I'm paying her to sit around all night, she might as well work for it."

Billy returns to where Evan, Lars, and Dean are standing.

"All right, I hooked you guys up. The studio is on me, you buy the engineer. Cool?"

"Cool," Evan says, "thanks."

"Don't mention it."

"Did you say Mica?" Lars asks. "Mica Morrison?"

Billy nods.

"Dude, you rock."

"Don't be intimidated," Billy says. "I'll drop in on you guys later on." He grins at Evan. "Evbee with a teenage son. Whack, yo."

Billy thumps fists with Lars and heads toward one of the doors that leads to some inner sanctum. As he reaches the door, Sybil hits the buzzer and the door miraculously opens for him. Then he is gone.

Lars smiles at Evan.

"Mica Morrison. Shit. She can make anybody sound good."

"Who's Mica Morrison?" Evan asks.

"Your studio is ready," Sybil says with an appetizing smile, pressing some secret button under her desk and releasing the electric lock on yet another door. Evan, Dean, and Lars step through and head for their first-class upgrade.

S TUDIO B. RUMOR has it that the Rolling Stones recorded a
track off their last album in Studio B. Rumor has it that Kenny
G, of all people, records only in Studio B. The studio isn't any different than Studios A or C, but it is the favored studio of Mica
Morrison, the famous engineer. A legend in her own time. A
mythical figure in the Seattle music scene. Occasionally she works
on an independent album as a favor or because she feels especially
charitable, but for the most part, she sticks to the majors. Major
labels, major artists. Apparently she's pretty hot. Apparently she's a
lesbian. All of this information is offered by Lars as he, Evan, and
Dean set up in the studio.

Evan appreciates Lars's banter, and indulges him in his engineering fetish. Lars makes it his mission to know everything he can
about engineering records. He memorizes lists of the top engineers, knows all the jargon, understands all the concepts, the mik-
ing techniques. It's his thing.

Lars immediately adopts Dean as his assistant, and they work
together setting up the drums, with Dean doing the heavier

work—fetching the pieces from Lars's van. Evan hauls his amp in and places it on a felt-covered wooden box to get it off the ground. He brought his Fender Deluxe tonight, one of the first amps he'd ever gotten and still his favorite. It isn't very big, but it weighs a ton, and it sounds just how he likes it. He takes his guitar out of its case, a '68 Stratocaster, and straps it on.

All the while this busy work is going on, and Lars is prattling on about drum mikes and phase cancellation, Evan's mind begins to wander. He tries to keep everything tight on the music, but his thoughts are scattered. It's kind of a big deal to make a demo, diminished only slightly by the fact that they're paying for it themselves instead of having a record company foot the bill. But that's okay. There's still plenty of excitement around making music on tape, or on computer, as the case may be. He remembers back in the day, years ago, when Dog Run recorded their album. A month of nonstop work in a cabin up on Dabob Bay, mornings spent scouring the beach for oysters, afternoons spent napping, nights spent working out their songs. And then two weeks of nonstop work in the studio. He was good then, but not *as* good. He had the energy without the technique. Now he has the technique without the energy. And he didn't have a reputation back then. He was just himself. Now he's a hired gun. They brought him in, a ringer, someone with a record, both figuratively and literally. They wanted what he brought them, an instant upgrade at a recording studio, for instance. Maybe someone takes a longer listen to their demo because "that Dog Run guy is on it." They fired their friend, the guy they grew up with, and brought in Evan, and Evan was expected to produce. And Evan *would* produce. Pressure? Nah. Pressure is growing up without a father. Pressure is having your mother crushed to death in a high-speed wreck when you're fourteen years old. What does Evan know of pressure?

He shakes his head quickly from side to side to get himself back into the room. The room. The studio. The session. Now is not the time to get lost in yourself.

Lars stops fiddling with his set and looks up.

"You okay?" he asks from his stool. He's gnawing at his thumbnail again. It's best when you let it heal for a few days and then go at it just as it's scabbing over.

"Yeah."

"You zoned, man. Where're Tony and Rod?"

"Dunno."

What's the matter? Feeling a little detached, are we?

That mind-body thing again. Dualism again. Evan doesn't like the concept of dualism. He wants monism. He doesn't want to feel that his body is just a vehicle for his mind. Because that's sometimes the first step. That feeling followed by the realization that the world could end tomorrow—doom—and the next thing you know you're standing in the middle of a big fat seizure with nowhere to go.

He has to have some pot before things go down the wrong road. A few hits should even things out, calm him down, make him forget about the possibilities. He glances around the room. Marijuana and sound studios go hand in hand. All musicians smoke and drink and screw and do all kinds of other illicit shit in a sound studio. Normally, Evan would just whip out his pipe and light it up. But Dean is here. Evan is Dean's father. Evan has to set some kind of an example. He has to find another place.

"I gotta take a leak," Evan says.

"Bleed the lizard," Lars says.

"Spank the monkey," Dean says.

Lars looks at him crookedly. "'Spank the monkey?'" he asks. "That's whacking off. He's not gonna whack off. You're not gonna whack off, are you?"

"Not that I know of."

"He's gonna take a piss. Get your vulgarity straight."

"Sorry," Dean says.

"Hand me my ride cymbal."

"Which one?"

"The big one," Lars groans. "It says 'ride' on it."

"Sorry."

"And quit apologizing. You're gonna make people think you're a pussy. The proper response is 'Shut your face.'"

"Shut your face," Dean says, handing Lars the cymbal.

"You're a good kid," Lars says. He turns to Evan with a wink. "He's a good kid. You should be proud."

"I am," Evan says, and quickly leaves the room.

He wanders the labyrinthine halls, venturing deep into the icy bowels of The Sound Factory. Most doors are locked, and the ones that aren't locked open into empty studios or mechanical rooms. That's the magic of The Sound Factory. There are no utility closets. Apparently, there is no need. The Sound Factory keeps itself clean by using high-tech ionizing defragmentors which vaporize all dust and dirt instantly. Crazy.

There's a men's room, but that's too public. There's somebody's office, probably a day-worker, but what if Evan gets caught? He tries one more door, his last attempt. It opens. It's dark inside. He flips on the light. Ah. The long awaited utility closet. Spacious and roomy. A ladder, a shelf full of light bulbs and paper towels, and the obligatory mop and pail. Perfect. He steps inside.

"Can I help you find something?" a woman calls out from the end of the hall. Evan hopes she isn't calling him. He looks around. She *is* calling him.

"I'm okay," Evan responds cheerfully.

The woman approaches. Evan's heart stops.

It's *her.*

The girl. Billy's girl. She smiles at him and waves. She remembers him.

He finds himself short of breath. She's wearing jeans, sneakers, and a tiny cardigan buttoned only once, revealing her navel, her taut stomach, a pleasant amount of cleavage, and a black lace bra.

"If you're looking for a light bulb, you probably should let me call Maintenance. They get kind of bent out of shape when a client tries to lift a finger around here. It's a union thing. You know."

She reaches Evan. She's shorter than he is. Her eyes are a deep chocolate brown that seem so calm and optimistic. Her smile offers only uncontainable joy, joy that works for her, and that she can give out as she sees fit. All in all, she's the kind of girl Evan could fall in love with. Instantly.

"Um," he hesitates, one foot in the closet and one foot out. "Listen, can I be honest?"

She nods, still smiling.

"I kind of wanted to find a place to smoke a little pot. Just a little bit."

"Ah. You can smoke in the studios. There are signs that say no smoking, but you can smoke. No one will say anything."

"But my son is in there and I don't really want to smoke around him. No one will mind if I just duck in here, will they?"

She shrugs. Evan smiles. "Thanks," he says. He steps into the closet and closes the door. But before he can get it closed, she slips in with him.

"You want some?" he asks. Why else would she join him in a utility closet?

"No thanks. That stuff makes me paranoid."

Evan locks the door and quickly loads his pipe. He lights the lighter and inhales the smoke. Relief. Relaxation. He can feel the tightness in his brain releasing.

"You were really great the other night," she says.

She remembers? Why would she remember?

"Theo was really into you. We went out after, and he kept on talking about you and laughing. He thought it was the greatest thing that a rock and roller would just get up and jam with them. He said you had to be pretty confident to get up at someone else's gig."

"Yeah, well. Confident? Maybe more like stupid."

"No."

She watches him as he reloads the one-hitter and lights up again.

"Smoking helps your music?" she asks. She's sitting on the step-ladder, hunched forward, looking at Evan. There's something about her, about the way she looks and the way she sits on a stepladder. And it isn't just the thin gold chain with the small gold medallion that's tight around her neck. (Evan has always found chokers sexy.) There's something else that gives Evan's heart a little lift.

Evan shakes his head no.

"You have a session and you're nervous?"

"Well, yes. But that's not why I'm smoking," Evan answers.

"Why, then? Just out of curiosity."

Does that count? Is that enough of a reason to justify being told the truth? That Evan has epilepsy?

"I smoke for medical reasons," Evan says. The same half-answer he gave to Dean, which, thankfully, Dean never pursued.

"Cancer?"

"No."

"Glaucoma? I've heard of people smoking pot for glaucoma."

"No."

Her shoulders drop, her face turns glum.

"AIDS?" she asks sadly.

Evan shakes his head, more to himself than to her. He's spent his entire life denying his condition to anyone who asks. When he was a kid at summer camp, if another kid saw him taking pills and asked why, Evan would make up a quick lie: allergy pills, for instance. In school, if a teacher punished him because he didn't answer her question in class, Evan wouldn't tell her he was having a seizure and was unable to speak, he would stand behind his behavior as an act of defiance. It was part of Evan's *fabric*. It was condoned by the officials of his life, his parents, the ones who made the rules. One time, way, way back, Evan was fourteen or so, and there was a family reunion at their house, everyone was there, cousins and aunts and uncles, people who hadn't been heard from or seen for decades, and Evan had a seizure. A full-blown status grand mal. The ambulance came. They took him to the hospital where he stayed for three days. The whole thing. Did Evan's mother take the opportunity to tell her family that Evan had epilepsy? Did she explain it all to them at that moment? Heavens, no. She told them that Evan was dehydrated. He was trying to lose weight for the wrestling team, she said. He'd been fasting. Sweating himself. That's why he had the seizure. All of which wouldn't have been so freaking pathetic if Evan had actually been *on* the wrestling team. He'd quit months earlier when Johnny Kruger tried to rip his arm out of its

socket and Evan cried and the coach slapped him and called him a
baby. Evan's entire life, since he was twelve, has been spent denying
one of the main things that defines him. His epilepsy. So why
would he tell this girl now?

"Fuck it," he says suddenly.

"Fuck what?"

"I have epilepsy," he says. "Sometimes pot lets me stop a seizure
I feel coming on."

"Wow," she perks up. "I've never heard of that. Really?"

"Yeah. It's a relaxation thing. Like asthma. When you get an
asthma attack, your fear and anxiety over the attack constricts your
capillaries and actually makes the attack worse. For me, sometimes
the stress of worrying about a seizure can bring on a seizure. So
smoking pot relieves the anxiety. That's the theory, at least."

"Interesting."

"There are other theories."

"Really?"

"But no clinical studies. You can imagine the issues . . ."

"Oh, sure."

"I wasn't even having an aura," Evan continues, enjoying his
newfound liberation. As long as he doesn't start explaining to her
what *status epilepticus* means. That'll make her bolt. Epilepsy is sensitive and quaint in a potential partner only if the seizures are
exceedingly mild. If every seizure is a near-death experience, the
idea of a long-term relationship dissolves pretty quickly. "I was just
afraid that maybe I would have an aura soon." He thinks about that
statement a moment, and realizes how it sounds. "All right," he says,
"it's a crutch sometimes. But it's better than a grand mal seizure, I
can tell you that."

"I'll bet," she says.

They stare at each other for a few moments, locking eyes. It
worked. He'd said enough but not too much. He could feel more
electricity circulating in the room than just the bare bulb overhead
and whatever excess was skittering around in his brain.

"What?" he asks.

"You have pretty eyes."

"You, too," Evan says.

"Not like you."

Again, the stare. The heated I-like-you stare.

"I should get to my studio. The guys must all be there waiting." She nods. "The guys."

Evan unlocks the door. He opens it and they step out into the hallway.

"I have no idea where I am," Evan admits.

"Where are you going?"

"Studio B."

"This way."

He follows her down the hall. The pot is having its effect. Not its seizure-defusing effect. That's already taken care of. But in the closet with this girl, Evan probably smoked more than he usually did and now he's stoned. He tries to focus on the hallway in front of him, but his eyes keep drifting down to this girl's ass, small and round, and the way her Levi's fit nicely around the curves, gapping a little at the small of her back to remind everyone that there's a naked girl underneath.

"What are you looking at?"

Evan looks up. They've stopped in front of a door.

Evan starts to answer, he tries to answer, but he really doesn't know what to say.

"Your studio," she says.

"You're working tonight?" Evan asks, realizing that she'll be leaving him soon.

"Yeah."

"Maybe we could get a cup of coffee during break or something?"

"Maybe."

"I mean, I'd like to see more of you—that's not what I mean." She laughs.

"You'll see more of me," she says. She opens the door to the studio and goes in. Evan is confused. He follows her into the room.

"How's everything going in here?" she calls out. Lars and Dean are there. So are Rod and Tony. "You guys find everything you need?"

Lars shoots up from behind his drum set. He rushes around his ride cymbal and heads toward the girl.

"Ms. Morrison," he stammers, his right hand outthrust. "I own every album you've ever engineered, and it's a real honor to be able to work with you."

"Just call me Mica," the girl says.

"This is Tony and this is Rod," Lars says, pointing them out. "This is my assistant, Dean. And this is our gem, our shining star, our brilliant guitarist, Evan."

Mica smiles at Evan.

"We've already met," she says.

MICA ASKS QUESTIONS about the band, their sound, how they want to handle the vocals, and so on. They all agree that they like a live sound, so they'll play together, in one room, without headphones. Keeping it real. The questions turn to more sophisticated sound issues: overdubbing, reverb, layering of tracks, filtering, boosting. Things that a novice band doesn't really know about because they haven't had the exposure. But Evan has had the exposure, having done all of this before, and Lars knows the lingo, so the two of them answer most of the questions.

She frowns when they tell her they don't have a producer, because that thrusts her into the role of producer pro tem, and she doesn't like producing, she mutters loud enough for everyone to hear. If she liked producing, she would *be* a producer. Evan looks at his bandmates and knows that they're feeling intimidated, which is what Billy warned against. He's feeling intimidated, too, but not by her rapid-fire questions. He's intimidated because whenever she glances at him his stomach flies into his mouth like he's on a roller coaster.

"Well, I guess we'll plow our way through it," she says hopefully, heading off to the control room door. "Let me get my panel set while you guys get warmed up."

She opens the door that leads to the dark room behind the glass wall and steps inside. The door sucks shut behind her.

"I'd like to plow my way through *her* sometime," Rod says when she's gone.

"Dude," Lars says, "don't be an idiot. She can hear you."

"Oh, shit."

Lars shakes his head in disgust. "You guys are a bunch of freaking amateurs. She fucking engineers The Rolling Stones. If you can't act professionally, at least keep your mouths shut."

"Fuck you," Rod snaps.

"Get in line behind your mother," Lars fires back.

Dean laughs.

"And what's with the midget?" Rod asks. "Who invited *him?*"

"He's not a midget, he's a kid," Lars says, standing quickly enough to knock over his throne. "And I invited him. And if you don't like it, you can fucking come over here and talk to me about it."

"Guys, guys," Tony says quickly, trying to stop the fight before it starts. "Relax. We're all a little freaked out. Let's just relax, let her do her thing, and we'll do our thing."

Calmed, everyone resumes fidgeting with their equipment.

Evan tries to peer into the control room, but Mica has the lights off inside so the glass wall is nothing but a mirror, reflecting the image of the band back at him.

He sees Lars, of course. Who could miss him? With his silvery crew cut and the dent in his skull he is, somehow, immensely likeable. He and Evan forged a bond the moment they met, and have been good friends from the beginning. The same can't be said for his relationship with Tony and Rod.

Tony is a good guy deep down, Evan is sure, though he usually walks in the shadow of Rod, the bass player. Tony is the band's front man, and he looks the part. He's of average height, but that's the only thing about him that's average. He sports a shaved head and a goatee and intense Charles-Mansonesque eyes. He is relatively conservative in terms of piercing—considering the vogue of the time—with only his ears and one eyebrow pierced by modest silver hoops. He's built like a rock, with massive tattooed arm muscles that are always on display since he never wears a shirt with sleeves, no matter what the weather. He wears tight leather pants and steel-toed boots and his fingers are covered with chunky silver rings that have been cast from the molds of small rodent skulls. He has thick lips and broad, flat cheekbones, and is brutally handsome in a way that attracts teenage girls.

He's a strange counterpart to Rod, the bass player and puppet master, who is definitely not attractive. If anything, he's the anti-Tony. He's a big guy, but Evan thinks he carries himself like a small guy. His face is marked with a permanent scowl that seems carved into his forehead. He wears black horn-rim glasses, plaid fifties shirts and Doc Martens. But it's Rod's hair that catches people's attention the most. It's dark brown, shoulder length, and matted into long, clumpy fingers—white man's dreadlocks—that dangle in his face, cover his eyes, and swing to and fro when he shakes his head, which he does often. This combination of styles gives people the impression that Rod is a kind of cross-cultural iconoclast, a Rasta Buddy Holly, and actually makes him seem more fearsome than Lars with his dented forehead, more fearsome than Tony with his bulging arms, and certainly more fearsome than Evan, who's pretty much the wimp of the group.

"Evan, can you come in here a minute?" a thin, disembodied voice asks. It's Mica, or at least a metallic facsimile of her voice that comes out of a black speaker mounted over the control room window.

Evan points at himself. "Me?"

"Yes, you."

He glances at the other guys, who grin at him with various degrees of letch. He goes inside.

The control room is warm and dark, like a cocoon. Its chairs are plush, it feels safe. Mica sits at a twenty-foot-long mixing panel full of dials, knobs, and levers that would make a 747 pilot feel right at home. She manipulates the controls; Evan waits patiently for her.

She looks like she knows what she's doing, flipping switch after switch with ease and dexterity.

"That's your son?"

"Yeah."

"Where's your wife?"

"I don't have a wife."

"Okay." Mica nods. "Where's your son's mother?"

"She died recently. Automobile accident."

"Oh, my God," Mica says, swiveling her chair around to face Evan. "I'm so sorry."

"Yeah," Evan says. "Me, too."

"So it's just you two."

"Yeah."

"Well, you seem to be getting along okay."

"We are. We're getting along very well, thanks."

They look at each other a moment, both sort of nodding their heads, taking in the gravity of what is in the past, tucking it securely away and gearing up for the future.

"Listen, I'm not a producer," she says turning back to the control panel.

"I know."

"Don't expect me to produce your demo. I'm not a savior."

"I know."

"A lot of people think I'm some magician. They think if they can get me to mix their tracks, they'll have a hit. That's not it. I listen to what's going on, that's all. I listen to the music and I listen to the producer and I put it together. A lot of what I mix becomes top-forty stuff because I work with really talented people. I just want you to know that."

"Okay."

"If you guys don't have a producer, one of you had better speak up when we listen to playback."

"Okay."

She stops working and turns around.

"Whose band is it, anyway?" she asks.

Evan cocks his head, momentarily confused. "It's ours—"

"Who's the leader? Just so I know. It's not Tony and it's not Lars."

She looks up at him, waiting for an answer.

"Rod," he says.

"The bass?"

"Yeah."

"Interesting look."

Evan follows Mica's eyes out to the studio where Rod is setting up his bass. It's true, Rod has an interesting look.

"Did he come up with it himself?" Mica asks.

"I think it came to him in a dream."

"Ha," she says, and smiles at him. "You want to get something to eat after this is all over?"

"Sure."

Now it's getting confusing. She's Billy's girlfriend. Why would she? . . .

"But, my son . . ."

"I don't mind if he comes," she says. "Oh, you mean it's too late for him?"

"No, no, I— Sure. I mean, I should ask him. But I'm sure he'd love to."

"Good. I'm asking now so you don't have to worry that I think you're a lousy musician or not a nice guy or anything. I kind of have a reputation for being a bitch during a session because I don't take any crap from anybody and because I know when someone's trying to get by without playing their best and I'll call them on it. So if I have to yell at you or something it's only because maybe I see you can do better. Don't take it personally. Okay?"

"Okay," Evan says.

"One more thing," she says.

"Yeah?"

"How'd you get that scar?"

She traces an invisible line on her own slender, unblemished neck that corresponds with Evan's scar, a thin, two-inch-long horizontal line on his throat just below his Adam's apple. Hardly noticeable. He's only been asked about it a handful of times in his life. It's a difficult scar to see, but once you see it, you can't forget it. It's a tracheotomy scar.

He smiles at her and touches his neck so they're both touching the same spot on themselves. She laughs when she notices what he's done, but not nervously. She laughs easily.

"I'm sorry, is that too personal?" she asks.

"No," he says. "A childhood accident, that's all."

She smiles and traces her finger up, over her chin, to her lips, across her cheek and to her ear, where she scratches briefly before taking it away.

"I predict . . ." she says, but leaves it at that.

"You predict what?"

"Hmm?" She pretends she's already dismissed it.

"What do you predict?"

"Oh. I predict that someday you'll tell me about that childhood accident. What do you think?"

What does he think? He shakes his head.

"Do you think I'll get you to talk, Evan? One day?"

"One day," he says, "maybe one day you will."

"Go."

Evan stares at her a moment longer as she turns back to her gear, rotates dials, flips switches, and stabs at the keyboard of her computer. Then he returns to the studio as if nothing has happened; he doesn't tell anyone—not a soul—that he's completely fallen in love with Mica Morrison.

"I'm telling you guys," Lars says giddily from his drum set, "Ev was hot!"

Tony nods in appreciation, plucking at his strings, tuning by harmonics. "So now you're sitting in with the big boys?" he jokes.

Mica comes into the studio and sets up microphones for the drums, guitars, and vocals. She moves with grace and purpose, no hesitation whatsoever. No one dares get in her way.

"It was insane!" Lars continues. "I walk in there, and Ev's up on stage with Lucky Strike! And he's walking around like unfrozen caveman guitar player with these guys—these . . . masters of jazz— and then they start to play, right, and Evan gets this look on his face, like suddenly it hits him: *what the hell am I doing up here?* And then it's time for him to solo, and he slams that guitar, I mean he bashes it for a few bars, just until he's got everyone's attention, and everyone in the room is silent at that point—I mean *silent*—you could hear an ice cube tinkle they're so silent. They're wondering: *who the hell is this?* And then he starts . . . sculpting . . . this solo, man. He starts weaving a goddamn tapestry of music! And everyone is on the edge of their seats wondering *where the hell is he going next?* Like they *have* to know. They *need* to know! And this is going on for, like, ten minutes."

"It wasn't ten minutes," Evan corrects.

"How do you know?" Lars shouts. "You were so into it up there, Theo Moody looks out at the audience and makes this face like, *should I stop this guy?* And the audience was like, *no fucking way!*"

"We get the picture," Rod grumbles.

Really? Evan doesn't get that picture. He was just playing. He didn't see Theo Moody ask the audience anything.

"I swear to God, man," Lars continues. "It was like the old days. It was like Eric Clapton when he still did drugs. It was fucked up and amazing at the same time."

"Yeah, yeah, we get the picture," Rod snaps. "Let's start playing."

"I'm with Rod," Mica says, finishing her mike job. "Why don't you guys run through your songs. I won't roll tape. I want to play with the levels and get a feel for your sound."

"Right on," Tony says. He turns to the band. "Let's start with 'Wheel Dance' and then go straight into 'Rainmaker.'"

"Hold up," Evan says. "Can Dean stay in here?"

"For now he can," Mica says. "But when we start recording, he should come inside with me."

Evan nods and reaches into his guitar bag. He pulls out a little plastic container and walks over to where Dean is sitting on an extra amp.

"Put these in."

"What are they?" Dean asks, eagerly uncorking the little bottle. His eyes are bright and he has a perma-smile on his face.

"Ear plugs," Evan says. "I've already ruined my ears, no need for you to do the same."

Dean looks disappointed. Evan frowns at him, and Dean, surprisingly, acquiesces without a fight. He squashes up the little foam plugs and slips them into his ears. He looks up at Evan when he's finished.

"Did I do it right?" he asks.

"You're a natural."

"Let's get it on," Tony says.

And off they go.

THEY PLAY THEIR two songs, and Evan is in a zone. He doesn't care that the songs they've picked aren't his. He doesn't care that these two songs don't showcase his talents as well as other songs do. He has no ego. He just plays. He plays truthfully and honestly. He feels the music in his heart.

He plays the notes, but he doesn't notice them. He plays the songs, but he isn't sure where they begin or end or how many times he's played each. Because what he's really playing is not notes or songs, he's playing a cosmic ballad, a universal love song that bridges over any preemptive halts to the music, any miscues, any flubs. He's playing what he feels, and what he feels is so strange to him. He feels he's been given two brand new things, two new toys, and he loves playing with them. But he knows he has to give them back. Dean goes back on Sunday, Mica goes back when the session is over. And his music reflects his feelings. It's joyous, but with an edge of melancholy, a kind of mellow hollowness that informs the music without upstaging it. The guitar solos, which had been locked in for weeks prior, take on a new depth, a new dimension. Not different, but deeper. It surprises his bandmates, and spurs them on. There's energy to spare. Call it inspired, if you want. The band is playing inspired music, and Evan is leading the way.

What Evan doesn't know is that behind that mirrored glass wall, in the control room, Mica is receiving all of Evan's energy, she's taking it in, and she likes it. She's there by herself at first. Dean joins her when they begin recording. Then Billy drops in.

"He's great," Mica says to Billy.

"He is," Billy confirms. "He is great."

"Who's great?" Dean asks from his seat behind the mixing board.

"Your pops," Billy answers.

"If he's so great, why isn't he famous?"

Billy and Mica exchange a glance.

"There's a difference between being good and being successful," Billy replies. "You need more than talent to make it. It generally helps if you know somebody. *And* you need to get real lucky."

Dean nods in understanding. "It's smarter to be lucky than it's lucky to be smart," he says.

Billy cocks his head at Dean, looking for clarification.

"It's what my Mom used to say," Dean explains.

Billy smiles and turns back to the window of the studio. He listens as the band flies through "Wheel Dance."

"Lars is pretty good," Billy says to no one. "A little white bread, but solid."

"The singer's voice is decent," Mica says after a moment.

"What's up with the bass player? Is it Halloween already?"

"Apparently it came to him in a dream."

Billy taps his foot to the beat and stares out at them, leaning over the console. When they finish the song, he stands up.

"Not bad," he mutters.

"What are you thinking?" Mica asks.

"I don't know," Billy says. "Maybe I'm thinking it's smarter to be lucky than it's lucky to be smart."

I T'S JUST PAST midnight and a bit cold in the control room. Dean has given up and is napping on the couch. The band is hashing over the songs, thinking and rethinking the mix. Mica rolls her eyes whenever someone suggests punching up the bass or pulling back the vocals or some other tweak. She doesn't believe in tweaking. She's instinctive, and she believes that if you get it right the first time, leave it be. You can only go downhill from there.

Evan's a little frustrated. He's tired, and tired is bad. He's hungry. He wants to eat, sleep, and dream.

"Why don't you guys let it sit," Mica suggests. "It needs to cure. Let it sit and come back if you want to play with it some more. It's all in ProTools, it's easy enough to pull up."

They make faces at each other.

"I'm with her," Lars says.

"Me, too," Evan votes.

Rod and Tony shrug. They'd like to stick around, but they sense the energy is down.

"Can we get some copies for reference?" Tony asks.

"Of course."

She picks up the phone and tells the machine room to run some dubs. Lars rousts Dean and they all file back into the studio and dismantle their equipment; Mica stows the microphones in a locker. Soon, Billy enters the room.

"You guys were sounding pretty good," he says. "Tight."

"Thanks, man," Tony says.

"If you want to hit me with a couple of copies, I could do you guys a turn and slide them to some heads I know."

Slide them to some heads? Give them out to record labels? Is he crazy?

"Hell, yes," Lars says. "Give the man some CDs."

"The mix isn't done yet," Rod says. "We just roughed it in. We have to tweak it."

Billy laughs. "Mica doesn't rough shit in, kid. And Mica doesn't tweak. And Mica doesn't stop until a job is done, so if she's putting equipment away, that means it's done."

"Then there it is," Lars says, cheerfully.

"I could of sworn the band has a say in how their music sounds," Rod grumbles.

"Hey," Billy says, "whatever you want. It's your sound. I'm just saying, I'm willing to put it in some hands for you. And when I put something in a guy's hand, he gives it a listen."

"You really think it's good enough to go out?" Tony asks.

"I wouldn't offer if I didn't think so."

"Then let's do it. We can always fuck with it later."

"Yeah, let's do it," Lars agrees.

BILLY LEAVES. TONY and Rod pack up quickly and take off. Mica's doing something in the control room. And Evan sits on an amp and waits for Lars and his assistant, Dean, to finish loading his van.

"Are you still hungry?" Mica asks Evan, coming into the studio.

Evan nods. "You?"

"It's late."

"Where are we going?" Lars asks. Evan looks at him. Dean is by his side. Each of them is holding a cymbal like a strange new kind of discus.

"I'm *starved*," Dean says.

"How about *Dick's* Drive-in?" Lars snickers.

"I can't have two *Dick's* in a week," Dean chimes in. "Let's go get a *Whopper*."

"Gemme somodat *special* saw-uce."

The two juvenile delinquents burst into laughter. Lars punches Dean on the arm. Dean punches Lars back. What a team. That brain damage of Lars's probably arrested his emotional and intel-lectual development at the eighth-grade level. That's why nobody really noticed. Most people only operate on the eighth-grade level anyway. But Lars's true colors emerge when he's around a real eighth-grader. It's like going home after years spent in a space sta-tion orbiting the earth.

"Seriously, though," Lars says, "let's go somewhere in the U-District so I can pick up a freshman and take her home to play Spin the Bottle."

"I know an all-night sushi joint in Chinatown," Mica offers.

Evan straightens up. "Sounds great. Let's go."

"I'm not eating any of that raw fish stuff," Lars warns.

"Sushi?"

"Yeah, none of that," Lars says. "But I do fancy a nice chicken teriyaki, I'll tell you that. And I like the big fried shrimp and the fried sweet potatoes."

"Tempura?"

"Yeah. I like that."

"Me, too," Dean agrees. "Big fried shrimp."

"All right, then," Mica says with a smile. "Big fried shrimp all around."

"IT DOESN'T LOOK like a restaurant," Evan says to Mica as they walk up to the unmarked door on King Street.

"It is. Look, they don't speak a lot of English here."

Lars balks. "I want to go to an English restaurant."

"It's okay, just let me do the talking, that's all."

She knocks on the door and a little hatch opens. She says a few words in Japanese, and the door opens from the inside. They enter.

Inside is a dark hallway filled with Japanese people smoking cigarettes. It's very loud and hot. Beyond the entryway is a crowded, well-lit sushi bar. The room appears to extend farther beyond that, but Evan can't make it out through the smoke.

A woman approaches them. She's wearing a slinky blue dress. She bows to Mica. They speak a moment in Japanese. Then the woman opens a door and leads the four of them through an empty hallway and up a flight of stairs. They emerge in a white corridor with sliding paper doors lining both sides. The woman opens one of the doors and motions for them to enter.

"Take off your shoes," Mica says.

They leave their shoes at the doorway and step into a tatami room, a small private dining room with a table sunken into the floor. They sit rather awkwardly at the table.

"Anything to drink?" Mica asks.

"Beer?" Lars asks.

"Coke," Dean says.

"Want some sake?" Mica asks Evan.

"No, thanks. Just water."

Mica speaks in Japanese to the hostess, who is kneeling at the doorway. The woman listens attentively, then rises and disappears.

"Are you Japanese?" Dean asks Mica.

"I'm half," Mica says. "My mother is Japanese."

"So you can speak Japanese?"

"Yeah. My mother made me learn it when I was a kid. My father was a jazz musician who died when I was little. He was black. That's not really a good combination in America. I'm pretty much the epitome of a minority: a black Japanese woman."

Evan laughs.

"After my father died, my mother remarried a rich Japanese man who owns this place. I would call it a restaurant, but it's more than that. It's an entertainment center, I guess. Anyway," she says, "free food."

"I like *that* part," Lars whispers to Dean.

A slight woman in a kimono appears with their drinks. She serves everyone and kneels down between Evan and Mica.

"You guys don't mind if I order for you, do you?" Mica asks.

They all look at each other and shrug. Mica speaks to the waitress who's waiting quietly at her side, and the woman leaves.

They chat about the recording session while they wait for their food. Mica tells them what she thinks Billy sees in them: the songs are pretty good, but it's the clean execution, she believes, that Billy likes. Songs and sound can be fixed; sloppiness never goes away.

"What about you?" Lars asks. "Working on anything big?"

"I have to go down to Jamaica soon to engineer a single for a movie soundtrack."

"Whose?"

"I can't say. It's part of the deal. They're kind of paranoid about publicity. You know."

"The Stones?"

Mica smiles and shakes her head. "There's a nondisclosure clause in my contract that says that if I leak a word about anything, even just a *hint* about anything, then I'm fired, *and* they'll sue me for damages. It's not that I don't want to tell you, Lars, it's that I can't."

"It's the Stones, isn't it?"

"No, Lars, it's not the Stones."

The food arrives. For Dean, a big plate of tempura. For Lars, chicken teriyaki. For Mica and Evan, a huge platter covered with countless pieces of sushi of every imaginable color, shape, and size. Mica directs Evan though the meal—try this, taste that, you'll like this one—and Lars and Dean look very contented with what they're eating, until everyone is stuffed.

"More?" Mica asks.

Lars laughs. "I have to pee," he says.

"That way," Mica points.

"So do you," Lars says as he stands, sticking his sweat-socked toe in Dean's ribs.

"No I don't."

"Pee with me, Dean."

"I don't have to."

Lars places a large hand on Dean's shoulder.

"Pee with me, or die."

Dean looks up at Lars the Hulk and realizes that it's not an invitation, it's a command, so he follows Lars out of the room.

Evan and Mica drift about in the wake of their departure. Evan knows they'll be gone a while; this is Lars's way of giving Evan and Mica a moment to get things started . . . or not. Where to begin? Or to begin at all? Evan is too nervous to speak. He looks up at Mica. She's watching him, smiling at him. She picks up a piece of pickled ginger with her fingers and eats it silently.

"I don't get it," she says.

"Get what?"

"Just about every guy who walks into The Sound Factory hits on me. And the one guy I might actually be interested in, apparently has no interest in me."

"Who's that?" Evan asks reflexively, before he thinks about what she's said. Before he realizes that she's talking about him.

She shrugs and sighs, almost melodramatically. "I guess I read it all wrong. My mistake."

"No—" Evan starts.

"No?"

"But . . . aren't you and Billy? . . ."

She waits for more.

"Aren't Billy and I . . . what?" she asks.

"You know. Dating."

"Dating?"

"You know, going out. Boyfriend and girlfriend?"

Mica blushes and laughs. She has a sweet laugh. It starts with her mouth, then moves up to her eyes, and then takes over her whole face.

"No, Evan. Billy and I aren't dating. Billy's like my brother."

"But . . . the Lucky Strike show."

"We go to shows together all the time. That doesn't mean we're dating."

"So, you're single?" Evan asks.

"Yes, I'm single."

"Well, in *that* case . . ."

He takes a deep breath and touches her hand, so soft and warm; he picks it up and holds it. He looks into her eyes.

"Will you marry me?" he asks.

Mica laughs again.

"I hate you," she says.

"Why?"

"You're skipping all the fun stuff."

"Like what?"

"Like this," she says, leaning forward and kissing Evan. Warm bubbles of flesh pressing against his lips, soft slippery tongue, a hand on the back of his neck, another on his arm. She tastes like ginger. Like thin strips of ginger, shaved and piled on a plate, sweet but with a bite. She pulls away.

"Wow," he says.

"What are you doing tonight?" she asks.

Tonight? Well, if he stays up any later, tonight he'll be having a seizure.

"I have to get Dean home and put him to bed," he says.

"And then?"

"And then *I* have to go to bed."

"You're not going to invite me over for a nightcap?"

"Oh, I'd love to," Evan says. "But . . . I'm not sure it's a good example to set. You know. For Dean."

Which is a lie. But Mica takes him at face value. She nods and pinches her lips together.

"I wasn't even thinking. I'm sorry."

"No, I didn't mean to imply—"

"But you're absolutely right," Mica says. "I was thinking about myself, and you were thinking about you, and 'you' is you and Dean.

That just shows what a good father you are, and what a horrible, horrible wench I am."

"Please," he says, and it's his turn to kiss her, so he does, and for a minute they stay like that, making out in a tatami room in a strange Japanese restaurant where the staff doesn't speak English.

"What are you doing tomorrow, then?" Mica asks through their lip clench.

"I was going to take Dean to the Center and let him spin his brains around all day on the brain-spinning rides."

"Sounds like fun. Can I come?"

"I wish you would."

And then several deliberate footsteps and a throat clearing signal the imminent arrival of Dean and Lars. Evan and Mica quickly pull away from each other and try to compose themselves, but it doesn't work. When Dean and Lars enter, they are smiling broadly—Evan's sure they've been lurking just outside the door for a while—and when Lars sits back down next to Evan, he leans over and whispers into Evan's ear.

"You dog," he says. "You dog, run."

Evan blushes, and Mica laughs, and Dean says, "Can I go to sleep now?"

EVAN SITS ON his bed and waits for Dean to finish brushing his teeth. He picks up his acoustic guitar and plucks at the strings. A good father. Ha. He sure has her fooled. Like he's ever thought of Dean first in his entire life. Little does she know the real reason he put her off: that he was afraid that if she came over they might get naked together, and if they got naked together, they might feel some kind of compulsion to have sex, and if they decided to have sex—and he somehow survived the minefield of exhaustion-induced seizures along the way—she would discover the true depths of his problems: the sun also rises, but Evan and Jake Barnes don't, if you catch my drift.

His fingers move on their own, it seems. They play things while he's thinking of something else entirely. And soon he is lightly strumming a melancholy Led Zeppelin song—you know, the one that starts off slow and then gets faster. Har, har. (Sometimes he cracks himself up!)

It may not be too late for him to be a good father, even though he was never a good son. Does that matter? Do you have to be a good son to become a good father? Or can you suck as a son and turn it all around when it's showtime? It wasn't like his own father was any good. He never set a good example, at least. To this day, he doesn't try to hide his true feelings. His father can't be in the same room with Evan without expressing his profound disappointment in him. He's allergic to Evan; he can barely look Evan in the eye. He can hardly sit at a dinner table alone with Evan. But is his father really a rotten father, or did Evan make him turn rotten? Maybe everything is Evan's fault. He's managed to ruin his father's life and his son's life in a couple of pretty effortless steps. (First, step in front of a car. Second, step away from your child.) Almost amusing. Here comes the fast part. *And a pocketful of soul.*

He looks up as he plays and there's Dean, standing there watching him. Evan stops.

"Sorry," he says, and puts his guitar down. "I got a little carried away."

Dean shrugs and leaves the bedroom. Evan follows him.

"Did you have fun tonight?"

"It was okay," Dean says, sitting on the pull-out couch and taking off his socks.

"I figured we'd go to the Center tomorrow. Mica said she wants to come, too. We can go on rides. The Science Center. EMP."

Dean doesn't respond. He pulls off his pants and climbs under the covers.

"It's what dads and sons do together, I've heard. And I thought, you know, me being a father and you being a son . . ."

"And Mica being a dad's girlfriend," Dean says.

"She's not my girlfriend."

"You want her to be."

"Well—" He couldn't very well deny that, could he? "You want me to tell her not to come?"

"No." Dean pauses a moment, then says, "You don't have to take me anywhere, you know. I could go back to that arcade tomorrow so you and Mica could go have a date or something."

"Don't be ridiculous. It's you and me tomorrow, bub. She asked if she could come, but I can tell her no. I'll call her now—"

"No, it's okay."

"Really?"

"Yeah."

Evan turns out the light and makes a move toward his bedroom.

"Hey, Evan?" Dean asks.

"Yeah?"

He stops and looks at the shape of Dean, a dark mound on a pathetic foam mattress, the lights of Wallingford sparkling in the distance. No shades on the windows. And it gets light early. It's clear: he's a rotten father.

"How long did it take you to learn to play like that?"

Evan thinks about it a minute.

"I started when I was a little younger than you, I guess."

"But how long did it take until you could play that song you were just playing?"

"That? That took a while, I guess. You have to learn chords first, then you learn finger work. *Then* you learn Zeppelin. Why?"

"I don't know."

The mound rolls over and snuggles in. Evan watches it for a moment.

"Goodnight, kid," he says.

"Frum-frumpf," the mound says back. And Evan goes into his room and closes the door.

A DO-IT-YOURSELF banner had been laced together with multicolored letters: WELCOME HOME EVAN! Quite a bit of his extended family was there, as were a few friends. There was cake and food. Some kind of "punch" mixed by his Uncle Bob, which meant it was way too alcoholic for the ladies, but they slugged it down anyway and smiled doing it. There were presents. There were the standard Swedish meatballs of which his mother was so proud ("All from scratch," she would say to anyone she saw eating one). There was even a thimbleful of caviar dwarfed by disproportionately large piles of egg, onion and Melba toast—a foreshadowing of the financial freedom Evan's father would achieve a few years later, when he would indulge himself by eating massive amounts of caviar out of a six-ounce tin. Everything was there that was usually there for major family celebrations, which were commonly held in honor of a graduation or an engagement or a significant anniversary, or, in this case, a homecoming. Everything was there but Evan's father.

"He got beeped this morning," Louise whispered to those who were meant to hear. "A donor heart flew in an hour ago. He *has* to take it. He's the only one who knows the history. He'll be out all night. I hope Evan understands."

Evan didn't understand, really. But, frankly, he didn't care, either. It was almost better this way.

The house looked different than it had weeks earlier. It was whiter. Oddly, it felt more sterile than the hospital room in which Evan had stayed for the month since the accident. Things had shifted slightly in his time away from home. A painting in the living room had moved, replaced by something new and more colorful. New photographs had replaced old in some of his mother's fabled silver picture frames which she kept on the entry hall table. (She'd been talking about updating those photos for a year.) The umbrella stand that used to be by the front door was gone. Where did it go?

"Glad to get home and get some of that good home cooking, eh, Evan?"

It was Uncle Bob and his red, puckered face. He'd sampled too much of his own punch, obviously. He should carry a spit cup like a sommelier.

"That hospital food is crap, isn't it? Like army food. I don't know how anyone can eat that crap."

Bob leaned in and breathed heavily on Evan's neck.

"Lemme have a peek, son. I want to see . . ."

Evan, who felt strangely detached from the scene, obliged, and pulled off the knitted cotton skullcap he was wearing, thus exposing his partially shaved head, a third of which was covered with a thin layer of fuzzy hair that did little to mask a gruesome red welt that started at the back of his neck, looped over the crown of his head, and dove toward his ear, stopping just above his hairline.

"Mother of God," Bob rasped, shocked at the brutality of the scar. Not that the scar was brutal by itself. No. It was just a scar. But it stood for something greater, something that was both brutal and offensive to anyone who stands by the Whole Skull Theory: the theory that holds, that a skull, to be truly effective, should always remain intact. For it was not simply a scar, it was a map, and by reading it, one was easily able to understand exactly what had happened. The flesh had been cut, the scalp peeled back. Drills or saws or both had cracked open the brittle bone casing. The brain had been exposed to the world, touched and fingered and fondled by people wearing rubber gloves. And then it had all been slapped back together hastily, as if the doctors had heard footsteps and were about to be caught doing something they ought not be doing, so they quickly shoved it all back in, sewed it up and hoped that no one would notice.

"Mother of God."

"Bob? Evan?" Evan's mother approached. "What are you two?—"

She stopped, appalled.

"Evan! What on earth? What are you?—Bob?"

"Oh, I—"

"Evan, come here."

Uncle Bob shuffled off toward the punch bowl, leaving Evan with a consoling grasp of the upper arm as he passed and grunting his refrain for the evening, "Mother of God."

"Put your hat back on," Louise whispered as she led him into the living room. "Don't take it off again. It upsets people." Evan knew that the person it upset most was her.

The living room was full of people talking and laughing. Evan was given an honorary seat on the couch, and he soon realized that little would be asked of him. Foods would be offered to him. Conversation would be directed toward him, carried on in his behalf. Drinks, forced laughter, strained good cheer. All he really wanted was to suck on a glass of crushed ice—never a dearth of ice chips in a hospital—but he didn't ask for it. His head hurt. All he really wanted was for all the people to go away. But he didn't ask for that, either. A plate of cake was set in his lap. People talked and grinned. He tried to grin back. He didn't bother trying to talk. . . .

He stood up quickly. He heard a soft bump and looked down. He'd forgotten about the cake. It lay, face down, on the carpet. But he didn't care. He felt nauseous. He rushed to the bathroom off the hallway, flung himself inside and vomited into the toilet.

Oh, god. The vomit kept coming until there was nothing but hacking dry heaves. His body felt awful, sick and drained, like it wasn't even a body anymore. It didn't measure up to minimum standards. They should send it back and he'll wait for the next available body. He slumped against the wall, half-wedged next to the toilet bowl. He noticed his mother standing at the closed bathroom door, lips pursed, holding a glass of water.

"It's the medication," she said quietly. "That's what made you sick. They said it might happen for a while, until you adjust."

He started to say something, but when he opened his mouth, more heaving came. Bile came. The smell of vomit wafted up from the toilet and made him sicker. He reached to flush, but couldn't find the handle. His mother leaned in and flushed for him.

"It's the medication," she repeated. "It's nothing to be ashamed of."

She led him up to his room and helped him climb into bed. The sheets were cold and good. The room was dark.

"When's Dad going to be home?" he asked.

"I don't know," she said. She stood in the doorway, silhouetted by the light in the hallway, one hand on the doorknob, the other on the jamb.

"He'll be home when he's finished with the operation. He's saving someone's life. You understand, don't you, honey?"

Evan didn't answer because he felt sick again and he thought that if he opened his mouth, vomit would fly out, and he didn't want any more vomit flying out of his mouth.

"I'll get back to the party," Louise said. "I'll tell them you still feel tired and you need your rest, okay? If you need to throw up again, I put your wastebasket next to your bed, just lean over. I'll check in in a little bit. I love you, honey."

"I love you," he said in reply, but he kept his lips closed because he was afraid of the vomit, so it didn't sound like "I love you." It sounded something like "I frumpf fru."

She left and he closed his eyes. He had a pounding headache. He felt so sick he didn't know someone could feel that sick and still be alive. Maybe he was dead. It was quite possible he was already dead.

He half-woke at some point. Later on? What time? He saw a figure standing at the end of his bed. Was he dead now? Someone had come for him. Could he give his body back now?

The figure stood there for what seemed like a long time. It was his father, a dark, silent figure. Evan tried to say something to him, tried to acknowledge him. He struggled hard against his sleep. But he was too tired, too many floors down, he couldn't make it to the surface. He wanted to see his father's face, he wanted to talk to him, but the fight was too great. He couldn't overcome it.

He gave up.

He opened his eyes again, later still, and his father was gone.

THEY MEET, AS planned, on the rim of the musical fountain.
"Hey, strangers," Mica says with a smile. She's wearing a celadon baby tee and faded jeans. "Where do we begin?"

They begin by watching young children run toward the center of the fountain to touch the base—which is studded with a hundred or so giant water cannons—and then gleefully retreat before being soaked by one of the jets, all while Stravinsky blasts throughout the plaza.

"Aren't kids cool?" she asks, an effectively rhetorical question since neither Dean nor Evan are sure how to answer. "But you like roller coasters," she adds, sensing their loss.

"Roller coasters," Dean echoes, and that's where they go.

They spend the better part of the afternoon spinning their brains out on the brain-spinning rides, just as Evan had planned. Teetering on the brink of nausea, they take a break and go into the Center House, where the food court offers a surprising diversity of foods, such that even Evan can find himself something to eat. It's the perfect day. And it isn't over.

"I have a surprise," Mica says. "Come on."

Off they go. Outside to a grassy bank that overlooks an outdoor stage. On the stage, a band.

"They haven't started yet," Mica says.

"Who?" Evan asks.

"Airto. Surprise!"

Airto Moreira, the famous percussionist, is giving a free concert in the park. Evan, Mica, and Dean lay back on the lawn and stare into space as Airto tinkles his chimes and plays his maracas, the ethereal music floating off into the afternoon sky.

When the concert is over, they switch into high gear and it's a track meet. They rush over to the Science Center where they watch the random ball-dropping machine line up its balls in a perfect parabola. (Evan remembers spending hours as a child standing in front of this same massive Plexiglas window, watching the balls fall, just as his son is doing now, discovering that randomness actually has a shape.) They rush to the roller coaster for another go, then to the top of the Space Needle, then a quick round-trip on the monorail, then back to the food court for dinner because they're so hungry and the day is almost already used up.

Evan is exhausted from all the rushing.

"How about a movie?" Mica asks.

"Great!" Dean yells. And off they rush.

They hop a cab to the Cinerama—Mica tells the driver to make it snappy—and barge into the middle of the latest James Bond movie. Mica buys Dean the largest size popcorn and soda and smaller ones for her to share with Evan. The giant theater is almost full, so they sit in the fifth row, leaning back against the seats and peering up Pierce Brosnan's nose.

After the movie, they cab it back to the Center to get their cars. It's ten o'clock. Evan and Dean are wasted. You have to be in good shape to keep up with Mica. She looks perky and up.

"I work out a lot," she explains. "Kickboxing. Plus, I'm used to working late."

"I bet she could kick your ass," Dean tells Evan.

"I'm sure," Evan agrees.

"No, *I'm* sure."

Dean climbs into Evan's car, slips on his seat belt and falls asleep with his head propped against the window. Evan turns to Mica, her face sallow in the sodium vapor lights of the parking lot.

"What's next?" he asks.

As if it's a question he deserves an answer to.

But he doesn't deserve an answer. Who is he to deserve an answer? Nobody. In front of him is a somebody. Mica. A girl. No make-up, casual clothes, her hair a mess. But eyes full of life, full of vigor. She's ready to go, she is. She looks up at Evan with her eyes that seem to reach out toward him. She's a girl worth keeping. A girl worth holding on to. A girl worth taking home to meet Mom.

"Dunno," Mica shrugs. "You tell me."

Evan doesn't say anything. He doesn't know why. It's a mistake. He wants to gush out at her, to cover her with kisses, to hold her tight. But he says nothing.

"Do we still need to set a good example?" she asks.

"You know, kids these days . . . they grow up so fast."

"Yeah."

Evan leans toward her and kisses her cheek.

"Did you just give me a peck?" Mica asks.

"I guess so."

"*You* gave *me* a peck?"

"Is that bad?"

"Yes."

He tries again. This time it's a full-fledged kiss.

"That's better," Mica says. She fans herself with her hand. "I'm going home. I need a shower very badly."

"See you later?" Evan asks tentatively.

"Do you really want to?"

"Yeah. I really do."

"Okay, then," she says.

She walks off into the thick yellow air to search for her car. At one point she turns around, looks at Evan, and yells, "Go home." Then she disappears. Soon after, he hears the whoop of her car alarm; and then, satisfied that she is safe, he drives Dean home and puts him to bed.

THE BUZZER SHOOTS through his brain like a dart. He bolts upright. Buzzer.

Buzzer, again, there it goes. Someone buzzing.

He looks at his clock. Midnight. He's still dressed, on his bed; his TV is on.

He stumbles through the living room. Dean is sleeping soundly on the couch. Evan picks up the intercom.

"Hello?" he asks.

"Open up."

Mica? Is it her? Evan presses the button that unlocks the downstairs door. What's going on? He waits.

Knock, knock, knock.

He opens his door.

Ah. It's her. Hair pulled back into a low ponytail, she wears a long peach-colored dress with so many little buttons on the front, the top five unbuttoned to reveal the heave of her breasts, the bottom twenty opened to create a provocative slit that exposes just enough-thigh per stride. She's holding a satchel. She has a big smile on her face.

"You're back," he says.

"You said, 'See you later.'"

"How did you find me?"

"It's called a phonebook. You should try it sometime. It gives you addresses, and it doesn't even need batteries."

He smiles so hard he thinks his ears might fall off. She's back. His heart is racing. He holds his finger to his lips, points to Dean.

He locks the door behind her, carries her bag as they tiptoe to his room and close the bedroom door behind them. They stand in the flickering darkness grinning at each other.

"I like your dress," Evan says.

"You do?"

"I didn't expect you."

"I know."

She moves toward him and kisses him, pushing him back with her body until he's fallen backward onto his bed and she's fallen on top of him.

"You smell clean," he whispers.

"I took a shower."

"I didn't. I must smell."

"You smell good," she says.

They kiss each other and the kissing quickly becomes passionate. They feel around; grope. She squeezes parts of his body like she's checking for ripeness, it's a squeeze that reads, "Am I gonna buy it or toss it back." It's firm and possessive. Her hand reaches for his crotch, squeezes.

"Hello!" he squeals.

"Do you like that?"

Like it? He loves it. He loves it because his dick is actually hard. *It's alive!* She has a magic touch. She unzips his jeans, slips her cool hand inside his underwear and takes hold of his—

"Wow!"

"Am I moving too fast?" she asks.

Moving too fast? No way. He's afraid if she doesn't move fast enough someone will take the air out of his erection and that will be it.

"No, no. It feels good."

She pulls her hand out and sits up.

"What?" he asks.

"Uncomfortable pause," she says.

He is confused.

"I thought about pre-doing this, but I figured that would be tacky. I didn't want to assume . . . you know . . . this would happen."

"I don't get—"

"Unless you've had your tubes tied . . . because *I* haven't."

"Ahh . . ."

"I'll be back in a minute," she says.

She climbs off and looks for her bag. When she finds it, she grabs it, goes into the bathroom and closes the door.

Jesus Christ. He's about to get laid. Holy shit! What should he do? In the movies the guy always takes off his clothes at this point. Is that what Evan's supposed to do? Strip down and get under the covers? He has no idea. Because, honestly, he hasn't had sex in a while.

Sometimes, Evan likes to think of his half-decade of abstinence as an aesthetic choice. Having felt the power of sex at such an early age, having experienced the truth about sex, that it is an activity specifically designed to create new human beings, it was only right for him to avert his eyes.

But that's just the façade. The real reason is that the anti-epileptic medication he'd been taking for most of his life stopped working five years ago, and suddenly Evan was having seizures all the time. The doctors scrambled to contain his brainstorm, and they tried dozens of drug cocktails until they found just the right mix. But the new medication, while effective at suppressing his seizures, also suppresses his libido. What a choice.

No doctor will admit the medication causes Evan's impotence, though they do agree that it may diminish his sexual desire to below "functional standards." Still, the onus of his impotence is placed squarely on his shoulders: he just doesn't want it enough. And, under these circumstances, they're right. He doesn't want it at all. It only takes a few failed tries at sexual encounters before you get a little gun-shy. Nothing quite as humiliating as having a naked girl pulling on your dick trying to make it come to life for you.

But that's neither here nor there. The fact is, right now he *does* feel aroused. And maybe if he and Mica work quickly enough, they can pull this thing off. As long as he doesn't focus on it too much. He should focus on something else. Like music.

Like what kind of music should he put on? Classical? Jazz? Maybe jazz. Or maybe not. He looks into the CD compartment of his boom box. Early Elvis Costello. Classical in his own way, but too dated for a date. He's so nervous. What if he goes limp in the middle of it? What if he stays hard but prematurely ejaculates? Christ, he doesn't have any condoms. She may ask to see an AIDS test, but he was never tested. What a disaster.

The bathroom door opens slowly. The light is off inside. Out comes a body, a figure, a long series of curves and bends, hips and ankles, a belly and breasts. It is completely, one hundred-percent naked. It is Mica, as she was meant to be seen.

She makes her way to Evan, taking her time. He is standing next to the boom box. She sidles up to him, kisses his neck, then bites his ear. He curls, but not away.

"You like that."

"Yes."

She rubs against him.

"We have a little problem," she says.

"What's that?"

"I'm naked and you're not."

She helps him off with his clothes. They work their way to the bed. Her flesh is cool and soft and resilient. They climb onto the bed; this time he's on top.

"How are you doing?" she asks.

"I'm so hot," he says, and immediately feels like an idiot. What a moronic thing to say. Jesus. *I'm so hot.* What he meant to say was: *you're* so hot, you're making *me* hot. But he didn't say that. He said something totally embarrassing. It just came out. Sex talk is the most absurd thing ever. That people say things and announce things that they never would under normal circumstances. Sex is a drug.

It makes you goofy. They might as well be doing whippets. He's mortified. She can see right through him now. She knows all. She's about to leave him.

But instead of leaving, she says, "I'm hot, too," and he realizes they both have the goofy sex disease.

He positions himself between her legs.

"Gentle, baby," she says.

She reaches down to help him in, and Evan could have died, right there, died a thousand times, ready to do it, make love to Mica, and she's holding onto his lifeless dick.

He slumps on top of her, buries his head in her hair.

"What's the matter, baby?" she asks.

"I'm sorry," he mumbles.

"About what? About that? Don't worry about it."

"I was hoping it would hold out."

"I'll get it up for you," she offers.

"It's my medication," Evan says. "It has an unfortunate side effect."

"Your epilepsy medication?"

"Yes."

"So . . . it won't go back up?"

"No."

"That's unfortunate," she says.

"Yeah." He shrugs. But that's life in the fast lane. You want to dance? You have to pay the piper.

He lifts himself off of her and rolls onto his back. He stares at the ceiling.

"Aren't there other medications?" she asks. "I mean, it's not permanent, is it?"

There are other medications. And they're all poisons. They will all kill him. He has been made effectively sterile by the giant pharmaceutical corporations. He is defective, and he should not procreate. Not even recreational sex. It could lead to more idiots who would run in front of cars and get hit and smash their skulls against the pavement and get epilepsy. Dumbshits. They should all be rounded up and killed.

"So, tell me about it," she says after a minute.

"What?"

"Your epilepsy."

"I can't."

"Why not?"

"I can't tell you about it right now."

"Why not?"

"I just can't."

She sighs, but accepts it for what it is, apparently, because she is Mica and she is enlightened. He is convinced of that. She is the Enlightened One.

"You remind me of my father," she says.

Evan raises his eyebrows, still looking at the ceiling, surprised by her comment.

"That's very Freudian."

"I didn't say you were *substituting* for my father. I said you reminded me of him."

"In what way?"

"Oh, when I was little and I would watch him play—"

"What did he play?"

"Alto sax—well, he played everything, but the sax was his instrument. When I would watch him play, he would get this far-away look on his face, like he'd left his body or something, like his soul was in a different place, where the music comes from, but his body was still there playing the instrument."

Evan glances at her.

"I look like that when I play?"

"It's hard to explain," she says. "A lot of people get faraway looks on their faces when they make music. But with my father, it was different. Maybe 'faraway' isn't the word." She struggles. "*Apart. Separate.* It's like he would break through to a different dimension to where—I don't know. . . . When he was dying he played all the time, all day long. I would watch him. I think it gave him some kind of comfort to be someplace where he existed without his body, you know? A place where only souls and music exist. It was his way of coping with the cancer."

"Epilepsy isn't fatal," Evan says with a quick, hard laugh.

"Oh, I wasn't—"

"You know, I'm not sure I'm into this thing about my being your father."

"Evan—"

"I don't have cancer and I'm not dying."

"Evan!" Mica says sharply. "Listen to what I'm saying. Listen. I'm not saying you're my father, or even anything like him. I don't want you to be. I'm saying that when I first saw you play, I saw something in your eyes that I used to see in his, and I realized that I already knew you—that we already knew each other—and then in the restaurant you asked me to marry you and I thought you felt the same way—"

"I thought you'd figure I was joking."

"I *know* it was a joke, Evan. I know." She sighs and closes up. God. He's screwed up another relationship.

"I'm sorry," he says.

"No. You've got a lot to deal with."

She gathers herself, gets to her hands and knees, slips her hand down, cups his balls.

"You may not be a rock, but I can still get you off," she says, moving down.

"No."

No? She hesitates. He hooks his elbow under her arm and flips her over on her back. Reversal: two points.

"I can get *you* off," he says.

He kisses her belly, moves down.

"Evan—"

"Shh," he quiets her.

"Evan—"

"Shh. Shh."

"Oh, Evan."

HE WAKES TO a tickle on his throat. The first sign of gray morning light is waiting outside his window. Mica is awake, propped on her elbow, watching over him, tracing his scar with her fingertip.

"Tell me," she whispers.

He shakes his head.

"I'll torture you."

"I'll never talk," he says. And he means it. She may be good at a lot of things, but he knows already that she's no match for him in the art of concealment. He'll wait for her to get desperate, and at just the right moment, he'll lie to her. And she'll believe it. And that will be that. Mica's a tough girl, but she wears her emotions on her sleeve. Evan wears his under many layers of scar tissue.

"No?" she asks.

He shakes his head. She sighs, stands; she's fully dressed.

"Where are you going?"

"We don't want to set a bad example," she replies.

She's too understanding for a normal person. Perhaps she's an alien. He starts to rise.

"Don't get up," she says, then, doing her best Arnold, she warns, "*I'll be back.*"

She gathers her things, gives him a kiss on the forehead, and slips out of the room.

He closes his eyes and urges himself back to sleep, but he can't quite get there. He hangs just on the edge of it. It's not uncomfortable. His body is, for all intents and purposes, asleep. But his mind gets no rest at all.

THE DAY PICKS up where the previous one left off. Mica returns with a box full of Krispy Kremes that she and Dean devour recklessly. They are a team. They are instant oatmeal: add water, make family. Evan is sure that, deep down, none of them are convinced of the legitimacy of their venture. But they are all having a good time, so who's Evan to burst their bubble?

They enjoy themselves without remorse. They laugh and joke as they explore Underground Seattle, take a ferry ride across the Sound to Bainbridge Island and back, watch the seals, eat lunch at the Aquarium. No one will let it end. One more thing, one more thing. Every time the afternoon begins to wind down, it is one more thing. Until they are standing in front of Market Seafood at the Public Market late in the day, watching the thick-handed men hurl twenty-pound salmon across the counter, bellowing words of caution as tourists cower in mock terror: sustenance as entertainment. Perverse, in a way. A twisted interpretation of the food chain. Sadistic performance art. But only if you're the salmon. Otherwise, it's good, clean fun.

Mica asks one of the flashy fishmongers to filet her a slab of red flesh. She turns with her catch and announces that she's cooking dinner for Evan and Dean. She buys produce at the produce stands, wine in the wine store, ice cream where ice cream is sold, and then they retire to Evan's apartment where she flies through the kitchen cooking furiously, cleaning nothing, until the sink is piled high with pots and pans and a frighteningly self-assured dinner is set on the table.

Evan and Dean exchange a look. It's an unfamiliar look of complicity between virtual strangers. She's pretty, she's smart, she's happy, she's motherly, she's sexy, she cooks. . . . If she does laundry, she's got the job. They laugh at themselves.

"What?" she asks.

"Nothing," Evan says with a giggle.

"Nothing," Dean repeats, same giggle.

She gives them a look, then concedes and sits. They plow into the food, which is wonderful, naturally. The conversation is lively and convivial because that's how they contrive it to be. And then it happens.

"What's that sound?" Dean asks.

"It sounds like someone talking," Mica says.

They listen carefully. Indeed, there's a soft mumbling in the background that sounds like someone talking. Who could it be? A neighbor? A television? Maybe a clock radio alarm that accidently went off due to a power outage? No. It sounds more like . . . an answering machine.

Oh, right. Evan had turned off the ringer in the living room because he didn't want it to disturb Dean's sleep. They're talking loudly, the music is on, they didn't hear the ringing.

"It's the phone," Evan says. He stands. "I'll see who it is."

He goes into his bedroom, and the voice becomes much clearer. It is a woman's voice. She is upset.

". . . I don't understand," she says. He knows that voice. Tracy? "You said you'd be here in the early afternoon. I haven't heard from you. Are you hurt? Should I call the police? You said you'd bring Dean home—"

Oh, shit, it's not Tracy's ghost, it's Ellen. He told her he'd bring
Dean home on Sunday. Today is Sunday. Oh, shit. He grabs the
phone.

"Mrs. Smith?"

"Evan?"

"I just walked in."

"Is everything all right? I've been worried sick."

"Oh, I totally . . . totally—"

"What happened?"

"—forgot. I'm so sorry."

A long pause that sounds remarkably like Ellen composing herself. Evan envisions her thin, pale fingers flitting through her hair.

"We were having such a great time," he adds for good measure.
She's pretty shaken, he can tell.

"I was so worried," she practically whispers.

"We were having a good time and the day just flew by. I don't
know how I could have forgotten."

"You could have called."

"I know, I know."

"I was worried you might have gotten into an accident," she
says.

"No, no. Why would you think that?"

"Oh, Evan," she cries, breaking down. "How could you ask me
that? My daughter was just killed in her car and you tell me you'll
bring Dean home and you don't arrive, how am I *not* to think that
you two aren't dead, also? Why *wouldn't* I think that? Oh, Evan."

She sobs uncontrollably into the phone.

"Oh, no, Mrs. Smith."

"Please, Evan."

"I'm really sorry."

"Oh, Evan," she bawls. "Please bring him home tomorrow.
Please."

Evan hesitates before he answers. He hesitates because he feels
somewhat caught. On the one hand, he wants to yield to authority,
give Dean back to his rightful owners. On the other hand, he's had
such a good time with Dean and Mica, he doesn't want it to end.

"Evan?"

But it has to end. Logically, that's what it must do. End.

"You'll bring him home tomorrow, won't you?" she begs.

"I'll bring him home tomorrow," he says. "I'll have him there by two."

"Really?"

"Two o'clock, Mrs. Smith. Dean will be on your doorstep at two o'clock tomorrow."

"Thank you, Evan."

Don't thank me. Thank the devil, who just got a soul real cheap.

He gets up from the bed and turns; he starts when he see Dean standing in the doorway.

Dean lets his presence be felt in the dim room; it's a clingy presence that seeps into the edges; as he grows more mature his presence will change; it will continue to develop until people who know him will call him wise, magnetic, charismatic.

"I have to go to the bathroom," he says cautiously.

"Sure."

"There's only one."

"I know. Go ahead."

Dean steps into the bathroom and closes the door.

What has he heard? What does he know?

He locks the door.

Ah. He's heard everything. He knows everything. Between a father and a son, sometimes, no dialogue is necessary. The simple act of locking a bathroom door can be enough . . . simple, but no less symbolic than the construction of the Berlin Wall, which, after all, was erected in a single, dark, lonely, Teutonic night. What does he know? He knows everything.

"WHO WAS IT?" Mica asks Evan.

"Dean's grandmother."

"Everything all right?"

"She was just checking in," Evan lies. He'll have to tell her soon. Right now she thinks that Dean is a permanent fixture in Evan's life. He'll have to burst that bubble, explain that he's shipping Dean out on the next slow boat. Then he'll tell her what *status epilepticus* means. The rhetorical version of a one-two punch.

"Listen," Mica says, "I have to confess something."

Confess? *She* has to confess?

"Remember when I told you guys I had to go out of town soon to mix a track for a movie?"

"Yes."

"Well, I'm leaving tomorrow morning. I'm going to Jamaica for about a week-and-a-half. I mean, it's not a big deal. Just so you know."

"Yeah, sure. Sounds like fun."

"Ugh. It'll be a *ton* of work, but . . ."

Jamaica. Evan wishes he were going. Ganja capital of the world. He'd like to stuff himself into one of Mica's bags and get air-freighted down there.

Dean emerges from the bedroom and skulks back into the dining room; he slides into his chair. He stares dully at his plate; he doesn't make a move toward eating; his arms are limp from the shoulder.

"Everything all right?" Mica asks.

"Yeah."

"I was just telling your dad . . . I'm heading off to Jamaica tomorrow morning. I won't see you guys for a couple of weeks."

"Oh?"

"It's work, not vacation. If it were vacation I'd blow it off in a second. You guys are too much fun. But I'm expected. There's a studio down there where some musicians like to record, and I've been requested."

"Oh," Dean says. "Okay."

They try to continue dinner, but the fun is all gone. Mica is full, Evan pushes some food around his plate, and Dean sits sullenly, staring at his fork.

"You feeling okay?" Mica asks Dean.

He shrugs.

"Stomachache?" She wonders.

"No."

"You look pale. Are you warm? Evan, does he have a fever? Maybe too much sun? You should drink some water."

She fills his glass from the water pitcher on the table.

"Maybe you want to lie down?" she offers.

Dean moves his head slightly—a move that might be construed as a nod—pushes back, scraping the chair legs on the floor. He hoists himself from the seat and trudges off, head hanging. Mica watches after him, then reluctantly stands and begins clearing the table.

"He's upset with me for leaving," she says.

Evan agrees that Dean is upset. But it's not what Mica thinks.

"I wish I could change it," she continues. "But I can't."

"That's not what he's upset about," Evan tells her. She's holding onto a stack of plates that she'd taken into the kitchen, but there's no place to set them so she brings them back to the table.

"What?"

"He's not upset about your leaving. He's upset about something else."

"What?" she asks. "*Us?* You and me?"

"No."

"Then, what?"

Now's the time to tell her. She walked right into it. If only everything were this easy. Ask a question, get an answer. Easy. Not like the many longstanding secrets he's kept from his parents. Things that are too complicated to unravel at a single gathering.

"You might want to sit."

Piqued, she sits. "I'm ready," she says.

Evan takes a big breath. "Dean is my son. He's been my son his entire life, but I've only known him for the past week."

Her eyes narrow and her jaw sets.

"Are you angry?" he asks.

"Go on," she says.

"His mother, Tracy, died. And I got a call. I went to the funeral and met Dean. And then his grandparents were having some kind of drama and his grandmother told me to get him out of there, so

I did. I brought him home with me. And now she just called and said she wants him back—actually, she called a couple of days ago and I told her I'd bring him back today, but I forgot because we were having such a great time. Now she wants him back and I think he overheard me talking to her, telling her that I'd bring him back tomorrow, and I think *that's* what he's upset about, not that you're leaving. Not that he wouldn't be upset about your leaving. But he's *more* upset about the other thing."

"That's interesting," she says. She's clearly seething, but her anger is masked behind a detached coldness; she might kill him right now, or she might walk away and let him suffer for the rest of his life. "But I'm more concerned about life *before* this past week. I'm interested in how it happened that you *didn't* see him for his entire life. How did *that* work?"

Oh, *that* part.

"I got Tracy pregnant," he says. "We were in high school. She moved away. I mean, her father moved them away, that's obvious now. She didn't want to move away, she wanted to go to Reed."

"Reed."

"College. Small, liberal arts, Portland."

"I know."

"Well, she wanted to go there. But she couldn't go with a baby. I mean, how could she? She wanted to go to college. You know, live in the dorms and stuff. How could she do that with a baby? She couldn't."

"So, she didn't."

"I don't know *what* she did. I mean, I don't think she went to Reed because they moved away, and she, obviously, had the baby."

"But the plan was for her *not* to have the baby."

"Well, the plan, as I recall it, was that she was using birth control and she wouldn't get pregnant."

"But you weren't."

"What?"

"Using birth control?"

"Sometimes. I mean, I was just a kid."

"Babies having babies."

"Look," he says, "the more you find out about me, the more you're going to hate me. Believe it. I'm a bad person. I'm stupid. I've wasted a perfectly good life. I've had every chance. I'm the eldest son of a famous, wealthy, white male heart surgeon. You can't beat that in America. I could have picked up the Old Boy Handbook and found myself listed as the number one pledge. I have no excuses. Everything bad that's happened to me is my own fault. So maybe we should cut it short and you can hate what I am and we can save ourselves a lot of trouble."

She looks at him crookedly.

"Boo-fucking-hoo," she says.

"I don't—"

"Evan. Listen closely. I don't know who your girlfriends have been in the past, but here's the deal: try that self-indulgent self-pitying bullshit with me one more time and you'll never see me again. You won't even see my shadow again. Got it?"

Evan nods. Message received.

"Now quit the whining and tell me what happened. You didn't want to go to Portland with her, you had your own life, you didn't want the baby."

"No!" Evan says strenuously. "No, not at all. No, no, no. I *wanted* the baby. I really did. I didn't care about college. I had no plan to go to college. I was in a band. Hell, the summer after I graduated high school all I wanted to be was a rock star. Are you kidding? I was willing to move down to Portland and marry Tracy and we'd raise Dean together. I'd go on tour when I had to. No, no—"

"Okay. So, what, then?"

"She wanted an abortion. That's what she wanted."

"How did you know?"

"Well, she said something like, 'I'm not going to college with a baby,' and then she said something like, 'I need money for an abortion.' It wasn't tricky."

"No, I guess not."

"So I gave her the money. But you have to understand, *I* wanted the baby. I asked her to marry me. I told her I'd move wherever she wanted, I'd quit the band, I'd get a job, whatever she wanted. She said no. She said she wasn't going to college with a baby."

"Ouch," Mica says.

"Yeah," Evan agrees.

"Fuck you, you liar!"

They turn, startled by the new voice. Dean is in the living room, watching them.

"I hate you," he shouts. "I hate you, you liar!"

Evan feels like he's been shot in the stomach. Dean's been standing there the whole time. Evan can't believe it. It makes him sick; Dean heard the whole thing.

"I hate you so much. I hate you so much I want to kill you. That's not what happened. You ran out on us. You're a dirty, stupid, drug-addicted liar. My mother hated you. She wasn't even sure you were my real father. She hated you and she knew you'd be a lousy father. I hate you so much."

Mica discreetly slips into the kitchen and begins to clean the dishes. Dean's face is bright red and his fists are clenched, but he doesn't move an inch as he speaks. His eyes are fixed and red with blood, his shoulders are rigid.

"You're sick, trying to get laid, so you're lying about my mother. That's the worst kind of sick. I wish she were here. I wish she were here. She'd tell you what happened. You tried to force her to have an abortion so she had to run away. I hate you so much. She used to tell me. You know what she used to tell me about you? She used to tell me that you can't make someone a father, and if you try to make someone a father who isn't, he just becomes mean and cruel and abusive and angry and that's what you are. And she was right. Telling lies about my mother. I want to kill you."

Dean's so upset he can't control himself anymore. Spittle flies from his mouth as he speaks. He's barely intelligible. He breathes in gasping breaths. His face is flooded with tears.

"I want to go home," he says desperately. "I want to go home. I want to go home."

And then, almost like he'd been clicking his heels together, he disappears in an instant, gone, back into Evan's bedroom, the door slamming after him, gone from the room, gone.

Evan doesn't move. He feels like someone has sucked his organs out through his mouth. Hollow man. He is empty. He sits in stunned disbelief for a long time, he doesn't know how long, for what seems like a long time.

"I'm going to go," Mica says softly in his ear; her hand touches his. "You two have to talk. I would stay if I could help, but . . . you have to talk to him. I'll call you from Jamaica."

Her lips lightly brush his cheek. He watches her cross in front of him and let herself out. He glances at the kitchen: it is clean. Still, he doesn't move. A minute later he hears the whoop of her car alarm through the window. How quickly we get to know people. How quickly they leave once we know them.

THE GREAT PUMPKIN had passed over Magnolia the previous week, leaving in his wake a world perpetually dark and wet, and a group of kids huddled together in conspiracy just down an embankment along a mildly steep road.

"Truth or dare, Charlie?" Penny asked, her reedy voice slicing through the dampness. "Truth or dare?"

Charlie hesitated.

"Truth or dare?" she demanded, this time taking an intimidating half-step toward Charlie.

"Dare," Charlie answered, unconvinced.

"Dare," Keith, the enforcer, echoed.

"Dare, then," Penny said. She glanced around at her minions, the other kids from the neighborhood who were silently thankful that they were not at the receiving end of the dare. "I dare you to run in front of the next car that comes down the hill."

Charlie glanced toward the road.

"Run in front of it at the last minute," Penny continued, "so it has to slam on its brakes."

Like a car slams on its own brakes, Evan thought. The driver slams on the brakes, not the car.

Charlie was confused by this last instruction.

"What if it doesn't stop?" he asked.

"That's the dare," Penny answered.

Charlie's lower lip began to quiver. He started to cry.

"Baby, baby, baby," Keith taunted. "Baby, baby, baby."

"Take the dare," Penny threatened. "Or you know what happens."

Everyone knows what happens. Keith holds your arms behind your back. Penny kicks you as hard as she can in the shins. She's wearing her tap shoes. Her kicks draw blood, leave scars. Evan has scars. He doesn't care, though. Evan can take it, the pain, the humiliation. But Charlie. Charlie is a baby. Keith is right. *Baby, baby, baby.*

"Do you give up?" Penny asked.

Give up? Pull out your eyes.

"Hold him," she said to Keith and Keith's friend, the kid who plays in the ice hockey league, the big kid without a name. They each took an arm. Charlie cried openly, he didn't try to hide it, he didn't try to be brave. He just cried. *Cry baby, cry baby, cry.*

"I'll do it," Evan said, stepping in front of Penny. His feelings of protectiveness over his little brother barely overcame his feeling of contempt for Charlie's whining. Play the game. Part of the game is getting kicked in the shins. You knew the rules going in. There are no surprises here. So suck it up.

"What?"

"I'll take the dare," Evan repeated. "Charlie's too little. He can't do it. I'll do it for him."

Penny glared at him, foiled again. She would much rather have extracted physical punishment from a babbling Charlie than have her dare fulfilled by a defiant Evan.

"So it slams on its brakes," she warned.

"I'll do it and then we're both going home," Evan said.

It was almost dark already; someone had stolen an hour of light from them. He could smell something sweet and meaty in the wet air, something like soup or stew with buttered noodles.

Penny signaled to her henchmen; Charlie was released. Evan climbed the bank to the road and waited for the next car.

The rest happened in flashes—or, rather, only flashes of what happened were imprinted on Evan's memory. He remembers only slivers: a car coming quickly down the hill; his foot slipping on the wet grass as he launched himself into the road; a chalky taste in his mouth, a taste of gunpowder, of tooth enamel; a woman turning him over and looking into his eyes and then standing back in such shock it made him cry.

"Am I going to be okay?" he asked her.

"What have you done?" the woman asked in response. "What have you done?"

Then there was nothing. Time devoid of color and light, but with warmth and dryness. There was nothing to see, but there were people around him. Hushed voices, but loud in their hush: angry, hushed voices.

". . . so stupid!"

"Carl."

"He did it to himself. *He did it* to *himself.*"

"No, Carl, no."

"It's so stupid. So stupid. He's thrown his damn life away."

"He'll be fine."

"He *won't* be fine! I'm a doctor! I know when someone will be fine, and *he . . . won't . . . be . . . fine!*"

"Carl. Please. It was an accident."

"It was not an accident."

"Carl—"

"It was not an accident, Louise." It was his father. His father and mother in a room with him. The bed felt warm; the sheets smelled of soap and were coarse under his fingers; he could wiggle his toes, so he wasn't paralyzed, and for that he was thankful; but for all intents and purposes, he was asleep to the world, held just under the radar of consciousness by one of many miracle drugs used by doctors, quite possibly his first taste of a Valium drip.

"It was *not* an accident," his father said again. "There *are* no accidents."

E VAN ENTERS THE room and finds Dean lying on the bed, staring at the ceiling. He is reminded of himself, as he has spent long
hours in exactly the same pose, thinking about things, or sometimes
not thinking at all, just existing. It's a good bed to exist on.

"Mica's gone," he says. "I guess we should talk."

"You lied about my mother."

"I didn't lie—"

"You lied! You're a liar!"

Dean heaves himself out of the bed and thunders past Evan, out
into the living room. He goes into the kitchen and throws open
the cabinets until he finds Evan's stash of plastic shopping bags. He
takes one back into the living room and fills it with his clothes, the
few things that Evan has bought for him.

"Where are you going?" Evan asks.

Dean shrugs as he roughly stuffs his feet into his shoes.

"Okay, so you don't want to stay here, I can understand that. So,
where? If you wait until tomorrow I can take you back to your
grandparents."

"I'm not going back there."

"If you don't want to stay here and you don't want to go back there, then where will you stay?"

"Who cares? The YMCA."

"Very funny."

"I'm not joking."

Dean moves toward the door. Evan heads him off.

"I can't let you walk out of here."

"Fuck off."

"Dean, I can't let you go. We have to sit down and talk about this. I mean, I don't know what your mother told you—"

"Shut up about my mother!" Dean shouts. "Shut up about her!"

He shoves at Evan, catching him in the sternum, knocking him back a foot. He grabs the doorknob, opens the door. Evan pushes the door closed and grabs Dean's shoulders. Dean twists out of the way and takes a swing at Evan. His fist misses Evan's face by several inches, but, on the follow-through, his elbow smacks into Evan's jaw.

"Shit!" Evan winces in pain. He feels his jaw, checks his bite.

Dean opens the door again; this time Evan kicks it shut hard. It booms into the frame. The wall shakes. It's a powerful enough gesture to temporarily stop Dean's thrashing.

"You hit me," Evan says.

"Yeah? Well, deal with it. You got to take my whole life off, so now you have to deal with it."

Dean gives up on the door. He heads for the phone.

"Who are you calling?"

"The cops. I'm being held against my will."

"You're fourteen. You don't have a will."

"Fuck you."

"No, fuck you, you rude little shit."

"Yeah, I'm a rude little shit. So deal with it. You never had to do anything for my whole life. You got to be in bands and sleep as late as you wanted while my mom worked all the time and I spent my life in daycare and we sometimes didn't even have a car, and I never had my own Play Station so I always had to go to someone else's house to play video games and for Christmas we did things like make each other paintings or get shoes instead of a bike because we didn't have any money, and *you* sat around the whole time in your rich house making albums that nobody ever heard, so fuck you. I hate you."

Evan rubs his face. He needs to find a way out.

"I'll take you back tomorrow," he says.

"I'm not going back there!" Dean shouts. "I hate them! I'm never going back there!"

"You have to do something, Dean! You have to go somewhere. You can't just go live on the streets. Now, you can come visit here whenever you want, but I'm not set up to have you stay with me forever. You're going to have to go live with your grandparents."

Dean stares at Evan. He looks like he's about to break, his face is fragile, his eyes red, he can't take much more of this; Evan wants to hold him.

"I'll kill myself," Dean says softly.

"Dean—"

"I'll kill myself if you send me back there."

"I don't understand—"

"My mother said I never had to see him again."

Oh, shit. It's Frank. How stupid can Evan be? Frank's why Dean doesn't want to go back.

"Does he hit you, Dean?"

"She said I never had to see him again."

"Does he abuse you?"

"She said—"

"*When* did she say this, Dean?"

Dean looks at him blankly.

"Did you see him before she died?"

No answer.

"How long before she died did she say you didn't have to see him? When was the last time you saw him?"

"Five years ago."

Evan closes his eyes and takes a deep breath. For crying out loud. Five years. The kid really is an orphan.

"What did he do to you?" Evan asks.

Dean doesn't answer.

"Tell me. Just tell me what's going on, Dean, and I can figure something out."

Still, Dean doesn't talk. Evan sees, though, that Dean isn't going anywhere. He's sitting limply on the couch. He won't try to escape. Evan goes into the kitchen and gets him a glass of water. Dean takes the glass, but doesn't look at Evan.

"He hit me," Dean says, after a moment. He holds the glass in his lap, but he doesn't drink from it.

"Where?"

"My face."

"Bad?"

He nods. His eyes are filling with tears, his mouth is trembling, he sniffles.

"Fuck!" Evan shouts, wheeling around and stomping across the apartment. "I'm not sending you back there, Dean. No way. You'll have to stay here for a while. I'm not sending you back. I'll figure something out. I don't know what, but I'll figure something out."

Dean takes a sip of water.

"You're not going to run away tonight, are you?" Evan asks.

Dean shakes his head.

"You won't try to kill yourself?"

Another shake. Another sip.

"I'm sorry I lied about your mother," Evan says.

Dean looks up at him, still trying desperately not to cry.

"You didn't lie."

THE NEXT MORNING, Evan calls Ellen with an ultimatum.

"I know everything," Evan says.

"Everything?" she asks.

"Everything. I know you haven't seen Dean in five years."

"Oh, that's not true."

What? Oh, crap. What's true and who's lying?

"When was the last time you saw him?" he asks.

"I used to see him every week, almost, Evan. Why are you asking about this?"

"Where did you see him?"

"I'd go meet Tracy and Dean in Richland, usually. We'd meet for lunch."

"Oh, I see," Evan says. "*You* would go. But when was the last time Frank saw Dean?"

"Oh, well . . ."

"Five years."

"Well . . ."

"I know everything, Mrs. Smith. I know Frank hit Dean in the face and that Tracy said he would never have to deal with Frank again. I know it all. And you expect me to bring him back to you? You should be ashamed."

A long pause.

"What do you intend to do?" she asks.

"I won't bring him back as long as Frank is there."

"What do you mean?"

"Dean doesn't have a problem with you. I'm sure he'd be willing to live with you, but not if Frank's around. So get rid of him."

"But . . . how?"

"Divorce him. Send him away. Get a restraining order, an order of protection, make sure he can't come within five hundred yards of your house. Get him out."

"Well, I can think about it—"

"What's there to think about?"

"Well, I don't really know how, but . . ."

"It's not that hard. Do it for Dean. He needs you."

"Yes, he does."

"Do it for Dean."

"I will, yes. I'll have to call a lawyer."

"Right."

"I'll have to call you back. This is all so confusing. The summer's almost over, school will be starting."

"Lawyers do it all the time."

"I'll call you back."

Evan hangs up and looks toward Dean who's eating cereal at the kitchen table.

"I'm only staying with you because Frank's dangerous," Dean says, "not because I want to. I don't have any other choice."

"I know," Evan says.

FREMONT GUITAR, THE biggest guitar shop in Seattle, is dead on Mondays, even in the summer when kids are out of school. That's because kids are never out of school anymore. Not like they were when Evan grew up. Back then, there were no day camps, no organized events. Kids had summer off; they spent it however they wanted, hanging out in guitar stores, whatever. Now, kids have everything programmed and planned, the result of either neurotic parents or a deadly bloom of psychopaths and rapists, waiting behind every tree to abduct our children and destroy them. Either way, it effectively kills the youth-driven guitar market on weekday mornings.

So, Evan and Dean hang around the store all morning doing basically nothing. Evan makes an attempt at getting Dean interested in a guitar or drum set, but Dean yawns whenever music is mentioned. It's tedious and difficult when there are more salespeople than customers in a store on a consistent basis.

Evan is buoyed a little bit, however, by the idea that he is no longer a father-for-a-few-days; he's a father-for-a-while. He likes Dean, and, though he doesn't have room for him and can't very well adopt him, he'd like to have him around a while longer. And he likes that he exacted a promise from Ellen that she would ditch Frank. That makes him feel good; he's done something that is good for someone. So, overall, aside from the incredible boredom of his job, Evan feels pretty good.

Dean seems to be doing well, too, aside from the boredom. He's joking with the other guys, doing the hang-out thing, flicking guitar picks across the showroom, stuff like that.

At lunch, Evan runs Dean over to the shopping mall where there's a video game store. It's a genius move on Evan's part. He plunks down his credit card, and it only costs two hundred dollars to outfit Dean with the latest Game Boy and a handful of game cartridges. The reward is practically instant: Dean, pooling his booty greedily in his hands, a grin smeared on his face as they order burritos at the Taco Time stand, a "Thanks, Evan, this is cool," which is about as much as Evan could ever expect, and then a quick lunch without distraction—Dean reading an instruction manual and Evan checking out the hot girls in the short shorts who keep walking by, wondering how old they are, knowing they couldn't come close to Mica if she were there, knowing, also, that she is far away, down in Jamaica where they got lots of pretty women who will steal your money and then break your heart.

"I was thinking," Dean says, gulping down a burrito supreme like a snake, one big bite, so that Evan imagines he can see the lump move through his son's body as it digests. "Maybe for Christmas I could get a Play Station 2. I can't really get a job until I'm sixteen, but I can mow lawns or something so I can earn enough to get games. But the system is the expensive thing. If I could get that as a present . . ."

"We might be able to arrange that."

"Not that I don't like the Game Boy. It's really cool—"

"The Game Boy is more of a portable," Evan says. "It's for hanging out while I'm working and stuff, until I can figure out how to get you in a camp or something for the rest of the summer. You know. It's a go-toy. But it's nowhere near the quality of a Play Station 2. You need a system for home."

"Yeah." Dean grins hard. "Yeah, you're right. This is my go-toy. When I get home, I need a home-toy. Yeah." He sucks down another burrito.

And the mystery of fatherhood is revealed to Evan. Forego all heart-to-hearts. Buy presents.

They head back to the shop and Evan sells three packages of round-wound bass strings to a cat who's too strung out to pluck them. Dean sits on a fifteen-hundred-dollar amp and plays Crash Bandicoot. And for the first time, Evan notices himself staring at the clock over the door. He's never paid it much mind because he's never had things to do. He works in a guitar store. He grabs some food, goes out with his buddies, listens to music late, and always wakes up glad that he's not hungover like his friends. But now, with Dean, Evan is waiting for the seven o'clock shift change so he can do something else, though he has no idea what he will do.

"Where's he going to school next year?"

Evan looks over. His co-worker, Randi, a die-hard punk in her mid-twenties, is standing next to him. Her face is a scrap metal scavenger's dream. She's a vegan. She doesn't shave her arm pits. Evan finds her hot, but not as hot as Mica.

"Not sure," Evan answers.

"Not sure?" She recoils. "He's registered, right?"

"No."

"You're screwed, then. Have you seen the enrollment? Way over. Totally understaffed. There are no teachers. There are no text books."

She has a son. He's ten. That would make her fifteen or so when she had him, which beats Evan's record handily. Where did he read that the youngest mother on record was eleven?

"What should I do?"

"Explain it to them. Beg for mercy. If he doesn't have a slot now, he might be bussed across the world. He could spend an hour-and-a-half commuting. What reference area are you in?"

"Reference area?"

"Do you know your cluster schools?"

"No."

She grimaces. "Go private, if you can afford it."

"Actually," Evan says, "he probably won't be going to school here."

"Really? Where will he go?"

"He'll probably go live with his grandmother. She's in Walla Walla."

"Oh," Randi says. "That's a long weekend commute."

Evan thinks about it. It's so long it's actually *too* long for a weekend commute. He wasn't thinking weekends, he was thinking major holidays, he was thinking a week here and there, maybe a three-day extendo-weekend thrown in for fun. Things are changing quickly and he's not keeping up. He's got to realize that he's not an uncle, he's a father. Any decent parent—even Randi, who cares so little about her own body that she's had gallons of India ink injected under her skin—would think about seeing his kid every single weekend. How can a weekend go by without seeing your kid? It'll mean a lot of time on the road, but of course he'll do it. How could he not?

"Well," he says, "you gotta do what you gotta do."

"Tell me about it."

THEY GO OUT for Thai food, and while they eat, Dean opens a whole new can of worms.

"When am I going to meet my other grandparents?"

Carl and Louise? He can meet them right after Evan tells them he exists. How's that sound?

"You want to meet them?" Evan asks.

"You showed me their house."

Yeah, but he didn't think he'd actually have to produce a face-to-face meeting.

"Sure. I'll give them a call and make a date."

"They don't even know about me, do they?" Dean asks.

Evan hesitates, searching for the right answer, which may or may not be the truth. Thankfully, Dean doesn't push it; he turns the conversation to something else as they finish dinner.

They get home and hang out for a while in front of the TV. Dean seems relieved to have things settled, or at least as settled as they are. Things feel settled, even though they aren't. Use Your Illusion, I and II.

Later that night, after they've both gone to bed, Mica calls.

"It must be late there," Evan says from the darkness, his sheets pulled up around his ears, blue light sneaking around the blinds of an otherwise empty room.

"It is, but I just got in and had something to eat. Traveling is a drag. How's everything going?"

"Pretty good."

"Tell me what happened with Dean."

He tells her everything, although when he's done he realizes that the way he's phrased it makes it sound as if he and Dean staying together is a fait accompli.

"She may dump Frank," he adds because he doesn't want to misrepresent the truth about how he sees the future playing out.

"I don't think so," she says. "But it still sounds great, Evan. I'm glad you two worked things out."

"So you're not mad at me?" Evan asks.

"No, I'm not mad at you Evan. But don't lie to me like that again. That was in the past. That was the old Evan. Don't do it anymore."

He promises he won't; they say their goodnights. And he goes to sleep feeling a little lonely, a little sad, but also a little happy and cozy and comfortable. It's strange having people in your life like a girl and a kid. It's kind of nice. He rather likes it.

E VAN BOLDLY CALLS his parents and asks if he can meet with them, he has something important to discuss. Sure, they say, we were going to dinner tonight, why don't you join us? Evan takes them up on their offer, not because he wants free food but because he figures a restaurant is, tactically, a good place for him to tell them about Dean: they won't yell at him in public. Theoretically, at least.

He drops Dean off with Lars, who, like the mensch he is, has arranged for an evening of pizza and indoor go-karting. He drives back downtown and arrives at the restaurant, Orsenigo's, right on time. He checks in with the hostess and discovers that he's the first of his party; yes, he'd like to sit, please. The woman shows him to the table—a prime spot next to the window—and he waits. He isn't surprised that he's the first to arrive. Carl and Louise Wallace always arrive fashionably late, even when there's no one to impress but Evan.

He glances around the dining room with the corners of his mouth turned down, and, admittedly, a bit of an attitude. Not at the restaurant or the patrons, who are all dressed quite nicely and speaking with enthusiastic yet subdued voices—cordial, affable, genial, perfect restaurant-mates, really—but at the idea that he will have to muddle through an Italian dinner—albeit one with a northern bent, without eating wheat or dairy. What he'd really like is a giant bowl of pasta with a pile of cheese on it.

Orsenigo's is a trendy little trattoria near the Public Market, which is always crowded, no matter what time of the night, no matter what day of the week. The owner/chef, Luigi Orsenigo, is a near legend in Seattle, an author of countless cookbooks, a guest on national talk shows, and a proud sponsor of any charity event that's even remotely related to food. The restaurant has a three-week waiting list, and those who are powerful enough to pull strings and get a last minute "day of" reservation, are thankful to be offered a choice between a five-thirty or a ten o'clock start time. His parents have chosen Orsenigo's simply because they can. They can choose it; they can change their reservation from two to three without a question. They can be assured that the table will wait for them, and never vice versa.

How this came to be is a story of its own. It seems that Carl and Louise were having dinner one night—having waited their three weeks—and Orsenigo's wife, Christina, a pleasantly chatty hostess, mentioned something about her brother who was on a waiting list for a liver transplant at Harborview Medical Center. She was dismayed that her brother was so far down the list that he would likely perish before a liver became available. Christina had no idea (or did she?) that she was speaking with Carl Wallace, King of the Hill, Head of the Harbor. You see, as chief surgeon, Carl basically ran the place like his own personal playground.

"Here's my card," he said to Christina. "Call me at home tomorrow morning."

She did. And wouldn't you know, suddenly her brother was on the short list for livers. Two weeks later, he was going in for pre-op. And wouldn't you know, Carl steps in and embeds the new liver personally. Damn.

Now the deal is, when you save the life of the owner's brother-in-law, you have about as much clout at a restaurant as you could hope for. Carl could call at eight o'clock on the eve of the new millennium and Orsenigo would give him the best table in the house, and toss in a free bottle of champagne for good measure. *That's* why Carl and Louise like to go to Orsenigo's. Not the food. Not the price. Not the view. The fact is, dining is a production, and you *do* get points for style.

Evan shakes himself out of his reverie. The bread boy has left a basket of bread on the table and, next to it, a shallow dish of rosemary-infused olive oil, a bit of cracked pepper and a pinch of sea salt. Evan would love to devour it. He's angry at himself for not bringing along any rice crackers. If he doesn't eat soon, he may starve to death at the table. His mother always tells him he's too thin, he should eat some spaghetti. He tries to tell her that if he eats spaghetti, his brain will do things he doesn't like. She doesn't understand. When he tells her the doctor said so, she understands.

He waits fifteen minutes, then flags down a waiter and asks to order. He's found it's generally better to order without his father around, anyway, since his father, the most conventional of all conventional Western doctors, dismisses dietary intervention out of hand, and invariably becomes agitated, if not downright pissy, when it comes to ordering time for Evan. The waiter is kind and understanding and assures Evan his meal will be safe, and Evan is left to struggle over his upcoming confession.

Ideally, he doesn't want to have to struggle over it. He wishes it would come out on its own, as part of a joke or something. But if that were possible, he knows, it would have come out as a joke at some point over the past fourteen years. The fact that he could hold out this long without telling them is just evidence of how deeply embedded the secret is. He likes Dean. He really does. And he would like to show Dean to his parents. But he's so petrified, so terrified about the actual moment of presentation, he really doesn't think he'll be able to pull the words from his mouth.

His appetizer arrives just as Carl and Louise enter the restaurant, a few ticks short of seven-thirty.

"Oh, good, you started," Louise says. Carl sits without saying a word. Doctors never apologize for keeping you waiting. They want to give you the impression that they were late because they were delivering a baby or binding the gushing wound of a stab victim or something equally important. Their time is more valuable than yours.

As soon as they are seated, a new waiter appears at the table. This one doesn't look as friendly as the first. He's thin, wrinkled, and has black, greasy hair.

"I am Mario," he says in heavily accented English, "the waitstaff supervisor. I will attend to you, personally. Would you like to see a menu, or may I order for you?"

There's a brief hesitation. Thank God Evan's already ordered. He knows Mario would totally screw up the concept of a wheat-free meal and dust everything with as much semolina as he could lay his hands on.

"I know what I'm having," Carl announces. "Veal chop, medium rare. Sauteed spinach, light on the oil. Green salad to start, lemon wedges on the side, no dressing. And a wine list."

Bam, bam, bam. Like navigating an operating room. Sponge. Suture. Clamp that bleeder! Scalpel, stat!

Louise doesn't have her act as together as old Carl.

"What are the specials?" she asks timidly. Evan can tell she wants to look at a menu—she certainly doesn't want Mario ordering for her—but with Carl having just ordered and Evan already eating, she feels the pressure to produce a decent order. Stat.

But there's no need for that, either. Because suddenly the man himself is standing at the table. Luigi Orsenigo, or just Luigi to his friends. A chubby young man with wispy brown hair, blue eyes, and a clean, heavily starched apron. Cute, without being overtly sexual. The women love him. The men don't feel threatened by him. The perfect person to pound your veal.

"*Buona sera, la famiglia* Wallace. *Come state?*"

"Luigi!" Carl bellows loudly enough so that the heads of other diners turn to catch a glimpse of the plump chef and the important people to whom he is attending.

"Your son was too hungry to wait for you, no? You were too hungry, no? Look at him, Dottore Wallace. He is such a good-looking boy. And look how he eats. Ah . . ."

Orsenigo loses himself in some kind of quasi-rhapsodic moment, absorbing Evan's presence. Then, suddenly, he snaps out of it.

"Mario," he barks at the gangly waiter. "*Per il dottore, la—*"

"No, Luigi—" Carl interrupts.

Orsenigo freezes, comically, mid-syllable, his hands grasping the air, his mouth fully open, about to form some wonderful Italian words to describe the dishes fit for a king he will produce for Evan's father.

"Carl's on a diet. High blood pressure," Louise explains.

"Ah. A diet. *Bene.* You must stay healthy, no, Dottore Wallace? You cannot operate on yourself, I think, ha, ha! *Va bene. Allora.*"

Orsenigo falls into thought. Who will be the beneficiary of his cooking prowess, his mastery of the kitchen? He fixes his eyes on Evan's mother.

"Signora?" Orsenigo asks slyly, with a hint of intrigue.

Louise blushes.

"*I'm* not on a diet, Luigi," she giggles.

"*Benissimo!* Mario. For la Signora Wallace, antipasto of wild mushrooms, sauteed in *extra-virgin* olive oil, topped with shaved parmesan cheese, and finished with olio di truffolo."

Louise is melting in this guy's butter. Notice how he emphasizes *extra virgin*. Evan is disgusted at the ridiculous cliché of a situation and his mother's participation in it.

"A *half* portion," Orsenigo leers. "The signora is concerned about her figure."

Louise blushes and Carl nods smugly, proud that his wife is being sought after by a genius cook. *You can look . . . but keep your truffle pickin' hands off her.*

"Next, a small serving of linguini con vongole—"

"I'm full already," Louise playfully chimes in.

"A tiny portion, *bella.* Because it is your favorite, no?"

"Oh, yes."

"Si. Ma, for the *secondo piatto,* she will have the whole red snapper, stuffed with olives, grilled until the flesh is perfect . . . firm, moist . . . fantastico. Fresh today. The best fish we have had all year. I will fillet it for you personally, *bella.*"

Louise is practically faint from this ordering process.

"*Allora.* And young Signor Wallace, you are fine?"

"I'm fine," Evan reluctantly admits, not really wanting to give this guy an inch.

"*Molto bene.*"

Luigi glances at Carl, who is studying the wine list.

"That wine list is no good to you here, Dottore. For your wine, I choose. You do not object to red, Signora?"

"Of course not, Luigi." Louise smiles.

"Luigi, this is too much," Carl protests. "You're running a business here."

"Ba. Nonsense. This is the family of the man who saved my brother-in-law's life. Food is food, *mi amico*, but blood is blood. As we say in Italy: *la famiglia cosi fa tutti.* The family is everything. *Basta*, I go."

And he's off, disappearing into the crowded restaurant. Evan watches as Orsenigo retreats. He smiles, he waves, he shakes the occasional outstretched hand. But he never makes a fuss even resembling the fuss he made over Carl and Louise. Which just goes to show you that if you work long and hard enough and you get some clout and some power to give a guy a new liver, some celebrity chef with a restaurant will kiss your ass.

"So, Evan," Carl beams across the table. "How's the band faring?"

He must have gotten caught up in the moment. He never asks about Evan's music. He must have figured he could soak up some of Orsenigo's residual charisma and pretend like he gives a damn.

"Great."

"Any *gigs* coming up?"

He says "gigs" like it's some kind of toy word, not used in the real world.

"Not for a few weeks. Sorry."

Carl and Louise share a proud smile, which makes Evan mad. They aren't really listening, obviously, or they would have heard the answer to the question, which didn't call for smiles. There's something very Stepford about this whole scene. Evan doesn't like it.

"Actually," he says, "there *is* something a little exciting. I got to sit in with Lucky Strike last week down at Jefferson Bank."

"Lucky Strike?" Louise asks. "Is that a band?"

"Yes."

"Never heard of them," Carl says.

"They're pretty well known in the music world. Theo Moody—"

"Did you get paid?"

"No, I didn't get paid. It was just a jam. But it was a full house, and everybody was really into it."

"Oh, that's nice, honey," Louise says.

"And we cut a demo. My friend, Billy Marx, is going to give it to some A&R people he knows."

"Do we know Billy Marx?" Louise asks Carl.

"Black fellow," Carl says. "Very friendly, as I recall. There was an article about him in the paper a few years ago. Seattle black entrepreneur of the year or something like that."

"That's him," Evan says.

"How do you remember all that, Carl?" Louise marvels. He shrugs in response.

"And I met a girl. I think I'm in love."

Both Carl and Louise drop their bread and stare at Evan, mouths agape.

"That's wonderful!" Louise exclaims.

"I can't tell you how long I've been waiting to hear that!" Carl says. "I was afraid you were gay!"

"Actually, she's a man. A transgender. She'll be a woman soon. Once she finishes the final round of hormone injections and gets her penis cut off."

"Oh?" Louise gasps, shocked.

"Compliments of il Signor Orsenigo," Mario announces. God only knows how long he's been standing there with that shit-eating grin, his greasy little hands wrapped around a hundred dollar bottle of wine.

Carl regains a bit of composure, pulls his eyeglasses out of his pocket and slips them on.

"Let me see that, Mario."

Carl takes the bottle and glances at the label.

"You were joking about that, weren't you, Evan?" he asks under his breath.

"Yes. She's a real woman. She is half black, half Asian, though."

"I'm not a racist, Evan. But I must admit I am a bit of a homophobe. It's something I should come to terms with, I know. I'd just rather not have to do it with my own son."

"She's a woman. I promise."

Carl nods, studies the label.

"That's a fine bottle of wine, there, Signora Wallace," Carl says. He hands the bottle back to Mario, who bows politely and uncorks it. He pours a splash into Carl's glass.

"Dottore, taste."

Carl lifts the glass like it's the holy grail and smells the wine. He savors the scent, examines the color, then sets the glass down.

"It's just fine, Mario."

"You do not wish to taste?"

"Tasting something that smells that good is pretentious, Mario. It feels a little cool. You must have brought it straight from the cellar. Let it be. We'll drink it with dinner."

Mario bows and vanishes into the throng of diners.

"So," Carl says, having fully regained his composure. "Where were we?"

Where were we? Evan was about to tell you that he has a son. Dean.

"I have one more exciting thing—" Evan starts.

"Mom has some big, exciting news—" Carl says over him.

"Oh?"

"—about Charlie."

Stalemate.

"Let Evan tell us his news first," Louise says.

"He's told us all his news," Carl objects. "He's got a girlfriend, and she isn't a man. What else is there?"

"Evan?" Louise asks.

"I can wait," Evan says, almost relieved at being cut off.

"He can wait, he can wait," Carl says excitedly. "Tell him."

Carl is grinning, his eyes are all lit up. Louise gives Evan a faux sheepish shrug—a *twist-my-arm-why-dontcha* expression—and clears her throat.

"Well," she says, pausing for a deep breath. "It seems that your brother, Charlie, and his wife, Allison, are pregnant with their second child."

Bam! Evan feels like he's been hit in the back of the head with one of Luigi's cast-iron frying pans. *Charlie and Allison are pregnant.* The words rattle through his skull like a mad wasp in a spittoon.

"Hoo, hoo!" Carl hoots. "Only *Allison* is pregnant, honey! Charlie's just the troublemaker!"

"Isn't that fantastic, Evan?"

"You'll be an uncle twice over, Evan. You'd better get started yourself, if you don't want to end up a bitter old bachelor with no kids to care for you in your golden years. Maybe this new girl of yours is the one. I know you'll be a great father when you finally decide to apply yourself."

But I am a—

"That's great," Evan forces himself to say.

"Isn't it, though?"

Already—

"I'm so happy for them."

What does he do now? How can he tell them about Dean? They wouldn't understand. They would take it wrong. They would accuse him of trying to sabotage Charlie's conquest. How could he tell them now that he has a fourteen-year-old son who will care for him in his golden years? First, they wouldn't believe it. Then, if he did manage to convince them, they would probably accuse him of one-upmanship, of timing his announcement to nullify the joy they were getting from Charlie. What a disaster.

Carl and Louise's appetizers arrive; Evan's empty plate is cleared; full of smiles, Evan's parents turn to him to present them with more good news.

"What is it that you wanted to tell us? You said you had more exciting news."

"Yes, son, and make it good!"

Evan feels like puking on the table. He's been totally shoved out of position, boxed out for the rebound. He wanted to go to dinner with his parents so he could be the center of their universe and tell them everything. But, once again, his brother ruined it. Here, take my dare for me—loser; now have a nice rest of your pathetic epileptic life while I ascend to the heavens. Well. All is fair in war and brotherhood, sure. But Jacob had better watch his back, because Esau has a major hard-on for him, and he ain't stopping until blood is spilled.

"Oh, right," Evan says, "it's not really news, so much, but if Billy hooks us up, we might actually get a record deal and then we'll need a lawyer, and I thought that since you guys—"

"Mike Fleischman," Carl blurts out, squeezing onto his salad the juice of Sicilian lemons wrapped in cheesecloth.

"Mike Fleischman?"

"My lawyer. If he can't do it, he'll dish it to one of his partners. Call Mike tomorrow morning. He'll take care of it. He takes care of everything."

Carl shoves a forkful of lemony greens into his mouth. To him, the case is settled. In Carl's world, things work effortlessly. Almost everything is as simple as "call Mike Fleischman." That's the world he's built around himself. He's a surgeon, after all. His job is to cut into people without flinching, to cauterize veins without hesitation, to remove the faulty valve without wavering. He can't stand distractions and deviations. Which are the two words that best describe Evan's life.

"I hope it's a girl," Louise says wistfully after a moment.

"Me, too," Carl agrees. "She would wear pretty dresses. Allison has a flair for that. She's a sharp dresser herself."

They work away at their plates, neither looking at each other nor at Evan, but at some blurry spot about eighteen inches before each of their faces where an invisible movie screen plays a wonderful home video of their new grandchild-to-be, recorded sometime in the future and broadcast to them by some benevolent deity.

"I've always liked the name Zelda," Louise says.

"Zelda was an insane woman," Carl rebukes her. "An alcoholic. Zelda Fitzgerald."

"I still like the name."

"I like Elizabeth," Carl says.

"Elizabeth?" Louise considers the proposition. "Eliza? That's nice."

"They could name her Tracy," Evan throws in, not really sure why he should nose into the middle of their fantasy film, but doing it anyway, maybe out of fear of disappearing entirely, of pulling an Alice and shrinking from sight. *Drink me.*

"Tracy?"

"Tracy?"

"It's a nice name," Evan says.

"Why Tracy?" Louise asks.

"He dated a Tracy once," Carl explains. "Didn't you? High school. A Mormon."

"Yes."

"Her father was a real pain in the ass. Called in the middle of the night once, claiming that she was in your bed. I told him that that was ridiculous. He cursed at me."

"How do you remember all that?" Louise asks.

"Mormons aren't allowed to curse, are they?" Carl wonders aloud. Then, with a shrug, he asks: "Hear anything from her? How's she doing? Is she well?"

"Actually, she's dead," Evan says quickly. "She died a week ago. I went to her funeral in Walla Walla."

"Oh, my."

Louise is shocked. Carl sets down his wine.

"Was she ill?" Carl asks.

"No. She was hit by a truck and killed instantly. Broken neck."

Evan doesn't know why he throws in the detail about her broken neck. He doesn't even know if that's how it happened, but he prefers to think of it happening that way. The alternatives are much too upsetting.

"Jesus," Carl mutters. "Poor girl."

"She was such a *nice* girl," Louise says.

"Was she married? Did she have children?"

"She wasn't married," Evan responds. "She had one kid. He's fourteen."

"*Fourteen*," Carl repeats, surprised. "I guess *she* didn't waste any time after high school."

"That's so sad," Louise sighs.

They sit in silence. The announcement of Tracy's death has cast a pall over the meal. If you're going to trump a conversation, you should trump it hard. Have no mercy. Crush all further conversation. There will be no more talk about pregnancies tonight. Death has settled over the table, and Death isn't leaving any time soon.

Perhaps Carl and Louise are honestly feeling the loss of someone they once knew. Perhaps they are being held silent by images of Tracy that are flashing through their minds. Hopefully good, but probably not. They never saw Tracy as Evan's first love, they saw her as Evan's temptress, the bad angel on his shoulder. They saw her leading Evan down the one-way path out of the Garden of Eden, a path which could ultimately have only one climactic result.

More likely, though, Carl and Louise are silent because they are feeling the loss of Evan's childhood, or, rather, the gap between what they thought Evan's childhood should have been and what it actually was. No one regrets a child's mistakes more than his parents, that's for sure. It's like thinking you're going to get a bicycle for Christmas, but all you get is a pair of shoes. You want to cry, but you smile through it, don't you? We can't be ungrateful. Some children don't even get shoes.

By the time the main courses arrive, Carl has recovered enough to perform a monologue, relieving both Evan and Louise of the obligation to speak. He comes through well, like a real trooper. He drones on and on about the hospital and other things that neither Evan nor Louise really listen to. And he does it courageously, without thanks. Because sometimes it is the duty of the father to do things like that. To talk when nobody else feels like talking, so that the entire dinner table isn't sucked down into the gray muck and never retrieved. Carl even has the wherewithal to banter with Orsenigo on the way out. What a guy.

They leave the restaurant and say their goodnights somberly on the street. Carl tells Evan to call if he needs Mike Fleischman's assistance. Then Louise hugs Evan tightly.

"Will you do me a favor, Evan?" Louise whispers in their clench. "Will you call Charlie tonight? Not for him. For me."

Evan shrugs as a way of saying yes. And as he pulls away from her he feels so sad. So sad that he hasn't told them, that they will go on not knowing. They should know about Dean and be as proud of him as they are about their grandson, Eric, and their grandchild-in-waiting. They should hook up their imaginary movie screen and see Dean, too, not just Zelda in a taffeta dress.

"Evan? Are you all right?" Carl asks.

Evan shakes his head. For some reason, he's on the verge of tears and he's struggling to hold them in. His father notices.

"Tracy's passing really hit you didn't it?"

He nods. But that's only part of it.

Carl puts his arm around Evan's shoulder and turns him up the hill. He guides Evan up the damp sidewalk toward First Avenue.

"It's hard to take the death of someone your own age," Carl explains. "Especially when you're young. It's your first confrontation with mortality, and it's hard to swallow."

Yes. They continue their abbreviated funeral march, Louise following at a discreet distance behind them, allowing father and son the privacy they need to have a heart-to-heart.

"And I'm sure that you're thinking about your own mortality right now, and where you are in this world. And, let me tell you, it's a big question, and it's not a question you should try to answer on your own, necessarily. Sometimes it's important to . . . If there's anything I can do . . ."

When they reach the top of the hill, Carl stops and faces Evan. He looks deeply into Evan's eyes and sees—what? What does he see when he looks at Evan?

"Dad," Evan says, breaking off eye contact, glancing at the ground, noticing how the neon sign in the coffee shop window behind his father reflects off the wet concrete. "Tracy's son . . ." He looks over his father's shoulder and into the coffee shop where a lonesome man sits huddled behind the counter. "Tracy's son . . ." He looks at Carl. "He's mine. He's my son." He feels a warmth inside him, a gushing, just the mention of Dean to his father has released so much. "He's staying with me now. Lars is keeping an eye on him tonight. But I want you to meet him."

Carl doesn't say anything. For a moment, he doesn't move, doesn't quiver. Then his color changes swiftly, his pinkish glow ashing over.

Louise joins them, then, assuming incorrectly that their heart-to-heart has reached a satisfactory conclusion.

"How are you two doing?" she asks.

Carl looks at her strangely, turns his body toward her, then reaches to steady himself on an iron chair that is behind him, a chair that belongs to the coffee shop and is intended for the comfort and convenience of its customers; he reaches for it so he can lean against it, so it can take some of his weight, but it darts away from him it seems, darts away and he can't catch it though his weight is already headed toward it; and he stumbles, his foot slips on the wet pavement, his leg buckles, his heft gains downward momentum, and he falls almost in slow motion, his temple careening recklessly into the iron table, partner of the iron chair, and opening up a gash which bleeds and bleeds and bleeds all over his new khaki raincoat.

A THREE PERCENT CHANCE of things going wrong. These things may include (but are not limited to) mortality, blindness, loss of memory, loss of speech, loss of motor skills, or infection of the bone tissue, which would mean we would have to insert a plastic shield in your skull so your brain won't leak out.

Seven years ago the maestros at Harborview Medical Center had given Evan that speech, after they had deemed Evan's epilepsy intractable. They were trying to bully Evan into brain surgery. They wanted to remove a macadamia nut-sized piece of brain, the source of Evan's electrical miswiring. Crack his skull open, cut out a chunk, sew him back up and off he goes, a placid little lobotomy patient, docile, well-behaved, ready to be sent to typing school so he can contribute to society, pay taxes, live out his natural life with some kind of dignity. Because having epilepsy is definitely not dig-nified. Always falling down. Drooling at inappropriate times. Those bothersome twitches. Who cares about art? Who cares about music? Who cares about what his mind will be like after the operation?

Evan didn't have definitive proof that removing a chunk of his brain would affect his creativity, but he didn't have proof that it wouldn't. And it seemed that this surgery was being pushed by Evan's neurologist at the behest of Evan's father. Too cozy. A spot just happened to open up. The brilliant brain surgeon has a free day and would be happy to help. You're a perfect candidate—say, can we stick these electrodes on your head again? Look at that EEG. Look at that. Perfect spikes. Just right. You won't feel a thing, although the sound of us drilling into your skull might be a bit disconcerting. We'll dose you with a happy drug so you won't be concerned that we're probing your gray matter with tweezers. The doctor has performed this procedure countless times. A walk in the park. Really.

Really. Evan was still living at home, so he got a full dose of it from his parents at the dinner table. Charlie was having his mind formed by the geniuses at Columbia Law, and Evan's parents wanted him to have his mind formed by the geniuses at Harborview. Just a little off the top, Doctor. It's an okay mind, just a little ragged. It just needs a trim.

But Evan said no. When push came to shove, it was his brain and he said no. His proffered reason was that he felt his creativity could be affected, that he could lose his musical talent, and that he couldn't stand a life without music. A perfectly legitimate concern, noble and true, and one that had to be acknowledged by his parents. However. There were other reasons that Evan dodged the knife. Fear, jealousy, anger, resentment, autonomy. Others, too. Shame.

Evan should have missed a year of school because of his accident. It happened in the fall, in early November. Evan didn't go back to school until late in February. His parents should have held him out the rest of the year, made him start over. But they were ashamed.

They pushed hard, they did. They hired tutors. They helped in other ways, too. They did Evan's homework for him if they had to. Poor grades they would accept. Being held back a year, they refused to accept. Push, push, push.

And not a soul knew what the Wallace family knew. That there was damage. Internal damage. The outside world knew that Evan had been in a coma for a time. They knew that he had gone through rehabilitation. But they didn't know that he was a different boy in one special way.

Well, to say not a soul is exaggerating. The principal knew. The nurse knew. But that was it. They, with Evan's parents, agreed that it was in Evan's best interest if his peers didn't know so he wouldn't be shunned, and, of course, that his teachers didn't know so he wouldn't be coddled.

Don't tell anyone. It's no one's business but ours. People are afraid of epileptics. People don't know what to do. Don't frighten them. Don't tell them.

A fine way to bring up a child. It makes your child dark inside. Able to keep secrets well. And able to punish his parents well. And that's what Evan did. He punished his parents by waiting until the eve of the surgery before announcing that he wasn't going through with it. By waiting until after the nurse had shaved his head. Until the OR had already been booked. Until the medical team had already been assembled.

What were they going to do? Strap him down and slice him open anyway? Nope. They were going to nod slowly and sigh and say we understand. They were going to say maybe you've made the right choice. They were going to say we love you and we want the best for you.

But they weren't going to believe any of it.

E VAN'S BEEN SITTING there for almost an hour when the door opens. He glances up at the doctor.

"It wasn't as bad as it looked," the doctor grins at him. "The scalp bleeds profusely. It's all those capillaries up there getting oxygen to all those hair follicles. He's all stitched up now. No concussion or anything, just a nasty cut and a bruise."

The doctor waits. For what, Evan doesn't know. But he towers over Evan for a moment, waiting. Evan feels childish sitting on the wooden bench in the hallway of Harborview drinking a can of soda.

"They'd like you to go in now," the doctor says.

Evan stands. The doctor lays his hand on Evan's shoulder.

"Evan," he says. He's an old friend of Carl's; Evan's known him forever but can't remember his name. "I suppose—" But he cuts himself off.

"You suppose?" Evan prompts.

"I suppose congratulations are in order," the doctor says, "as belated as they may be."

He purses his lips, taps Evan's cheek lightly with his palm, and then walks off.

CARL SITS ON the examination table wearing a hospital gown that is stained with blood on the left shoulder. A massive bandage is held in place on his left temple by a gauze headband. Louise is standing near the window.

On their faces is that look, a somber, agonized look, the same look he's seen a million times when they've come to pick him up at the hospital after a seizure. The shoe's on the other foot.

"You okay?" Evan asks when nobody says anything.

Carl nods and touches his bandage gingerly. He looks to Louise. She nods back to him.

"We've discussed your situation," Carl begins.

Obviously. That's why they didn't want Evan in the room with them while Carl was being repaired. So they could discuss his situation.

"And I think we've reached some kind of conclusion."

Great. They've reached a conclusion about Evan's life. He can hardly wait.

"This is how your mother and I will help you with your son," he says deliberately. "You'll sell your apartment, and then you and he will move in with us where we can help you raise him."

"We've got plenty of space," Louise adds. "You can sleep in your old room and your son can sleep in Charlie's old room."

"Does that sound fair?" Carl asks.

Evan is too stunned to even answer. He knows that his parents think of him as totally incompetent and unable to perform the smallest task without assistance, but this is ridiculous. Move in with them? Why? What kind of person would even suggest that as a solution?

"It sounds stupid," Evan says.

Carl and Louise look at each other, surprised by Evan's response, which, evidently, comes as a shock to them.

"What do you mean?" Louise asks.

"Why is there an assumption that I need your help?"

"Why did you tell us about it now if you weren't asking for help?"

"I wanted you to *meet* him," Evan blurts out. "He's your grandson. I wanted you to meet him. He wants to meet you."

"Oh, that's rich," Carl hisses. "Fourteen years this boy has existed and you tell us about it *now* because you want us to *meet* him, not because his mother has died and you have to grow up and act like an adult."

"What are you talking about?"

"And just how long do you think you'll last by yourself, Evan?" Louise asks pointedly. "Do you know anything about raising a child? It's a lot of work, *hard* work—"

"I'll say," Carl agrees.

"I think you have some fancy notion that you and this boy will get by eating Beef-a-Roni for the rest of your lives. But it's not like that."

Evan fumes. His parents' assumption that he couldn't raise Dean competently if he chose to is infuriating.

"You know nothing about being a father, Evan. It's a full-time job. How are you going to raise your son and play your music at the same time? How is that going to work?"

"I can make it work—"

"You've got late-night gigs," Carl points out.

"I can get a baby sitter if you're too busy."

"Rehearsals at all hours."

"You should come live at home," Louise blunders on, caught up in her own world. "Your father and I will raise Dean so you don't have to worry about it. You go on doing whatever it is that you do. We'll take care of him for you. But I insist that you live in our house."

"You'll need all your extra money for expenses," Carl says. "You can't afford to maintain an apartment."

"I *own* the apartment," Evan snaps. "Grandpa left it to me. I don't owe any money on it, just the common charges."

"He needs his father around," Louise goes on, almost talking to herself, trying to convince herself. "But if I'm going to start cooking again every night, take him to school in the morning, shuttle him about every day to music lessons or sports or whatever it is that he does, then I insist that you make it easier for me by being close by. I'm not as young as I used to be, I can't drive all over Seattle anymore. If I'm going to do all the work of raising another child, I insist that you meet my conditions."

"What are you talking about?" Evan asks angrily.

"I insist!" she cries brittlely. "I insist!"

"No, Mom! No. It's not happening that way. I'm not moving in with you. He's my son, *I'll* raise him. *I'll* cook his dinner. *I'll* drive him everywhere he needs to go—"

"You'll *drive* him?" Carl mutters. "You shouldn't be *living* alone, no less *driving.*"

"What's that, Dad?"

"What if you had a status seizure in your apartment? What would you do then?"

"Dad, I know in advance. I always get an aura. I can call someone—"

"You're killing us with worry, Evan," Carl says. "What if you don't call in time?"

"I've taken care of myself so far."

"But you've got your hands full, don't you? And now you want to be responsible for someone else? That's ludicrous!"

"I don't need you to take over my life. I don't need you to live my life for me."

Carl doesn't respond.

"I can be a damn good father if I want to be. I can be a damn good father. You know why? Because I know how to listen, that's why. And I know how to be flexible. And Dean knows how to listen and be flexible, too. And when he meets you, he's probably going to ask if he can mow your lawn so he can earn money to buy games for the Play Station 2 you're going to give him for Christmas, and I'd appreciate your giving him a chance. He and I are going to be a good team, and we don't need to live with you to do it."

Louise and Carl exchange a look. Then Louise turns to the window and looks at the city that sparkles outside.

"We've discussed this," Carl says flatly. "And we feel very strong-
ly that we either go through this together, all of us, or you go
through it alone."

It's a second before Evan fully understands what his father is saying. When he does, it's like a blow, like being punched in the gut
by Frank.

"You mean I either do it your way, or I can go fuck myself,"
Evan says.

There's no answer. His mother looking out the window, her
back turned. His father staring him down, unresponsive. Evan is
alone in the room. The only thing that keeps him there is the shock
of it. That they would create such a world in their minds and then
expect him to comply without so much as a whimper.

"Then I guess I have to choose the latter," he says.

He leaves the examination room and walks down the hallway.

He hears his father behind him. Coming into the hall, calling
after him. *"Evan! Evan!"* He doesn't respond, doesn't look back.
"Evan, come back here!" But he doesn't. He doesn't go back.

DEAN IS ASLEEP on the couch. He's on his stomach, his face
pressed into the pillow. Evan wanted to be home before Dean got
there, but he failed. He has an excuse at least. He sits on the edge
of the sofa bed and gives Dean a nudge.

"You asleep?"

"Yes," Dean says into the pillow.

"Sorry I'm late," Evan said. "My father slipped and fell down in
the street."

"Is he all right?"

"He cut his head and had to go to the hospital. A few stitches,
no big deal."

"Did you tell them about me?" Dean asks after a moment.

"I did."

"When do I get to meet them?"

"Maybe next weekend. Their plans are up in the air. Possibly
next weekend. If not, the weekend after that."

"Are they nice?" Dean asks.

"Yeah, they're nice."

"Do you think they'll like me?"

"Yeah," Evan says. "Yeah, I'm pretty sure they'll like you."

LATER THAT NIGHT, much later, in the wee hours, long after Evan has tucked Dean in, he calls his brother, because he promised his mother he would, and he always keeps his promises to his mother.

"Hello?" a sleepy voice croaks.

Evan looks at the clock. It's after one. Charlie was sleeping.

Charlie. The model citizen, model father, model husband, model brother. He never once said a thing about the accident that changed Evan's life. Not to Evan, not to their parents. Evan lay bleeding on the street, a charcoal sky pressing down, headlights from the offending car illuminating the scene. An ambulance arrived, but not before Carl, who had come home from work early, it seems, and had been summoned by a neighbor to attend to his unconscious son. ("What happened?" Carl had demanded, Evan later learned from Penny. "He broke his head," Charlie had answered.) And Charlie standing mute against the truth. Not a word.

In the hospital. Days of coma. Days of uncertainty. Not a word. After he wakes, weeks of recuperation. Not a word. The accident never spoken of. Why it happened, not a question. How it happened, who cares? Evan left to drift around in a raging sea without someone to throw him a line. If they had only asked how it had happened. How? And if Evan had only told them. Or if he had not. If he had held his tongue, and, later, Charlie had gone to them, head in hands, and confessed that he was to blame. But Charlie didn't say a word. Carl and Louise never asked. Evan was never given the chance to tell. *It wasn't my fault,* he wanted to tell them. *It wasn't my fault.* But, apparently, they had no interest in hearing.

"Hello?" Charlie repeats.

Evan says nothing. He's angry with himself. Angry that he's getting sucked into ridiculous bitter memories about his own past instead of concentrating on Dean. And forced to call his brother? Now? Just because his mother wanted him to?

"Hello?"

He wants to hang up on Charlie, but the pause has already gone on too long. Charlie would know; he has caller ID. Evan has to say something.

"Sorry, Chuck, I didn't realize it was so late. I'll call you tomorrow."

Charlie yawns into the phone.

"Once you breach the sleep/wake barrier the damage has already been done," he says, hushed. "Let me take it into the other room so I don't wake Al."

Sleepy shuffles, a closing door.

"What's up?" Charlie asks.

"I just called to say congratulations."

"Oh, right, you had dinner with Mom and Dad? How'd it go?"

How'd it go? Should Evan tell his brother what he told his parents? Or should he keep Charlie in the dark, let him find out by back channels, like Evan found out about the pregnancy?

"It had its moments," Evan says, and then, to avoid any probing questions, he launches into an animated retelling of the scene: an evening of fawning and groveling simply because their father had shown favoritism in organ allocation.

"Dad's a cardiothoracic surgeon," Charlie says when Evan has finished. "He doesn't do livers."

"Yeah, whatever," Evan says. "But I mean, Dad bumped Orsenigo's brother twenty spots up the liver list so he could get a good table and a free bottle of Pellegrino on a busy night. Isn't there something wrong with that?"

"That's not what happened, Evan."

"No? Well, what, then?"

"He told me," Charlie explains. "Dad reviewed the records. Orsenigo's brother-in-law was much sicker than the charts had shown. Dad reevaluated the guy's condition, that's all. It turns out he really would have died if Dad hadn't reclassified him. And Dad didn't perform the surgery, either. He was in the hospital making rounds and he scrubbed up and observed. He always observes surgeries. That's practically all he does. I don't think Dad has actually performed a surgery in years, and when he *did* perform surgeries, they were *heart* surgeries. You remember things all distorted, Ev. You have selective memory."

"Yeah?"

"You have selective memory that makes people look bad."

"Really? Maybe so."

Evan wonders. It's probably so. Charlie remembers things accurately. Evan remembers things emotionally.

"Well, anyway, I just wanted to say congratulations. Mom and Dad are all excited. They've got a list of names for you."

"I figured. Hey, I have to get up early and get to the gym. You wanna work out tomorrow? I'll leave you a guest pass at the WAC. I'll be there at six."

"What about Eric?"

"What about him?"

"Don't you want to have breakfast with him?"

"Ha. That's a good one, Evan. Eric has breakfast with Spongebob every morning."

"I guess you're working late tomorrow, too?" Evan asks.

"Yeah, I am. I'm working like a dog lately. I'm up for partner. I think it's a pretty done deal."

"That's great," Evan says, trying to sound enthusiastic.

"It's ninety-nine percent sure. But I've got to bust my balls for the next couple of months to show that I really want it. It's like getting into a frat."

"I didn't go to college. Remember?"

"You've seen movies, though."

"Yeah."

"So, you know. It's a universal metaphor. Hazing."

"Yeah."

The conversation stalls for a moment.

"Do you remember Tracy Smith?" Evan asks.

"Your old girlfriend, Tracy Smith? From high school?"

"Yeah. She died."

"What? How?"

"A car accident."

"Oh, you're kidding. Man. I'm really sorry."

Evan wonders how much Charlie knows about Tracy and Evan's relationship. Charlie was on a different wavelength in high school—the academic fast track; he wasn't too clever about observing people's comings and goings. Most likely he never saw or heard a thing of Tracy's late-night visits to Evan's room.

"You know," Evan says, "Tracy was the first girl I ever slept with."

"Really? I didn't know that," Charlie says. "I thought you were still a virgin."

"Ha, ha."

"Were you *her* first?"

Evan stops, surprised by the question.

"Yeah," he answers. "Why do you ask?"

"Nothing. It's nothing."

"That means it's something, doesn't it, Chuck?"

"No—I shouldn't have said anything. She's dead. You shouldn't gossip about someone who's dead."

"Go ahead, Chuck. Tell me what you were going to say."

"Well. I heard she slept around, that's all."

Evan bristles, but he forces himself to laugh. He'd like a little more information before he makes Charlie swallow his fist.

"You never heard things in high school, Chuck, you know that. You were too much of a nerd. How could a guy like you have heard anything?"

"I heard enough things," Charlie says.

"You're talking out of your ass, Chuck. She didn't sleep around. She was either with me or she was studying. She was a hell of a lot smarter than you, you know. What did you get on your SATs?"

"What does that have to do with it?"

"She's my old girlfriend and she's dead and you're dissing her, that's what it's got to do with it. So shut up."

"Sorry, Evan. Let's drop it."

Evan considers dropping it for about half a second.

"If you're so sure, then tell me who she was fucking."

"Ev, just drop it, man. Forget it."

"*How* do you know, Chuck?" Evan demands. "You're a lawyer, present your evidence. *How* do you know? Give me names. Dates."

Evan feels Charlie stiffen against this comment.

"Look, Evan, Tracy was a nice girl. I'm very sad that she died. Let's leave it at that, okay?"

"Fuck you, Chuck. You're a prick to throw out some bullshit comment like that and then not have the balls to stand behind it. You're a pussy."

"All right, fine, then. I'll tell you. I don't care. She had a baby right after she graduated high school, less than nine months after you two broke up. Okay?"

A lump shoots up into Evan's throat, making it impossible for him to speak. Charlie knows about the baby.

"Okay?"

"What about it?" Evan asks.

"Well, if you're *not* the father, then I guess she slept around. If you *are* the father, then . . ."

"Then?"

"Then I guess you're an asshole," Charlie says, "because I heard that the father abandoned Tracy and the kid." Then, after a pause, he asks: "Are you the father?"

Evan goes numb. He doesn't know why. He's already told his parents, which means that Charlie is less than twelve hours away from knowing. So why does he feel sick? It's already in motion, the steel balls have been released, randomness is being formed.

"Are you the father?" Charlie repeats.

Evan can't answer because Charlie is picking at fourteen years of scab, and it hurts.

"I didn't think so," Charlie says. "Look, I've got a breakfast appointment tomorrow with clients. Call me tomorrow, okay?"

"Fuck you, Chuck," Evan says, releasing everything. "I'm his father, and his name is Dean, and Tracy didn't sleep around, and if you say another bad word about her I'll come over there and beat the crap out of you in front of Eric."

"Are you serious?"

"I'm his father. I have a fourteen-year-old kid. Didn't see that one coming, did you?"

"Holy shit! Do Mom and Dad know?"

"They know."

"What did they say?"

"They said they thought it was really great. They were very happy for me."

"You're joking."

"Yeah, I'm joking."

"Oh, man," Charlie says, "I can't—"

"Believe it?"

"I mean, I . . . Look, I really have to go to sleep. I have a big meeting . . . Oh, shit. Can we talk about this later? Tomorrow isn't good. Maybe the next day? Lunch or something. Shit, I don't know what to say."

"You don't have to say anything, Chuck. We don't have to talk. I just wanted to tell you firsthand rather than have you hear it from Mom and Dad."

"Wow. Yeah, thanks. We'll get together and you'll tell me the whole story from the beginning, right?"

"Sure, Chuck."

Evan wonders what time frame Charlie has in mind for this get together—next month? Next year?

"All right, then. Goodnight, Ev."

"Goodnight, Chuck."

Goodnight, goodnight.

E VAN WORKS HARD for the next few days. Not hard at his job, hard at Dean. He tries to entertain Dean as thoroughly as possible. Nary a moment passes without some scheduled activity. They hang out at Fremont Guitar together, then they go for dinner, then to a movie or to see a band somewhere or to hang out with friends. Or he drags Dean to Lars's house, wherein the band hangs out in the basement and listens to the demo over and over, talking about what might become of it, while Dean spends the evening upstairs in the den playing Gran Turismo. With so much to do, Dean seems bored.

A full week passes like this. Evan doesn't call his parents and they don't call him: the "go fuck myself" comment probably was too much for them. He doesn't call his brother and his brother doesn't call him: Charlie has always been famous for being able to block out the little nuisances in his life (his brother, his son, his wife . . .) in order to better concentrate on his work. He talks to Mica briefly a couple of times, but she's on the go, go, go.

And then a funny thing happens. Evan takes Dean down to the indoor skating park near Safeco Field, where Evan is forced to act fatherly for maybe the first time when he tells Dean that, no, he won't buy him a two-hundred-dollar pair of new blades, and, yes, Dean *will* have to use the junky rental skates; and, while Evan is watching Dean grinding any rail he can find and landing some precision airs, being smooth on his transfers and even adding a three-sixty to the tail of his frontside gap (like Evan knows what *that* means; but the kid sitting next to him in the bleachers with the cast from his wrist to his shoulder is busy doing a competent play-by-play: "One day I'll work for ESPN and cover the X-games," he says), his cell phone rings. Caller ID: an area code he doesn't recognize. Jamaica?

"I found you."

For a moment he thinks it's Mica, and that thought makes him practically cry: she found him. A statement that resonates so deeply. No one has ever said that to him before. No one has ever found him before.

"I've been waiting," he says. It sounds kind of romantic.

"I can't do it."

What? It's not Mica. It's someone else.

"Who's this?" Evan asks.

"It's Ellen. I can't do it. I can't do what you ask."

Oh, shit. Ellen. Ellen. Evan gets so focused on certain things that other things go on and he doesn't even think about them.

"What do you mean?"

"I believe you," she says. "I agree. I loved Tracy and I love Dean. I would love to take care of Dean, to raise him. But I have to agree with you that it would not be good to raise Dean near Frank. And I know that Tracy would never have it that way. Never. She would prefer Dean be with you."

Evan watches Dean, suddenly detached from what he's hearing. Dean's like a little mongoose with wheels on his feet. He's so damn quick, and he shoots up those ramps, it's positively dangerous, but Evan signed the waiver and Dean insisted that he knew what he was doing.

"Check it out!" Cast Kid shouts, punching Evan's arm, "alley-oop topside soul! You know that kid?"

"What are you saying?"

"Frank has his problems, Evan, I know. I know. But I love him all the same. And as much as I would love to have Dean with us—"

She's stopped by her own sobs. She's crying.

"As much as I would love that, it wouldn't be right, because I loved Tracy, and I would never, ever, *ever* do *anything* that would betray her."

"Mrs. Smith?"

"If Frank doesn't have me, he has no one, Evan. If Dean doesn't have me, he still has you. You see that, don't you?"

"Oh shit! He's down! He went for a five-forty and he's down!"

Evan leaps to his feet. Cast Boy flies down the bleacher steps and hops the railing into the pit. Dean tried something too hard. A five-forty. It was too much. He was showing off. He's down. He's in pain.

"I won't contest anything. I'll have our lawyer deal with Tracy's estate. We'll sell the house, put everything into a trust fund for Dean. You will be the trustee. I just want you to know we won't fight you, you have our support."

Evan makes his way down to the railing.

"Mrs. Smith—"

"Take care of him, Evan. He's just a child. He's fragile. Please take care of him like Tracy would."

The line goes dead; Evan looks over the railing at his son who is pooled on the floor of a concrete basin with three strangers attending to him. He climbs over the railing, throws himself down into the pit, and, thank God, as he approaches, Cast Boy looks up and gives the thumbs up. Dean isn't hurt. Thank God, he isn't hurt.

ICE AND HEAT. Ice and heat. That's the proper way to deal with contusions and deep muscle bruises, both of which Dean has. Thankfully, he was wearing pointy-parts body armor—elbows, knees, wrists, and head were all protected—which only left his ribs and his left thigh open for injury, and both areas got injured pretty good.

Dean spends the next day nursing his wounds. Evan spends it on the phone with the Seattle School District. He makes the calls from his bedroom with the door shut; he still hasn't told Dean.

"I'll mail you out an enrollment form and an immunization and medical records form. When was his last physical exam?"

"I don't know."

"He'll need a new physical, probably, unless his old doctor examined him recently. Do you know who his old doctor is?"

"No."

"You should find out. He'll have the immunization records. Do you claim a religious or philosophical exemption?"

"I don't know."

"I see. And, of course, we'll need all school records from his old school district. Can you get those sent directly to us? They will only process the request if it's made by a parent."

"Yes."

"I'll mail this out today, although it will be faster if you come to the office and pick it up. Do you know where we are?"

"What school will he go to?" Evan asks.

"Well, we'll have to see where we can place him."

"I pay taxes."

"I'm sure, but—"

"There's a school right up the street on Queen Anne."

"Yes, Mr. Smith, I'm sure there is—"

"Wallace."

"Yes, *Wallace*, I'm sure there is, but—"

"No, *Mr.* Wallace. I mean, *Evan*. I mean, *his* name is Smith. He took his mother's name. Dean Smith. Her name was Tracy. My name is Wallace. Evan Wallace."

"Mister . . . Wallace? . . . I'm sure there's a school quite close to you."

"He's going into the ninth grade. It's a high school. I see the kids all the time."

"I'm sure you do. But, Mr. Wallace, we do our enrollment in April. The classes have already been filled. Now, since you do pay your taxes, we will find a place for your son, but at this late date, I cannot guarantee *where* we will find this place. It might very well be at the high school up the street. It might be in another cluster or another reference area. All I can say, Mr. Wallace, is that we *will* find a place for your son, and we *will* provide transportation for him as needed."

"Transportation?"

"Either yellow bus or a Metro bus pass."

Evan sighs.

"Do you think any private schools nearby would take him?"

"I'm sure they've all filled their classes, too, Mr. Wallace. It's a little late in the season."

"A bad time of year for someone's mother to die."

She waits a respectful amount of time.

"I'm sure any time of the year is a bad time for someone's mother to die," she says.

"But this is the worst season."

"Yes," she reluctantly agrees, "in terms of school placement and moving to a new city, I suppose I have to agree with you, Mr. Wallace, *this* is the worst season."

His next call is to a real estate broker, and her response is much more encouraging.

"I can sell it in a heartbeat, sight unseen," she boasts. Her voice sounds as if it might reach through the phone and smack him in the face.

"It's not very big," he says.

"Location, location, location, Evan. Feel your heartbeat. Do you feel it?"

"Yes."

"That's how fast I can sell your apartment for you."

"Don't you need to see it?"

"Of course I need to see it. And I need to have a deep-cleaning crew work it over. And I need to take all your unnecessary furniture and put it in storage. But I know I can sell your apartment in two weeks, a month, tops. I work at six percent, exclusive only. I'll drop the paperwork by this afternoon and pick up a key and we'll move this property, Evan, I promise you. We'll move this property and get you into something better suited for you and your new-found life with your son."

He staggers from his bedroom, finally feeling the true impact of Ellen's phone call. It's one thing to play dad for a week, but to *be* dad . . . that's a little shocking. Meanwhile, Dean is somewhere in the icing cycle.

"You need heat?" Evan asks.

"I just started ice."

"Stay with ice."

He sits down next to Dean and they watch a bass-fishing derby on OLN.

"Do you fish?" Evan asks.

"No."

"Do you *like* fish?"

"You mean, to eat?"

"I don't know. I'm wondering why you're watching a bass derby."

"I find it restorative," Dean says.

Evan nods as if he understands completely, yet he's really wondering where in the hell Dean came up with that one. *Restorative?* Must have been on a standardized test or something.

"I was thinking maybe you wanted to head back to Yakima for a few days," Evan says after some famous fisherman bags a bass and stuffs it into a special lifesaving box where it will be kept alive until the end of the tournament, at which time it will be weighed and released back into the wild, now a deranged and psychotic victim of post-traumatic-bass-stress-disorder. "You could get your good skates and stuff."

Dean measures up Evan good and long.

"Okay," he says cautiously.

"Clothes. Personal items. You must miss it—"

Shit, he shouldn't have said that. He must miss it. He must miss his mother, since she's *DEAD!*

"Yeah?"

"Let me be straight with you, kid," Evan says, sucking it up. "I was kind of thinking that you would stay with your grandmother most of the time. You know? You'd go to school out there and I'd come and spend weekends with you, and maybe you'd even spend most of the summer with me or something. But that's not the way it's going to work out, apparently."

Dean waits for Evan to explain the way it will work out.

"Apparently, your grandmother can't leave your grandfather— or, she doesn't want to. And, frankly, I'm glad about that. But even if I gave you the choice, and you said you wanted to go live with them, I wouldn't send you back there with Frank around, because . . . because I just couldn't do it. I *wouldn't* do it. Because I know he did some things. But, more importantly, because I know Tracy—your mother—didn't want you there for some reason, and

I don't need more than that to know what to do. Do you understand? You're going to stay with me for a while. Even if you don't
want to. You're going to stay with me."

Dean watches Evan for a long moment. He has an innocent,
almost angelic look on his face. Because he's crossing the line. He's
still a boy, not yet a man.

"Are we going to live in Yakima?" he asks.

"I—"

Evan feels a surge of panic, followed by guilt. Why would he
assume that Dean would assume that they would live in Seattle?
Where is it written that a son has to move to the father and not
vice versa? Shouldn't he continue to grow up with his own friends,
in his own house, with his own memories around him all the time?

"I don't know. I—we can discuss it. We can think about it. But
I'm not sure how I can live in Yakima and still make a living. I'm
not sure it's practical."

A dark, perplexed look falls over Dean's face. He turns back to
the TV. He works his lips, chews the inside of his cheek; he's trying not to cry.

"Dean?"

"I miss my mom," he says, and he looks at Evan and tears are in
his eyes, and Evan doesn't know how to handle it, what to do. He
reaches out awkwardly, puts his hand behind Dean's neck, and that's
the right thing to do, apparently, because Dean responds to it by
leaning forward, tipping himself, folding himself into Evan's shoulder and becoming a limp little kid crying on his dad. Evan
embraces him and feels Dean's tears, warm and wet, as they soak
lightly into his T-shirt, and Evan can't really do anything but sit
there and hold him and think, poor kid. He misses his mom.
Poor kid.

THEY GET INTO his car and drive. East out of Seattle via Interstate 90, an awe-inspiring highway that plows up Snoqualmie Pass like a great Roman road, full of majesty, a masterpiece of engineering that reduces the Cascade Mountains—at one time a fearsome and perilous range—to a mere speed bump, nothing more than a brief ear-popping transition for the masses. South at Ellensburg onto Interstate 82, which veers through the Yakima River Valley and into Yakima itself, a small agricultural hub with delusions of grander things: upon reaching Yakima, the traveler is met with a roadside billboard proclaiming the city THE PALM SPRINGS OF WASHINGTON. So be it.

Dean directs Evan off the freeway and through a ghostly commercial district, distinctive because of the hundreds of empty boxcars stenciled YAKIMA VALLEY APPLES, or YAKIMA TOMATOES, which are piled five-high alongside the handful of railroad tracks that run through the center of town, up a broad avenue and into a neighborhood called Nob Hill. It's an old neighborhood with pretty tree-lined streets and nice houses. It's not a wealthy neighborhood, but it's not poor. It's a neighborhood of people who care about their houses, tend their own gardens, pay the neighbor's kid to mow their lawn. The lots are small, the houses neatly arranged behind white picket fences. Kids play in the street or in front yards, dogs wander without leashes, the roads are peppered with Neighborhood Watch signs designed to ward off burglars and thieves.

Dean's house is light blue with white trim. There are rose bushes in the front yard, but they haven't been cut back recently. The dead heads cling to the vines, little bundles of withered petals that stay the growth of new buds trying to emerge. Strangely, the grass is uniformly green, as if it has been watered regularly for the past week by a computer-controlled sprinkler system that works ceaselessly, even in the face of death.

Dean hesitates before getting out of the car, as if he's having second thoughts.

"You okay?" Evan asks. "You want to go in?"

Dean nods slightly.

"Maybe this isn't such a good idea," Evan says. "If you need some things, just tell me where they are and I can go in and get them and we can go back to Seattle."

"No," Dean says quickly, turning to Evan. He looks afraid. Not of ghosts, but of what he is feeling. They get out of the car and walk up the flagstone path to the front door. Dean takes out his key and lets them in.

"Make yourself at home," Dean says with deliberate casualness as he turns and heads off down the hallway, disappearing behind a closed door.

Make yourself at home. Easy enough to say. But Evan can't. He can't move, he can't even step into the house. He is struck, standing in the foyer. His feet are rooted to the tiled floor. He is overcome with a horrible creepy feeling. Dean may not be afraid of ghosts, but Evan is.

The house is of generic, inexpensive construction. The décor is run of the mill. Wall-to-wall carpeting, a fireplace of laid sandstone, ornate brass-plated light fixtures, overstuffed Levitz furniture; not bad, but not good either. The art on the walls consists primarily of framed posters. Again, not bad, but not great. It's all very Tracy, though. That's what gives Evan the creeps. Everything cries out *Tracy*. And Evan isn't really sure why. He tries to recall her home in Seattle, when they were in high school together. Maybe that's it. This house has the same kind of feeling. It's a feeling that Evan has always taken note of, since, growing up in his parents' house, which was immaculately decorated with expensive furniture and art-work—posters only allowed in the kids' bedrooms, and barely then—he noticed the difference when he went to other people's houses. Upon reflection, Evan suspects that the furniture in front of him may very well be the same furniture Tracy's parents used to have. It's hard to furnish a house on a limited budget—parental hand-me-downs are acceptable.

And then . . . here's Evan assuming that Tracy was on a limited budget when he doesn't even know what it was she did for a living. So many things, so much weirdness rushing through Evan's mind. He doesn't feel totally comfortable with it, with the idea that he is looking at his parallel universe, where he might have been living for the past however-many-years had he gone down a different path. Very Twilight Zone. It disturbs his equilibrium. He needs to walk to keep his balance.

He walks straight through the living room toward the back door. The kitchen and breakfast nook are to his right. Something smells of dirt or mildew, and it seems to be coming from that direction. He doesn't want to confront the smell. Not yet, anyway. Because that smell is the echo of death. A house, suddenly abandoned. Food left on the counter—*I'll be back in a minute, honey*—and a silly miscommunication, a "You go right, I'll pass left," resulting in a collision of powerful, heavy metal boxes that twist and deform in grotesque ways after impact, and then what was inconceivable is quickly woven into the fabric of the universe by small Turkish girls who have been waiting patiently for instructions as to which design to make, which patterns to use to illustrate the story of your life, their little fingers so adept at tying intricate silken knots, the humidity of the coastal summer making them furrow their brows, the workings of the massive loom casting skeletal shadows across their laps. Evan opens the sliding glass door and steps out into the backyard. Outside, there is no smell.

The yard needs some work. A kind neighbor has mowed recently, but that's about all he's done. Weeds are running rampant in the flowerbeds, and some kind of creeping vine has ransacked a couple of low bushes, all but strangling the life out of them. But even with a Gray Gardens feel, the yard is kind of nice. A small brick patio, an ivy draped arbor overhead to give shade, a playable patch of lawn, a bird bath with green water in it, a couple of bird feeders hanging from the trees, a barbecue grill: propane, not charcoal. A small, round glass-topped table with a closed umbrella sticking out of the middle and four vinyl-webbed chairs around it.

Very nice, very nice. A nice little life. No glamour, very few frills. Neat and tidy. Functional. Efficient. Pared down, in a sense, to provide the least amount of padding between parent and child. Quite unlike Evan's backyard when he was fourteen, which was full of balls and bats, bicycles, basketball hoops, golf clubs. Tools. Weapons. Things used by father and son to bridge the gap of intimacy. Things to do that can then be talked about. Never talking about feelings or thoughts. Talking about the shot just made in a game of Horse, or how to chip from the fringe. Men are genetically engineered to behave in this way. Since the beginning of time, back in the caveman days, fathers didn't chat with sons about poetry or music. They took their sons out to the savannah and stalked okapi. You don't talk about sonnets on the savannah or the okapi will escape. You are silent. A single spear is thrown, dartlike, through the air, piercing a heart. The men rush to the fallen prey. They stand over the kill. They talk about what a good throw it was, how it could be thrown better the next time. They do not talk about their feelings.

He reenters the house. The smell is worse, if that's possible. It smells like wet dirt. He ventures into the kitchen, a narrow galley bookended by the entry hallway on one side and the breakfast nook on the other. He glances around for something offensive smelling. Nothing jumps out at him.

He returns to the living room. Nothing. He looks down the hallway. A light is on in the bedroom at the end. Must be Dean's room. Dean isn't inside. Evan hears movement from the other direction. He quietly walks toward the sound.

The hallway is dim and ends at a single door which is open. Evan looks inside. It's Tracy's room. It's pretty big, a double bed, a large dresser, a writing desk, a TV, a bathroom off one corner, a lot of closets. It's warm-feeling, decorated with tans and browns. It's sophisticated, not frilly. It's like the backyard: there is no extra junk, but it still doesn't feel empty. It feels full, but full of something other than objects. It feels, strangely, full of soul. It feels like it was lived in by someone who enjoyed living in it.

Dean stands silently at the dresser, his back to the door and to Evan. He's looking through Tracy's jewelry box. Evan watches for a couple of minutes as Dean opens each small drawer and pokes through her belongings. Occasionally, he removes something, a ring or a bracelet, examines it, feels its heft, considers it, then sets it back in the box. At last he takes a necklace, a thin chain with a locket on it. He holds it up and stares at it as it glitters in the sunlight from the window. Then he gathers the chain into his hand. He closes the jewelry box door without replacing the necklace.

"I should probably go to the store," Evan says.

Dean starts. He jerks around.

"What?" he asks, clearly wondering how long he's been watched.

"I should go to the store and get some supplies. You want to come?" He hadn't meant to startle Dean. Just the opposite. He wanted to console Dean. He wanted to share Dean's thoughts.

Dean doesn't answer. Evan walks toward him. He can see the pain on Dean's face from being in his mother's room. He wants to hold Dean, to hug him. He wants to tell Dean he's there for him. He reaches out, touches Dean's shoulder.

"You okay?" he asks softly.

Dean jerks away.

"Let's go," he says.

He brushes past Evan. As he walks toward the door, he slips his hand to his jeans pocket. He tries to stuff the necklace into the pocket, but it falls to the ground. Dean quickly kneels and scoops the chain off the carpet.

"What's that?" Evan asks.

"I didn't steal it," Dean says quickly, standing.

"I know. I just wondered what it was."

"Nothing. It's just a necklace."

He slides the necklace into his pocket, and then stands with his back to Evan, not moving. He's being interrogated. He's waiting to be dismissed.

"Was it your mother's?" Evan asks, and immediately feels like an idiot. *No, it belongs to someone I've never met, but my mother keeps it in her jewelry box.* Duh.

Dean shrugs and looks at the wall. He doesn't want to talk about it. Yeah, Evan thinks. Sometimes he feels exactly the same way.

"So let's go," Evan says.

Dean nods and leaves the room without looking back at Evan.

THEY GO TO THE local supermarket and buy the junk you would expect them to buy: potato chips, corn chips, popsicles, cereal. They return to the house and Dean wants to go Rollerblading. His injuries feel much better and he wants to get out on his good skates like in the old days. It's early, and the late July heat has dissipated enough to make the evening almost idyllic. Evan gives his blessing, partly because he knows that if he doesn't, Dean will go anyway, so why fight it.

Dean dons his helmet and blades and takes off; Evan goes into the kitchen to put things away, and the smell is so intense now, it almost knocks him down. He sees what it is instantly. Sitting on the counter is a bunch of rotten bananas. Really rotten. Blackened bananas, sitting in a pool of their own rotten banana juices. A million fruit flies are swarming in a cloud above them, dipping down in intervals to suck up the sugary mess. It's absolutely foul.

He finds a garbage bag, scoops the mess into it with a wad of paper towels and seals the bag shut along with most of the fruit flies, who have chased the banana frappé into the bag. He cleans the counter briefly and then commences putting things away. He picks up the frozen waffles and popsicles and turns toward the refrigerator, where he notices a piece of notepaper held to the refrigerator door by a magnet. He looks closer.

It's a note from Tracy:

Dean—

There's a pizza in the freezer and carrots in the fridge . . .
EAT THEM! I'll be a little late.

Love you,
Mom

Evan cautiously opens the freezer door, not wanting to see what he knows is there. Inside are ice cubes, ice cream cartons, various unmarked containers. And there's a small frozen pizza in a box—pepperoni—and Evan is suddenly overcome with sadness, like falling into a pool of warm water, it's suddenly all around him, inside him, without him feeling the change. Just a stupid pizza, that's all. Nothing to be upset about. But it's proof. The day she died, Tracy wrote a note to her son telling him about dinner, telling him that she would be home late, probably working overtime or attending a community board meeting or something, and she was probably driving to that meeting to drum up support for a new playground or new after-school activities or a firmer anti-drug program in the high schools when her car was hit by a truck and she was killed. The truck driver probably walked away from the accident unscathed, unmoved, angry, even, at the scratch Tracy's puny car had made on his front left fender. But Tracy was dead, and her plan—that Dean would eat a frozen pizza and some carrots for dinner—was scuttled once and forever.

Evan drops the note into the garbage can and looks around the kitchen, hoping to see something that will make him feel better, or at least make him feel not so alone. He walks to the hallway and looks toward Dean's room, but Dean isn't there, he went skating; Evan can't try to connect with him. He can't call his parents or his brother. He tries calling Lars, but Lars is out. He tries calling Mica in Jamaica, but she's not in her room. There's no one. He's absolute-ly alone, just him and Tracy's ghost, and she's got such cold hands, they make him shiver.

WHEN EVAN WAS sixteen, he took the bus to his grandfather's apartment once a week to play the guitar for the old man. It was a forty-minute ride, but Evan didn't mind it. These private recitals were something they both enjoyed, even though Evan had long suspected that his grandfather was too deaf to hear.

His grandfather was old, eighty-seven, but he was still a spry lit-tle man who got around as best he could and refused every offer of help. That was why, the week before he died, Evan was surprised by his grandfather's question.

"Is there anything I have that you want?" he asked Evan.

"No, Grandpa," Evan smiled. "Nothing."

"Come, Evie, there must be something. When I die, I want to leave you something. What will it be?"

Evan looked at him and felt so horribly sad that he felt ill. His face must have registered powerfully, for his grandfather didn't wait for an answer.

"That wasn't a very good question, was it, Evie?" he said quick-ly. "Let's pretend I didn't ask it."

That was on a Monday. The following Monday, Evan let himself into the apartment with his key. He found his grandfather lying on the carpet next to the coffee table. He was dead. Around his head was a dark, circular stain.

Evan was overcome. He didn't know what to do. He called 911. Then he called his father.

"You didn't call emergency, did you?" Carl asked.

"Yes."

"You did?"

"Yes."

"Why?"

Evan didn't know why. He thought that was what he was sup-posed to do.

"I'll be right there. Don't let them in if they get there first."

Thankfully, Carl arrived before the ambulance. He immediately started in with the questions. When did you find him? When was the last time you spoke with him? Did you move the body? So many questions.

"It was an accident," Carl then announced to Evan. "He fell and hit his head. A terrible accident."

The intercom buzzed. Carl let the medics in. Then he took Evan by the arm and led him into Grandpa's room. He shut the door on Evan.

Evan could hear them through the door. The medics, the police. A lot of talk. Carl telling them that he was a doctor and he had already examined the body. Carl telling the ambulance guys that he would ride with them to the hospital and sign the death certificate. The police not really caring, going back to work. Evan could hear them hoist the body onto a gurney, take it outside, and then the door closing and everyone was gone.

Everyone.

After a few minutes, Evan realized no one was coming back. He had been left there. His father had forgotten him.

He waited for an hour before he went outside to catch a bus. An hour after that, he got home. When he walked in the house, he found his mother and father and Charlie together in the kitchen, crying. His mother looked up with tears in her eyes and said, "Grandpa is dead," and Evan could do nothing but stare at them blankly. He couldn't join them. He couldn't cry with them. He wasn't a part of them, he wasn't one of their group. He retreated to his room to play his guitar, as he had planned to do that afternoon, for his grandfather.

Evan never knew what happened. He wondered if his father ever remembered how he had forgotten Evan that afternoon. He didn't even know if his father remembered who had found Grandpa. His father never said a word about it. Neither did Evan.

"What are you doing?" Dean asks.

"Setting up the bed," Evan replies. And, indeed, that is what he's doing. He's in the study, the office, whatever you might call it, unfolding a sofa bed, tucking sheets around a three-inch-thick foam mattress.

"Why?"

"So I can sleep. I'm tired."

Evan knows that's a false answer. It's true, but it doesn't answer the real question, which is, why are you sleeping in here and not in Tracy's room? And that answer is a bit too complicated to tackle at this time. It's probably something like, because he's afraid of Tracy's ghost, he's afraid of Dean, and he's afraid of himself. In a den on a sofa bed, at least he can concentrate his energy on his own discomfort and thereby avoid becoming overwhelmed by other things.

"You can sleep in her room."

"Thanks, Dean, that's a generous offer, but—"

"I'll help you change the sheets."

Dean turns and walks away from Evan, stops at the linen closet to pick up clean sheets, and then heads off toward Tracy's room. Evan follows him; they make the bed together.

"Thanks, Dean," Evan says when they've finished, but Dean doesn't make a move to leave. He lingers by the bed.

"You want to watch some TV with me?" Evan asks.

Dean shrugs a yes. Evan turns on the TV and the two of them slip off their shoes and sit back on Tracy's bed. Evan takes control of the remote and puts on MTV for some mindless programming, then they watch *Iron Chef*, then Letterman. Sleep sneaks up the side of the bed and takes them both by surprise, first one, then the other; they drift off silently; neither stirs all night.

EVAN THROWS TOGETHER a little barbecue dinner for two. A grilled, marinated chicken recipe he picked up from his buddy, Emeril, who has a TV show and often talks about how to cook dead things. They sit on the back patio and eat off of paper plates because eating off of paper is cool; they drink out of glasses, however because beverages taste better out of a glass.

"Can I go out?" Dean asks as they clean up.

"Did your mom let you go out on weeknights?"

"There's no school tomorrow."

"So that's the criterion?" Evan asks.

"Yeah."

"Okay. Be back before dark?"

"Mom always said I had to be back by nine-thirty."

"Okay," Evan says. "I'll believe you. Where are you going?"

"To play street hockey."

"Street hockey? That's a little rough, isn't it? You're injured."

"It's not rough. Plus, I feel all right."

"Let me see the bruises," Evan says.

Dean pulls down his jeans and displays the bruise on this hip. Not that bad. He lifts his shirt and reveals the larger bruise on his lower back.

"That doesn't look good."

"It looks bad, but it doesn't hurt," Dean says, sensing Evan's reluctance. "Matthew's dad puts up cones. We wear helmets. It's really safe."

"Well . . . I guess. Can I come and watch?"

Dean doesn't answer. What kind of question is that, anyway? *Can I come watch?* A bit dorky. Surely the answer will be no.

"I don't care," Dean shrugs and leaves the room; Evan continues cleaning up. Dean reappears two minutes later holding his stick, pads, and skates.

"I don't want to be late."

"I'm ready," Evan says, surprised, quickly drying his hands. "I'm ready."

AT THE BOTTOM of the cul-de-sac are fifteen or twenty kids on Rollerblades. They're carrying hockey sticks and wearing helmets. Half of them are wearing orange vests, like soccer kids wear. There is a man on Rollerblades, too. This must be Matthew's father. He wears a whistle around his neck.

The street is blocked off by orange cones, as Dean had said. Two portable nets are set out. White lines indicating the playing area are painted on the street, as is a center line and two off-sides lines. No doubt the paint job is courtesy of Matthew's father, who seems to take his officiating rather seriously. Dean slips on an orange vest and takes his place on the sidelines, waiting to be rotated in.

Evan leans against one of the cars parked adjacent to the hockey field. Most of the cars have been moved away, probably to avoid being smashed by a flying kid with a stick. And they *are* flying, these kids. Spinning and weaving, firing an orange ball among them. It's a fast game. When a ball shoots out of bounds into the low ivy that surrounds the cul-de-sac, Matthew's dad simply dips into a bag he wears around his neck that holds an apparently

endless supply of new balls. No time to search for the errant ball.
We'll gather them up later.

And Dean is in. He is one of the smaller boys, some of them
being older, sixteen, maybe, much more muscular, football players,
probably, but made to look Neanderthal by Dean, so agile and quick
as he darts around them like a little bug, flicking the ball this way
and that, the unselfish guy, flick, flick, flick, it's off his stick and—

Goal! Goal! Goal!

Dean has scored. Fresh into the game, and he's changed the
entire complexion of it.

He does a dance. His comrades beat on him. High fives. High
tens. Hugs. Jumping.

"Good to have you back, Smith," Matthew's dad bellows across
the pavement, smiling, his deep voice booming off the houses that
encircle them, the dark houses, residents obviously knowing of the
daily, weekly, or monthly game and clearing the heck out of there,
diving into the local Red Lobster for the nine-ninety-five all-you-
can-eat special on batter-fried-prawns, hoping against hope that
there is no overtime.

Ssshhhheeeeeeee!

The shrill squeal of a whistle and the attention is back at center ice.
"Rotate!"

One boy from each team reluctantly skates to the sideline,
replaced by someone new and energetic. What a system. Matthew's
father runs it all. Rules, a judge, painted lines, a rotation system—
what's that?—Evan realizes that Matthew's dad has a stopwatch.
Brilliant. He's timing the rotations. Maybe on a goal they auto-
matically rotate. Who knows? Dean is still in.

Swish, swish, flick, flick. The ball skirts along, hits a rock and
bounces up a bit, a foot off the pavement; the big guy, the one on
the other team wearing a New York Rangers jersey, takes a swipe
at it. Why not? *Swack!* Misses the ball and catches nothing but shin.
Dean's shin.

Dean crumples to the ground. Evan moves toward him, but holds
back. Dean's big enough to take care of himself. He clutches his leg.

The other boys stay away, skating in circles. Matthew's father skates
to Dean and examines his shin.

"Shake it off, Smith," Matthew's father commands. "Shake it off.
No blood, no pain. You want out?"

"High sticking," Dean blurts out through his gritted teeth.

"I saw it, Smith. Not intentional. No penalty. You want out?"

"No," Dean responds loud and clear.

"Shake it off, then. The clock doesn't stop for injuries."

Dean shakes it off and keeps skating. They play on.

A few moments of affected limp, and then Dean is at full speed,
calling for the ball. Swish, swish, flick, smack—

JUST WIDE!!!

Good shot, though. Good shot. Dean is the man. He is obviously the talent. It makes Evan so happy to watch him. How clever
he is skating through the other boys, dodging, head-faking. Feint,
feint, spin move, he sends the ball to another boy, wide open,
swack—

Misses completely. Whiffle Ball City.

Matthew's father wings around, skates up beside Dean and grabs
him affectionately around the neck.

Ssshhhheeeeeee!

"ROTATE!" Matthew's father bellows, releasing Dean and
preparing for a face-off.

Dean is still in. He's a ball magnet. The other kids look for him.
They send it to him. Everyone wants the ball on Dean's stick. He
directs. He motions. He's setting something up. Off he goes, up the
left sideline.

Whack!

The big kid—the Rangers kid, the one who nearly broke
Dean's shin—whacks at the ball and catches Dean's skate. Dean
flies forward, face first, and lands hard, skinning his forearm on the
asphalt. This time there's blood. Road rash.

Matthew's father skates over.

"Tripping," Dean complains.

"He was going for the ball," Matthew's dad says.

"He did it on purpose. Tripping."

"I didn't see it that way, Smith. You want out?"

"No."

"Take a breather, Smith. Settle down. You just got back, you're getting tired. Rotate out, Smith."

"No."

Ssshhhheeeeeee!

Another face-off. This time Ranger wins the battle. He has the ball. Dean skates over to him. Bumps him. Ranger bumps back. They skate up the sideline, jostling. But Ranger is much bigger. He's shoving Dean around. Dean is quicker and dodges for the ball. There's confusion. Who has control? An elbow. Dean is caught in the mouth. He hesitates momentarily, feeling his bloodied lip, then wheels around, his stick at shoulder height, and slashes at Ranger, cracking down on Ranger's forearms with such force Ranger screams horribly and falls. Dean stands over him.

"Don't fuck with me, Matthew!" Dean yells. "Don't fuck with me! Quit with the cheap shots, Matthew! I'll take you out!"

Matthew's father is there in a second, shoving Dean out of the way. He attends to his son. (His son!)

"You're out, Smith!" Matthew's father shouts. "You're out. Misconduct! Ejection and two-game suspension. Think about that, Smith. You're better than that."

"He tripped me," Dean says in his defense.

"He was going for the ball, Smith. Game misconduct. You're outta here."

Evan can't take it any more. He rushes the playing field.

"I saw the whole thing," Evan yells. "Your son tripped my son because he scored."

Silence hits the cul-de-sac like a tornado, swift and sudden. All faces turn, small faces tucked into hard plastic shells; smooth, round faces with dark circles under their eyes, the first signs of sleep deprivation and sugar addiction showing. Evan realizes that they've been expecting him.

"You're Dean's father?" Matthew's father asks, rising. He is the first to regain his composure. He voices the question they all want answered. He is the Lord of the Flies. He puts the pig's head on the stick.

"Yes," Evan confirms.

There is no response. Evan is not sure where this is going. He turns to see Dean, his equipment in hand, slowly skating off. Evan starts after him.

"Hey," Matthew's father barks, leaving his son, Matthew, writhing on the street, still in agony. He follows Evan. "Hey."

Evan doesn't stop.

"Hey," Matthew's father says again, skating up to and catching Evan, laying a thick hand on Evan's shoulder. "You probably know Dean better than I do, but he doesn't play like that."

He waits for a response from Evan. None is forthcoming.

"He's the best kid out here. He's too good to take cheap shots like that."

"Your son took a cheap shot first," Evan complains.

"Look, if he gets his wrist broken because he's an asshole, that only hurts *him*. He's quarterback of JV. He should be more careful than that. I'll deal with him later."

Evan, settles down a bit, turns away.

"Hey."

Evan looks back.

"I'm sorry about your . . ."

His what? Wife? Ex-wife? Girlfriend? What? Evan nods.

"But this is a place for everyone to have fun. You tell Dean that if he wants to appeal the suspension, he can come to me. I'll listen to him. But Dean doesn't play like that. I don't allow that."

Evan nods and walks away.

"Nice to meet you," Matthew's father calls out. "My name is Brian."

Evan turns. "Evan."

"Nice to meet you, Evan. I wish we could have met under better circumstances."

They look at each other, Evan and Brian, for a moment, as fathers look at each other, imagining themselves in each other's shoes, wondering what it would be like to be father to a different child. Or are children all the same? Just different names and hair colors and sizes, but all the same on the inside, nascent souls fighting against the terms of their confinement: a lifetime imprisoned in a fleshy container.

"I have to get back to the game," Brian says.

"I hope your son is all right," Evan offers.

"I hope *your* son is all right," Brian says.

Ssshhhheeeeeee!

The whistle blows. The game is on.

EVAN WALKS QUICKLY, hoping to overtake Dean, but he's too far ahead and Evan can't see him.

He feels something like a father now, having stood up for Dean in a pinch. Having experienced irrational defensiveness, he thinks that must be what separates real parents from pretend parents: the ability to set aside reason in order to protect your kin. Something with which he has had prior experience, having run in front of a car to protect his brother, though his brother was in no imminent danger at the time. Still, he responded in a visceral way to the possibility of Charlie getting hurt and acted by throwing himself in front of the bullet. In this hockey incident, too, the danger wasn't imminent, but if it had been, Evan would have been there for Dean.

He sees him up the block, skating slowly—more slowly than he needs to. Evan picks up his pace and catches up to him.

"Wait up."

"Why, so you can yell at me?"

Evan doesn't take the bait; they continue along in silence. Dusk is creeping into the neighborhood, the trees are dark.

"So, start yelling," Dean says after a block or so.

"Why do you want me to yell at you?"

"I don't *want* you to yell at me."

"So?"

"So," Dean says, considering. "You're *supposed* to yell at me. You're a father now. Fathers yell."

"Ah. Well, I'm not very good at it, apparently. Maybe I should get some Oprah tapes. Study up."

Dean cracks a smile.

"I don't get it," he says. "Did you read a book on how to come to terms with the child you abandoned at birth or some thing?"

"No."

"No, you're not a reader. An audio book."

"No."

"No. That would take too long. You read an article in *Newsweek*, one of the little sidebar things that's in the gray box?"

"No."

"Saw it on *20/20*?"

"No."

"I give."

"I just don't feel like yelling at you," Evan says.

"You're going to yell later?"

"I'm not going to yell at all, Dean. You didn't do anything that deserves yelling."

"But I slashed Matthew. I did it on purpose."

"He took two or three shots at you first."

"But I shouldn't have retaliated. I should have turned the other cheek."

"Sometimes you run out of cheeks to turn, Dean. I understand that."

"But I lost."

"You lost because you're still a kid, Dean. For some reason you think that because Matthew's father saw it all and knew what was going on he was going to be fair. But the fact is, you slashed his kid. He's not going to be fair. He told me his kid deserved it. He said that to my face. But it's his kid. You can't fight that kind of power structure. You shouldn't fight it. You'll lose every time."

"So you *are* yelling at me."

"I'm not yelling. I'm just pointing out that things aren't always fair, and things are often loaded up in someone else's favor, and when that happens, you have to decide how you're going to han-dle it. I mean, what did you get? You got beat up and suspended for two games. Do you think Matthew got suspended? No. So you lost."

"My mom didn't lose," Dean says quickly.

Evan is taken off guard. So confident he was with his sociological assessment that he is nonplussed.

"I don't know . . ." he stumbles.

"When she worked for the union, she fought and won," Dean challenges, sensing Evan's confusion, pushing on.

"What union?"

"She was a lawyer for the Pickers and she beat the Growers down so hard they had to hire her just to stop her."

"I didn't know—"

"They used to slash her tires in the parking lot when we went out to dinner. One time they sent a guy to beat her up."

"What? What did she do?"

"Mace."

"Well—"

"I saw it. She sprayed him right in the face."

"That's—"

"If someone's gonna try to bully me down, I'm gonna fight him. I'm gonna fight."

"That's okay," Evan says warily. "You just have to be careful."

"Mom said there are some things you can't let go. You can't let them back you down. She never backed down."

And now she's dead, Evan thinks. Maybe the car accident was a fix. Maybe she was taken out by the Growers. No. Not even the best hit man in the world could orchestrate that. But maybe Tracy had become so used to trouble that she could find it wherever she went. Maybe that's why it was her car that ended up face-to-face with that truck.

"I didn't know your mother like you did," Evan says, "but if she was fighting for a cause, that's one thing. You were playing hockey. It's not worth fighting over a bad call in street hockey, Dean. Not when the referee is the other kid's father."

Dean sucks in his cheek and looks away.

"Yeah," he says. "That's what my mom would have said."

Inside, Evan gives himself a high five. Scored a goal on that one.

"Would she have said anything else? I don't want to miss anything."

"She would have told me the sport was too rough and that I was smaller than everyone else so I shouldn't be playing it at all. Maybe I should try out for the swim team. Then I'd be competing against myself."

"Really?"

"Probably."

"Is it okay if I skip that part?"

"Yeah."

They round the corner onto their street. Perfect timing.

EVAN WAITS UNTIL Dean is long asleep before he sneaks down the hallway and into Tracy's office. He closes the door quietly and takes a moment to orient himself. The fold-out bed is against one wall, opposite a desk with a computer on it. Next to the desk is a large file cabinet, on which sits a printer/fax/copier/waffle iron. The sliding doors of the closet reveal winter clothes hanging in dry cleaner bags, winter boots on the floor, and file boxes on the shelf above.

Evan doesn't know what he's looking for. Clues, maybe. Evidence of a life lived. Something that will lead him somewhere, tell him something, show him a side of Tracy that he can use to solidify his burgeoning relationship with Dean.

He opens the file cabinet; her files are orderly. Her life is neatly chronicled in individual, alphabetized, color-coded folders. One by one, he removes them and examines their contents. He checks each piece of paper for clues, each invoice that is marked PAID with a little red stamp and a check number and date written in ballpoint pen, each mortgage statement, each brokerage report. He learns everything about her. Her mortgage originated two years ago: a five-year ARM. She has an investment portfolio with thirty-thousand dollars in it, half in mutual funds, a quarter in the money market, a quarter in stocks. (Why so much in the money market?) She has an IRA with eighteen-thousand dollars in it, a custodial account for Dean with five-thousand, probably planning ahead for college. There are bank statements, medical insurance bills, charitable giving—she gave a thousand dollars to a home for battered women, bought a hundred-dollar ticket to a Cancer Society fund-raising dinner, donated $225 worth of old clothes and furniture to a church thrift shop.

He gives up on the file cabinet and turns to the closet. He takes down the banker's boxes on the top shelf. They are filled with papers, files, literature, photos from trips to the Columbia River Gorge, tape recordings of lectures from college. (But not from Reed. From Central Washington University. Interesting . . .)

The desk drawers are crammed with paper-clips, pencils, envelopes, stationery, deposit slips, certified mail receipts from tax returns sent to Los Angeles half a decade ago, dried-up Sharpies, an old cell phone, emery boards with nail tracks on them, an old *New York* magazine that proudly proclaims "Where To Eat Now" on its cover, catalogs from a million different catalog stores, a transcript from high school, clear laser labels of different sizes, more boxes of staples, Post-its, a bottle of Scotch (from which Evan thinks hard about having a pull), a disposable camera with three exposures left . . .

. . . an old Rolodex.

He takes the Rolodex and flips through it. The cards are dog-eared and yellowed. He finds himself. He's in there. She has his address listed as his parents' house, but his parents' phone number is crossed out and his apartment phone is written below it. Next to the number is a date: the month and year Evan moved into his grandfather's apartment. He still finds it hard to believe that he owned the place for eight years before he finally wrestled free of his parents' insistence that he live at home.

Who else? Other names, none of which he knows. SMITH, FRANK AND ELLEN. A Yakima address. A second card with their Walla Walla address. Interesting. SMITH, BRAD. COOS BAY, OREGON.

Coos Bay. So that's where Brad is. Evan picks up the phone and calls Coos Bay Information. The woman gives him the same number that's on the Rolodex. And then, before Evan knows it, the computer connects the number. And before Evan can stop it, the phone is ringing. He quickly glances at the clock. Two A.M. Welcome to the Thunderdome.

"This better be good," Brad answers. "I'll count to three: one, two—"

"Evan Wallace."

Long pause.

"Evan. What took you so long?"

"Screwing up my courage."

"Ah, yeah," Brad groans. He's sitting up in bed and rubbing his eyes, Evan can hear it.

"Coos Bay," Evan says.

"Coos Bay."

"What are you doing in Coos Bay, Brad?"

"Why are you calling me at two A.M., Evan?"

"I asked first."

The line goes dead. Evan was just joking around and he hangs up? Short enough fuse? He dials again.

"What do you want, Evan?"

"Sorry, I was just—"

"What do you *want*, Evan?"

"I want to know what happened," Evan says. He's got the oracle on the phone, now he has to get the prophecy.

"You're a smart kid, Evan," Brad says. "You know what happened. You tell me."

"Tracy got pregnant. She had the baby. Your father moved you guys away. That's all I know. That's what happened."

Silence. As if Brad is waiting for more. "Okay, Evan," Brad finally chuckles, "if that's the way you see it. Okay."

"What, then?"

"Nothing, man. It is what it is. So why are you calling me, then?"

"I need to know about Tracy. I don't know anything about her. What did she do? Who was she?"

"She was Tracy. That's all. The thing about Tracy was that she was always Tracy. Nobody could ever make her be anyone else."

"I don't—"

"She was a lawyer, Evan. Is that what you want to know? She was a lawyer. After high school, she moved with my parents to Yakima. I left when they all moved. That was my chance; I took off. She moved with them. How could she not? She had a baby. After a couple of years of dealing with the kid, she went to college. CWU, in Ellensburg, not far from Yakima."

"She wanted to go to Reed," Evan says.

"We *all* wanted to go to Reed, Evan. How many of us went?"

"So?"

"So after college she started working with single mothers in Yakima. She got really involved; she was a social worker for a year or two, until she got fed up with everything and got into law school at Washington State. She wanted to change the world. Our mother raised Dean while she was away. She came back, changed the world, did good things, everyone lived happily ever after. Right?"

"You skipped something," Evan says.

"What did I skip, Evan? Tell me."

Evan thinks hard. There's something wrong with the time line. She left high school. Took care of Dean for a couple of years. Went to college. Worked for a couple of years. Went to law school . . . That's about eleven years. Dean is only fourteen years old. Dean hasn't seen Frank for five years. At some point—

"Where's the flaw, Evan? Tell me."

"Dean hasn't seen his grandparents for five years."

"That's good, Evan."

"There's not enough time for her to have finished law school while your parents were looking after Dean. She never could have finished."

"You're smart, Evan. That's right. There was a small problem, wasn't there?"

"What was it?"

"You tell me," Brad says.

"Frank," Evan says.

"What about Frank?"

"Abuse?" Evan asks.

"Okay, I'll say 'warm' when you're getting close and 'cold' when you're going the wrong direction: your hand is on fire right now."

"Frank was beating Dean."

"Ouch. Put out the fire, Evan. You're too close."

"He was just a kid," Evan says.

"Yeah, you're right. Think about that for a minute, Evan. He was just a kid. *Your* kid. And you weren't protecting him."

"I didn't know."

"Sure. The Germans said the same thing. They didn't know."

"Go on," Evan says. "Tell me."

"So Tracy came home one vacation and saw what had happened."

"What happened?"

"You don't know? You know."

"Frank hit Dean."

"'Hit' is a good euphemism."

"Punched?" Evan ventures.

Brad doesn't answer for a moment.

"You ever watch boxing, Evan?"

"Yeah, sometimes."

"Yeah, well, you know how it's illegal for one guy to hold the back of the other guy's head while punching him?"

"Yeah."

"Do you know why?"

Of course Evan knows why. Because if a fist hits a head and the head recoils, the energy of the blow is diminished. But if someone is holding the head, there's nowhere for the energy of the blow to go but *into* the head.

"I know why," he says.

"Okay, then. Next question."

"Is that what happened?"

"Next question."

"Brad, is that what happened?"

"Don't make me hang up on you, Evan. I won't answer again. *Next question*."

Evan takes a deep breath. He wants more information. He can't piss Brad off yet.

"Did she finish law school?" he asks.

"She did."

"That must have been hard."

"It was."

"That's when Frank and Ellen moved to Walla Walla?"

"Good," Brad says. "You're doing great."

"Then what?"

"You tell me."

"I need help," Evan says.

"She started out working for the union, the apple pickers union. She did a great job. Too great."

"What do you mean?"

"The growers sent someone to have a little talk with her. She defended herself fine, but she realized that it wasn't worth it. She didn't want to worry that one day her house might get burned down because some disgruntled grower was pissed that she got an extra five-minute bathroom break for the pickers, you know?"

"Which house?" Evan asks. "The house I'm in now?"

"You're in Yakima? Good for you. No, not that house. She was renting a dump somewhere else. The house you're in was her reward."

"You lost me."

"It wasn't worth it," Brad says "*I* told her it wasn't worth it. So she took their offer."

"The growers."

"They weren't stupid. They knew how smart she was, so they offered her a bunch of money to join their side. They created some new post for her, 'worker advocate' or something. It was all a sham, of course, but it was an irresistible sham. She jumped ship. Everything that she stood for. She chucked it all for money. Money does strange things to people, Evan. But I cut her slack on that. She had Dean to worry about, after all. And Dean didn't have a father."

"That was two years ago," Evan says.

"Very good, Evan."

"When she bought her house. She bought her house two years ago, didn't she?"

"Excellent."

"Suddenly she had a lot of money. Investment account, IRA, college account for Dean."

"You've been doing research, Evan. I'm impressed. Can I go back to sleep?"

"No," Evan says.

"There's something about you, Evan," Brad says. "I don't know. I can see what she saw in you, to a certain extent. I mean, you seem like you don't know what's going on, but deep down you know exactly what's going on, don't you? That's the double-edged sword, Evan. I like you for it, but I also hate you for it, you know?"

"She was really smart," Evan says. "Go on."

"Yeah, she was smart, but she was also stupid. He used to beat the crap out of me, but the second I had a chance, I was out of there. He used to hit Tracy, too, but she never left. Why not?"

"He never hit her."

"Yes he did, Evan."

"No—"

"Body shots. Nothing that couldn't be covered with a T-shirt."

"No—"

"Dude, what's your deal?" Brad suddenly shifts, the tone of his voice changes.

"My *deal?*"

"Your deal. What is it? I mean, you gave her money to have the abortion, she told me all about that."

"Well, yeah."

"And then you stopped calling. You never called her. She was up all night, every night, crying, trying to hide being pregnant, and you never called her. What were you thinking?"

"She wanted the abortion."

"She *said* she wanted the abortion. Theoretically she wanted the abortion. But did she *really* want the abortion?"

"Well, how am I supposed to know something like that?"

"I don't know, Evan. By *calling* her and asking?"

"But I—"

"Hey, Evan, did I tell you I heard your song on the radio? They were playing it all the time for a while. Remember that?"

"Yeah."

"Tracy heard it, too. She called me and was practically crying into the phone she was so proud of you, you fuck."

"What?"

"Why didn't you ever call her, you fuck?"

"She—"

"Fuck you. She didn't do anything. You came to see her in the hospital, which was totally inappropriate, by the way. I saw you there. I saw you pressing your nose up to the nursery window. I saw you running down the hallway, trying to escape. What were you thinking?"

"I—"

"Shut up, Evan. You know? Why didn't you ever look for her? You knew she had the kid."

"I tried."

"Bullshit, you tried. Did you hire a P.I. to look into it? Did you canvass the state with flyers with her picture on it? Did you put her face on the back of a milk carton? Did you contact the real estate company? Call the phone company? Try sending her a letter with 'please forward' written on it? Did you make *one single effort* to find her?"

"No."

"Then tell me, Evan, *how* did you try?"

"I—I asked around."

Brad laughs bitterly. "Passive-aggressive theater," he says. "You asked around."

"I was just a kid."

"Yeah. So was she. But she was a kid with a baby."

Brad pauses for a response, but he doesn't get one.

"You know how Frank found out?" he asks. "You'll like this. I mean, you understand that Frank *had* to find out. If Frank hadn't found out, she would have had the abortion and that would have been that. But since she didn't want to have the abortion, she had to let Frank find out, because she knew he would stop it, and she would have the baby, which is what she wanted—but, of course, you didn't *know* that because she never *told* you that. So, you'll like this, Frank got drunk one night—"

"I thought Mormons didn't drink."

"Welcome to Planet Earth, Evan. He got drunk one night and he was mad as hell, and she said something at dinner, I don't even remember what, but it was obvious that she was jerking his chain. I mean, looking back on it, she had it totally set up. She mouthed off to him and he told her he was going to beat her, and she broke down, she said she was pregnant and she didn't want him to kill the baby. Oh, man, he blew. He asked her who the father was because he was going to kill him. She started crying; she wouldn't tell because she had to protect you. So I made a stupid crack: I told him it was me. I was just trying to deflect the energy, you know? But he beat the shit out of me that night, Evan. I took it for you. He knew I wasn't the father, but he knew that she would never tell, and he was mad, so he beat the shit out of me. I still have scars from that, Evan."

"I don't know what to say. I'm sorry."

"Yeah. Listen, Evan, I've always liked you. But you think you're the victim in all this, and you're not. You're the one who got away clean. You owe me one, Evan. One day I'll call you on it."

"Yeah, okay," Evan says, completely rattled by Brad's claims.

"I gave you Dean," Brad says. "I put him right in your lap. You think they would've called you? Think again. I gave him to you."

"Thanks, Brad, I owe you one."

Brad laughs derisively.

"Fuck you, Evan," he says. "Take the one you owe me and shove it up your ass, you pompous fuck. Don't call me again."

The line goes dead.

• • •

EVAN IS BLOWN away by his conversation with Brad. Is everything that Brad said true? All of it? The beatings, mental anguish, the way it all came to be? He staggers to Tracy's room and throws himself on the bed. It doesn't make sense. Frank would punch Tracy in the stomach? No. Evan saw her with her shirt off plenty of times. Not on a regular basis, maybe, but often enough, when they would fool around. Although sometimes they didn't fool around, she didn't *feel* like fooling around—Wait. This is crazy. She kept her shirt on because she was covering up her bruises? No.

And the idea of punching Dean in the face. That *can't* be true. Just can't be. What kind of a human being would do such a thing? Who could hit a child at all, no less a clay-handed ogre hitting a nine-year-old kid? No.

There's no point in trying to sleep. It won't happen. He's too upset. He turns on the TV, hoping to drown out his thoughts with electronic white noise.

HE'S STARTLED AWAKE by a rustling sound in the hallway. He leaps out of the bed. Is someone in the house? Burglars? Thieves? His heart pounds. He checks the clock; it's three-fifteen. He feels especially dazed.

He walks across the room and peers down the hallway. Someone is there. It's hard to see. Someone in the dark hall standing at a door. It's the door to the linen closet. The person doing the rummaging is Dean.

"What's going on?" Evan asks.

Dean mumbles something that Evan can't hear. He walks toward him.

"What?"

"I have to change my bed," Dean mumbles a little louder.

"Why?"

"I threw up."

Evan reaches Dean and sees, in the dim glow of the yellow bug light that spills through the front window, that Dean is practically green; he's quite ill.

"Let me help."

Evan takes the sheets and goes into Dean's room. It smells awful; foul, rank, dark vomit is splattered on the sheets and blankets.

"You couldn't make it to the bathroom?" Evan asks.

He looks back at Dean who's swaying in the doorway, barely able to keep himself upright. Dean shakes his head slightly, then retches, tightens his lips, but a few drops spurt out; he turns and runs to the toilet, Evan hears the vomit come; he hurries to help. He waits until the round is over.

"Is it a flu? Are you sick?"

Dean shrugs listlessly, leaning against the wall of the bathroom, his legs splayed out around the toilet bowl.

"How do you feel? Are you achy? Feverish?"

"My back hurts really bad."

"How bad?"

"Bad, bad."

"What part?"

"Here."

Dean points to his lower back, his kidney.

"One side, or both sides?" Evan asks.

"One side. It hurts real bad. I think I'm dying."

Evan takes a moment to think. Projectile vomiting and severe pain in left kidney. What could that be? Kidney failure? From what? Poisoning? No—wait. From a blow. A severe blow to the kidney. Holy crap.

"Which side did you land on when you fell at the skate park?"

"I don't know," Dean moans. "This one." He points to his left side.

Oh, man. Evan's stomach drops. Dean's done severe damage, internal bleeding, urine is backing up, he might die—

"Let's go!" Evan commands.

"I'm sick."

"I'll carry you. Let's go."

"Where?"

"To the hospital."

• • •

THEY FLY THROUGH the black streets without hindrance; everyone in Yakima, including the police, sleeps at night. They fly, fly, fly to the hospital. Dean groans and turns uncomfortably in the backseat, one second lying, one second sitting up, one second heaving into a plastic garbage bag Evan has brought along. The town is silent. There is nothing to hear but the sound of four tires on rough pavement and the uneven rhythm of a boy vomiting.

The hospital comes into view, a yellow brick building all lit up like a beacon of hope for the frail and sickly. Evan skids into the parking lot and stops at the ambulance entrance. An empty ambulance is parked by the curb. The lights under the awning are so bright they hurt his eyes. Two-foot-tall red letters announce the importance of the portal: EMERGENCY ONLY.

Evan leaps from the car, rushes in. A woman sits behind a desk and is startled by Evan's entrance.

"My son. He's having kidney failure. He was hit. He's vomiting. He's in the car. I can't carry him—"

Bam! She hits a button somewhere because in an instant, two giant orderlies come rushing at him.

"Kidney failure in the car outside," the woman barks. "Get him into triage, stat! How old is your son, sir?"

"Fourteen."

"Does he have any history of kidney failure?"

"No."

"Has anyone in your family ever—"

"No, no."

"Why do you think it's kidney failure, sir?"

"He fell really badly, in a skate park, you know, where they jump off ramps and spin around. He hit his lower back and got a giant bruise. He seemed fine, but then he started vomiting everywhere and he can't move and his back hurts so much—he can't even walk, I had to carry him to the car—he's probably bleeding to death internally—"

"Please, sir, don't panic."

She picks up the phone and dials.

"Dr. Katz, we have a fourteen-year-old male with a blunt force trauma to the lower back, suspected internal bleeding and kidney damage. He is extremely ill, vomiting, lethargy, acute localized pain, inability to ambulate. Yes, sir. Of course, Dr. Katz. Very well, sir."

She hangs up.

"Dr. Katz is our attending trauma doctor," she says to Evan. "He's instructed me to bypass triage. He's on his way."

The gurney bearing Dean is wheeled through the lobby at high speed. Dean groans horribly. He's covered with a sheet and is belted down.

"Prep Two," the woman shouts at the orderlies. She turns to Evan, "The best thing you can do is relax. Why don't you fill this out for me?" She hands him a clipboard. "Do you have your insurance card?"

Insurance? Clipboard? His son on a gurney? No. It's too much for Evan: he's suddenly assumed the role of his parents, the sit-and-wait role, and he doesn't like it. It's easier to be the patient than the one who waits.

"Sir?"

His head starts to spin. He's tired. Very tired. And stressed. Oh, god. Is that rubber he smells? Burning rubber?

"Is something burning?" he asks.

"No, sir. Are you all right?"

He feels not-so-all right, actually. A little dizzy. His insurance card. A clipboard. Dean disappears down a hallway. Evan hears metal rings scrape against a metal rod as a privacy curtain is snapped shut. He hears a wail of pain from Dean.

"Sir?"

"I have epilepsy," Evan says to her. He holds up his hand, shows her his bracelet. "Please call my neurologist in Seattle. He will tell you exactly what to do."

"Sir?"

"Don't do anything until you've called him."

"Are you all right?"

"Don't touch me until you've called him. Do you understand me?"

"Sir?"

And then the blow comes, the blunt end of an axe swung hard by a big, strong man intending to chop down a tree with one magnificent swing; the blow comes, striking him just below the base of his skull; his head snaps back, his arms flail, his legs go rigid; he falls.

E VAN GAVE HER the money she asked for one afternoon as they walked home from school together: he handed her the envelope he had gotten from the bank, blue with a white stripe and holes neatly punched in it for some unknown reason.

He offered to drive her to the doctor, to wait for her, to drive her home. She said no. He asked her if there was anything he could do. She said no. He asked her if there was any way she would reconsider, if there weren't some way they could grow up quickly, keep the baby. She said no.

"Tracy, I—"

"What, Evan?"

"I want . . ."

"You want what, Evan?"

He wanted so much. He wanted to be older and more mature and to tell her again that he wanted to keep his child. Even if she didn't want him, he wanted to keep the kid.

"Are you sure we can't try to make it work?"

"And if it doesn't work out, Evan, what do we do *then?*"

She smiled sadly when she saw that he had no answer.

"You can't force someone to be a father, Evan," she said. "My mother forced my father, and look at him. Bitter and mean. I won't do that."

But it wouldn't be forcing anything. She wouldn't have to force.

"Go, Evan," she said, "follow your dream. Be famous. Make me proud."

"But I—"

"But what, Evan?"

What could he say to her? That he didn't want to be famous? No. She was giving him a gift, releasing him, giving him a mission. Go, be famous.

She turned and walked up the street, flat and dry, dirt for sidewalks and ditches to collect the rain.

"Go," she said. "Go home."

"But, I—"

"*Go*, Evan."

But, I—

"**Y**OU'RE A VERY fortunate young man."

Evan blinks his eyes open. He's in a hospital bed. That's more like it. He looks over. A doctor.

"I see you've had a tracheotomy before. Your seizures sound remarkably like a collapsed trachea. I can imagine how that could confuse an EMT."

White coat, blue scrubs, mid-forties. He has a long, flat face with a broad chin and speaks with an accent, a hint of Australia. Possibly New Zealand? He never says "mate," but Evan can feel the word lurking at the back of his throat.

"I'm glad you showed the nurse your Medic Alert bracelet. We called your neurologist; he gave us a detailed medical history. In all, you were seizing for less than ten minutes. Very fortunate."

Evan doesn't respond; the doctor doesn't leave. All doctors do that. They linger a moment. What do they want? Thanks? Thank you for giving me life? The doctor as God. Maybe that's the real reason God cast Adam out of Eden. He didn't say thanks.

"Where's Dean?" Evan asks.

The doctor steps aside and presents the other bed in the semi-private room. In it lies Dean.

"He's asleep," the doctor says.

"Is he all right?"

"Gastroenteritis. Food poisoning. Probably salmonella, but we won't know until the cultures come back from the lab. Acute, painful, but his kidneys are just fine. Did he eat any contaminated food recently?"

"I don't know."

"Think about it later. Don't worry about it now. Once he wakes up and we get your blood levels back from the lab, we can release you both. Dr. Melon wants to see you as soon as possible, of course."

"Of course."

The doctor turns to go. At the door, he stops, thinks a moment with his back to Evan. Then he turns around.

"Do you ever wonder about something like this?" he asks. "You must. You have *status epilepticus*. Very rare. You must wonder about these sorts of things."

"What's that?" Evan asks.

"Your son would have been perfectly fine at home. He'd have vomited and vomited and vomited and eventually fallen asleep, slept for a day or so, and then he'd be over it. But if you'd had that seizure at home, you might have died. The only reason I mention it is that Dr. Melon told me how intelligent you are, and that you have a very clear understanding of your epilepsy. And epilepsy fascinates me. I wonder. Did you ever think that maybe your assumption that Dean was in a life-or-death situation was really your brain's way of fooling you into going to the hospital?"

Evan considers it for a second, but it's hard to consider anything because he feels drugged and tired.

"You don't have to answer," the doctor says. "I'd be interested to know, but it's really not my business. If you were to ask me, though, I might say that, consciously, you brought your son here to save him, but, subconsciously, you brought your son here so you could save yourself."

He steps out into the hallway.

"Very fortunate," the doctor says to himself. "You're a very fortunate man. And you have a very fortunate son."

And he is gone.

HOURS LATER, EVAN awakens. Dean is sitting up in bed, sucking on ice chips, watching TV.

"You want some ice?" he asks.

Evan nods. Dean presses his buzzer. When the nurse arrives, Dean says, "Could you get my dad some ice, please?" The woman nods and heads off.

"It was the chicken," Dean says. "Bad chicken. Someone came and asked if we wanted TV. I said okay. Is that okay? There's a fee. Is it okay?"

"It's okay," Evan says.

"I can't believe we both got sick off of that chicken. We should sue Emeril."

Oh, wait. Dean thinks . . .

"I mean, it tasted fine going down, but it sucked coming back up, right? I feel pretty good now. How do you feel? I feel good. Just take it easy for a couple of days. That's what Dr. Katz said. Just take it easy."

The nurse returns with a cup of ice chips.

"How are you feeling?" she asks Evan discreetly as she tucks in his sheets and fluffs his pillows.

"Pretty good."

"You've been admitted for observation. They'll let you go in the morning. I'm on duty all night."

Evan wonders if she is propositioning him. He wants to ask her if there's a sponge bath in his future.

"Are you hungry?" she asks.

He looks over at Dean, who's shoveling ice chips into his mouth like popcorn and flipping the channels like it's a Play Station 2.

"Maybe for something sweet," he says.

She smiles at him knowingly, turns to Dean.

"You want a popsicle?" she asks brightly.

"Sure!"

She leaves. Dean smiles at him like it's some special vacation, and Evan doesn't say a word, not one thing. Not about the seizure, not about what Brad told him. He smiles at Dean, but he keeps his mouth shut.

"WELL, OKAY," DR. Melon says. "Why don't you come in and we'll take some blood levels."

"I'm in Yakima."

"When will you be back?"

"I don't know," Evan says. "I'm not sure."

"Well, come in as soon as possible. In the meantime, raise your dose of Tegretol by one pill a day. And no driving."

"I have to drive."

"No driving, Evan."

"I always get an aura, Dr. Melon. I always know when it's going to happen. I can pull over."

"And what happens if the next seizure is one that isn't preceded by an aura?"

"I know I'm safe," Evan says. "I know it."

"Evan, as your doctor and your friend, I am legally and morally compelled to tell you not to drive. That being said, you are an adult, and your decision on whether or not to heed my advice is yours alone. However, I will tell you that I will not sign your license renewal form until you're seizure-free for six months. Got it?"

"Got it."

"Good. Anything else?"

"I want off my medications."

Dr. Melon laughs heartily.

"Seriously," Evan says.

"You can't do that, Evan. You know that."

"Why not?"

"Well, for instance, in addition to all the other medication you take, you've been on heavy doses of phenobarbital for twenty years now. If you stop cold turkey, you'll die. Your body will go into shock. Withdrawal. It's a horrifically addictive drug. I'm serious when I say it could kill you."

"So I'll go off everything else."

"But the other things are what keep you from being a zombie because you're on so much phenobarb. You know that."

"Uppers?" Evan asks.

"Uppers to counteract the downers. The downers to counteract the seizures. The mood enhancers make you feel almost normal. The marijuana takes the edge off. You're a twentieth-century pharmaceutical cocktail, you know that, Evan. You're a toxic dump. You're the true test-tube baby. They made you, they destroyed you, now they're making you able to deal with your own destruction. You're Robocop after they drilled his brain out that second time, you know?"

"Who's this 'they'? *You're* my doctor—"

"You know, the second one. *Robocop II.* The one with the psycho kid, where they give the guy open heart surgery while he's still awake."

"Yeah, yeah, I know. But *you're* my doctor. You're the one who's giving me the drugs."

"Because you came to me too late. If I only could have had you when you were twelve, right after the accident, Evan. I could have saved you. I could have done things. I would have stopped them from pumping that garbage into you. I could have protected you."

"But you weren't there," Evan says.

"No, I wasn't. My great regret."

"Mine, too."

"No one was looking after you, Evan. The doctors said, 'Give him this,' your parents said, 'Okay,' and the nurses gave. No one thought of how it might damage you later in life. No one wanted to help you. They just wanted to stop the seizures."

"But you could have—"

"*I* could have stopped them. I *would* have."

"You would have stopped the assault to my system."

"That's right. I would have stopped the assault. I would have helped your body heal itself. It would have been hard, sure. It would have demanded sacrifices. No more McDonald's, for instance. But is that such a great sacrifice, considering the condition you're in now? Is it worth becoming a toxic waste dump, a pharmaceutical depository, just so you can go to a fast food joint and stick more polluted foods into your body, irradiated corn and antibiotic-saturated meats?"

"No."

"No. But what's done is done. Ours is not to condemn the past, but to improve upon it. You want to undo it now? You want to get off all your medication? I told you, Evan. You've been on this garbage for twenty years. Give me twenty years, and I'll get you off of it. That's how long it will take. May those brain butchers burn in hell. You were just a child."

"I don't believe you," Evan says. "It wouldn't take twenty years."

"I suppose not," Dr. Melon agrees wistfully. "It might not take *someone* twenty years, but that's how long it would take me. I'm old, Evan. I'm too entrenched in the Medical Establishment. Oh, I have a leaning toward holism, yes, and if I had found a different path as a young man, I would have traveled it. But you need a true naturopath now, one who has the tools. If you truly want to be free, there are people who can help you. I know people. I can give you names."

"I have a girlfriend."

"Ah."

Ah. Dr. Melon fathoms the depth of Evan's request now. Behind every action there is a motive. Look for the source. Always look for the source.

"I can give you Viagra," he says. "That would help."

"Viagra?" Evan exclaims. "I want *fewer* drugs, not more."

"It's an answer. I don't like it, either, but it's an answer. I told you, Evan, as a medical doctor, I have an obligation to inform you of all your options. We could also give you a penile implant. You could pump."

"Pump?"

"Stiffen it up a bit. You get semi-erect, yes?"

"Yes."

"So. Also, there are various apparatuses on the market. Sex toys, as it were."

"What?"

"They make a dildo that straps onto your thigh. It would satisfy your partner, though it wouldn't really help you . . ."

"Dr. Melon, I don't—"

"Oral sex is a fine answer. You know, most women don't climax during penile penetration. The angle is wrong. Mutual masturbation is a wonderful experience. Many fully functioning couples practice this by choice."

Evan groans. Sex talk with a New Age neurologist. Where else but Seattle?

"Doctor Melon."

"Yes, Evan?"

"I have to go."

"Come see me as soon as you get back to Seattle so we can take a look under the hood, Evan. I can give you some names then, if you like."

"I'll call you," Evan starts to hang up, but then stops. "Doctor?"

"Yes?"

"Could you really have saved me if you had gotten me when I was twelve?"

Dr. Melon considers the question long and hard.

"*Someone* could have saved you, Evan. I might have been that someone. But I suspect I would have been too afraid to try, just as I'm sure your parents were."

A COUPLE OF days later and they're both feeling fine. They're in a groove and the thick layers of Dean's resentment and anger have been shed like so many molted skins. Being sick together was good for them. It was the father-son experience they'd never shared before: *Remember that time when we ate that chicken and got so sick we went to the hospital because we thought we were dying? Ahahahaha.* Little does Dean know it's all a big lie.

He doesn't know and Evan's not going to tell him. Evan's going to let it ride, because when you're at the table and the dice are rolling your way, you should never do anything to break the flow.

Dean is out with his buddies for the day, having taken only lunch money with him when he left. Evan is out in the yard, in the baking sun, weeding the garden. He finds it pleasant work. He wears a broad-brimmed hat that he found in the closet. He uses tools with orange plastic handles he found in the garage. He drinks homemade lemonade when he's thirsty and mops his brow with a kitchen towel when he sweats. He feels the earth under his fingernails. It is moist, crusty on top, but damp underneath. It is dark and rich in color, like coffee grounds. It smells of dirt and decay and nutmeg. There is something alive and crawling in every handful; there is something dead.

A slightly familiar car pulls up to the curb outside Tracy's house. Evan's seen the car before, but he doesn't know where. Out steps a familiar woman. He's seen her before, too; but, like the car, he doesn't know where.

She walks toward him, a slight woman wearing sunglasses and a hat rather like the one Evan is wearing. She's wearing slacks cut from some ultra-artificial fabric that looks much too hot for the day; in contrast, her flowery blouse looks quite cool as it billows in the breeze. She takes off her sunglasses; he recognizes her. She removes her hat; he knows who she is. She speaks:

"Hello, Evan."

It is the second time Tracy has appeared to him in the form of a ghost. And it is the second time the ghost of Tracy has dissolved into Tracy's mother.

"Mrs. Smith," he says. "What are you doing here?"

"I DON'T KNOW when Dean's coming home," Evan says uncomfortably. Ellen is sitting on Tracy's couch, drinking Evan's lemonade. She still hasn't told him why she's here. "Did you come for a visit?"

She nods.

"He won't be home until dinner, probably. Do you want to wait? You drove all this way."

"Evan," she says, "I came to talk to *you*."

"Oh?"

"Frank has been transferred to Coeur d'Alene."

Now *this* is something to talk about. Frank has been transferred. If she's come all this way to tell Evan that, then there must be strings attached.

"I hear it's beautiful there," he says with a smile. He doesn't add that he also hears it's infested with ultra-right-wing psychotics. "I'm sure you'll love it."

"I'm not going with him."

Ah. Just as he suspected. So many strings attached it's a freaking ball of twine two stories high.

"We've legally separated," Ellen explains. "We've filed the papers. We'll get divorced once we sell our house."

"And then what will happen?"

"That's what I came to talk about."

Of course.

Evan stands up and makes a face at her, but he says nothing. What is there to say?

"I've done what you asked," Ellen says. She looks to put down her glass, but she can't seem to do it; there are no coasters on the coffee table and she can't bring herself to set a sweating glass on a wooden tabletop without a coaster. She resolves to hold it. "I've done what you asked. I'm getting divorced from Frank. I love Frank, but you forced me to examine my life and our relationship and think about what *I* really wanted, what was most important for *me*, and what was most important for Dean. It think the answer is simple: I'll move here and raise Dean. It's best for everybody involved. It's closer to Seattle for you to visit whenever you want; you can keep a room for yourself here. Dean can attend his old school, keep his old friends. It will be as close to the way it was before the accident as we can make it. It will be back to normal, almost."

Yes. That's true. Back to normal.

What's only slightly funny is that a week ago Evan was desperate to have Ellen sit before him and tell him she would take Dean off his hands. Now, it makes him queasy.

He and Dean have gotten someplace. They have a history. Evan's not so sure he wants to give it up. What's to prevent *him* from moving to Yakima and raising Dean in this house and his old school and all of that? Not much. A flimsy job at a guitar store. Not enough.

"No," he says.

She freezes. Then a quick thaw. She sets down the glass in spite of herself and her hands, little birds, flutter to her face.

"Evan, I—"

"I'm sorry, Mrs. Smith. But I'm keeping him."

Jesus Christ, what is he saying? He's keeping a *kid?* Is he *joking?* Does he understand the implications of what he's doing? He can unload Dean right now, no worries. What on earth? . . .

"But I left Frank."

"I'm sorry, Mrs. Smith."

"I left him. I'm all alone."

"I'm sorry."

"But I did what you asked!"

She tips her face into her hands and holds it while she cries. *"I did what you asked,"* she repeats over and over again.

Yes, she did. But things change, things are different. Evan has cleaned up Dean's vomit. He's cooked Dean's meals, washed Dean's clothes. They've spent time in the hospital together. They've fallen asleep on the same bed watching TV. They have a history now. A short one, but a powerful one. They are father and son. Evan knows it. He knows it to his very core.

"No," he says firmly. "No."

She looks up at him, her face a mix of shock and despair and anguish.

"What?" she asks. She needs to hear it again, to galvanize herself, somehow wrest herself out of the stupor she's in. "What?"

"I'm keeping him."

"But, I—"

"It's the way it is. I'm his father and he's my son, and that's the way it is. I'm sorry. I know this must be hard for you."

"But, I— But you— *You just met him!*"

"And you haven't seen him for five years! So?"

"No, no, no. I saw him all the time. We'd meet. We would. Tracy would bring him to Richland and I'd meet them there. We'd eat in a little restaurant. Or we'd pack a lunch and eat in the park, it's very pretty, you can see the bridge. I saw him all the time. Every week. Every Wednesday unless he had a dentist appointment. Every Wednesday. Every Wednesday."

"I'm sorry, Mrs. Smith."

"No!" she cries. "No! You have no right! You didn't want him! You wanted her to have an abortion!"

Evan stares at her incredulously. *He didn't want an abortion!* How many times does he have to say it? First Brad, now Ellen? Everyone pushing his own truth. Well, Evan's got his truth, too.

"That's not true!" he yells. "That's a lie! When she told me she was pregnant, I told her we would get married and raise the baby ourselves. I told her we could do it. But she said no, so I gave her money. She insisted on the abortion and took my money, and then she didn't do it; and then you stole Dean from me!"

Ellen, shocked, clasps her hands over her mouth.

"Oh my God," she says through her palms. "Is that true? Oh my God."

"Yes, it's true. And then you went into hiding."

"We didn't go into—"

"You stole him away from me."

"We didn't steal . . . Tracy said . . ."

"What did she say?" Evan demands.

Ellen stands; her eyes are wide and they search the room distractedly.

"Oh my God," she repeats. "This is all a terrible mistake. A terrible mistake."

"Mrs. Smith—" Evan starts, but he doesn't say more. Her search has become more frantic. She is desperate to find something. She doesn't see Evan and doesn't hear him.

"A terrible mistake," she repeats in a hoarse whisper to herself. "Terrible."

And then she finds it. The door. Her eyes lock on the door and draw her to it; her hand turns the knob. She glances at Evan. "A terrible mistake," she says again. And then she leaves.

Tracy said what? Evan wonders. What did she say?

And when did she say it? Did her story change over time? Did she tell Frank one thing in the heat of battle and tell Dean something else entirely, when he was older, nearly grown-up, ready to know the truth?

Or did she take the truth to her grave?

Perhaps she was waiting to tell Dean soon. Maybe even that fateful night. A mother-son discussion over pepperoni pizza and carrot sticks.

Who knows what, and when did they know it, and what were they doing when they learned it? This is the Rashomon that is Evan's life.

He knocks on the door to Dean's room and opens it without waiting for a response. Dean is lying on his bed reading a book. Evan looks around.

The room is dim: the shades are pulled down even though the summer evening is still bright outside; the overhead light seems to be missing a bulb. The bed is unmade, clothes litter the floor. The room is decorated with several posters, including an R.E.M. concert poster, which Evan is happy to see. There are two large bookcases filled with books, next to which stands an open file cart filled with neatly arranged road maps. There is a desk with a sizeable computer on it, a mini stereo system, and a clothes hamper that obviously isn't often used.

"Can I help you?" Dean asks, looking up from his book.

"I wanted to talk to you, if you've got a second."

"I'm busy."

Dean goes back to his book; Evan wanders over to the bookcase and looks at the titles. Fiction, mostly, except for a few reference books.

"What are you reading?" Evan asks.

"You mean, what am I *trying* to read?"

"Are you having trouble?"

"Yeah, someone keeps interrupting me."

Evan smiles. Smart-ass kid.

"What are you *trying* to read, then?"

"*Crime and Punishment*. Ever read it?"

"I think I was sick that day. Is it good?"

"Let me guess," Dean says, "you're going to bug me with stupid questions until I say I've got a second, right?"

"Basically."

"Okay," Dean says, putting down his book. "Go ahead."

Evan takes a deep breath and sits backwards on the desk chair. It's time for him to have a little talk with Dean. Ellen and Brad don't really matter. They can think whatever they want about Evan and how it all happened. But Dean's opinion matters. Dean has to know the truth. He has to know Evan's side of the story.

"Dean, a lot of things happened in the past that weren't really supposed to happen the way they did."

Dean looks at him unblinkingly.

"I mean, with how we got into the situation we're in. I don't know what your mother told you—"

"What are you talking about?"

"Well, your mother must have told you something about me, about why I wasn't around, right? At some point you asked who your dad was, and she told you something, and you asked why I wasn't around, and she gave you an answer. I just want to set the record straight. I mean, you should hear both sides. You've heard what *she* told you, but you should also hear *my* side of it."

"Okay. So what's your side?"

"Well, why don't you tell me what your mother said first?" Evan says. "Then I'll tell you my side."

Dean shakes his head.

"What did your mother tell you about me?" Evan repeats.

Dean makes a pained face. He lifts his book and starts to read it, then puts it back on his lap facedown and runs his fingers up the spine deliberately; he scratches his nose; he doesn't answer.

"She must have told you something about me," Evan continues. "Maybe not about me, personally, but about why she was raising you by herself. I'd just like to know what she said, so if I think anything's wrong, I can tell you what really happened."

Dean shakes his head again.

"What did she say?" Evan asks.

"Nothing," Dean answers.

"She must have said *something*."

"Nothing. She never said anything."

"*Never?*"

"No."

Evan considers it a moment.

"I don't believe you," he says. "Did she tell you I abandoned you? Is that what she said?"

"No."

"What, then?"

"Nothing."

"Did she tell you I didn't want to keep you? Because that's not true and I—"

"Yeah," Dean breaks in. "That's what she said. She said that."

"What? That I didn't want to keep you?"

"Yeah. She said you gave her money and told her to go have an abortion and then you told her you never wanted to see her again."

"She said that?" Evan exclaims. "Why would she say something like that? That's not at all how it happened."

"Well," Dean says, "that's what she said. Sorry."

Evan leans back in the chair and stews.

"I can't believe it," he says.

"Sure, you can."

"I mean, yes, I can. She told your grandmother some things, so I guess—but I thought she would have told you the truth, you know?"

He looks up at Dean, who's looking a little smug, enjoying Evan's pain.

"What else did she tell you?"

"She told me you had rich parents who never gave you anything," Dean says, "but who gave you money for the abortion, but they were too cheap, they should have given more."

Evan is confused.

"Why would she tell you that?" he asks. "They didn't give me money—that was money I saved by working summers."

"And that you were so stupid, she had to help you with your homework all the time."

"One time!" Evan cries. "*One time* she helped me. Did she really tell you that?"

"Yeah. And you know what else she told me? You aren't my father. It was some other guy she was dating, but he moved away and she needed to find someone. You acted guilty so she picked you."

"What?"

"And I met my real father, too. He's a really rich stockbroker who lives in Tokyo and wants me to come live with him. He's sending me a ticket—"

"You're making this all up."

"All I have to do is get a passport and then I'll go."

"You're lying about everything."

"I'll go live with him. He has a really nice summer house in Fukagawa—"

"Stop lying, Dean," Evan says, standing angrily. "Knock it off."

"And we'll eat wild cherries in the orchard while he reads me haiku he's written over the winter—"

"Stop it!" Evan shouts. "Shut up, Dean! Shut the hell up!"

Dean shuts up. They glare at each other. Evan is so angry, he doesn't know what to do. All he wanted was to have a real talk with Dean, and it exploded in his face.

"I mean, Jesus, Dean. I wanted to have a man-to-man talk."

"So go find another man," Dean snaps.

Evan instantly decides he's not taking any crap from Dean.

"I don't want to make your mother sound bad," he says, "but I need to tell you what happened. She was a senior and I was a junior; she was a year older than I was."

"Stop talking. Get out of my room."

"Spring of her senior year. It was an accident. She told you that. It definitely wasn't a planned parenthood."

"Stop talking about my mother. It's none of your business."

"She was going to a really great college. It made sense. We discussed it. Neither of us *wanted* to do it, but it made sense—"

"Shut up and leave me alone!" Dean shouts. He jumps up off the bed up and confronts Evan. "Get out of my room!"

"You need to be told the truth, Dean," Evan shouts back. "I wanted to keep you. Do you understand that? I gave her money, yes, but I only did it because I loved her and I thought that was what she wanted."

"Get out of my room! Leave me alone! I hate you."

"I would have married her and raised you with her, but they stole you away."

Dean lets out a scream of frustration; he stomps his feet and wheels around in a tight circle, screaming. When he stops, his face is bright red and his eyes are teary.

"Stop talking about my mother. You never even knew her!"

"Dean—"

"I'm only here because Frank's dangerous. I don't want to be with you. I don't even like you."

"Dean—"

"I don't want to be with you!"

"Well, who the hell do you want to be with?" Evan asks sharply. "Tell me who you want to be with and I'll try to arrange it."

Dean's just barely holding himself together. It's all he can do to remain standing. Evan lets him off the hook; he walks to the door, pauses, tries one more time.

"I wish I knew what she told you about me," he says.

Dean looks up at him. He's been broken. Tortured to the breaking point, there's nothing left for him to hide.

"She didn't tell me anything," he says quietly.

And Evan is hit with the realization: Dean is telling the truth. He's been telling the truth the whole time. Tracy told him nothing. She never said a word.

"Dean—"

But Dean's lower lip quivers, and Evan sees that he's just a little kid. Smart, but a kid: *So go find yourself another man.*

"Would you please leave my room?"

Shit. She never said a thing. There were no lies to correct, there were no minds to change. And Evan, soulless Evan, rushed in and destroyed the one thing that Dean really owned: the pure memory of his mother, which now lies amongst the rubble, like a felled statue of Lenin in Red Square.

"Please leave."

THE NEXT MORNING, Evan wakes up with the previous night's encounter spinning in his head. To distract himself he checks in with Lars.

"What do you want first, the good news or the bad news?" Lars asks.

"Oh, let's go for good," Evan says.

"Okay. Remember when Billy said he'd pass our demo around?"

"Yeah?"

"Well, he did. And we got a call."

"Really? From whom?"

"Template Records."

"No way," Evan says, genuinely surprised. Template Records is huge for a Seattle-based independent label. Almost Sub Pop. "They're interested?"

"Very. You've heard of Mel Kidd?"

Evan's heard of him, seen him around, been introduced to him a couple of times, but Mel Kidd would never remember Evan.

"Yeah."

"Well, Mel called Tony and told him that he wants to take our demo to CMJ in New York in the fall. And he wants us to go with him."

CMJ? The ultimate independent scene? Too cool for words.

"He's going to sign us?"

"Well, maybe. There's a catch."

Oh. The bad news. "So what is it?"

"The catch is that you need to come back to Seattle next week so we can meet Mel, meet his publicist, take some photos, and play a gig for him so he can see how we perform."

"That's not a bad catch."

"That's cool, right?" Lars asks.

"Very."

"You're into that whole thing, right?"

"Very."

"Cool."

"So, what's the bad news, then?" Evan asks.

Lars chuckles.

"I stopped into Fremont Guitars today. I saw your boss."

"Yeah?"

"He wants me to give you a message. He says you're fired."

EVAN CALLS HIS boss, Ehud, and, indeed, he's been fired. It turns out that Angel, Evan's substitute, hasn't shown up for work for three days. It's only logical that Ehud should fire Evan for that. Evan doesn't like it, but he understands.

And, after some thought, maybe he does like it. He definitely finds it liberating. So much has changed. He's taken his son back from the people who stole him. His band is about to sign a record contract. He might as well wipe the slate clean and start all over.

When Dean comes home from his day as a street urchin, they eat. After dinner they retreat to their respective rooms. Once in Tracy's room, closed off from tender young eyes, Evan decides he might be able to sneak in a little marijuana. He doesn't need it—

he's not having an aura. But since the fight with Dean about his
mother, there's been a cooling between them, which is upsetting to
Evan—upsetting enough to overshadow Lars's good news, so he
needs a pick-me-up. (This is how the line gets blurred, he thinks,
as with professional athletes and their painkillers: when the ritual
becomes habitual . . .) He opens the windows, lays a rolled-up towel
at the foot of the door to prevent fumes from escaping into the hallway, and lights up his pipe. *Mmm, that smell.*

It's always the same, that smell. The first hit of the day. There's a
brightness to the scent, an extra tanginess that vanishes with sub-
sequent puffs. He takes a few hits and puts the pipe away. He doesn't
want to get wasted, just a little high. Take the edge off his sunburn,
cozy him up a bit.

The phone rings loudly. Evan looks at it. Is he supposed to
answer? It rings again. Then it stops. Dean must have gotten it.
Huh. Oh, well. He lies back on the bed, closes his eyes and lets his
mind wander.

BAM, BAM, BAM.

He's startled out of his reverie by a knocking at his door. He
leaps to his feet, stows the pipe in the cigar box.

"Yes?" he asks frantically, his heart racing. He's been caught
totally unawares. He panics. Where is he? What time is it? Was he
asleep?

"I'm going out. Is that okay?" Dean says through the door.

"Hold on a sec," Evan replies quickly. He closes the box and
sticks it under his pillow. He throws open the door and tries to act
casual.

"Where are you going?" he asks breathlessly.

Dean looks at Evan strangely.

"You reek," he says.

"Reek?"

"You've been smoking weed," Dean observes.

"What are you talking about?"

"I smell it. It smells like weed."

"How do you know what weed smells like?" Evan asks with a sheepish look sweeping over his face.

"I know."

Evan turns and walks across the room decisively. "Where are you going?" he asks. "Was that a friend who called?"

He grabs his wallet from the dresser. People who are stoned always act deliberately because it takes special effort to act not-stoned when you're stoned. A stoned person's momentum is in favor of all motion stopping. So the stoned person often overcompensates and moves quickly from place to place.

"Yeah. We're going to the mall. Is that okay?"

"I guess so," Evan says, taking a twenty out of his wallet.

"Mom always wanted to know how I was getting home," Dean says with a shrug.

"How are you getting home?"

Evan turns and sees Dean sitting on the bed with the cigar box in his lap, holding the plastic baggie of pot that Evan keeps inside. Over an ounce of pot. Maybe an ounce-and-a-half. Good pot, too. Dean opens the baggie and smells it.

"Hey," Evan shouts. He charges across the room and snatches the box out of Dean's hands.

"Can I have some?"

"No, you can't have some." He stuffs it in the drawer of the bed-side table.

Dean rolls his eyes and stands.

"Dirt weed," he mutters as he stalks across the room.

"It's not dirt weed, my friend. That is some of the finest marijuana on the planet. That's hydroponically grown Indonesian sin-semilla, all female, all bud. That ain't starter weed like you delinquents smoke here in Yakima."

"Ooh, I'm impressed," Dean says mockingly. "Rick's father is driving us. Can I go?"

"Yes," Evan says, holding out the twenty. "Here."

"What's that for?"

"Food. A movie. Whatever."

Dean takes the bill and looks at it comically, like it's some kind of moon rock.

"Wow," he says. "Big spender." He stuffs the bill in his jeans and walks down the hallway toward the door.

"Your mother never gave you any money for the mall?" Evan calls out toward him.

Dean stops and cocks his head at Evan, a slightly puzzled look on his face. Evan has no idea what Dean is thinking. Just a strange, bemused gaze.

"She gave me money," Dean says simply. He continues his puzzled stare at Evan for another beat, then shakes his head to himself and disappears.

IT's NINE-THIRTY and Dean still isn't home. Evan is slightly worried. Did Dean say he'd be home by nine-thirty? Or was that on hockey nights? Does curfew change for the mall? What if Rick's father didn't show up to take them home and Dean decided to walk? Would he think to call Evan?

Evan knows that Dean has a key, so he's not worried about not being home for him; he gets in his car and goes looking.

The streets are quiet. Deserted. Nothing but big, thick-trunked trees whose roots buckle the sidewalks, their heavy branches draping over the streets. Nothing but green lawns with sprinklers. Nothing but silent cars parked underneath ominous Neighborhood Watch signs. The streetlights are on, but there's still a touch of light in the sky, enough to see by. And he cruises through the neighborhood, not really looking for Dean but looking at the same time. Simply driving up and down the streets. Finding nothing while not looking for anything at all. Hoping, perhaps, to happen upon Dean and his friends walking home as a group, or shooting a few hoops on a streetside rim. But he finds nothing.

He stops at a 7-Eleven he passes on one of the bigger avenues; he'd like to get himself a soda. He parks and sees a group of teenage delinquents hanging out by the Dumpster at the side of the parking lot. Kids still hang out in the parking lot of the 7-Eleven? That's a throwback. Evan thought they all played video games these days. He gets out and starts inside.

"Hey, mister." A carbuncular young man in baggy jeans and large sneakers and an oversized Cypress Hill T-shirt approaches him.

Evan turns, surprised by the interruption.

"Hey, mister, buy me some cigarettes?"

The kid holds out his upturned fist. Inside, presumably, is money to be used to procure the contraband.

Evan, slightly astonished by all of this, shakes his head.

"No," he says.

Evan turns to go into the store.

"I'll suck your dick for some beer."

Evan looks back at the kid.

"Faggot," the kid sneers and walks away.

Jesus. What kind of kids are they raising these days? Is that a devalued sense of humor, or what?

Evan grabs a seltzer and goes back outside. The kids have moved closer; they're leaning against the store window, right in front of Evan's car.

"Did you get the beer?" one of the kids yells at Evan as he gets in his car. All the other kids laugh. Evan remembers his own high school life and the disgust he'd felt for kids like this, the tough ones who hung out at the 7-Eleven, smoking and talking about drugs and girls. Evan was never friends with them. He was too busy practicing his guitar. And he was already having sex, anyway, while kids like this just talked about it.

"Come on, mister, buy us a Philly so we can roll a blunt."

Evan looks up as he opens his door.

Holy crap. Is that Dean?

He looks closer. In the back. Hunkering down. Trying not to be seen. Dean.

"Hey," Evan says, pointing toward Dean. "Get in the car."

A murmur buzzes through the group.

"I said, get in the car," Evan repeats sternly.

A big kid steps forward.

"Fuck you, faggot," he bellows.

Evan boldly moves toward them, ignoring the big kid. He points at Dean.

"Dean," he says. "Get in the car. Now."

Dean? At the mention of a proper name, the murmuring stops. Eyes turn. The kids part like a sea and reveal Dean, who is angry at being thusly exposed.

"Now!" Evan shouts.

Defiantly, Dean starts toward the car.

"Dean, who's that, man?" a kid whispers.

"My dad," Dean explains with a roll of his eyes.

Dean tries to look tough as he circles behind the car and opens the passenger door.

"Dean's daddy came to get him. What a puss."

"*You* told him you'd suck his dick."

"Shut up, fuck face."

"Hey," Evan barks, "what, are you tough guys hoping to work your way up the ladder and get a job behind the counter here?"

Blank faces.

"You have no excuses," Evan says. "This is America. If you piss away your life, it's your own damn fault. Go home and read a book, get an education, and maybe you can aspire to do something a little more relevant than stocking the 7-Eleven with candy bars."

Silence.

Dean is sitting in the car. Evan gets in and starts it up. As he pulls away, he looks in the rearview mirror. The kids are making all kinds of obscene gestures at him, giving him the finger, grabbing their crotches, pumping their fists. Sick, sick, sick. That his son would be one of them. Sick.

EVAN PULLS UP to the curb and stops. He and Dean are both silent.

The wind is blowing. Evan can see it through the windshield, though he cannot hear it. It's blowing the trees back and forth, the long dangling willow vines, the dark, somber oak leaves.

"You told me you were going to the mall," Evan says.

"I lied. So sue me."

"How about I ground you instead?" Evan snaps.

"So ground me. I don't care."

"You're grounded."

"Ooh, I'm really scared," Dean taunts. "You're so fucking *Leave It To Beaver*. You're pathetic."

"Don't swear."

"Fuck, fuck, fuck."

"You're seriously grounded this time," Evan says.

"Oh. *Seriously* grounded. As opposed to the last time when I was only *play* grounded? Now I'm *seriously* grounded. What exactly does *seriously* grounded entail, *Dad?* No flying around the house?"

"You know," Evan says, "this is probably the first time in your life you're trying on how to be a real prick. And you're good at it. But, trust me, it gets tired real quick. And some day, someone's gonna pop you in the nose."

"Bullshit."

"Don't swear so much. It makes you sound stupid."

"Bullshit, bullshit, bullshit!"

"I see you got your father's mouth."

Dean twists in his seat to glare at Evan.

"I got my father's eyes, too," he snaps. "And I got my father's ears. And his face and his hair and his body. I got my father's lack of responsibility. I got my father's Attention Deficit Disorder. And I got my father's basic loser nature. So what else are you going to give me? Pearls of wisdom? 'Don't swear so much?' Fuck you."

Evan tries to center himself.

"You're a nasty kid," he says.

"You're a lousy father."

"Well, I'm a lousy father who's taking you back to Seattle next week."

"I'm not going."

"I have to go for work. It's important."

"So, go. I'm staying. Hire me an au pair."

"You're going," Evan says.

"I'm not your fucking suitcase," Dean says. "Go fuck yourself." He gets out of the car, stomps up the walk and into the house, and leaves Evan wondering what the hell a real father would do right now.

A REAL FATHER probably wouldn't take this moment to try to get laid, but Evan calls Mica in Jamaica. She has checked out. He tries her in Seattle. She's there.

"I'm tired," she says.

"Sorry to bother you."

"No, no."

He unravels the Dean dilemma for her, but she doesn't have anything to offer. He can hear her steady yawns; it's torture to keep her awake.

"You should go to sleep."

"I'll come out tomorrow morning, okay? I got Dean this really cool diver's watch. It was a little expensive, but I figured it was worth it. It's really cool. He'll like it, won't he?"

"I'm sure."

"Do you miss me?"

"I miss you a lot."

"Really?" she asks.

"Really. What should I do about Dean?"

"He'll be okay. He's a kid. He needs to do that kind of stuff. I wouldn't worry about it. You guys are tighter than that. People fight. It's part of growing up."

"Yeah?"

"Sure. Don't sweat it. I'll see you in the morning."

"Okay."

EVAN SITS IN the kitchen reading the Saturday morning paper and drinking coffee. He's rather hungover from the verbal abuse he received from Dean the previous evening. He was supposed to be the one doing the yelling; instead, he let Dean curse him out. Wimpy father material. He hears Dean in the foyer strapping on his skates. *Click, click, click.* Then the other boot. *Click, click, click.*

"Where are you going?" Evan asks from the threshold.

"Out," Dean responds without looking up.

Evan knows where Dean's going. He's going to play hockey between the cones that Matthew's father puts out.

"Out where?"

Dean glances at Evan as he stands in his skates. He picks up his hockey stick.

"Out."

"Mica's coming over this morning. Don't you want to be here when she arrives?"

"No."

"Why not? She said she brought you a present from Jamaica."

"I don't want it."

"Why not?"

"Where's she staying?" Dean asks sharply. "Not in my mom's room."

"I—"

"She's not staying in my mom's room. So where's she staying?"

"I'll find a place for her," Evan says.

"I bet you will."

"What's that supposed to mean?"

Dean doesn't answer. He gathers his bag of equipment and reaches for the door.

"When are you coming home?" Evan asks.

"None of your fucking business, *Dad.*"

Evan feels a flash of rage. His face flushes. He understands that Dean is deliberately challenging him, but this is out of control. Things have moved out of the rational realm and into the emotional. Before he can stop himself—indeed, before he even knows what he's doing—he rushes Dean and grabs him by the collar. He pushes Dean backward, pinning him against the wall.

"It *is* my business," Evan yells at Dean, whose eyes are wide. "You may not like it, but I'm your father and you're stuck with me. So learn to show me a little respect."

Dean is taken momentarily by surprise. He's afraid of Evan and this sudden anger. But then, when Evan doesn't follow through, when there's nothing after the initial burst, Dean regains his composure. He's not intimidated. He correctly assesses Evan's attack as bluster. Then, taking Evan quite by surprise, Dean spits in Evan's face.

Spit? Can Evan believe what's going on? Did Dean just spit in his face? Suddenly, Evan isn't in control of his own body, his arm is a club attached to his shoulder, a spring-powered catapult that's been cocked, and someone looses the firing pin, someone cuts the string, and his arm leaps forward in an instant and the heel of his hand careens into Dean's jaw, his palm into Dean's cheek, his fingers the side of Dean's head, and the sound it makes is so loud, like someone clacking two-by-fours together as hard as he can, a crack. Dean loses his footing, his skates go out from underneath him. With a mad scramble he goes down.

He sits, stunned for a moment, looking up at Evan. The left side of his face blushes a deep scarlet. Tears well on the edges of his eyelids, but they are not tears of pain; they are tears of shame, of frustration, of anger, of humiliation.

"Take off your skates and go to your room," Evan says. "Don't come out until I tell you to."

Evan doesn't know who's doing the talking. It certainly isn't him. He would never say something like that. He would never act like that. What has happened to him? What has he become?

"Now!" he shouts at Dean.

Dean angrily complies. He skates down the hall and kicks open his door; he slams it. Once safe behind the closed door, he shouts: "I hate you! I wish you were dead!"

WHAT HAS HE done?

He couldn't help himself. Dean was pushing him too hard. Dean spit in his face. He *made* Evan hit him. That's what he did.

And he hit him hard, too. That wasn't a love tap. That was as close to a full-out hit as it gets. Thank god he didn't close his fist. That would have been a disaster.

He's no better than Frank. He and Frank are cut from the same cloth. They are brothers in crime. Abusers. Bullies. He thinks he's sensitive, he thinks he'd make a good father, but he's no better than the next thug; when your back is to the wall, come out swinging.

Is this how he deals with discipline problems? Bone-crushing blows for no reason, with no warning? Evan is a bad man. He can't control himself. At some point he might go crazy and beat Dean to death in the night. *Bam, bam.* Open hand. *Bam, bam, bam.* No fist. *Bam.* Until Dean's face is so swollen he can't see, can't talk, his teeth loose, blood trickling from his ear. *Bam, bam.* Like a pile driver. Evan, the pile driver. Relentless. *Bam.* Until Dean is dead. *I didn't mean to hurt him*, Evan would say to the judge. And the judge would shake her head sadly, bang her gavel once, and, tears in her eyes from all her pent-up compassion, pull a Nanny-Murder-Trial upset and reverse the jury's verdict, sentencing Evan to time served—two days—for the bludgeoning death of his own son.

"HEY, LOVER."

Evan starts. He's sitting on the patio; she's standing before him.

She's radiant. She's smiling a brilliant smile. Her skin is glowing and her hair is tinged with a salty lightness. She's alive.

"Welcome back," he says.

"Miss me?"

"Oh yeah."

"Prove it."

She leans down and lets him kiss her. He tries hard to be passionate with his kiss, but he's not sure he pulls it off. She lifts her face from his and beams at him; it worked.

"Where's Dean?" she asks. "I want to give him the watch. Check it out. It's pretty cool."

She hands a box to Evan and he opens it. Inside is a sophisticated diver's watch with a yellow dial and every kind of chronometer one could imagine.

"That's cool," Evan says. "I want one."

"Oh. You'll get your present. You be patient. Where is he?"

"In his room. Straight through the kitchen, take a left. Look for a closed door."

"Be right back."

She snatches the box and bounds into the house. She comes back too soon.

"He's not there," she says, disappointed.

He's not there? He was told to stay there until he was released, and he's not there? Evan fumes.

"He must have gone out," he says.

"He'll be back," she replies with a smile.

Evan's not so sure.

LATER IN THE day, Mica is resting and Dean is mysteriously back in his room, acting like he'd never left.

"You were supposed to stay in your room," Evan says.

"I was here," Dean replies defensively.

"No, you weren't."

"Yes, I was!"

"Mica came in to see you and you were gone."

"Well, I must have been on the toilet, *Dad*. Solitary confinement doesn't allow for bathroom breaks?"

He's got Evan there. Maybe he was in the bathroom. Honestly, Evan never checked.

"We're going out to dinner," Evan says. He wants to believe Dean. He really does. "So get ready."

"I'm not going."

"Yes, you are. Mica came to see you. She has a very nice present she bought for you. And you're going to go to dinner and be nice. You can hate me all you want, but leave her out of it."

"I'm sick," Dean says.

"No, you're not. Get dressed."

"I am. The reason she didn't see me in my room is that I have diarrhea. I've been in the bathroom all day. I must still have food poisoning."

"I don't believe you."

"What, now I need stool samples?"

Damn. Crafty kid. Where did he pick that up? Probably from his mother.

"Let me feel your head."

Evan presses his sweaty palm to Dean's forehead and prays for an epiphanic lightning bolt, one that will tell him what a fever feels like. But Dean's forehead is cool.

"You don't have a fever."

"It's a gastrointestinal disorder."

Evan takes a step back and stares down at Dean. He considers the situation.

"I'm sorry, okay?" he says. "I lost control. I never should have hit you. I'm really sorry."

Dean doesn't reply.

"So will you come to dinner?"

"I'm sick."

Evan throws his hands up.

"Look! I'm a horrible father. I did the worst thing a father could do. I hit you. It was stupid. It was bad. I'll beg your forgiveness forever. Just come to dinner."

Dean takes a moment to size Evan up.

"I'm sick," he says.

Evan groans, realizes he can't win, walks toward the door. Then stops.

"Listen, Dean. Your grandmother stopped by the other day. She's divorcing Frank."

Dean is surprised by this information; he sits up.

"So Frank's out of the picture," Evan says. "You have to decide. Who are you going to live with? Maybe you'd really rather be with your grandmother."

Dean seems to change before Evan's eyes. Evan has seen both his faces: wise young man and lost child. Evan's gotten to know Dean's faces and recognize them for what they are. But now Dean is like a strange Star Trek creature; his face changes by the second: wise, lost, wise, lost . . .

"Is that what you want?" Dean asks. He can't answer the question by himself. He's just a kid.

"It's not my decision, Dean. It's yours. But you obviously don't like me. And I have to go back to Seattle, and you don't want to go. And I have to live in Seattle, and you don't want that. So, you know . . ."

Dean thinks about it a minute. It's a lot for a fourteen-year-old to think about. A lot for anyone.

"What do you think?" he asks.

"I don't know, Dean," Evan says, exasperated. "I mean, we're not happy together, are we? You give me a real hard time, and I guess I probably ride you pretty hard, too. If there were no other options, I guess we could get through it. But I'm not Butch and you're not Sundance. We're not standing on a cliff, and a posse isn't chasing us down. We don't have to jump."

"What are you talking about?"

Evan has just made himself a permanent old man by dating himself with an old-man movie.

"I don't know," Evan says, "maybe a cooling off period would be right. I *have* to go to Seattle next week."

Dean nods. "A break," he says.

"Just a breather," Evan says. "We can clear our heads and then get together again later and try it again, you know?"

"Yeah, I know. A cooling-off period."

"I'm just thinking. It's been really intense. And you haven't seen your grandmother for a long time, really. Frank's not a threat. Maybe you could spend some time with her before school starts in the fall, then you can make a decision where you want to live, you know? Maybe you'd like to be in Walla Walla—"

"Doubtful."

"Or here. She said something about moving here. You could live in this house, stay in your old school. I'd come visit all the time. You'd come to Seattle for vacations. Maybe that's the way to play it."

"Yeah, I see what you're saying."

"I mean, we're feeling pressure right now, and there's no need for pressure. Both of us. I'm doing it, too. We're pushing. We should take a minute. Go with the right decision, not what we *think* is the right decision."

Dean nods considerately. "A cooling-off period," he says.

"Yeah. Maybe. What do you think? We don't have to do it."

"Just for a while."

"Yeah. A few days. A week. A couple of weeks. Whatever."

A year. A decade. A lifetime . . .

"Is that what *you* want?" Dean asks.

Evan is on the spot again. How come really important decisions always come back to him? It doesn't seem fair.

"Yeah, I guess. For a little while. Not long."

"A cooling-off period," Dean says again.

"That's all," Evan agrees. "A cooling-off period."

And that's it. Agreed upon right there in Dean's room, both of them together. They look at each other and nod; they mentally shake hands. They agree: a cooling-off period.

But they both know, deep down, that it isn't a cooling-off period at all. It's the end. The experiment is over. They tried and failed. When Dean goes to stay with Ellen, he will stay with her forever. Evan will make his visits. Many at first. More seldom as Dean grows older. Until they are few and far between.

They agree, right here in this room: Dean isn't feeling well, Evan is taking Mica to dinner, and their brief flirtation with a serious and lasting relationship is over.

S HE'S LIKE A supercharger. That's what Evan likes about her.
Wherever she goes, everything speeds up. Everyone pays attention to her. Her beauty, her exotic looks. She must be someone famous, people think. She needs extra attention.

At Julep, a downtown-Yakima steakhouse, the help is all in a tizzy. They don't have two pound-and-a-half lobsters. Unfortunately, three pounds is the smallest they have.

"That's okay," Mica laughs at their fawning waiter. She has a hearty laugh, a deep, full-bodied laugh. "We'll take two of the big boys, then, *fra diavolo*. You do *diavolo*?"

A confirming nod.

"Salads and whatever sides you can think of, and a bottle of Cristal."

The waiter bows himself away from the table.

"Don't worry about how much it costs," Mica says, leaning in to Evan. "My treat."

The waiter pours the champagne. Evan takes a sip, no more. Mica takes a long draft.

"I want to go with you to The Castle in Jamaica," Mica says excitedly. "You and Dean. When can we go? He has school soon, doesn't he?"

He does. In a few weeks. The summer is winding down already.

"Maybe at Christmas we can go. I'm sure they're already booked for Christmas, but I can probably call in a favor. It's expensive, but it's amazingly beautiful, and secluded. You don't have to worry about how much it costs, though. I can pay for it and write it off on my taxes. We'll get a two-bedroom suite, and as long as I check in at the studio a few times, it'll be a business expense. If you have any solo material, we can lay that down, too. I bet Dean would get a kick out of that. Are you teaching him the guitar? When he grows up, I bet he'll be a sexy musician, like you. You both have sexy hands. It'll be fun. We'll have a blast."

"I have money," Evan blurts out, blowing a hole in the good mood at the table and wiping the smile off of Mica's face.

"Sure," Mica says hopefully. "Okay. I didn't mean anything by it."

"I have plenty of money. I can pay. My treat."

"Sure, Evan, sure thing."

Mica looks down at her salad, the life crushed out of her by Evan's tone. She silently picks at the greens on her plate.

"I'm really sorry, Evan," Mica says after a minute. "I'm used to musicians being poor, that's all. I'm just so happy to see you and all. I wanted us to have a good time without worrying about how we're going to pay for it. I shouldn't have assumed."

Evan gives her a half smile. Mica half-smiles back. All is forgiven.

"You're upset about Dean?" Mica asks.

Dean. Yes. He's upset about Dean.

Dean brightened for Mica. Accepted her gift with proper gratitude. Actually seemed happy to see her. He even suggested that she stay in his mother's room. But then he quickly pinched out the flame, declared himself ill for the night, and hid from sight. And then, while Mica got herself ready for dinner, Evan changed his life with two short phone calls: he told Ellen she could pick up Dean on Sunday, and he told Lars he would be back in Seattle on Monday. The canyon growing wider, both Evan and Dean knowing it, both of them helping it along.

"Where are you?" Mica asks.

Evan smiles at her. "Just thinking."

"He's a good kid," she says. "He's probably just a little confused right now. He needs a little time to find his place."

"Yeah," Evan agrees. "That's probably it."

Or, more likely, he needs a little time to pack his bags and get the hell out of town.

They fall silent again for a few minutes until the lobsters arrive; then they eat.

AFTER DINNER THEY drive through downtown, up First Street, which has come alive with light. Neon signs above every hotel and restaurant glow in plasticky colors, illuminating the strip for as far as the eye can see, until it vanishes into the flat landscape, leaving only the heat of summer in its wake. Neon and glitter. Desert heat. Yakima. The Palm Springs of Washington.

"Let's get an ice cream," Mica says dreamily, her head resting on Evan's shoulder and her eyes closed. She's pretty drunk: they'd finished the bottle of champagne and he'd only had one glass, and that left the other nine gallons for her.

"You must be tired," he says.

"I am."

"I'll take you home."

"No," she moans. "Ice cream."

He parks across from the Yakima Mall and they go inside. Mica comes alert at the TCBY, and orders herself a large cup with toppings. Evan doesn't order anything. They sit under the fluorescent lights, the crowded mall echoing with conversation and footsteps and the rustle of countless plastic shopping bags.

When Mica is finished, they stroll through the mall, ending up in a bookstore, where they split up and browse on their own. After a few minutes, Evan has nothing, but Mica has a couple of books.

"I'll meet you outside," she says, getting in line.

"Okay."

He steps out into the mall to wait. It's nine-thirty, and the place is full. Where America goes to socialize. People of all ages, families, older folks, groups of teens. Evan glances over at a gang of young men gathered around a palm tree, which is the centerpiece of a bench arrangement. They're hanging out, chilling, as it were, drinking Dr. Peppers and howling at young girls who walk by. What a life. Evan's glad he didn't grow up in the Age of Malls.

But then he notices something very disturbing. The kid sitting on the bench under the palm tree eating a hotdog. That's Dean.

Evan's heart drops. Dean. Not so sick after all. Evan can't believe it's happened again.

Evan stares at his son. Maybe he's wrong. He glances over his shoulder into the bookstore and sees Mica stepping up to the register. Then he looks back at the kid who resembles Dean. The kid looks up. Their eyes meet.

The mall freezes in place. Time stops. No sound, no movement. It's Dean. Evan's sure of it. It's Dean and they're staring at each other. They both know.

"Hey!"

Evan turns. Mica is tugging on his arm.

"I got you something," she says. She takes a book out of her bag and hands it to Evan. "A present. Surprise!"

Evan looks at the book. *The Ten-Minute Garden*.

"A gardening book?" he asks.

"You said you found gardening restorative," she says, flipping open the book as Evan holds it for her. She finds a page. It's a bright, colorful photograph of a million little yellow flowers.

"I thought it was so pretty when I saw it. I wanted you to have it."

Evan looks at the page distractedly. "It's nice," he says.

He looks over to Dean. The kids are leaving. Dean stands up, glances at Evan one last time, and then loses himself in the crowd and is gone. Evan looks down at the page again.

"Very pretty. That was so nice of you," he says. He gives her a peck on the cheek. She looks at him strangely.

"I don't know where you are sometimes," she says.

• • •

"TAKE ME HOME."

"It's too early," Evan says.

He pulls the car out into traffic and they head down First Street again. Another cruise down the strip. He can't bear getting home and not finding Dean in his room. He won't do it.

"But Evan," Mica leans in to him and nibbles on his ear. "I need to screw your brains out," she whispers.

That sounds great, but not at Tracy's house. There's too much going on there, too much baggage. And the issue of Dean. And the issue of the use of Tracy's room for sex. No. Too much.

"Dean might not be asleep yet," Evan says, hedging. "And I don't want to act inappropriately in front of him."

"Oh, I see," Mica laughs. "We're back to that again, are we? Well, what do you have in mind? I'm not doing it in the car, you know."

"Not in the car."

"Where, then? Remember, it's three hours later for me than it is for you. I can't wait much longer. I'm pretty tired."

Where, then? Evan has no idea, so he keeps driving.

Then he sees it. Neon and glitter. Perfect. Evan quickly turns across traffic and swerves into the parking lot of the Bali Hai Motel. The perfect place to screw your neighbor's wife.

"What's this?" Mica asks.

Evan jumps out of the car and runs into the office. He comes back with a room key.

"Oh, Evan," Mica coos. "You're so sexy. You're gonna fuck me in a motel? That's so spontaneous. I'm all hot."

"Are you mocking me?"

"Poor, insecure baby."

They drive to the room and park. They go inside. As soon as the door closes, Mica jumps on Evan, grabbing his face and shoving her tongue into his mouth. After a furious kiss, she breaks off.

"I'm drunk," she says.

"That's okay."

"So you'd take advantage of a drunk girl?"

"If she kissed me like you just did, I would."

Mica makes her way to the bed, kicking off her shoes. She slips out of her dress, leaving herself in only black lace lingerie and stockings. She lays back on the bed.

"I'm so tired," she says, closing her eyes.

"We don't have to do it now. We can wait."

"No, I want to do it now. What are you doing by the door? Come here and look at my tan lines."

She absently reaches behind her back and unclasps her bra, exposing her breasts, a shade or two lighter than the surrounding, nut-brown flesh.

"Look," she says. Her eyes are still closed. "Your beautiful presents."

"Very beautiful," Evan agrees.

"You're not just saying that?"

"No."

"I've been saving them for you."

Evan smiles at his poor naked girlfriend who can barely keep herself awake. Too much champagne, too much jet lag.

"Let me just wash my hands," Evan says. "I smell like lobster."

He heads toward the bathroom.

"Your father's a doctor, right?" Mica mumbles.

"Right. Why?"

"Obsessive hand-washing."

He turns on the water and scrubs up to his elbows, like he imagines his father would do it.

"You're very clean," Mica says from the bed. Her words are slurred and thick. "That's what I first noticed about you. Even when you were smoking pot in the closet, you seemed very clean. I think personal hygiene is good."

Evan turns off the water and dries his hands with a towel.

"You've dated a lot of guys lacking in that department?" he asks, stepping back into the room.

But he gets no answer. He looks across the room. Mica is asleep.

Evan lifts the bedspread over her warm body and tucks her in. He grabs his wallet and steps out of the motel room.

There's barely a touch of color in the sky. It's almost ten. The sun has set behind the mountains and the valley has fallen into a strange twilight, the cobalt sky stretching broadly over the hot pavement. It's still hot, the warmth coming from below now, not above, the earth giving back the heat it has absorbed. He walks down the breezeway to the soda machine to get himself a club soda.

After the machine dispenses the sweating blue can, Evan looks up at the sky again. It's an unusual color. Black, mostly, but energized with purple and blue, like transparent layers of sky material draped over the world. Light, wispy clouds high above the earth add depth and contrast. It's shocking, in a way. It's one of those moments when you see Nature at her absolute best.

"What are you looking at?"

Evan is startled. There's someone else at the Bali Hai? A middle-aged businessman, hair thinning, wearing a white shirt and a loosened tie, holding a can of Coke, stands looking up at the sky.

"Do you see something?" he asks.

Evan looks up again.

"I was just looking at the sky. The color."

They stand there for a minute, the two of them, gazing at the sky.

"Yakima Blue," the man says.

Yakima Blue? Evan looks at the man. The man looks back and smiles. Evan shakes his head, an indication of confusion.

"Pretty," the man says.

Evan nods, looks back at the sky.

After a moment, the man says, "If they made a crayon that color, they would call it 'Yakima Blue.'"

Evan laughs to himself. "They would," he agrees.

Another moment, then Evan turns to go.

"Good night," he says as he walks back to his room.

"They *should* make a crayon that color," he hears the man say behind him. "My kids would love it."

They would, Evan thinks. They would.

AT ELEVEN, EVAN shuts off the TV in the motel room, dresses Mica, and carries her to the car. He drives her back to the house and puts her to bed in Tracy's room.

He walks silently through the house, down the hall. He opens Dean's door a crack. It is dark. Warm. It smells of someone sleeping, the humid breathiness of sleep. He opens the door wider and looks toward Dean's bed. In the darkness he sees little, but he detects movement, a tensing of muscles, if only slight. He knows that Dean is awake. He feels it.

"Are you awake?" he asks.

No response.

"Dean?"

Nothing. Nothing at all. Maybe he was wrong. Maybe Dean is asleep.

He pauses in the doorway for several moments, as long as he can stand it, waiting for Dean to sit up or say something, move, interact with him in some way so that he could say, *Stop, stop it all, let's stop it all.* He holds his breath and waits and waits until he's all out of air; he exhales silently.

He steps back into the hall, and as he closes the door he hears something, a slight movement, and he thinks about opening the door again, but it is already pulled shut, so that all that is left for him to do is release the knob and allow the latch to set. Was Dean actually awake? Should Evan have spoken? Would Dean have said something if Evan had stayed a moment longer?

He releases the knob; he hears a soft click; he turns and walks away down the dark hall.

E VAN READS THE Sunday *New York Times,* which, like so many other things, simply gets delivered to Tracy's house without request. Once you're in the computers, there's nothing that will stop them. Kind of an unpleasant reminder that when you die, the world will continue its ceaseless expansion into the dark emptiness that surrounds our universe.

Dean skulks into the kitchen in baggy shorts and a baggy T-shirt. Evan can't tell if this outfit is Dean's pajamas or the latest in gentrified hip-hop propaganda. He pours himself a cup of coffee.

"Are you allowed to drink that?" Evan asks.

"Allowed by whom? By you?" Dean retorts.

Dean takes a carton of vanilla ice cream out of the freezer and spoons a big blob into his cup. He returns the carton to the freezer and stirs the coffee.

"By your mom. Did she let you drink coffee?"

Dean sips his concoction. "Yes," he says. "But she's dead, so I guess you'll just have to take my word for it."

Dean takes a box of Cheerios from the cabinet and reaches for a bowl. He prepares his cereal deliberately, using orange juice instead of milk because there is no milk. He sits at the kitchen table, reaches for the sports section, and eats almost resentfully, shoveling Cheerios into his mouth silently, spoonful after spoonful, like a Cheerio-eating machine, orange juice spilling sloppily out of his mouth and back into the bowl, all the while reading, or pretending to read, the news of the latest Mariners triumph or debacle, the end of one losing streak or the beginning of a new one; it's always one or the other.

"Hey," Mica chirps, bursting into the room. She's wearing Evan's pajama bottoms and a microscopic tank top that exposes most of her midriff and her ribs. "How are my two favorite boys?"

"Morning," Evan says cheerfully.

Dean says nothing. He just stares in awe at Mica, the hot babe in the breakfast nook.

"What are we doing today?" Mica asks.

Evan shrugs.

"You're not wearing a bra, are you?" Dean asks from out of nowhere.

Mica is momentarily surprised, but she recovers quickly.

"No, I'm not," she says. "Why?"

"Because I can see your nipples."

"Hey!" Evan snaps. "That's enough!"

"She's showing them, not me," Dean says in his defense. "What, am I supposed to do, lie and pretend I don't see them?"

"That's rude and out of line. You apologize to her—"

"Evan," Mica breaks in.

"Apologize. Now."

"Or what?" Dean challenges. "You gonna hit me?"

He leaves out the word "again," but Evan hears it.

"No, Dean," Mica says. "He's not going to hit you. It's my fault. I'll go change."

"I didn't say I didn't *like* it," Dean mutters.

"Hey!"

"Evan," Mica chastises. "Stop with the 'heys.' Hay is for horses."

"A nicely phrased aphorism by the pretty lady with the nipples," Dean smirks.

Evan clenches his fists. He has no idea how to handle an asshole kid who's provoking him. He wants to hit. Another quick smack to let him know who's boss. So tempting.

"What are you gonna do?" Dean taunts. "You gonna ground me? Tell me I can't leave the house? Go ahead. Ground me."

Evan is almost blind with frustration. It starts in his chest and throbs its way up to his temples. He can't ground Dean. He has no authority. If he were to ground Dean, Dean would just laugh at him.

"You're not grounded, Dean," Mica jumps in. "Evan, he's not grounded, is he?"

Evan looks to Mica. "I guess not."

"Now listen," Mica says to Dean. "I want you at the front door with a swimming suit and a towel and a bottle of sun block in a half an hour, okay? We're going on an outing."

She turns to Evan.

"You. I need to speak to you. Come with me while I change into something less revealing."

"MY BEING HERE is a direct challenge to Dean," Mica says, peeling off her tank top and dropping her pants, suddenly so naked in the bedroom. "I'm a challenge to his mother and to his relationship with you and to almost everything. I mean, I'm sleeping in his mother's bed. That has to have a lot of significance to him. He imagines that you're having sex with me in this bed. That must conjure up some resentment. And, also, if you go along with the Freudian thinking that every fourteen-year-old wants to sleep with his mother, and I'm standing in for his mother, then he *really* wants to sleep with me because he can pretend he's sleeping with his mother when he really isn't—I'm an obtainable stand-in for his mother. Do you understand?"

Evan nods.

"You're completely naked," he says.

"Yes. Does that distract you?"

"Yes, it does."

"You can imagine how my nipples might distract Dean, then."

"I can."

"*Plus*," Mica goes on, "his verbal assault on me is really an assault on *you*. Understand? He was challenging you to hit him or ground him. He's becoming a man. He's struggling for control of the herd, in this case, me. I mean, if I had thought about it for a second before I came out, I would have put on a big robe or something. Sometimes I take my sexuality lightly. I don't spend a lot of time around teenagers. I usually spend time with drugged-out rock stars who couldn't get it up if I sucked on their dicks for a half hour because they're on so much black tar heroin. It didn't occur to me that my nipples might give Dean a hard-on that he'll have for the next two years."

She stops, one hand on her hip, the other, palm up in a plea for understanding, completely naked, and completely unfazed by it.

"You're giving *me* a hard-on *I'll* have for the next two years," Evan says.

"I'm happy to know I'm stronger than your medication. We can deal with your hard-on later. Right now I have to get into the shower. We're going to the water park."

She turns and goes into the bathroom. Evan follows.

"There's a water park around here?" he asks.

"I read about it in my handy guide to Yakima Valley," she answers, turning on the shower.

"You have a guide to Yakima?"

"I got it last night at the mall, along with a very pretty book about gardening that I gave to you but you don't care about."

She steps into the tub.

"I'd invite you in, but I told Dean we were leaving in a half hour and that doesn't give me enough time to wash myself *and* you. You'll have to do that on your own."

She closes the shower curtain with a snap, and there Evan stands, once again awestruck by Mica, concerned that she can see what's going on so much better than he; convinced, further, that he is not meant to be any child's father.

IT'S A SMOKIN' HOT Sunday morning. Ninety-two degrees, not a cloud in the sky. Perfect for watersliding. The park is crowded, teeming with kids and adults, each flying down one of the seventeen extended slides and plunging into one of the six vast pools of overheated, overchlorinated water.

It takes Dean one twisty slide and dunking to come out of his funk, and that goes for Evan, too. Within minutes, they are laughing and having a ball together. Just like the old days.

In the morning they play. In the early afternoon, they eat lunch from a snack bar. Evan breaks his diet: chili dogs and root beer. Then Dean asks permission to hit the slides again. Again, his unbridled enthusiasm and joy for life having been unleashed by Mica.

"Too soon after you ate," Mica says. "You shouldn't swim for thirty minutes."

"I won't swim. I'll go down the slides and get right out."

Mica smiles at him.

"Okay. But no swimming. And if you vomit in the pool, don't say I didn't warn you."

Dean grins at Mica without restraint and then bounds off for the slides. And all of this—all this manic behavior—bothers Evan. The joy that Dean is experiencing bothers Evan. The fun that Mica is having bothers Evan. The fact that Mica looks at Dean with such pride and love bothers Evan. Because in Evan's mind, the break has already been made. It's one-thirty. In two-and-a-half hours, Ellen is coming to take Dean away, and for some reason, Evan can't get past the fact that this is a permanent change.

He knows, of course, that if he confided in Mica, she would fix it. She would fix everything. And he half-suspects that Dean knows the same thing. In that sense, Evan and Dean are co-conspirators. They both know that if either of them told Mica about the imminent transaction, she would smite the very core of the idea to powder, whip both of them into shape, have everyone hugging and in tears, and, when Ellen showed up to claim her prize, Mica would plant a tornado kick on her temple that would drop her like a dead halibut on a dock. It's all over but the gutting, as they say.

But they are mute. They, both Evan and Dean, knowingly let the day slip through their fingers without alerting Mica of what is to be. A silver Honda rolling up Nob Hill. Dean climbing in, closing the door after himself, leaving Yakima.

"I love kids," she says as Dean bounds up the steps to the top of a slide.

Evan shakes himself awake. He's been drifting.

"I said, 'I love kids'," Mica says again, leaning in to Evan. "Don't you?"

"Sure."

"Sure," Mica repeats. "Sure. I hate men. *Sure*. Men say 'sure' like it means something. Sure."

Evan stops, puzzled.

"I'm sorry?"

"Oh, nothing," Mica sips at her water.

Evan nods. Men are also willing to take "nothing," and "never mind," at face value.

He sees Dean in the distance, reaching the top of the slide, waiting in line. Then it's his turn and he goes, his body hurtling down the ramp at high speed, turning over and over, down and down and down, shooting into the pool at the bottom, squirting underneath the water, and then his little brown head popping to the surface; he climbs out and heads for the top again.

"Are you at all interested in having another kid?"

"I don't know," Evan answers cautiously. "Why?"

"You didn't raise Dean," Mica says. "Are you at all interested in raising a child from birth?"

"I don't know. Why?"

"Just asking," Mica shrugs.

Evan catches sight of Dean again. Barreling down the slide, this time feet first, spinning over and over and flying out into the pool.

"I need two things," Mica says. A new approach. "I need love, and I need a family."

Evan nods and turns to Mica.

"Sure," he says.

Mica frowns at him. "You're not listening to me at all, are you?"

"Sure, I am."

"No. You're in a whole different world," Mica says regretfully. "Where are you, anyway? What are you thinking?"

What is he thinking? He's thinking about how easy things have become since Mica returned. How it's like being a kid again. Mom announces where we're going: to the water slides. And we go. The logistics of it, the where and how, are details for an adult to worry about. Not for a child who just lets things flow, whose primary job is to have a good time wherever he is.

". . . I'm not trying to freak you out," Mica says, always the perceptive one. "We only just started, I know that. But I thought that you're not the kind of guy who would get freaked out by this. You're not, are you?"

Evan shrugs, suddenly panicked. Shit, he really was far away that time. He has no idea what Mica was talking about. How long has she been talking? What did she say? It's the heat. The damn heat.

"I need some water," Evan says tightly. Mica offers what she's holding, a liter of something bottled.

"I freaked you out, didn't I?"

"No, no. How hot is it?"

"It's supposed to be in the mid-nineties today."

Mid-nineties. That's raisin-making temperature. *Dis heer's seizsure weathir. Beck home, we us'ta git heet lik dis, 'n' dem epolepticks us'ta git dem fits so mich, ya coodn't hardlie tek a step wit'out squashin one a dem boodies, squigglin roun onna groun lik a skinn'd snek.*

Evan looks for Dean. He desperately wants to see Dean on one of the slides, standing on line, or in the water, or somewhere in between. But he can't find him anywhere. The heads of a million children and adults bob around like wet rats. Human cannon ball after human cannon ball, bursting out of a tube and skittering across the water. God only knows why there aren't more broken necks at a place like this. They must carry a billion dollars in liability, that's for sure.

"I'm old," Mica says.

Evan swings his head around. Mica reaches for the water.

"How old do you think I am?" she asks.

"Twenty-six," Evan offers. Mica scoffs.

"Try thirty-eight," she says.

Thirty-eight? Jesus. Those carrot sticks and sit-ups really work.

"Listen," Mica says. "Can you hear it? Tick-tick-tick. That's my biological clock."

She takes Evan's hand and holds it to her breast.

"Feel," she says.

He can feel her heartbeat. Or is it his own? He doesn't know. But he definitely feels blood pounding through his ears. He feels tight. Suddenly overheated. Suddenly confused. Please, please, please. Please let this not be a seizure. He hasn't called Dr. Melon. He's been driving. He's been doing all the wrong things. Please, God. Please.

"I don't want to put pressure on you, Evan. I know how guys are. As soon as you mention something like this, they take off. But you're different. You aren't afraid of me. And I'm not talking right away, anyway. Just soon. At some point soon. We can have fun now. Tons of fun. Trust me, I'm full of fun. But soon. I have to know if there's a possibility, at least, because I'm getting old."

Evan takes his hand away from Mica's chest. He looks at her with glassy eyes.

"Are you okay?" she asks.

She puts the back of her hand to his forehead.

"You've been in the sun too long," she declares. "You should go inside."

Evan nods in agreement.

"You go to the lockers and take a warm shower, okay? Don't take a cold one, it could shock your system."

Right. We definitely don't want to shock the system right now. Right now we want to calm the system.

"I'll find Dean," she says. "When you're done, go into the entry area where we bought the tickets. It's air-conditioned in there. Okay?"

Okay. Right. Good.

Get to the showers. Evan can manage that. Get to the air-conditioning. Get home. Get some weed. Get some sleep. Sure. He can handle all that. No problem. He feels for his Medic Alert bracelet. He turns it around his wrist. He has a fleeting inclination to show it to Mica as she walks off toward the pools, point to it to let her see it; maybe then she would look out for erratic behavior, maybe she would be aware of the possibilities. But she wouldn't know what to do. He's never briefed her on what to do. He's never briefed anyone. Almost nobody knows. They all do the wrong things.

He walks slowly to the showers, and he doesn't feel half bad as he goes. Maybe it was that he'd been sitting so long. Activity, food, then becoming sedentary. Makes all your blood pool in your feet. Makes you light-headed. The heat, dehydration. Not a seizure. Just a little bout with heat stroke, which is okay. Anything but a seizure. Anything.

THE PATTERN FOR Evan is this: he gets an aura. Sometimes it stops there, but not usually. Usually, it progresses to a simple partial seizure, a state in which he may act confused, lose his ability to talk (but not to follow a conversation), and he can quickly lose track of time. Usually, it stops there. On relatively rare occasions, he will have what is called a secondary generalized seizure, or a secondary grand mal. Usually, people who suffer from grand mal seizures do not suffer from simple partial seizures. They're different seizure disorders altogether. It's not often that they meet like they do in Evan's brain. Evan is one of the special few.

There is a benefit to having secondary generalized seizures, and that is that they are preceded by an aura, whereas primary generalized seizures—generally speaking—are not. In other words, Evan has time to pull over.

Not always, but a significant majority of the time, Evan's secondary generalized tonic-clonic seizures have "gone status." A status seizure is a repetitive loop, a string of seizures, a seizure that feeds into another seizure that feeds into another seizure until either the cycle is stopped by a massive dose of drugs, or the body finally gives out and dies. Evan has never died, but he stands much closer to the edge of death than most.

SOMETIMES, PEOPLE WITH simple partial seizures act drunk and confused. Sometimes they are arrested for drunk driving. They don't know what they're doing. They don't know why they've been arrested. In some states, if you drive with an unsealed bottle of medication, whether or not it has been prescribed to you by your doctor, you can be arrested. The reason being, naturally, that the police officer has no idea what that particular prescription does to you. Maybe it's dangerous for you to be driving with that particular medication. Maybe you could get in an accident. So it's standard procedure to arrest, confiscate, detain, and wait until the next morning when the prescribing doctor can be contacted.

The problem is, often if the person with epilepsy could have one of those little white pills, he or she would be just fine. But the cops won't give it over. It's not policy.

Evan has never been arrested for suspicion of DUI. He has never been arrested with an unsealed bottle of medication in his car. He has never had an accident because of a seizure. That's because Evan knows when his seizures are coming, and he refuses to drive. He simply won't drive if he thinks there might be a problem. Because he's been hit by a car before. He knows how quickly it can ruin a life.

So as they walk toward the car in the parking lot, Evan hands his keys over to Mica.

"You all right?" she asks.

"Yes," Evan says. "I am now."

Liar.

She looks at him curiously.

He shakes his head and smiles. "The shower made me tired," he says.

So afraid to tell the people who matter. So afraid that someone will hate you for who you are. That's why you don't ever let anyone in. That's why you pushed Tracy away. Blame your parents if you want. Go on. It takes the pressure off you. You're still a liar. Dean and Mica: They don't know where your medication is. They don't know who your doctor is. They don't know how to contact your parents in case of your sudden death. You don't tell anyone anything. Blame it on conditioning. Blame it on how you were raised, if it makes you feel better. Go ahead and blame everyone else. Blame Charlie. But you know the rules. Keep the epileptics away from the pools. Keep the epileptics out of the cars. Keep the epileptics in nice cool zones where they don't sweat too much. You know that. The shower made me tired. *Right. You just didn't want to kill everyone but you were afraid to say it. You're talking to the girl who wants to bear your children, and you can't even tell her the truth. Afraid she'll leave. Shame on you. Shame on you, Evan Wallace. You don't deserve her and you don't deserve Dean. You are hereby condemned to a life of solitude. May you die alone, face down in a mud puddle, chewing on your tongue, nobody there to turn you over, nobody to stop you from breathing water.*

Shame on you.

E VAN GOES STRAIGHT for the bedroom and closes the door; he reaches for his cigar box.

His pot is gone. Where did he put it? Where's his pot? He must have stashed it somewhere else. In the sock drawer? Not there. In the bathroom? No. Maybe under the sink.

"Wow, that sun really knocked me out, too."

Evan whips his head around. Mica.

"What are you looking for?"

He can't tell her he's afraid he might have a seizure. It was easy to tell her about using pot to stave off seizures when he didn't really feel in danger of having one. But now that one's knocking at the door, he can't tell her. It's too real. She thinks she understands, but she doesn't. It's easy to say you understand and say you'll help out when you're needed, but when push comes to shove, they always back off. It's too much stress for a bystander to manage. A body beating itself up like that. It's not something people should see.

"I'm gonna lay down for a little bit. You want to snuggle with me?" Mica asks.

Yes. No. Not yet.

"Where's Dean?" Evan asks.

"In his room. He's tired, too. I didn't realize the sun was so strong east of the mountains. It just sucks the strength right out of you." She falls back onto the bed and rolls over. "Let's all take naps," she adds.

Not yet. Evan hustles into the living room. Did he leave it out? When was the last time he smoked? He needs to know where it is.

He tears through the living room, the kitchen. Nothing. It's okay, it's okay. He sits down at the kitchen table. It's somewhere. He probably put it in a shoe in the closet or something. Why would he even take it out of the cigar box? His medication is still there— three bottles, three pills, three times a day. But his pot. Well, pot is pot. It's replaceable. Still, though. It would be nice to know where it all was.

Evan relaxes a little. He crosses his arms on the table and rests his head. The house is dark and reminds him of the third grade when it got hot out and they would turn out the lights and make the kids put their heads down. Other kids disliked these rest periods, but Evan always liked putting his head down in class. There was something so peaceful about it. Cool and dark and quiet.

"She's here."

Evan lifts his head. Dean is standing in the foyer. Several bags are at his feet: a large suitcase, two duffles, and a giant bag full of hockey equipment.

"I guess I'm gonna go," he says.

"I'll call you tomorrow?" Evan asks, trying to hide the fact that he'd fallen asleep.

"Okay."

"And then we can decide, you know, how long you'll stay with her. You might like it."

"Where's Mica?"

"In the bedroom."

Dean trudges down the hall and sticks his head in the room.

"Bye, Mica," he says.

Evan can hear Mica rustling on the bed, trying to rouse herself.

"What?" she blurts out, confused.

Dean disappears into the room briefly, a little kiss on the cheek. What a good kid.

He reappears in the hallway. He opens the door and drags his bags out onto the porch, and, with a pained smile at Evan, he leaves the house, closing the door tightly after himself.

"Oh, man, I really passed out," Mica complains, entering the living room.

Evan is sitting on the couch watching tennis. Andre Agassi is playing someone else. If Evan had to be an athlete, he would have been Andre Agassi. He isn't sure why. The fallible hero. He and Evan are a lot alike.

Mica crosses over to Evan and gives him a big, enthusiastic kiss, which he does not return so enthusiastically.

"Where did Dean go?" she asks.

For the past fifteen minutes, since Dean left, Evan has been beating himself up about Dean's leaving and wondering how he was going to explain it to Mica. Now it's time.

"He went to visit his grandmother," Evan says.

"Is she okay?" Mica asks casually, walking into the kitchen and opening the refrigerator. "Do you have any fruit or vegetables around here?"

"Who?"

"Dean's grandmother. Is she sick or something? Why did he suddenly go see her?"

"Well, she's kind of sick."

"*Kind* of sick?" Mica questions, reappearing with an orange which she peels. "*What* kind of sick? Is it contagious? Will Dean catch it?"

Good question.

"I don't know," Evan answers.

Mica shrugs and eats a section of orange.

"Is he going to be home for dinner? I was going to cook. It's not too late, is it? Just point me toward a supermarket and I'll take care of it. You should rest. You look wasted." She walks past Evan to the foyer. "I remember passing a supermarket at some point." She picks up her handbag. "You okay?"

"No."

"What's wrong?"

Mica puts down her handbag and goes to Evan. She sits down next to him on the couch. She looks at him for a long time, but he doesn't look back. He watches the tennis match. Agassi is losing. Big surprise. He'll come back, though. He's a fighter.

"Come clean," Mica says softly.

Evan turns to her. He wants to confess, he wants absolution. So he tells her what happened between Dean and him.

"You *hit* Dean?" Mica asks, stupefied.

"I couldn't help it."

"Yes, you could have. You just don't do it. Didn't you say that his grandfather abused him?"

Evan nods.

"And so you thought it was appropriate to hit him?"

"You have to understand the situation," Evan says in his defense. "He was pushing so hard. He spit in my face."

"Oh, Evan," Mica shakes her head angrily. "There's something weird going on here. You're acting very strangely. You know why Dean spit in your face, and you know why he said he wanted to go to his grandmother, but you're denying it for some reason that I can't figure out."

"You're giving me too much credit," Evan replies dryly. "I play checkers, not chess."

Mica smiles at him oddly.

"That's funny, Evan."

"Why?"

"You've never played checkers in your life. You play bridge or some really sophisticated game with six decks of cards. You play a weird game with hidden hand signals to your partner. Evan, you're on a whole different level of game-playing."

Evan doesn't respond.

"You're too smart for this argument, Evan," Mica goes on. "You know exactly what was going on with Dean, don't you?"

"I don't think I do."

"Dean was testing you, Evan," Mica says. "He was testing you and you failed the test. He wanted you to make him stay. He wanted you to need him."

"He's going to see his grandmother for a few days, Mica, for Christ's sake. Can't you understand that he may have a good relationship with his grandmother?"

"What about his grand*father?*"

"What about him?"

"Evan, you turned him over to a pathological child-beater," she says harshly. "That's not what I would call a vacation."

"Frank isn't there any more," Evan says.

Mica raises her eyebrows; her eyes open wide.

"He moved to Idaho," Evan explains. "He and Ellen have separated."

Mica laughs bitterly and rises.

"What's happening here, Evan? Why are you telling me all of this after the fact? Why did you send Dean to visit his grandmother? Is it because of me? Is it because you're afraid you don't have a chance with me as long as you're living in Yakima with Dean? Is that it?"

No. Not at all.

"Because if that's what's going on here, you've got me so wrong you don't even deserve me."

That's not it at all.

"You may have only met Dean a few weeks ago, Evan, but as far as I'm concerned, you two are a pair, so you'd better just go over to Walla Walla and get him back, because if you don't, I'm not staying."

Mica waits for an answer.

"I can't do that," Evan finally says.

"Why not?"

Because none of this is meant to be. Dean, Mica. They are simply two more mirages in Evan's life. They don't really exist. He's been dreaming them the whole time.

"Why not?" she asks again.

Because, goddamn it, his entire life he's wanted all of one thing and he's never gotten it and now he wants it, even if it's just for a day, just for a few hours, he wants to feel it, to live it, he wants to know that in a different world, a parallel universe, one in which he left the muddy embankment a moment earlier, just sneaked by the chrome fender of the car, made it safely across the street and went home to eat dinner and laugh with his family at the table, in that universe he is a rock star, and in that universe, everything is different.

"Evan?"

Evan shakes his head.

"I have some business to attend to," he says coldly, detached. "In Seattle."

Mica doesn't move. Not an inch. But Evan would swear on his life that something about her changes; something gets very cool and calm inside her; she sinks a little lower to the ground.

"What kind of business?" she asks.

"Billy sent the demo to Template Records and they're interested. I have meetings. We have a gig at General Tso's on Wednesday."

Mica glares at Evan for a moment.

"So postpone it," she says.

"I can't."

"So take Dean with you."

"It's too important."

Mica frowns. Then she turns and marches away. When Evan catches up to her in the bedroom, she's shoving her clothes into her bag.

"Where are you going?" he asks stupidly.

"I'm not interested, Evan. I'm checking out."

"Why?"

She glares at him. "Are you joking?"

He watches her shove her clothes into the bag, jamming them with force, as if she were mad at the bag and the clothes. She stomps into the bathroom, reemerges a moment later with her travel kit.

"I just have some business to take care of, that's all," Evan says.

Mica doesn't acknowledge the comment.

"It's temporary. A cooling-off period."

She angrily zips her bag shut and looks up.

"You may be good at lying to yourself, Evan, but if you think it's working with me, you can forget it."

"What are you—"

"It's too perfect, Evan. Look at how it lays out. You wanted to give him back from the beginning, you only kept him because you were trying to protect him, and now that he's safe, you get rid of him. Then you tell me about it after the fact. I'm not stupid. You were afraid I would stop it. But I would never stop you from doing anything, Evan, because if I stopped you, you would hate me for it. So do what you want. Just don't count on me being a part of it. Goodbye."

"It's about the band!" Evan shouts. "I need a break so I can take care of the band. It's just about the band!"

"Bullshit, Evan. It's not about the band and you know it."

"It is!"

"Then tell me about the band, Evan. Tell me about the damn band. What's so great about the stupid band that's worth trading your son for?"

"I didn't trade him. We're taking a break."

"You're lying, Evan! Tell me the truth. I deserve that. You were hoping to ditch Dean on his grandmother, go off to rock superstardom with The Last, carve out your place in the Rock and Roll Hall of Fame, and fuck me on off weekends. That's the truth, isn't it, Evan?"

Evan flinches. She's cutting a little close. She caught flesh on that one.

"Fuck off," he fires back, out of ammunition, out of his league, fresh out of trump cards, just needing some power shots in the form of anger to hold her off.

"Do you have any idea how it works?" Mica snaps. "Do you have any grasp of the fundamentals of this business that you're so desperate to be a part of? Billy says something one day, the next day everyone is calling you, and three days later the phone is dead and you're nothing. You're nowhere. It's called hype, Evan. Have you listened to what these guys are saying? Do you hear how desperate these people sound, these little people trying to make money off of you? Evan?"

Evan doesn't respond. He hates what she's saying, and he hates her for saying it.

"I can think of five bands off the top of my head that would love to have you, Evan. *Five* bands. One of them—*maybe*—one of them might go someplace. And every one of those bands is twenty times better than The Last."

Evan burns inside. He wants to believe that maybe things are different with this band. Maybe things don't fit into Mica's mold so easily. Maybe this is the exception. And he hates Mica because she doesn't see that The Last has a chance, that Evan has a chance.

"You want to be a rock star, Evan?" Mica asks. "Let me put you with some people who are real musicians. Let me hook you up with a band that isn't worried about how quickly their buzz is going to die. A band with integrity. Then you can go get Dean. You can have Dean, you can have me, you can have your stardom. It just might take a little longer, that's all."

Evan seethes.

"You know," he hisses at her, "your little 'been there, done that' attitude really makes me want to puke."

Mica catches her breath. It not so much what Evan said, but how he said it, looking out from under his eyebrows, his eyes dark, his face as emotionless as a serial killer's.

"You should save that shit for someone else," Evan continues, "because *I* know the truth. I've been there. I've had a top ten single, if you remember, and it turned to shit in a heartbeat. So don't tell me to be patient. I've been waiting eleven years for another shot. You think I'm going to pass this one up? Well, fuck you."

Mica doesn't speak; she stares at Evan, shocked by his rant.

"This is my chance, damn it," he yells at her. "This is my chance and I'm taking it!"

"What's wrong with you?" Mica asks.

"I'll tell you what's wrong with me. I've been to the emergency room more times in my life than you've been to the dentist. All my life, people have told me what to do, what's good for me, what will make me better, what will make my life easier. And you know what? Everything that they say is what will make my life easier for *them*, not for me. Do you have any idea what I'm talking about? Every day that I wake up alive I thank God that I didn't die in my sleep. Do you have any idea how that changes your perceptions? I'm the fucking Elephant Man, okay? And I'm living my life now. And if Dean has to stay with his grandmother another year or two years or five years, and after that I can have a nice respectful adult relationship with him, then great. It's better than what we had, which was nothing. And the reason we had nothing was because they took him away from me, yet more people deciding things about my life without consulting me. Do you have any idea what I'm talking about? Do you have one clue? Or in your sheltered lit-tle famous musician's world do you think the worst thing that could ever happen to you is your father dies of cancer?"

He stops. His heart is pounding, he's out of breath. He sucks air across his dry lips and over his heavy tongue. His eyes are burning.

Mica moves toward him, tries to hug him, but he steps back.

"What do you want?" he demands.

"I'll stay," she says. "You're all over the place. You need me to help you. I'll help you."

She reaches for him again, but he knocks her arms away.

"Get away from me," he snaps.

"Evan—"

"Get away."

"I understand," she says. "It's not about the band. I know. It's about so much more."

"Get away! It *is* about the band!"

"Evan, it's okay, Evan."

"It's *not* okay!" he shouts. "It's not okay! Leave me alone! I don't want you here. I don't want you around. Get out of here, now!"

"Evan—"

"Go!"

He lunges at her like a crazy man. She flinches.

"I don't understand," she says, suddenly vulnerable.

"Get out!"

He grabs her bag off the bed; with her following, he marches to the door, opens it and tosses the bag out onto the lawn.

"What are you doing?" she asks.

"Go!"

"What's the matter with you? This isn't really you."

"No, Mica, this *is* me," he barks at her. "This is the real me. Get a good look. Ugly and mean and selfish. Now get out of here and leave me alone!"

She shakes her head and starts to go, but she stops. She turns back. She waits for him to look at her, waits for him to say something. But he doesn't acknowledge her.

He rubs his face with his hands and pulls at his hair. He's sick and tired of everyone wanting things from him. He's tired of disappointing people.

After a moment, she picks up her bag.

"You can treat me like this," she says. "I don't care. But Dean . . ."

"Dean's got nothing to do with it," Evan counters.

"Yes he does, Evan. He's got everything to do with it."

She smiles sadly and leaves.

HE DOESN'T TAKE anything but his wallet and his car keys. He knows he shouldn't, but he does it anyway: he gets in his car and drives to Seattle.

E VAN'S MOTHER CALLED only once while he was away. Had things been normal between them, she would have called at least eight times.

He opens the windows of his apartment and inhales the familiar smells. There's nothing like returning home on a midsummer's night. A few kite-flyers in Gasworks Park hold out against the encroaching dusk; soon it will be too dark for them to see the colors of their kites. A steady stream of sailboats cruise eastward toward the cut, heading home after an afternoon on the Sound, their passengers trying to shake off the euphoria of the day, trying to get a handle on the reality of bagging the sails, battening down the hatches, putting the kids to bed, giving the wife a quick lay before a few hours of sleep and another long, hot week of bad traffic and boring meetings. Already looking forward to good weather the following weekend, maybe a regatta or a leisurely sail up through Deception Pass and onward to Roche Harbor for a candlelight dinner and an overnight at anchor.

He calls his mother. She answers on the third ring.

"Where have you been?" she asks.

"In Yakima."

"Oh."

A long pause settles in between them.

"Where are you now?" she eventually asks.

"Here. In Seattle."

"Oh? We'd love to meet your son."

Yes, they would. Of course, they would.

"Do you have any time?" she asks.

"I'm pretty busy," he says. "I have a lot of meetings this week, and then I have to head back to Yakima."

"Oh."

Another pause, this one shorter.

"He isn't here, anyway," Evan says. "He's staying with his grandmother in Walla Walla."

"I see."

It's like trying to talk from inside a black hole: the gravity pulls all the words back inside before they can get out.

"Well, when it's convenient, we'd love to meet him," she says. "We'd be happy to drive to wherever you are . . ."

But the rest of her idea is sucked back inside by the gravitational pull.

". . . and your girlfriend, too," she manages to get out.

It's hard, but she's putting forth a great effort. She deserves a reward.

"Yeah," Evan cheers up a bit. "Maybe next weekend."

"That would be nice," Louise responds in kind.

"We could come over and Dad could barbecue or something."

"Oh, Evan. Dad would love to."

"I could call Charlie," Evan goes on, feeding on his own enthusiasm, "tell him to come with Allison and Eric. A family reunion."

"That sounds like so much fun," Louise agrees. "I'm sure Charlie would love to come."

"Kind of a weird family reunion, though," Evan says. "Charlie, with his traditional family. Me, with my non-traditional family."

"A family is a family, Evan. Tradition doesn't matter."

"Kind of pathetic, though."

"Evan," Louise says firmly, "you are my son. In your whole life, you have never been traditional."

"I guess not." Evan laughs weakly.

"Are you going to call Charlie and ask him? It would be better if you called, so he doesn't think I'm forcing anything."

"I'll call now."

"We love you, Evan."

Of course they do.

EVAN SITS BY the phone for an hour, thinking about how absurd it was for him to offer a family reunion when he has no family at all. Not even a non-traditional one. He cast aside both his son and his girlfriend before they had really started. So what, then, is this mirage of a family barbecue that he has concocted?

He could take it a step further. He could call Charlie, get all enthusiastic, convince Charlie to bring his wife and kid over, and, a few days later, they could all stand around in the backyard eating grilled skirt steak sandwiches and rosemary roasted potatoes and arugula salad with oranges, fennel and shaved Parmesan. But there would be one problem. Dean and Mica wouldn't be there.

Some reunion.

THE NEXT TWO days are difficult for Evan. He sits alone in his apartment, practicing his guitar obsessively. He doesn't go outside; he has food delivered. His phone rings periodically and he always lets the machine pick it up. Generally, it's Lars calling to make some amendment to the Wednesday plans; Wednesday is the intended day of wine and roses.

Then a strange thing happens: his brother calls.

"Hey, Ev," Charlie says into the machine. "Mom said something about a barbecue this weekend? Listen, I want to apologize for the way I acted the last time we talked. You just really surprised me with that—"

Evan picks up.

"I'm here," he says.

"Oh, yeah? Screening?"

"Always."

"But you've got to pick up for an apology from me," Charlie jokes. "Right?"

Evan laughs with him. It almost feels good to laugh.

"Anyway," Charlie says, "sorry about the way I acted. I should have been more understanding."

"I dropped it on you like a bomb," Evan says. "You didn't have much choice."

"I could have done better, but I was totally stressed out that night. It's killing me, Ev. It's killing me. This economy. Things are really tight at the firm. I was supposed to make partner by now; now I might be on the short list of who goes, you know? Plus Eric . . . and Allison is sicker than a dog—"

"Chuck, Chuck. We were talking about *me.*"

"Right. Sorry. Look, I think it's great that you've got a kid. I mean, I wish I knew about it earlier."

"Don't we all."

"Well, Mom and Dad do, that's for sure," Charlie says.

"I'm not so sure."

"Oh, no, Ev. That's why I'm calling. I mean, Mom is all shaken up. Dad is too, but he would never show it. They're really upset about how you guys left off. They didn't mean to give the impression that—"

"Yes, they did," Evan snaps. "They meant to give every impression they gave."

"Yeah," Charlie agrees reluctantly. "Well, Mom is all excited for this family-reunion-barbecue thing. I guess it's Saturday? She's all freaked out. She wants to know if Dean has any food allergies she should know about."

"No," Evan says.

"Well. So. I'm anxious to meet him. Does he look like you?"

"Spit and image."

"Really. That's great. Okay, then. See you Saturday, right?"

"We'll be there," Evan says. Then, hit with a sudden inspiration, he adds, "I actually have a gig tomorrow night at General Tso's. You want to come?"

"Uh . . ." Charlie hesitates. "What time? I probably have to work late."

"We're scheduled for nine-thirty, which means ten."

"Oh, not until ten?"

"We're opening for someone who's opening for someone. It's kind of an audition gig. A big indie label is watching us."

"Really? That's great."

"So, you want to come?"

"Um, look, I'll try to get away . . ."

"It's all right. Don't worry."

"No, I'll try to get away. But I can't guarantee anything."

"I'll put you on the guest list," Evan says, confident that his brother will never show. "Look for me."

THAT EVENING, EVAN leaves his apartment for the first time in almost forty-eight hours to go for a drive. He doesn't have direction or a goal when he leaves, but one soon finds him. He ends up at his parents' house in Magnolia.

It's obvious what he's doing there, so he doesn't fight it. He lets himself in and finds his parents upstairs in their room getting ready to go out to dinner, something they do well and often. They attend social events. Benefits, awards ceremonies. Their formal attire is always pressed, their minds always filled with relevant topics for conversation. They welcome Evan's visit, but they're busy getting ready.

Evan sits on the edge of their bed stroking the matted fur of Ralphy, who's looking a little the worse for wear. Louise sits at the vanity in her spacious bathroom, carefully applying the elements of her makeup. Carl is walking around in a T-shirt and briefs with his black tux socks on, debating whether to wear the wing collar or the standard.

It brings back memories for Evan. Memories of his childhood, when his parents would go out and he and Charlie would sit on their bed, watching them get ready. There was always something exciting about watching his parents prepare for a formal event. The layers of clothing, the attention to detail. Evan would insert one of his father's cufflinks, Charlie would insert the other. They would take turns with the studs. They would check the back of his braces to make sure they weren't turned. Louise would walk around in her slip, her lips painted bright red. Charlie would zip up her dress. And when they were all ready, they would stand together, and Carl would ask: "How do we look?" And Charlie and Evan would reply in unison: "Like Mom and Dad in fancy clothes." And they would all laugh.

"Put in my cufflinks?" Carl asks.

Evan looks up. His father is standing in front of him with his tux shirt on, holding out his hands. Evan takes the cufflinks and slips them into the slots.

"Thanks. Any movement on that record deal?"

Evan shakes his head. He doesn't want to tell them anything until the deal is done. "We're kind of bogged down right now."

"Why?" Carl asks.

"We're just bogged. We're stuck in a bog. No real reason."

Carl nods understandingly. "A shitty business, eh? Ah. All businesses are shitty, I suppose." Carl slips into his slacks, reaches for his suspenders.

"Say," he continues. "If you ever want to come to one of these galas, grab that girlfriend of yours and we'll double-date. I hate these things. I don't even know what this one is for. The opera, I think. Or maybe some theater company raising money for a new theater. They're all the same. Are my braces straight?"

He turns his back to Evan.

"Straight as an arrow," Evan says.

"Clean as a whistle," Carl replies. He takes his bow tie off the bed and loops it over his neck. He stands before the dressing mirror next to the closet.

"You tie it like a shoelace," he mutters as if he isn't quite convinced it's that easy, even after all these years.

Evan watches him and is taken by how gentle they all are with each other—he, his father, his mother—considering how close they were to disaster at their last meeting. Carl has had his stitches removed; the wound looks good, tucked neatly against his hairline. No mention is made of their last, violent words. The white elephant, Dean, is nowhere in sight. Time is the longest distance between two places.

Louise emerges from the bathroom wearing a dressing gown.

"We're looking forward to Saturday," she says. "Charlie called me a little while ago and told me you'd invited them. What did you say your girlfriend's name was?"

"Mica."

"How do you spell that?"

"M-I-C-A."

"What a beautiful name."

And then she does something strange. She reaches out and touches Evan's cheek lightly.

"Such a pretty boy," she says faintly, almost inaudibly.

She smiles a closed-lipped smile at Evan. She looks better when she smiles with her lips apart, but she's ashamed of her teeth. She'd grown up poor and with crooked teeth, so, as an adult, she'd trained herself to smile with her lips together. Evan feels a little bad for her and her smile. She could have that corrected. They make adult braces. They're invisible.

"Your father's going to cook a butterflied leg of lamb on the grill. Won't that be nice?"

She goes into her closet, a large walk-in, big enough for a small family of immigrants.

Carl grimaces and mutters to himself: "Tie it like a shoelace, goddamn it."

Louise reappears in a moment wearing a slip.

"Allison's going to bring her macaroni salad. I love her salad. And I'll make vegetables, or a green salad—would a green salad make too many salads?"

"Who cares?" Carl groans. "Do I have a clip-on?"

"A surgeon who can't tie his own tie," Louise frets. She takes charge of the silken ends. "Does Dean drink soda, or juice? Does he have a favorite dessert? I remember you and Charlie used to love mud pies from Baskin-Robbins. Every night in the summer. Every night. I wonder if they still make them."

The tie is done, neat and tight.

"Thank you, dear," Carl says, relieved, kissing her cheek.

"I don't think Dean's coming on Saturday," Evan says, and the rides in Fantasyland grind to a halt, the children cry, Carl and Louise stare at Evan.

"Really?" Louise asks. "Why not?"

Good question. Why not?

"He wanted to stay with his grandmother in Walla Walla."

They look at him hard for a moment. Then Carl breaks the spell: "I can understand that," he says. "The boy is going through an awful lot."

"Yes," Louise agrees. "But I was so looking forward to seeing him. Charlie says he looks just like you. When is he returning from his visit?"

"Well," Evan says, "he may be staying with his grandmother from now on. It might be better for everyone. She's willing to live in Tracy's old house so Dean can go to his old school. I can go visit whenever I like; I can even have my own room there. And he can spend holidays here, and a few weeks in the summer. We could go on a family vacation together. But I'm not sure that I'm up for taking him full-time. You said so yourselves."

Ah, the white elephant emerges from the bushes. How long would they have gone on ignoring their previous encounter? How long would they have denied the reality of having expelled Evan from the family. Who knows?

"It sounds like the most sensible thing, Evan," Carl declares, tugging at his tie. "The best for everyone involved."

"Yes, I suppose so," Ellen says. She disappears again to finish dressing.

That's it? No protest? No regret? A second of thought, and then it's like cutting off the foot to save the leg—only the amputee will feel the lingering ache of the missing toes.

"She seems motivated," Carl says, "and devoted. I think you've made the right decision."

Evan laughs to himself. Everything in his life has been done only to gain the approval of his father, and now that he has it, he can't rejoice. How can he? He is made sick by their impassiveness. They tie everything neatly in a bundle and stick it in the closet. It's all about reducing the amount of trouble.

Carl slips on his jacket, buttons it. He looks at himself in the mirror.

"But don't you think you could prevail upon his grandmother to bring him over for a visit this weekend?" he asks. "She's welcome also, of course. We could have a real party." He meets Evan's eyes through the mirror, and for maybe the first time in Evan's life, he sees vulnerability in his father's eyes.

"I'm not sure," Evan says. "I'd have to ask."

"It would mean a tremendous amount to your mother. She's been looking forward to this barbecue since you mentioned it. I can't tell you how much she talks about it. She desperately wants to meet your son."

"What about you?" Evan asks. "Do you want to meet him?"

Carl turns to face Evan, surprised by the question, or maybe he didn't hear it at all. But it doesn't matter because Louise steps between them: she's ready.

"How do we look?" she asks, taking Carl's arm.

How do they look? Like angels, like demons, like torturers, like saints. How do they look? Like his parents, only older.

"Like Mom and Dad in fancy clothes," Evan says.

Louise glides across the room with a smile on her face—is it a smile that disguises her feelings?—and kisses his forehead.

"There's food in the refrigerator," she says.

"Turn on the alarm when you leave," Carl adds. "And could you do me a favor and take Ralphy out and lock him in the kitchen when you go?"

They slip out of the room and out of the house.

Evan takes Ralphy for a run in the yard. The moon is full and bright. It lights up the entire Sound. Ralphy joyfully, relentlessly chases after a madrona stick that Evan throws.

Why is he disappointed with the outcome of the night? What did he expect? Did he really think they would react like Mica, that they would yell at him and tell him to go get Dean back?

No. He expelled Dean, and then he expelled the person who told him to retrieve Dean. That leaves him with the people who told him he never should have had Dean in the first place. It's just like Mica said: it lays out perfectly; the way is clear; he can now go and become famous, like Tracy wanted.

He throws the stick for Ralphy until Ralphy finally gets tired and starts eating rocks. Then he takes the old dog inside and gives him some water. He kisses Ralphy's nose. Ralphy looks up at Evan just once, then falls asleep on his soft, round pillow.

Evan watches Ralphy sleep for a few minutes, locks the kitchen gate, and turns on the alarm on his way out.

WHEN EVAN CLIMBS out of the taxi in the parking lot, Lars howls like a banshee and rushes at him. He grabs Evan's head with his hands, huge and clammy like slabs of beef, and plants a kiss firmly on Evan's lips.

"You are the man. *You* are. Nobody else, baby. Just you."

Lars is glowing with excitement, and he's bigger than Evan remembered. Only away a week and Lars has grown a couple of inches. His stick-straight polar-bear hair is short and standing at weird angles. Definitely styled. His cheeks are red. He looks like he's dropped a couple of pounds.

"Are you on a diet?" Evan asks.

"Yes. Absolutely. The camera adds ten pounds. I've been starving myself since last week. What do you think of my hair?"

"It's nice."

"My mom sent me to her hairdresser, some twinkle-toes at the Lake Forest Park Mall. But he knows how to use the gel, right?"

Lars smiles down at Evan. "You came," he says.

Evan smiles back. Yes, he did. He put everything aside, his foundering relationship with Mica, his floundering relationship with

Dean. All aside for this. So he could stand in the barren parking lot of The Sound Factory at ten-thirty A.M. with Lars kissing him.

"Everyone's inside," Lars says. "Let's go."

Inside they go. Evan has his guitar and amp for the beginning of the day's events. The plan calls for them to play for an hour or so, for the benefit of a writer from *Entertainment Weekly* who's up from L.A. to do an article on Peter Buck, but was willing to stop by as a special favor to Mel. Then they'll junket together to a slate of meetings and introductions with key players in the Seattle record biz, then on to a photo shoot and the gig.

They quietly greet Sybil, who looks a little dazed to be behind the reception desk at such an early hour, but who manages to form a mousy smile at Evan as they pass. They march straight to Studio B, where Rod, Tony, Mel Kidd and a sweet little thing of a girl in a teeny, sheer dress await.

Mel, the precocious president of Template Records, is a slight man, with a full head of dark curly hair and perpetual razor stubble on his face. To call him a man might be a stretch. He isn't *actually* a man—he's only twenty-four—but he plays at being a man very well. And he certainly *looks* like a man when he wears his too-cool black suit and floppy collared shirt from agnès b. (sans tie) as he wields an awfully large expense account around the Seattle music scene wooing pre-emergent bands with tales of his prowess. He knew about the demise of Soundgarden before it demised. He knew about the death of Kurt Cobain before he died. He knew about the birth of Eddie Vedder before he was born. He's a magus man. He's the one who brought the myrrh. He's the one who sold his watch, cut off his hair.

"Evbee!" he shouts enthusiastically. Evan winces. He's only met Mel in passing twice, so he would hardly call them close, so what's with the "Evbee?" Billy is the only one who ever calls Evan "Evbee."

"Hi, Mel," Evan replies with a smile. "Good to see you again."

"Lars told me you were holing up in Yakima. A little spiritual revitalizing. Honing your edge. Well, welcome back to civilization. How's everything? How's your son? How's that girlfriend of yours? I bet she rocks your world, huh? What a body! I heard she's forty-three."

"She isn't," Evan says.

"*I* heard she's a lesbian," Lars adds with a phony grin.

"She isn't," Evan grins back.

"I heard she's fucking Keith Richards," Rod says.

Evan glares at him, not knowing how exactly to respond to that one.

"Evbee, this is Tumi," Mel says, indicating the waif of a girl in the corner. "From *Entertainment Weekly*."

The girl steps forward.

"Nice to meet you, Evan," she purrs.

"Likewise," Evan replies.

"Delightful," Mel says with a wink at Evan. "Well, you people all have work to do," he announces. "I'll be on my way for now. Remember, the van is picking you up in one hour to take you to lunch. Don't be late. I'll see you at the gig. Just leave your gear here, I'll make sure it all arrives at the club and is set up for you."

He pauses flamboyantly, as if he expects applause or a fanfare or something.

"I've done my job here," he adds, when he realizes he isn't getting whatever it is he wants. "Now you people: make magic!" And he rushes out of the room.

There's silence in his wake, then giggles.

"What a freak." Rod laughs, shaking his head.

And then suddenly everyone is all over Evan. Rod and Tony giving Evan hugs, welcoming him back. Tumi hitting him up with a couple of quick questions. Lars smacking his drums as Evan tries to answer her, which, of course he can't do very well because he can't hear himself talk with the drums beating. Tumi is snapping pictures of the band—but concentrating on Evan, mostly—with a camera that's so big it seems to swallow her face every time she puts it to her eye. And suddenly, before Evan is really ready, a jam starts, just like the old days, the early days of the band when they didn't really know each other and they actually listened to what everyone else was playing. They just start up, which is maybe the most surprising thing to Evan. That Rod and Tony are making eye contact with Evan. That they *smile* at him. Which, he figures, has to be because Tumi is there, recording it all for posterity. You have to present a unified front to the media, after all.

And all of this sudden energy in the room, all of it, Lars throwing himself around behind the drums, Rod jumping up and down as he plays, and Tumi dancing to the music like some kind of eighteen-year-old groupie (she whirls and whirls and tosses her hair around her face and the guys wiggle their eyebrows at each other because when she whirls her short dress blows up and you can see her underwear), all of this instant energy makes Evan forget what's been on his mind for the last sixty hours, since he threw Mica out, since he cast Dean overboard, that while he's in Seattle to be with his band, he is really very much alone.

Evan forgets it all. How numb the drive was from Yakima; the sense of an ending without closure. How ugly he'd felt standing at the window in his apartment—his grandfather's apartment—looking out at Lake Union as Dean had done not long before. How he had woken up Monday morning yearning to go sailing with Dean somewhere, exploring somewhere. How he wonders, every minute, where Dean is and what he's doing and if he's all right; fearful that today of all days, Dean may decide to go Rollerblading without his helmet, he may trip and fall, his head may kiss the corner of a curb, his life may be altered forever.

All that is forgotten.

As they pile into a ratty, blue passenger van, Tumi rubbing her naked thigh against Evan's jeans and smiling at him slyly, as the van bursts up Airport Way toward town, toward the "M" Hotel and lunch with Sally Roebucks, publicist *extraordinaire*, as they adjourn their meeting with Sally to meet with Sam Max, the flashy video director who somehow hitched a ride on a rocket going straight to the stars and was completely hot and completely famous even though he had done little more than make a silly short film that Roman Polanski said was too daring to show in the United States and therefore had been shown absolutely everywhere in the United States. As they are photographed by Philip, the famous rock-and-roll photographer who spends much of the afternoon recreating images from the greatest album covers of his time, which he claims was the seventies, although he seems to be too old to be hip as recently as the seventies. ("A millennial version of *Abbey Road*." "A millennial version of *Who's Next*." "A millennial version of . . .")

As the day flashes by him. As the wheels of the van squeal around corners, zig and zag past Hondas and Suburus and Volkswagen Jettas, driven by bland people with beards and Patagonia shirts. As the Frappaccinos are guzzled, as a heavy buzz of sugar and fat and caffeine settle on the group. As people talk and point while Tumi snaps pictures, flashing away helplessly, trying somehow to alter nature's giant flashbulb in the sky. As his dream of rock stardom sits in his lap like a warm orb, a big ball of heat, Tumi sticking her tongue in his ear while the fun-house faces of Lars and Tony and Rod grin at him and laugh and laugh.

"Hey!"

Evan looks up. He shakes off his daze.

"Want some chowder or something?"

What? Lars. They're parked outside of Ivar's on the waterfront.

"What time is it?" Evan asks.

"Seven. You okay?"

Okay? Sure. Fine.

"I must have fallen asleep," Evan says.

"Really? I told the guys you were meditating."

"Where is everyone?" Evan asks, suddenly realizing the van is empty.

"We're out on the dock getting some food before the gig. We're over there. Want something?"

"Yeah," Evan mumbles, sitting up in his seat.

"I'll get you something. Fried clams? Chowder? New England or Manhattan?"

Evan looks past Lars to the sky, a blue sheet, Seattle Blue. My kids would love a crayon that color, yes they would. Giant white gulls diving down, landing on the pilings, eating french fries. A sign: KEEP CLAM.

"Ev?"

"Yeah. That'd be great. Thanks."

Lars shrugs and walks away.

Evan gathers himself together.

What happened? He'd fallen asleep? Or was it a seizure? Did he miss his big day because of a seizure? Not just one. Not a big one, anyway. A long string of little ones. Simple partials. A lot of ins and outs, snippets, a day of broken fragments that he doesn't really remember. Just fuzziness. Images. Why can't he remember?

He starts to climb out of the van, but he can't manage to get himself out. He sees Lars with a tray of food. Lars points at Evan, then at the food, then at a table where everyone sits. Evan sinks back in his seat. Where is Mica? Where is Dean? He sinks lower and he feels reality settle on him like a crushing weight, pinning him to the upholstery. His day. His dream. What he had wanted. None of it is his. It isn't his because he has no one to give it to.

Because nobody knows. Because he hasn't told anyone.

Because he is so tired of it. Because he is just too tired of it to go on.

THEY WANDER TOGETHER into General Tso's, the hip Capitol Hill nightclub, feeling somehow more powerful when taken as a group, as a band, as the Next Big Thing. Evan is feeling better, and the sudden camaraderie is nice to have. Rod seems to have embraced Evan. Maybe only temporarily, but it's a start. Tony is relaxed. Lars is nothing short of joyous at the events of the day and of his rosy future. Tumi is the lone dissenter, feeling disappointed at Evan's lack of response to her advances; upon entering General Tso's, she quickly excuses herself and begins prowling for her friends, many of whom are in attendance, or so she boasts.

They work their way backstage, down a hallway, and to a large, dim green room that smells of yeasty beer. Everything is there, just as Mel promised. All the accoutrements of fame. Chubby men in black jeans and T-shirts to help them with their gear. Slender girls in tight black pants and tank tops to provide them with bottled water. Trays of cold cuts. Bottles of vodka. Other musicians in various stages of readiness.

A muscular guy with a gray crewcut and reading glasses approaches them, looking at his clipboard.

"You The Lost?" he asks.

"The *Last*," Tony corrects.

"Right. You've got twenty to set up your shit, so you'd better bust a nut."

"Is Mel here?" Lars asks.

Clipboard Guy peers over his glasses.

"Who the fuck is Mel? This is my fucking backstage. Your shit's already out there. You've got twenty."

He turns and walks away.

Lars, Tony, and Rod shrug at each other and head to the stage. Evan follows and looks out toward the audience. The room is filling steadily; it's a large space and it holds a lot of people. Evan tries to ignore them as he sets up his effects pedals; the sound guy mikes his amp, Evan takes his guitar out of its case, slips the strap over his head, tunes, and he's done. Ready to rock. Lars is working fast, and he's got two guys helping him with his drums. Tony and Rod are wound up tight and burning their energy, fiddling with crap. And Evan doesn't want to be near any of them.

He goes back to the green room and notices a roadie in one corner smoking a joint. He goes over and bums a hit. Then another.

"Big crowd out there," Evan observes.

"No shit."

"I don't even know who we're opening for," Evan says.

"Foo Fighters," the roadie says.

"Seriously?"

"There's Dave, right over there."

He points with his chin. Sure enough, Dave Grohl is standing by the buffet table, eating a melon ball.

"*Ev.*"

Evan looks around. His brother, Charlie, walks up. What a surprise.

"Hey, Chuck. We're about to go on. Glad you could make it."

"Yeah."

Charlie's eyes are bloodshot. He seems upset.

"You okay?" Evan asks.

Charlie covers his mouth with his hand and breathes in. Then he quickly slaps his cheek several times.

"Yeah," he says with forced enthusiasm. "Great!"

"What's up, Chuck?"

"Nothing. When are you going on?"

"In a minute. Are you drunk?"

"Drunk?" Aha. He's been caught. "Maybe a little."

"You don't get drunk, Chuck. What's wrong?"

"Nothing. We'll talk about it later. You have a show."

Charlie looks around nervously. There are maybe fifty people backstage, tons of sound equipment, cables everywhere. A girl in a tank top walks by, Evan catches her eye.

"How long until The Last?" he asks her.

She looks at her watch and shrugs. "Now," she says.

"I've gotta go in a minute," Evan says to Charlie. "Is something wrong?"

"I got fired," Charlie says.

"Oh, shit. When?"

"Four hours ago."

"Why?"

"I don't know. I told you, I was up for review. I mean, I've been there for seven years. They were supposed to offer me partner, right? So I finally get called in and they tell me they can't afford to make me a partner even though I deserve it, and rather than make me hang around for a couple more years, they want to let me go find my place with another firm."

"Oh, shit. What are you going to do?"

"I don't know. I mean, I'm totally overextended on the house; the contractor started working on the basement last week and the sprinkler guy just finished and I owe him money, and Allison is on some kick to get all the lead paint removed from the win-dowsills, which costs a fortune. I put down a fucking grand on a car that's coming next month but I won't be able to afford it, and now I get shitcanned with nothing but a three-month package and a To-Whom-It-May-Concern, Charlie-is-a-Nice-Guy letter. I'm fucked, Ev. I'm totally fucked."

"Jeez, Chuck, I'm really sorry."

"Yeah. I didn't want to tell you before you went on—"

"No. That's okay."

"I didn't want to bring you down."

"I can handle it, Chuck. It's only money, after all. It's not like Eric is really sick or something. It's just money."

"Yeah," Charlie agrees, seeing the light. "You're right. It's just money. But if we have to sell the house, Allison will kill me."

"You could always move in with Mom and Dad."

"Promise me you'll slit my throat if that happens."

They laugh.

"Hey, I got an offer on Grandpa's apartment," Evan says. "If you need some cash quick, I can help out."

"You're selling your apartment?" Charlie asks. "Why?"

"A lot of reasons," he says with a shrug. "I was thinking about Grandpa a while ago. The way he died. You know."

"How do you mean?"

"I'm not sure," Evan says, struggling with his thoughts. "The way he predicted his death."

He looks to Charlie for confirmation, for recognition. There is none.

"The week before he died," Evan explains, "he asked me if he had anything I wanted. Like he knew he was going to die."

Charlie squints at Evan and shakes his head. The girl walks by again. "I think your band is looking for you," she says.

"What's so surprising about that?" Charlie asks.

"He *knew* he was going to die," Evan says again.

"Right."

"Right," Evan repeats. "There's something weird about it, almost magical. How did he *know*?"

"Well," Charlie says, slightly baffled, "you knew he had cancer, right?"

"What?" Evan is stopped dead. Stunned. "He had cancer?"

"The doctor told him he'd have to start chemo or he'd be dead in six months. So Grandpa called Dad, he told Dad it was time, Dad understood and prescribed him the medication, Grandpa took it. He died."

"He fell and hit his head," Evan says.

"Right," Charlie agrees, "*after* he took the pills. It was actually good that he fell and hit his head. Everyone thought he died because of a stroke or something. No one would have thought Dad had given him pills to do it. You know who signed the death certificate, don't you? Dad did."

Evan feels suddenly removed from anything familiar. Like he's been lifted out of his body, pulled into the air by some tractor beam. Like he's hanging above the earth. He looks around. Lars, Rod, and Tony are on the steps that lead up to the stage. Lars beckons him. Evan holds up one finger. The show is about to begin.

"You okay?" Charlie asks.

No. Nothing is what it seems. That's not okay.

"I'm fine. I just have to go."

He isn't angry. He isn't even surprised. Grandpa committed suicide. It makes sense. Knowing Grandpa, it makes perfect sense. But why didn't he tell Evan? Why didn't anyone tell Evan? Charlie knew everything, but no one told Evan.

Evan starts toward the stage, then stops; he starts again.

"You're acting a little strange," Charlie says. "Are you having a seizure?"

"A seizure?" Evan asks, confused. "No."

"An aura?"

An aura? Evan stares at Charlie. Charlie. Mr. Know-it-all. Grandpa committed suicide. Like everyone knew. Right. An aura. Like Charlie knows. He knows nothing.

"No, no aura," Evan says. "I have to go to the bathroom."

Evan wanders off toward the men's room. Lars rushes up behind him.

"We're on," he says. "Come on, Ev!"

"I have to go to the bathroom. I'll be right there."

"Hold it in, Evbee, it's only a thirty-minute set. Hold it in. Come on."

"I'll be right there."

He goes into the restroom, turns on the faucet, splashes water on his face.

Grandpa committed suicide. How odd. How interesting. Utterly fascinating. More proof that Evan has been treated like an invalid his entire life. Since the accident. No one has trusted him, no one has confided in him. He's been labeled as damaged. By his own parents. By his brother. There's nothing to be ashamed of. You're just the egg in the carton that looks okay from the top, but when you lift it you see that it's broken. That's nothing to be ashamed of.

"You okay?"

It's Charlie. He's followed.

"I'm fine."

"You sure?"

Evan stops. He glares at Charlie.

"What is it, Chuck? You want me not to be fine?"

"No. I'm just concerned."

"Really?"

"Are you okay?"

Evan shakes his head in disbelief.

"No, Chuck, I'm not okay. I have epilepsy."

"Are you having a seizure?"

"No."

"Are you having an aura?"

"No."

"Then what's wrong?" Charlie asks, as if this were the limit of his ability to comprehend wrongness. A seizure or an aura. Everything else is okay.

"I have epilepsy," Evan says.

"Are you having a seizure?" Charlie asks again.

"No."

"I don't understand," Charlie says, genuinely confused.

"I have epilepsy."

"I know."

"I know you know," Evan says. "I have it because of you."

Charlie stops. Cocks his head.

"What do you mean?"

"I took your dare."

"My dare?"

"Your dare," Evan says. "I ran out into the street."

"That wasn't *my* dare," Charlie says. "That was *your* dare."

Evan. Stunned again. *Whose* dare? His own brother, a Stepford. They're all Stepfords. They should just change their names and get it over with.

"No, Chuck, it was yours," Evan says.

Charlie scratches his head.

"No," he says.

"I remember it vividly, Chuck. I do."

"You remember it wrong," Charlie says.

Evan wants to lash out. He wants to strike his brother, bash him. But he doesn't act on his impulse. This is nothing to him. Evan knows the truth. He knows how it happened. Although, if Charlie remembers it some other way, at least that would explain why he never went to their parents to tell them what really happened.

And does it really matter, anyway? For his entire life, it's mattered. All the hatred. All the resentment. But who really cares? Who cares why Evan has epilepsy? Who cares who took the dare for whom? That's beside the point, isn't it? The fact remains the same. Evan has epilepsy. It's time to stop assessing blame. All this time he's been waiting for something from Charlie, an apology or a thank-you or something, anything. But he will never get it. Does that mean what he did for his brother was any less significant? No. He did it out of love. He did it to protect his little brother. He made a sacrifice for Charlie, and that sacrifice was its own reward.

"Chuck," Evan says, grabbing Charlie behind his neck in some kind of Sicilian grasp of friendship and brotherhood. "Chuck, I am your brother, and I will protect you."

Charlie looks confused.

"I am your brother, and I will protect you," Evan repeats.

That's how it happened. One cold, wet November evening. Dusk settling on the road. The smell of fireplaces. The smell of stew.

One more dare and it would be over. Charlie had the last dare. One more dare and we could go home.

"I am your brother, and I will protect you," Evan says again.

But Charlie cried. Charlie cried, so Evan stood up for him, that's what he did. He didn't want his little brother to get kicked in the shins by Penny and her tap shoes. He didn't want Charlie to cry. So Evan stood up for him.

"I am your brother . . ."

Evan took the dare. It was raining. The road was wet. He hadn't factored in the wet roads. He didn't think about the extra distance needed to stop on a wet road.

". . . and I will protect you."

When the car hit him, he was so surprised. Like it was a strange, surprise gift. *Thump.* And the funny thing. None of it hurt. Not the car hitting him, not his landing on the road. None of it hurt. Even seizures don't really hurt. It's not the seizure that hurts. It's after the seizure that hurts. When you wake up. That's when you feel bruised and broken. That's when you feel most alone. When you feel like no one is there for you. Not even your parents, who are standing at the foot of your bed watching you like you're some kind of a freak. They aren't really there. They can't really help you.

"Evbee."

Standing in the doorway is Mel.

"On stage, *now!*"

Evan leaves Charlie—who is thoroughly a wreck, as if Evan has cast some kind of magic spell on him—and follows Mel toward the stage. He hears music. It sounds like The Last.

"They've started?"

"Yes, Evbee. And, for the record, you're every bit as good as Billy and Mica say you are, but Eddie Van Halen you ain't. If you pull a stunt like this again, I'm dropping the band. Now get your ass on stage and play."

Evan bounds up the stage, plugs in his guitar. The song is halfway done. How long was he in the bathroom with Charlie? Tony makes a gesture of relief toward him. Evan waits . . . waits . . .

waits . . . and when his cue comes, he rips into his guitar with so much force that all the people in the club are blown backwards at least a foot, their eyes forced wide, their mouths agape, they are compelled to listen because there is no way to avoid it. They are convinced by Evan and his guitar to believe—with more faith than they thought they had in their souls—that The Last has arrived, and that The Last will never open for another band again.

I T IS WHEN he plays guitar that he feels absolute clarity. He can't explain it; he doesn't know why. But there is a point at which he is the instrument and someone or something is playing *him*. Something larger. Something outside of all of us. Call it the Universal Mind, if you like. But when he feels it, he knows that the people listening feel it as well. They are all tapping into the same thing. They all understand.

Absolute clarity. He sees a young boy on his father's shoulders near the foot of the stage, and it is clear. It is late. It is smoky. But there is an astrological event in the room, and it is the music. The boy is dancing, as is the father underneath him. They are dancing separately, but they are one dancer. Because a father and a son may be separated, but they are never separate. They cannot deny each other. They may have never seen each other in their lives, yet they still influence each other.

And it is clear to Evan, now: the difference between what is and what has been done; the present and the past. He sees that what he does and who he is isn't based on the past unless he wants it to be.

It is clear: he doesn't have to hide his decisions behind false issues: the need to protect Dean from Frank; guilt over Tracy's life and death; his assumption of his own incompetence; the fear of his epilepsy that he projects onto Dean. No. That is the past, which has been seen differently through many different eyes and has become hazy and unclear, like a pond when stirred with a stick. Only the present moment is clear and free from prejudice.

And so, playing this particular guitar on this particular stage on this particular evening, freed from his own history, Evan asks himself: What does he want?

He answers: To be with Dean.

He asks: Why?

He answers: Because he is Evan and nothing else. Because he is Evan and that is enough.

ABSOLUTE CLARITY.

There is Tracy: he's always maintained that she wanted the abortion and he didn't, but that isn't true. She didn't really want the abortion (as Brad said); she was waiting for Evan to fight to keep the child. But he didn't fight. He agreed so easily. He thought he was agreeing to cause her less pain, but he caused more: if he had insisted on keeping the baby, she would have been relieved and thankful; instead, he went to the bank and cashed a check, and she was sorry.

He gave her the money so he could feel morally justified that he'd made the right decision—deferring to Tracy's wishes—while assuring that the issue was dealt with quickly and easily. Yes. He'd spent all of these years telling himself that he really wanted to raise a child with Tracy, but he was kidding himself, and Tracy was smart enough to see through him.

She left in order to spare him the uncomfortable visits with her family, whom he used to call "white-trash Mormons" to her face. She would laugh, but the words were hurtful and offensive. By calling her parents those names, Evan was signaling to her that he didn't want to marry her. He was vetoing any concept of permanence in their relationship. Sure, he was.

Oh, he created it all. When you dissect it, it becomes obvious. Like Brad said, Evan acts like he doesn't know what's going on, but he knows everything. To date, his plan has worked to perfection. It was the perfect design, executed masterfully, and the result has been Evan's perfect, masterful, mediocre life of nothing.

And things would have gone on that way, too, Evan knows. Forever and ever. Except for two chance meetings that crumbled his worldview. The chance meeting of Tracy's car and another's on the freeway. And the chance meeting of Evan and a girl, who suggested to him that he sit in with a band called Lucky Strike.

AFTERWARD, THEY GO out to celebrate. Evan tags along for as long as he can stand it, but he knows when it's time to go. There's no reason for him to continue dragging from club to club in Belltown. Sure he wants to be one of the guys, sure he wants to hang out with their new producer, but he also has to get the hell out of town first thing in the morning. He has to go. He's standing at the back of the Crocodile Lounge, but in his head he's already packing his bag, setting his alarm, trying to catch some sleep. He's already halfway to Walla Walla.

He tells Lars he feels sick. An easy excuse. And he slips out of the Crocodile and onto the cool street. There's a group of kids waiting to get in. He's made space for them and they're thankful.

"Check you later, Evan," the bouncer says. Evan's never seen him before, never met him. How did he know Evan's name?

He rounds the corner, out of the glare of the big green sign.

"Yo, Evbee."

Evbee? Only one person calls him Evbee.

"Hey, Billy."

"I heard your set tonight," Billy says. "You sounded good."

"You were there?" Evan asks. "Why didn't you find me?"

"I was with people."

Billy breaks off from his friends and approaches Evan, but his greeting isn't as enthusiastic as usual. There's no hip-hop handshake, for instance.

"I gotta jump," Evan says. He points over his shoulder with his thumb. "We need to talk."

"I've got to get up really early in the morning, Billy. Can we talk tomorrow?"

Billy moves to within striking distance. He doesn't blink.

"Let's take a walk," he says.

He takes Evan's elbow and guides him away from the Crocodile and down Blanchard Street. As soon as they're away from Second Avenue, the street plunges into darkness.

They walk several blocks—longer than Evan is comfortable with—without speaking. He's concerned that Billy may kill him, stuff him in a Dumpster somewhere.

"We need to talk about Mica," Billy finally says.

No, he's already screwed up his relationship with Mica. He screwed up his relationship with Dean, too, but for some reason he feels he can salvage it. Maybe it's blood. But with Mica, he went too far.

"I love Mica, Evan," Billy says. "She's like my little sister, and I love my little sister. Understand?"

"I fucked up," Evan says.

"That's what she said," Billy says. "Let me give you some advice about Mica."

"It's too late, Billy—" Their eyes meet, but they don't speak for a moment. "She makes me so afraid," he says, finally.

Billy is silent.

"She looks at you and she sees all of your lies," Evan says. "You can't lie to her."

"That makes you afraid of her?" Billy asks.

"That scares the shit out of me."

"Why?

Evan tries to assemble his thoughts.

"My life is a fraud, Billy. You know when you tell a lie and then you have to tell another one to make the first one stick, and then you tell a third and it goes on like that?"

"Yeah."

"My life is like that. My entire life. I've been telling lies since I was twelve years old. You know? And I'm good at it, Billy. I'm fucking good. And Mica walks in with her goddamn laser vision, and blows it all apart. That wouldn't scare you?"

Billy thinks about it. "It might make me happy," he says.

"Only after the fact, Billy. I mean, if you're clinging to a piece of wood in the middle of the ocean and you don't know that a mermaid is waiting to rescue you and take you down to her mermaid castle, you're scared shitless of letting go of that wood, right? *After* you let go and she saves you, you can be happy. But *before*? You're scared. Right?"

"I see your point," Billy says.

"I wasn't ready to be exposed," Evan says. "That's why I acted like that. I can't live up to her expectations. I can't tell her everything about me. She doesn't understand."

"Did you give her a chance?"

Evan doesn't answer. They walk another half-block, Billy nodding to himself. They wait for a walk light at a corner. When it turns in their favor, they don't cross. Billy looks at Evan.

"We go way back together, don't we, Evbee?"

"We do," Evan says.

"Way back."

"Hey, Billy, thanks for the help with Mel."

Billy acknowledges Evan's gratitude with a nod. "You gonna sign with him?"

"I think so."

"Do you know why I helped you out, Evbee?" Billy asks.

"No," Evan admits.

"I did it because you gave me my start, man."

"What do you mean?" Evan asks, surprised.

"You inspired me to open The Sound Factory, Evbee. When we were in Free Radicals, all you guys were better musicians than I was. I could see that. And you could play that fucking guitar like crazy, man, and I woke up one day at rehearsal and I realized that I was just an overachiever, Evbee. My whole life, I just worked hard at things like playing the drums, or whatever. I never had any talent for it. And that's okay, you know, in a sense. A lot of people go through life like that. But I realized that if I was gonna have to work hard for whatever I got, I'd rather work hard in a profession where I could make some money, you know? Musicians don't make any money. So that's why I quit playing and opened my place. And you know what? I found out I had a real talent for something, and now look at me. So I quit playing because of your talent, and I found my place because of you. So I knew if I could pay you back someday, I wanted to do it, you know?"

"I appreciate it, Billy. I really do."

"Come here for a second."

Billy leads Evan across the street and toward an old, brick apartment building on the opposite corner. He mounts the three short steps up to the vestibule door. He presses a buzzer on the intercom.

"Hello?" a girl's voice crackles.

"Yo, doll, it's Billy. Lemme up."

The door unlocks with a buzz and Billy pushes it open a crack. He looks over at Evan.

"It's your move, Evbee."

Evan considers it. He knows he has to deal with it, but he was kind of hoping to put it off until later. Maybe until never.

But with Billy leading him there by the hand, how can he say no?

He takes the door from Billy and steps into the entryway.

"Be straight, Evbee," Billy warns as Evan passes. "If you break her heart, I don't want to see you around anymore. Seriously. She's my little sister, and I don't want her heart broken. Cool?"

"Cool," Evan agrees.

"Good looking-out, Evbee," Billy says, followed by the special handshake; he turns and walks away.

HE CLIMBS THE dimly lit stairs to the third floor. As he walks down the hallway, he hears the muffled sounds of people's lives behind their doors: a dog whimpering, a TV blaring, music playing; he smells Chinese food. He finds her apartment and pushes the doorbell.

After a moment he hears soft footsteps, then the pivoting of a little round metal disk on its hinge. Light briefly flashes through the peephole, disappears, then returns. The door opens.

She doesn't welcome him in. She doesn't step aside and usher him to her bed. She simply stands in the doorway, the door still mostly closed, only one-third of her body in view.

"Where's Billy?" she asks.

"He left."

"Why are you here?"

"Because Billy wouldn't let me run away."

She watches him carefully, trying to detect signs of deception. There are none. She lets him in.

Her apartment is small and dark. It's a one-room studio. The floor and trim are darkly stained oak. The walls are French vanilla. It's messy and cluttered; clothes lie in piles on the floor surrounding a futon; books and magazines cover a square kitchen table that acts as a buffer between the room and a kitchenette, which is filled with every imaginable cooking item.

Mica pads across the room and picks up a water glass from the floor. She stands next to the window and drinks. She's in her pajamas.

"Were you sleeping?" Evan asks.

She turns toward him, and she seems so vulnerable. So small and delicate. He's always seen her as larger-than-life, as powerful and poised; now she seems almost childlike. He feels awkward next to her.

"My grandfather committed suicide," Evan says. "He died ten years ago, and I just found out tonight that he committed suicide."

She watches him but she doesn't speak.

"It's so obvious, looking back on it. It should have been obvious to me then. But it wasn't because I didn't want to see it that way. I saw it the way I *wanted* to see it; I only looked at the parts I wanted to see. I didn't see that he had cancer. I didn't see that when he asked me what belongings of his I wanted that he was telling me he was going to kill himself."

She listens, but she doesn't respond.

"Did I ever tell you how I got epilepsy?"

She shakes her head.

"It was a dare. We were playing Truth or Dare. Charlie got a dare, but he chickened out. I took it for him, and I got hit by a car. Stupid. Dumb. The point is not how it happened, but that my brother—all this time—has thought the dare was mine. It wasn't mine. It was his. But his way of dealing with it was to believe that it was mine, and that explains why he never said anything to my parents. That's another major thing that I learned tonight."

"Evan—"

"But they're not the only things. Things have become so clear."

"Why?" she asks. She's still standing by the window, cupping one elbow with the opposite hand. She still looks so small.

"I was on stage. I was playing and I saw a kid . . ."

"And that made it clear?"

"No. It just became clear on its own."

"And the kid? He made you think about Dean?"

"No," Evan says. "He made me think about you. A rare lunar eclipse."

He sees on her face that his comment affects her, but she tries to fight it off.

"What do you mean?" she laughs cautiously.

"Will you forgive me?" he asks.

She smiles at him and shakes her head.

"I'm such an asshole," he says. "I wanted to fail—with Dean—and you weren't going to let me. You were going to stop me. So I said horrible things to make you go away. And you went away. Simple. Effective."

"And now?"

"Listen, Mica, I acted like an idiot. I have no defense. I said horrible things to you. I'm not here to get you back, but to apologize to you and to tell you that tomorrow morning, as early as I can wake up, I'm going to Walla Walla to get Dean back. Not because of pressure from you, but because that's what I want. I'm not asking you to accept me, but I am asking you to forgive me."

"You don't want me to accept you?"

"I do," he says. "Yes, I do. But I don't expect you to."

She turns away.

"Will you forgive me?" he asks.

"Evan, I forgave you a long time ago. I forgave you before we even had that fight. I forgave you before you were born, before either of us had bodies, when we were still lost souls floating around the universe looking for what to do next, when I first met you out there, a hundred million years ago."

Evan goes to her and embraces her. He lets himself feel her warmth, this strange woman in his arms. Her warmth flows over him.

"Do you forgive yourself?" she asks.

Is she asking about their fight? Or is she asking if he forgives himself for all the other things? For Dean. For running in front of the car. For not measuring up to his own standards. Maybe she wants to know if he forgives himself for being himself. If he forgives himself for existing.

"Do you?" Mica asks.

Does he? Maybe now he does. Maybe now.

He holds his wrist up in front of Mica.

"This is my Medic Alert bracelet," he says. "It says I have a seizure disorder. There's a telephone number on it that you can call to find out what kind of medication I'm taking, how to contact my neurologist, and how to contact my next of kin. If I have a seizure and it lasts more than ten minutes, you *have* to call the ambulance, you have to insist that they take me to the hospital, and you have to insist that they call the number on the bracelet. If I have a seizure, I can't swallow my tongue, that's a myth. It'll sound like I'm choking, but I'm not. Roll me over on my side and put something under my head so I don't hurt myself. Don't ever stick anything in my mouth or I'll bite down. It's a reflex. I almost took a woman's finger off once. If you ever ask me a question and I don't answer but I smile at you or I wave my hands like I'm eating something hot, I'm having a little seizure. It'll pass, just give it time. If I'm driving, I may pull over and ask you to drive. One day you'll probably witness me having a grand mal seizure. It'll upset you more than it will upset me. You may look at me differently afterward. You may decide that you can't have an emotional attachment to someone like me. I'll understand. Just tell me that. Don't tell me that it's something else. Tell me the truth. That's all I ask."

He pauses. Throughout his speech, Mica listened intently. Now she curls up the corners of her mouth as if in question.

"I love you," Evan says. "And I think I have to let you know what you're dealing with if I want you to return my love."

She kisses him deeply, and he accepts her kiss; then he breaks away, moves toward the door.

"Stay," she says.

"I can't. I have to go get Dean in the morning and I need sleep."

"Okay. Call me, then."

"I will."

He opens the door.

"Evan," she stops him.

He turns.

"I'll return your love," she says. "And I won't look at you differently. And I'll always be there to put something under your head so you don't hurt yourself."

He smiles at her and leaves.

HE WANTS TO call her the second he walks in the door. He picks up the phone and notices that there are two messages on his machine.

"Hi, Dad. Are you there, or are you in Yakima?"

It's Dean. Dean has never once called Evan "Dad" without a massive dose of irony. Something's wrong.

There's some background noise, then: "If you're there, pick up."

A long pause. Then Evan can hear him say to someone else: "He might be asleep, or maybe he went to the store. Can I call back in a little while?"

Then the beep of the answering machine. Message over.

Evan sits up and listens closely. Something was definitely wrong about that call.

The second message is much more clear.

"Look, Dad, it's me, Dean. I'm in jail."

(Another voice in the background says: "It's not jail. You're at the police station.")

"I'm at the police station," Dean corrects himself. "I'm in a lot of trouble. Can you come and get me?"

(Background voice: "Give him the number.")

Dean reads off the telephone number.

(Background voice: "If he doesn't call soon, we'll call your grandparents. You can't stay here overnight.")

Then, Dean, almost at a whisper: "I know you don't want me around, but you have to come and get me, Dad. They said if you don't come soon, they'll call Grandma. She's been talking to Frank. They're getting back together. He came back today. He's gonna kill me. I stole your pot and they caught me with it. The cop said I could go to jail for dealing. I didn't know how much it was, I've never smoked pot before, I just took it and showed it around, I didn't give anybody any of it, I didn't smoke any. You have to come and get me. Please. I'm afraid."

Beep.

Oh, my God. He replays the messages. The first call was at nine-ten. Shit. The second call was at ten. He dials the number Dean left.

"I'm calling about my son, Dean Wallace Smith," Evan says quickly when the man answers.

"And who is this?" the man asks.

"His father."

"Hold."

Dead air space. Crap. Dean was arrested. No wonder Evan couldn't find his pot. Dean took it. Oh, man. That was more than an ounce of pot. That's a felony.

"Mr. Smith?" a new man says into the phone.

"Wallace. Evan Wallace. He has his mother's name."

"I see. Where's his mother?"

"She's dead—"

"I'm sorry."

"We all are. Look, I'm on my way. Don't call his grandmother. I'm on my way."

"She's already been called."

"Don't let him go with her."

"She picked him up an hour ago, sir."

"You're kidding! Was Frank with her?"

"Frank?"

"Her husband. He beats Dean."

"Sir?"

"Dean's grandfather beats him. If he finds out about this, he may kill Dean for all we know."

"Does he have a record?"

"No—I don't know—"

"Any history?"

"Plenty of *history*. I just don't know if it's recorded in any of your files, okay?"

"The best I can do is have a squad car do a pass-by," the cop says.

"Well, park a fucking squad car in front of their fucking house until I get there."

"Sir, don't use that kind of language—"

"And make sure Frank Smith knows it's there!"

"Sir, I can't do—"

"Do it!" Evan shouts into the phone. "Do it! Do it! *Do it!*"

"Sir!"

"If that man hurts my son, so help me God, I will spend the rest of my life making your life a living hell."

"Are you threatening me, Mr. Wallace?"

"That's not a threat," Evan hisses. "That's a plain fucking promise."

He slams down the phone.

Shit. Double-crossed by Ellen, of all people. She gets Dean and the first thing she does is call in Frank. *Shit*.

Dean's in serious trouble this time. And where is Evan? Five hours away. Powerless.

He dials Ellen's number. It's midnight. The machine picks up. Damn. He hangs up, dials again. No answer. He dials again. Nothing. *Shit*.

He throws on his shoes. No time to find a thermos. No time to make coffee. He'll have to stop at a truck stop or something. He has to get out on the road right away.

What a mess. Dean stole his pot. Well, why the hell wouldn't he? Evan had declared that it was the best pot on the planet, so why wouldn't Dean want to steal it?

Evan rushes out to his car. He heads for Walla Walla.

THE NIGHT AIR is thin and dry; it's not really dark at all because of the moon, which hangs menacingly over the valley like an angry god. He stops for gas just outside Yakima. It's two-thirty. Making pretty good time, considering . . .

To tell the truth, he doesn't feel altogether great. He feels a little nauseous; this news about Dean has made him physically ill, like he wants to puke his guts out on the dashboard. He buys a cup of coffee from the station store, but maybe he should buy some Pepto-Bismol instead. His stomach is unsettled, his head hurts, the beginnings of a headache. There's something wrong.

No. Now's not the time for waffling. His son's welfare is at stake. He starts up his car and pulls out of the station. It looks like the service road parallels the highway for a while before it feeds back on. Is he going in the right direction? Or is something wrong? There are no cars on the road, so he leans on the gas a little, doing sixty in a thirty-five zone. That's a ticketable offense.

He feels a slight twinge in his neck as he passes through an intersection. Another twinge as he pulls onto the entrance ramp and that's when it occurs to him that something is wrong.

Something is wrong. Evan doesn't get twinges. Something is happening and there isn't even an aura. A thought flashes through his mind that he should pull over, that maybe this is an aura, but before he can act on that thought, he realizes that he has no control of his hands. Or his arms. They are his limbs, true. They are gripping the steering wheel, true. But he can't make them turn the wheel. And as quickly as he realizes this he hears a sound, a gurgling sound, a choking sound, and he knows that sound is coming from him, and there's something wrong. His head snaps violently to the side; snaps again; a third time and he hears a deafening crack, a head-splitting sound followed by a roar and he thinks his head must have been torn clean off his shoulders, nothing left for him to see, a tenth of a second of darkness, and then nothing, not even darkness, just nothing. Nothing.

There's something wrong.

WELL, THE GOOD news is that he doesn't wake up dead.

The bad news is that he wakes up in a hospital bed with an IV stuck painfully in the back of his hand.

The room is semi-dark. There are many beds. Intensive care. Machines are beeping all around him.

An electric pump attached to a stand next to his bed keeps careful track of the drugs being leaked into his veins. Lying on his chest is a small plastic tube with a button on one end and a wire that leads to a pump at the other end.

He is wearing a hospital gown. It is white with little pale blue flowers on it.

His left eye is swollen; his face aches terribly. His arm is strapped to his torso. His shoulder screams.

He doesn't know how much time has passed—if it can be measured in hours or days—but he knows he is late. He was supposed to be somewhere, and he is very late.

He tries to sit up, but he can't. He doesn't have the strength. There are too many drugs in his body keeping him down. He picks up the tube and pushes the button to call the nurse. The electric pump beeps; almost instantly he feels the rush of a sedative. That isn't a call button; that's a PCA. *Damn.* He drifts off to sleep, angry at himself for breaking his promise to his son.

THE SECOND TIME he wakes up, there are people in his room. Someone is speaking: "As soon as we get his blood count back from the lab and it indicates that he's stable, we'd like to operate."

That would be a doctor. Evan recognizes the tone.

"It's important to do it now. You understand. We either do it now or we wait until it's healed and break it again. It's your call, of course. I've paged our chief surgeon, Dr. Richard Wald. You may want to airlift him to Harborview. It's your call."

Evan can't see him, but he sounds young. He sounds afraid.

"I sat in on a lecture of yours at the University of Washington when I was pre-med there. You were giving a talk at the Medical Center about repairing ventricular septal defects. Absolutely fascinating. It was the defining moment in my life really. It tipped the scales for me. I was thinking of dropping medicine and going into law. But when I heard you speak, I knew I had to be a doctor. Is he awake?"

"Hello, Evan."

Evan closes his eyes. This is a bad dream, right? This can't be happening. The apple doesn't fall close to the tree. No, the apple tries to get as far away from the tree as possible, it's just that the goddamn tree keeps following.

"Can I have some more of the happy juice?" Evan groans. "I think I'm feeling another seizure."

Evan, eyes still closed, hears the young doctor scramble to his side.

"Are you having an aura?" he asks, practically hyperventilating, reaching for Evan's pump. "I can begin the drip immediately!"

"Relax." Reee-LAX! That would be Carl. Dr. Dad. Never loses his cool. "Dr. Boukas, I'm afraid that's my son's idea of a joke."

Evan opens his eyes. Carl. What a guy. Got to give him credit. He went to the trouble to don a white coat for the hospital. Doctors. So afraid that people will forget they're doctors.

"A joke?" the young Dr. Boukas asks.

"Evan?"

Evan smiles, but when he does a searing pain flares up on the left side of his face. "Hi, Dad. What brings you here?"

"Can we have a moment?" Carl asks Dr. Boukas, who immediately excuses himself.

"He's a pleasant young man," Carl announces after Boukas is gone. "Too bad he doesn't know that airlift helicopters are reserved for things like critical burns and severed limbs. Shattered collarbones and facial contusions simply aren't given the same priority."

He smiles tentatively at Evan. His idea of a joke.

"I have a shattered collarbone?" Evan asks. "Is that why I feel like my chest has been caved in?"

"Yes."

"Anything else?"

"Nothing else is broken, as far as they can tell. Do you feel any pain?"

"Only when I live."

Carl sighs and sits on the edge of Evan's bed, his back to Evan. All Evan can see is Carl's hunched frame, his large head of gray hair, his broad white jacket.

"Evan. What have you done?"

Here we go again.

"Just another fuck-up in a long line of fuck-ups, Dad."

Carl nods slowly.

"I get a call at four in the morning from Yakima Memorial Hospital telling me that my son has been in a terrible accident and could I please come right away. Thank God you were wearing your Medic Alert bracelet."

"I never leave home without it. You never know when you'll end up in a ditch somewhere."

"Yes, well, you didn't end up in a ditch, you ended up wrapped around a telephone pole. Thank God you didn't hit someone and kill him, a poor, innocent bystander."

"As opposed to me, a guilty participant, who deserves to die."

Carl scowls at Evan.

"I have to go," Evan says abruptly. "Can you unplug me?"

"Go?" Carl asks.

"I have to go right now."

"Where?"

"I have to go get Dean."

Carl takes a deep breath and turns away from Evan. He pinches the bridge of his nose with his finger and thumb.

"My grandson," Carl sighs. He turns slightly to Evan. "How old is he?"

"Fourteen."

"Fourteen," Carl repeats thoughtfully. "Who would have thought that I had a fourteen-year-old grandson named Dean?"

He pauses, waiting for an answer from someone. But Evan doesn't have an answer. Maybe Carl is waiting for God's reply. He covers his face with his hands.

"I wanted to buy him a present on the way over," he says.

"Did you?" Evan asks.

Carl looks over his shoulder at Evan.

"Nothing's open at four in the morning. And, besides, I don't know what he likes. I don't know him. I've never met him. I didn't know he existed until a few weeks ago."

Evan thinks he sees a tear running down Carl's cheek.

"Why?" Carl asks, turning away. "I don't understand. Why?"

Evan shrugs. "It's inexplicable."

Carl repositions himself so he's facing Evan.

"No, Evan, I think it *is* explicable. I really do. I just think you don't want to take the trouble to explain it."

Carl looks at Evan directly. Evan doesn't know what to say. That it all started on a cold, rainy evening in November, many, many years ago? That he didn't want to let them down again, so he didn't tell them? That he felt sorry for himself, so he tried to hide his own disappointment? No. There is no explanation. It's inexplicable.

"He's a good kid," Evan says of Dean.

"I know," Carl nods, then, suddenly, sobs, trying to suck it back inside, hide it inside, not let it out. "I know."

Evan wants to reach out to his father, take him, hold him. But he can't do it. Not because he doesn't want to. Not because he doesn't need to. He just can't. Carl is sitting on his IV tube. Evan can't move his arm. He can't sit up. He wants to laugh about life's little compromises, but he doesn't.

"I'm sorry," he says.

"No," Carl shakes his head, shifts his weight. The IV tube is pulled tight. Evan feels a shooting, burning pain in his hand. He tries not to react.

Carl sighs.

"I don't like getting calls like this, Evan. You're my son, and I don't like getting calls in the middle of the night that you're in the hospital. It makes me feel like I've let you down, somehow."

"You haven't."

"I feel like I've failed you."

"No, Dad—"

"I've failed you."

"You haven't failed me, Dad."

Carl nods, looks up at the lights hanging from the ceiling.

"We put Ralphy down the day before yesterday," he says.

Evan starts. His heart races. Ralphy. Gone.

"He was old," Evan says.

"Not old enough, I think."

"He was sick."

Carl smiles a tight smile of agreement. He's a very sad man.

"So," Carl says loudly, getting up off the bed, thankfully, taking the pressure off of Evan's tube, stopping the pain. "Your mother would like to see you before the surgery."

Evan can see how hard his father is working to keep it all in. All the tears. Evan rarely, if ever, has seen his father cry. This is as close as Carl gets. Using his supreme powers of restraint to bottle it all in, hold it tight, only letting a sob out occasionally, eyes red, nose running, sucking it all back in.

"Why didn't she come in?" Evan asks.

"Intensive care. Only one visitor at a time."

Please.

"They would have broken the rules for you," Evan says.

Carl shakes his head.

"There are other people to think of, Evan. Other patients. We have to respect their privacy."

Oh, yeah. Right.

"She wanted to be here when you woke up, but the timing didn't work out. She'll be in. They'll operate on your collarbone this afternoon. No reason to go to Harborview. I know Dick Wald, the chief surgeon here. Top notch fellow. He'll do a great job."

"No," Evan says.

Carl pauses.

"No? No, what?"

"No operation."

Carl, seemingly lost, stares at Evan a moment. Then he laughs.

"Why not?"

"I have to go, Dad. I have to go right now. Send in Dr. Boukas. Tell him to unplug me."

"You have a compound fracture, Evan. If you don't let them operate now, it will have to heal as it is. It will be painful, it may even get infected. Then, in six months they'll re-break the bone and reset it. And that will be more painful than anything else, believe me. Is that what you want?"

"I don't care," Evan says. "I have to go."

Carl is silent. He picks up the plastic tube and presses the button. The pump beeps.

"No—"

"This will help you sleep," Carl says, pressing the button again.

"Dad, stop. I don't want to sleep."

And again.

"Give that to me," Evan says, grabbing for the tube, but Carl holds it beyond his reach.

Beep.

"Why are you doing this?"

"You'll feel differently when you wake up."

A fog rapidly descends on Evan; suddenly, he is asleep.

H E ISN'T IN a recovery room, which is good. He's in a private
room with lavender walls and tasteful sconce lighting, a television suspended from the ceiling by a large bracket, and a tray
table with some food on it: green Jell-O, oatmeal, cottage cheese,
juice. Invalid food.

He doesn't feel differently. He feels angry.

His parents aren't there. No nurses, no doctors. He climbs out of
bed, which is difficult because his right arm is immobilized in a
sling that's held tight to his body. He feels a drug-induced hang-
over. He's still got an IV in his wrist and a bladder catheter slith-
ered up his urethra. He checks the label on the IV drip. Saline,
thank God, no more narcotics. He reaches underneath his gown
and slides the catheter out slowly, not an especially pleasant sensation, but something that has to be done.

He tries the phone, but he can't get an outside line. He buzzes
the nurse's station. A pretty Hispanic woman soon arrives.

"You're awake. How do you feel?"

"Did they operate on me?"

"Operate? No."

"Where are my parents. Are they in the waiting room or something?"

"No one was here when I came on duty. Are you sure you have visitors?"

"Trust me. I have visitors."

"They must have gone home."

"Their home is in Seattle. Kind of a long trip."

"I don't know."

No. She wouldn't know.

"This phone doesn't work."

"You have to get it turned on."

"Is there a payphone around here?"

"There's one in the basement, right next to the cafeteria."

"Forget it," Evan grumbles.

He looks around the room and immediately spots the cabinet. He's been in enough hospital rooms to know that in each there's a secret cabinet with all the good medical stuff. Cotton balls, bandages, rubber gloves, face masks. He opens the door and digs around. Alcohol swab, cotton ball, and a Band-Aid.

"What are you doing?" the nurse asks, concerned by his pillaging of her secret cabinet.

"Removing my IV," Evan says.

"You can't do that."

Evan ignores her and takes a moment to assess the difficulty of his project. He could ask the nurse for help—she could do it in a second—but she doesn't look like the type, if he can divine her character from her appearance: all business. His right arm is held tight to his body by the sling, but his hand and fingers are free, so he should be able to manage. It's like a sequencing test in kindergarten. First, he tears open the Band-Aid wrapper with his teeth and holds the Band-Aid between his lips while he removes the adhesive backing. Next, he holds his left hand to his right and disconnects the vein catheter from the IV feeder tube. Then, he peels the tape off of his wrist, exposing the tube entering his vein. Slowly, he eases out the thin plastic straw. Ah. It feels like someone's squeezing a balloon inside his arm.

"You can't do that," the nurse says, but she says it without authority; clearly, she's fascinated by Evan's sequencing abilities.

With the tube removed, he holds a cotton ball over the bleeding wound. Finally, he takes the Band-Aid from his lips and applies it to his wrist, holding the cotton ball in place. Finally, he takes the catheter and drops it in the red bio-hazard box on the wall.

"I could be in Cirque du Soleil," he says ironically.

"I'm calling security," the nurse warns.

"Why?"

"You can't remove your own IV."

"First of all, it was saline," Evan explains. "Nothing vital. Second, I'm checking out and I don't think the hospital would want me to walk out with its precious portable coat hanger. It probably lists for four hundred fifty dollars or something."

"You can't check out."

"Why not?" With his good arm, he rummages through the closet next to the night table. His clothes are rolled up on the top shelf. He removes the roll and places it on the bed.

"The doctor has to sign off."

"That's your problem, not mine."

"You can't leave without the doctor's approval."

On the one hand, Evan feels like an asshole, but he's also a little mad that no one ever teaches these people anything. You can't keep someone in a hospital against their will. It's unethical and illegal. If a patient wants to leave, he can leave. The doctor does not have to approve.

"Do you have my insurance imprint?" Evan asks.

The nurse shrugs. That's a yes.

"That's all you need. If my insurance chooses not to cover this because I left the hospital AMA—against medical advice—they know how to find me, I promise. The hospital will get its money."

He unrolls his belongings. He raises his boxer shorts by the waistband. The leg holes have been cut up the side, rendering them unwearable.

"You need to sign an AMA release form," the nurse says.

"No, I don't. Did they cut *all* my clothes?"

He unrolls his jeans, which are sliced up the outside seam of each leg.

"Do I get reimbursed for these?" he asks.

"You have to sign a release."

He flaps his jeans, exasperated.

"No, nurse," he says, "I don't have to sign anything. Listen, I've gone through this before, I know my rights. I've walked out of bigger hospitals in bigger cities. There's nothing you can do to keep me here short of trying to kill me with a scalpel, and then *you'll* be the one security is looking for. Okay? So, could you do me a favor and help me with this?"

He grabs a roll of medical tape out of the cabinet. He slips into his ripped jeans and tries to tape the seams together as best he can. The nurse doesn't help. He manages to get them strapped on, but they look pretty silly. He reaches for his T-shirt, but it, too, has been shredded beyond repair. So he takes a pair of scissors from the cabinet and crops his gown at the waist. His socks are cut, as are the laces of his sneakers.

"What is it with you people always cutting my clothes off?"

"Standard procedure in cases of seizure," the nurse says. She hasn't moved to help Evan, but she hasn't moved to have him arrested either, so that's a step in the right direction.

"Well, it's a stupid standard," Evan says.

"Have you ever been an emergency medic?" the nurse snaps. "Have you ever been on the floor of an ER? There's a lot of tension and a lot of stress. The last thing you need to worry about is someone's blue jeans."

Evan looks at her coldly. There are a lot of buttons you can push with Evan; that's not one you should try.

"Have you ever had a status seizure?" he asks her softly.

She shakes her head.

"Then what can you tell me about tension and stress that I don't already know?"

The nurse withdraws momentarily.

He glances around the room one more time. His wallet and money and keys aren't there. His parents must have them, or they're in the hospital safe. There's nothing else of his here. He's ready to go. He walks toward the nurse.

"Are you going to call security?" he asks.

She doesn't answer.

"When I was twenty," Evan says, "I had a seizure in a restaurant. A status seizure. Someone called nine-one-one. The medics came. They thought I was choking on a french fry. They thought I was seizing because I was in shock. So they gave me a tracheotomy—they were excited, it was probably the first tracheotomy they'd ever done. *After* they got the tube in, they saw that I was wearing a Medic Alert bracelet. *After* they had cut my throat open, they decided to check to see if I had any jewelry identifying my medical condition."

He pulls down the neck of his gown and reveals to her his tracheotomy scar, the one Mica was so desperate to know about. A thin, two-inch line of scar tissue just below his Adam's apple.

"Every night, when I wash my face before I go to bed . . . every morning when I shave . . . every time I button up a shirt in the mirror, I look at this scar. And do you know what I think? I think: Why do they need to cut my shoelaces? Why can't they just untie them?"

"I'm sorry," she says, surprising Evan.

"You don't have to be sorry," he says. "But please let me go and find my son."

She doesn't respond. He walks past her and she doesn't say a word. He reaches the elevators and pushes the button. When the doors open, he looks back. She's standing in the doorway to his room, watching him.

HE RIDES THE clean, spacious, brightly lit elevator to the ground floor and marches down the disinfected hallway. He makes his way through the main lobby, newly remodeled, full of local artwork, large acrylic-on-canvases of tomato fields. He sees the outside beckoning him, the bright sunshine, the air that has not been filtered through the hospital's superior air-filtering system. He is almost free.

But he's stopped short. Before he can escape the hospital, he's stopped by his mother and his father, who are entering the lobby together. They have come for him, but he's already left.

Evan sees the look of surprise on his mother's face and the look of anger on his father's face so clearly, he's sure he could paint them with acrylic on canvas if he wanted.

"Where are you going?" Carl asks.

"Where were you?" Evan asks in return.

"We were getting lunch," Louise explains.

"Where are you going?" Carl repeats.

"I'm leaving. Where's my wallet? Where are my keys?"

A moment of silence.

"Here."

Louise has Evan's personal affects. She hands them over.

"Where are you going?" she asks.

Evan hesitates. He doesn't feel comfortable with them because they are the enemy. They want to stop him, make him stay in the hospital, keep him from doing what he needs to do. He doesn't want to be near them. Still, they look so tired; they've been up all night.

"To get some clothes," he says.

"Where?"

"At Tracy's house."

"How are you getting there?"

"Taxi," Evan says.

"Let us drive you," Louise offers.

"No."

"Please, Evan."

"No."

Louise moves to Evan's side and touches his arm.

"*Please.*"

Evan would rather take a cab, leave his parents behind. But it's hard for him to refuse his mother, especially to her face. So he nods, and they all go out to the parking lot to find Carl's black Mercedes.

• • •

No one speaks as they drive to Tracy's. He'll take a cab to Walla Walla; he has no idea where his car is, but he imagines it isn't in very good shape. And he really can't drive now, anyway. It was pretty stupid of him to have tried it before. He's lucky he isn't dead. Look at the bright side.

Evan directs Carl to Tracy's house and they park out front. Evan starts to get out of the car.

"Can we come in?" Louise asks timidly.

Funny, he assumed they would. Nice of her to ask.

"Yeah," he says, heading up the walk, his parents following.

They step inside.

"It's quite nice," Louise says, surveying the living room quickly. Carl is silent, smoldering.

"Make yourselves at home," Evan says as cheerfully as he can. "I'm sure there's some spoiled milk in the refrigerator, and I *know* I saw some Cheerios the last time I looked."

Louise smiles painfully at Evan's bad joke, while Carl ignores it, settling himself heavily on the couch.

Evan goes into Tracy's room to change. Fortunately, he has a shirt in his bag that's large enough to fit over his sling. After he struggles into his clothes, he calls Ellen. But as he anticipated, there is no answer at the Smith's. Not even an answering machine. Which leaves him no other choice. He has to go and find Dean himself; he opens the Yellow Pages and calls a car service.

He returns to the living room in time to catch Louise examining a framed photograph she's picked up from the mantel. It's a shot of Tracy and Dean outside somewhere, a horse ranch or something. It's a pretty recent picture. When she hears Evan approach, she guiltily replaces the frame.

"It's a lovely house," she says. "Tracy did a nice job decorating it."

Evan smiles. His mother is such a liar. Tracy didn't decorate it, she used it. It's a house of comfort and utility. It isn't decorated. Not like Carl and Louise's house with its color-coded rooms and door knobs that match the cutlery.

"Dean is very good-looking," Louise goes on, gesturing toward the photograph. "That's him, isn't it?"

"Yes."

"He's very handsome. Carl, did you see?"

"No," Carl grumbles, unmoved, making it clear to Evan and Louise that he has no intention of seeing.

"And Tracy took quite good care of herself," Louise blindly continues, pushing through Carl's antagonism, ignoring Evan's impatience, just trying to get a firm hold on the situation, which, after fourteen years of secrecy, is suddenly, awkwardly, writhing in her lap. "I don't see a wrinkle on her face. It thinned some, didn't it? Her face, I mean. It thinned out since you were in high school. She had a layer of baby fat then, didn't she?"

She glances back at Evan, who stands motionless, struck by his mother's odd presence. She seems old in a way that he's never noticed before.

"Say," Carl blurts out, grabbing the attention of the room. "That sure was a fast one you pulled, Evan. Leaving the hospital before they could reset that bone. That's a real 'I gotcha!'"

"How's that?" Evan asks.

"Well, you know, I made arrangements to keep you there. I wanted you observed. I'm a little concerned about this seizure business again. I thought your medication was handling it."

"It is."

"I suppose not."

"A breakthrough seizure is just that, Dad. It breaks through. Get it? You could keep me comatose on your medication and a breakthrough seizure would still break through. That's why they call them 'breakthrough seizures.' Pretty simple concept."

Carl nods, pursing his lips tightly. "Pretty simple concept," he repeats. "And now, suddenly, it's *my* medication?"

"Did I say that?" Evan asks, oh so innocently.

"Yes."

"Well. Mea culpa, Dad. *Mea culpa.*"

Carl blinks hard. Evan tries not to enjoy watching his father strain to contain his emotions.

Which is what his father does for a living, after all. He's a containment specialist. Contain the disease. Isolate and remove. Slice and dice. Sew it up. You can do that with emotions, too, if you want. Don't cry, don't laugh, don't get mad. Contain it. Lower the temperature of your emotion until it stops beating. Put yourself on an artificial heart, a mechanical pump. And there you go. Just once, Evan would like to see his father blow up. Just once.

But he doesn't get the chance. Louise jumps into the conversation, hoping to head off any potential conflict.

"Where are you going now?" she asks Evan quickly. "Home? We could drive you. Maybe you could see this doctor of yours—"

"I'm going to get Dean," Evan interrupts.

"From his grandmother? From Tracy's mother?"

"Yes. So if you'll please excuse me . . . Stay as long as you like." Evan starts to leave.

"We can drive you," Louise offers. "Carl. We can drive Evan, can't we?"

"I suppose we have to," Carl says, rousting himself from the couch.

"No," Evan says. He glances out the front window. No car yet. Damn. He really has to go.

"Well, you can't very well drive yourself," Carl says sternly. "Not in your condition."

"I'm not driving myself, I called a car."

"We can save you the carfare," Louise pipes in.

"No, Mom," Evan groans. "Dean is in some trouble and I don't want you two around. It's nothing personal." Or is it?

"What kind of trouble?" Louise asks.

Evan roars in frustration. "What part do you want to know about, Mom? The fact that his grandfather who beats him has just moved back into the house, or that he was picked up last night for possession of marijuana?"

"Tracy's father? . . ."

"Yes. He's a child-abuser. I have to go get Dean."

"Well, your father—"

"No."

"What about this marijuana?" Carl asks.

"Yes," Louise says, "does he have an addiction? Is this an ongoing thing? Maybe he should be in treatment. Your father knows many doctors who could help—"

"Mom!" Evan snaps. "It wasn't his pot. It was mine. He stole my pot to show his friends. He's never smoked pot before, he told me."

"*Your* marijuana?" Louise takes an involuntary step back, horrified by this news.

Evan throws up his good hand.

"Oh, Jesus Christ, Mom, you know I smoke pot. I've been smoking it for years."

She holds her hand over her mouth, her eyes wide, looking at Evan in such shock.

"Dad, tell her, for Christ's sake. I take it for seizures, Mom. I know you guys know about this. Dr. Melon is a New Age marijuana neurologist. Dad, you know. Everyone knows. Why do I have to deal with this now? I have to go get Dean."

Evan looks to his father in a plea for sanity, but Carl rebuffs him, takes the opportunity to stick it to Evan, lowers his eyes and doesn't say a word. A little dig at his own son. You can't miss Carl's son; he's the one twisting in the wind.

But Evan knows that his parents know. They have to know. Carl, at least, has to know. He knows every doctor in Seattle. He even endorsed Evan's switching to Dr. Melon. Certainly, Carl knows about Dr. Melon's medicine of choice.

Evan looks again to his mother, who's a quivering mass of near-tears, shaking, trembling at this unexpected news—that not only is her son a pathetic epileptic with a broken collarbone and a hidden fourteen-year-old son, but that he's a chronic substance-abuser to boot. It's too much for her.

He glances toward the door. The car has arrived, thank God.

"Look, I have to go get Dean. The car is waiting."

"Evan," Carl says calmly but forcefully as Evan starts out, "before you go."

Before you go. There's always something, isn't there?

"In light of all these recent events, your seizure—which carries with it an automatic license suspension—"

"I know, Dad. Dr. Melon has already suspended it."

"Yes, well, with your car being totaled, and now this revelation that Dean has been arrested on possession and that you smoke marijuana regularly . . ."

"What's your point, Dad?"

"I believe that we should revisit our earlier proposal that you and Dean move in with us. I don't know what your relationship is with this girl of yours, but from what I gather, she's very successful in her job. I'm sure she doesn't want to spend her days looking after a fourteen-year-old boy."

"*I'm* looking after the fourteen-year-old boy, Dad. He's my son."

Carl makes a face. He looks to Louise, who's snapped out of her funk and is now glaring at Evan.

"I don't see any other way," she says. "No other way."

"You guys don't change, do you?" Evan asks. "I don't need you to fix it. All you do is try to fix everything in my life. But I don't need you to fix it. What I need is your support, your faith. I need you to *help* me. I don't need you to *fix* me."

"We raised you," Louise says.

"What does *that* have to do with it?"

"She's right," Carl agrees.

"She's right about what? You get to run my life because you raised me? That's bullshit."

"That's a shitty thing to say to your mother," Carl barks.

"But it's not a shitty thing to say to you, is it, Dad? Because you know that it's true."

"Now you listen—"

"No, *you* listen! I'm leaving now to get Dean!"

He storms toward the door.

"Any concern for your collarbone?" Carl shouts after him. "They want to insert screws—but you have no concern about that, do you?"

"No concern."

"How about your blood levels? Any thoughts about seeing your neurologist? Or *any* neurologist for that matter?"

"Nope."

Carl nods slowly, angrily, chewing his lip. Evan reaches for the doorknob.

"Are you trying to kill yourself?" Carl asks.

Evan stops, hand on knob, and turns to face his father.

"Hey, Dad," Evan says sweetly, "see this? This is the front door. Be sure to close it on your way out."

Carl seethes.

"I hope your son never treats you like you've treated me," he hisses.

"My son won't treat me like that because I haven't treated him like you've treated me," Evan fires back.

"You haven't treated him like anything at all, have you, Evan? True to your colors. You back off and let someone else raise him, then step in when all is said and done. If it doesn't work out, whose fault is it, Evan? Not yours, I guess."

"Hey, Dad, let me show you something," Evan says, taunting. "See this? This is the front door—"

Carl rushes to Evan and sticks a finger in his face. At last, a reaction!

"Listen to me, you little shit—"

"Carl!" Louise shouts. "Evan! Stop fighting, right now."

"We aren't fighting, Mom. Dad is just trying to explain to me why it's my fault that my life is worthless."

"You make your own choices," Carl mutters.

"Like epilepsy was my choice," Evan snaps.

"You ran into the street!" Carl shouts. "You ran into the street, that was your choice. It's too bad you have the personality of a daredevil, Evan, but you do, and you ran into the street because you thought nothing could hurt you. You never thought anything could hurt you."

"I ran into the street for Charlie!"

"You made the choice—"

"I ran into the street for Charlie!" Evan yells again.

"You learned your lesson, didn't you. A perfectly good life you had, and you threw it in the gutter, didn't you. Almost out of spite, I think sometimes."

"Fuck you."

"Yes! Out of spite."

"Yes, Dad, out of spite! Out of spite for you. Because I hated you. I never wanted to be a doctor. I gave myself epilepsy so I wouldn't have to be the son you wanted me to be."

"You were never going to be a doctor, Evan. Never. You're too selfish. You don't have empathy."

"Goddamn you! Goddamn you, Dad! I have so much empathy, I *bleed* empathy. It's you who doesn't have any empathy. It's funny that the world's greatest heart surgeon doesn't even have a heart!"

"Oh my God," Louise shrieks. "Would you two stop?"

They both look at her.

"Stop it! Stop it! We'll leave, Evan. Is that what you want? We'll leave. Just stop fighting."

Evan is suddenly struck by all of this, all of the yelling. He turns away from his father, walks absently into the living room and drops down on the couch. He stares blankly at the lifeless TV.

He didn't want to act this way toward his parents. He didn't want to fight. After the gig, talking with Mica, it was all so clear: do not blame other people for being themselves, you will only be frustrated by it.

But he couldn't help himself. He let them draw him into a fight. He let them get to him. Why? Why couldn't he have just walked away?

There's too much, too many years for it to happen easily, he guesses. It will take a lot of time. With Mica and Dean he can change his story, because they hardly know him. But with his parents, it will take years. It may never happen.

"Carl," Louise says, "let's go."

"No—"

"Carl!" Louise says more firmly.

Carl takes a few hesitant steps toward Evan, aware, perhaps, that something has just happened. Sensing that, in an instant, their entire family has changed.

"Can I take a look at your collarbone?" he asks Evan gently.

"No," Evan answers.

"Evan—"

"No," Evan repeats. He looks up at his father. "No. There's nothing for you to fix here. I don't even know why you're still here."

"Because we're your parents," Louise says. "That's what parents are supposed to do. We're supposed to be here when everyone else has gone."

Evan doesn't reply. He returns his gaze to the dark TV, afraid they might see his face.

After a moment of silence, Carl nods, his head heavy. He turns and motions to Louise, who, dismayed, walks to the door. They hesitate a moment, perhaps hoping for a reprieve. And then they leave.

AS THE BLACK car creeps along the highway, Evan leans back and fails to relax; there is too much fight ahead of him to relax.

He takes out his cell phone and tries Ellen's number; he's startled when she answers.

"It's Evan," he says.

"Evan," Ellen replies cheerfully. "How are you?"

"Tell me Frank hasn't beaten Dean yet, Ellen. Because if he has, I will personally murder you both, and I'm quite serious about that."

"Frank?"

"If he's raised a fingernail against Dean, I will make sure I arrive with squad cars. Tell me Dean's all right."

"He's fine, but—"

"Then why the hell did you bring Frank back!" Evan shouts. "You told me you'd never let Frank near Dean! Why the hell is he back?"

"Evan, he—"

"There is no possible explanation that will satisfy me. I'm on my way to Walla Walla right now and I'm taking Dean back to Seattle. We'll stay as long as it takes to clear up the marijuana possession charges, but then we're leaving and that's the end of it. I can't believe you would do this to Dean!"

"Evan, Frank isn't here."

"Well, not right now he isn't. But he's *there*, believe me. I know."

"How do you know, Evan?" Ellen asks.

"Dean told me."

"I see. Well, Evan, Frank *was* here, that's true. He came by two days ago to pick up the rest of his things. He was here for several hours loading some furniture into a pickup truck. Then he left. He's never coming back. I don't know what Dean could have seen that would make him believe Frank was staying here, but he isn't, I assure you."

"But I thought—"

"He *isn't*, Evan. I assure you."

Oh, man. Could Dean have gotten it wrong? Could he have misinterpreted something?

"I'm sorry," Evan says. "My mistake."

"And what's this about marijuana possession charges?"

"Well, that I *know* is true. Dean called me from the police station. He was arrested."

"He wasn't *arrested*, Evan. I swear, I don't know where he's getting these stories. He was *detained*. For loitering. In the parking lot of a 7-Eleven."

There you go with the 7-Eleven again.

"But there *was* marijuana, right?" Evan asks. Now he really doesn't know *who* to trust.

"Yes, there was."

"See!"

"They found a bag in the garbage bin. The police don't believe it came from the boys because there was so much, and apparently it's not the type they see on the streets around here. I'm not much of a marijuana expert. They believe it was only a coincidence: the boys may have unwittingly stumbled onto a drug deal and frightened the culprits who dumped their marijuana in the garbage to escape."

Thank God the cops didn't put the puzzle together differently. Obviously *Dean* stashed the pot in the Dumpster before he was caught. Clever kid

"So there's no arrest?" he asks.

"No."

"And Frank isn't threatening to beat him to death?"

"No."

"So I drove all night across the state, had a seizure and drove into a telephone pole for nothing?"

"Oh my! What happened?"

"I had a small accident."

"Are you all right?" she asks.

"I'll survive."

"Well, Dean misses you tremendously; he talks about you all the time. He's spent most of his time in his room."

"Really?"

"Yes. And he's made his Christmas list. He would like a guitar and some lessons, he told me. What do you make of that?"

Yes. What does he make of that?

He looks out the window of the speeding car. Outside it is vast and dry. Hillier than he'd remembered; hills that roll about playfully on both sides of the highway. He notices a marshy area and a large man-made lake, the back end of a reclamation project. There are farms and farmers, trucks and tractors, and irrigation systems with giant wheels that drive watering pipes around a central hub. There are fields of fruit which soon change over to fields of grain. There are fields of lazy cows and fields of galloping horses. Fields of futuristic windmills, whipping their blades around to provide even more electricity for the surrounding communities. There are road-side towns that look like they belong in a different age altogether. There are rivers that rush up to the highway and run alongside it for a little while, like a friendly dog, only to veer away quickly. There are children riding dirt bikes through a makeshift BMX course on the side of a hill. There is the road, relentless and sure, flicking its yellow tongue quickly before them, smelling its way to their destination.

EVAN GETS OUT of the car and feels the brilliantly hot air quickly attach itself to his skin. One hundred three degrees in Walla Walla, ladies and gentlemen. One-oh-three. The sidewalk seems to grab Evan's shoes as he walks. Each time he lifts a foot he hears a sticky sound, like peeling a label of a jar. It's so hot, the streets are melting.

Evan's shoulder hurts whenever he takes a breath. He wishes he had gotten some pain pills from the doctor. He steps up on the porch and rings the doorbell. After a moment, Ellen appears behind the screen. When she sees him, her look changes to concern.

"You poor boy," she says. "Dean's around back"

Evan nods and starts off the porch.

"Will you stay for dinner, Evan?" Ellen asks.

Evan is startled by the question; then he considers it for what it is.

"Yes, thanks," he replies.

He steps down onto the walk.

"You're welcome to stay the night if you like."

"We'll see. Thank you, Mrs. Smith."

"Will you be taking Dean with you?"

Evan turns and looks up at her. He can't tell if she asked with a hint of hope in her voice.

He nods at her slightly. And she nods back more vigorously. She wipes her hands on her apron.

"A boy needs his father more than he needs his grandmother," she says, and she fades into the darkness of the house.

He hears something, a strange squeaking noise. *Squeak, squeak.* Like bedsprings. Someone bouncing on a bed.

As he rounds the corner of the house, he can see into the back-yard, and there he is. The Boy Wonder. Tossing a baseball into a springy net backstop that tosses the ball back to him. *Squeak, squeak, squeak.*

Evan opens the gate and approaches cautiously. Dean doesn't notice him until he's only a few feet away. When he does see him, he catches the ball and looks quizzically at Evan.

"What happened to your arm?"

"I—" He stops. How does he answer? "I broke my collarbone."

A half answer at best.

"How?" Dean asks.

What can he say? How can he tell Dean that he drove into a telephone pole, knowing full well that Dean's mother died less than a month ago in a high-speed automobile collision?

Dean senses Evan's reluctance.

"You crashed your car, didn't you?" Dean asks. "You can say it."

"I crashed my car."

Dean nods and throws his ball into the backstop.

"I was driving over from Seattle and I crashed."

Dean catches the ball and throws it again.

"I'm sorry," Evan says.

Dean shrugs, catches and throws the ball.

"Did you have any trouble with Frank?" Evan asks.

Dean catches the ball and eyes Evan suspiciously.

"Grandma made him go away," he says. "He won't be back."

"Oh, that's good. What about the pot thing?"

"I guess they let me go or something."

"Oh, yeah? Do you think they'll give me my pot back?"

Dean cracks a smile, but doesn't share it with Evan.

"Can I play?" Evan asks.

"Sure," Dean says. He removes his glove and hands it to Evan with the ball in the webbing. Evan takes it with his good hand. "Knock yourself out."

He walks away and sits on the porch steps.

That wasn't exactly what Evan had in mind by play. He follows Dean to the porch.

"Look, Dean," he says, "you didn't have to have an emergency to get me here."

"What are you talking about?"

"I was coming anyway, you know."

"What do you mean?"

"I was already on my way. You didn't need to be in trouble to get me here."

No response. They're silent.

"Somebody made an offer on my apartment," Evan says after a moment. "I'd have to talk to your grandmother about this, but do you really have to live either here or in Yakima?"

Dean shrugs.

"Because I was thinking, you could sell your mom's house in Yakima, I could sell my apartment, and then maybe we could get a little place near Green Lake or something. Nothing big. The schools are good around there, and we could get a windsurfer or something. They have a ton of soccer teams there. And I'm sure *someone* plays street hockey, right?"

Nothing.

"It doesn't have to be a parent-kid thing. We could write down rules. We'd both abide by them. You know. It would be like a partnership thing."

"What about Grandma?"

"Well, we can talk to her. Maybe she'd want to move back to Seattle. You know, she lived there when your mother was growing up. She might not even like Walla Walla."

"She hates it."

"See? Or we can make sure to get a house with an extra bedroom so she could visit whenever she wanted. We can figure something out."

Dean studies the palm of his hand for a moment.

"So now you want me again?" he asks.

"Dean, I've got to be honest. I got scared. I got really scared that I would ruin you, you know? That I would make all the wrong decisions and say all the wrong stuff. When you tried to push me away, I let you do it, like I let your mom do it a long time ago. Instead of thinking about it a minute, I threw it back in your face. And when I hit you, it scared the shit out of me, honestly. I panicked."

Dean doesn't respond, but he switches hands and studies the other palm.

"People make up stories about themselves, Dean," Evan says. "They tell themselves stories, and then they try to make those stories come true. Sometimes the stories are good, but sometimes people make up bad stories about themselves because maybe someone told them something once and they believed it. It's easy to believe, Dean."

Dean nods at his feet.

"But you can change the story. You can take a bad story and make it good and try to fulfill it, take responsibility for it, and then nobody can do anything to hurt you unless you let them."

They sit for several minutes thinking about what Evan has said, and about the sky and the brown grass in the backyard, about the dilapidated fence at the end of the yard that needs replacing or at least painting, about the man across the yard who's shingling his house with a rhythmic banging that teaches an elementary lesson in physics: light travels faster than sound. What he's said sounds a little ridiculous, a little simplistic, a little moralistic. But it makes sense, especially to a fourteen-year-old. Which is what Evan is. Which is why he can relate.

"So, what do you think?" Evan asks. "You want to rewrite our story?"

Dean shrugs a nod at him, again, not meeting eyes, again not speaking, just reaching down and pulling at his shoelace, tucking a small stone into an eyelet.

I feel like I've failed you.

No, Dad, you haven't failed me.

"I'll start," Evan says. "I have epilepsy. Did your mother ever tell you that?"

Dean shakes his head no.

"Do you know what epilepsy is?"

I feel like I've failed you.

Dean starts to nod, then shrugs, then pulls at his shoelace again. Evan holds up his wrist.

You haven't failed me, Dad. But my head is broken and you can't fix it. Nobody can fix it.

"This is my Medic Alert bracelet," he says. "There's a telephone number on it that you can call . . ."

Dean glances at the bracelet, then looks at Evan, who is struck by his eyes, glowing at him like giant emeralds. And his ears. And his cheeks and his mouth. His hands and arms. He is Evan. He is Evan incarnate. Evan made him.

Dad, Mom, Brother. You haven't failed me. But you have all grown up. You have all grown old. And I'm still the same. I'm still fourteen-years-old. And I'm just now waking up.

ACKNOWLEDGMENTS

Lori Ames, Kristen Bearse, Tina Bennett, Bryan Devendorf, Yale Fergang, John Field, Douglas Fleming, Muffy Flouret, Wallace Gray, Tom Hobson, Lynn Hoffman, Ted Houghton, Laura Hruska, Soyon Im, Juris Jurjevics, Douglas Katz, David Katzenberg, Peter Kenney, Roy Kimbrell, Dena Jo Klingler, Jennifer Lager, J.R. Lankford, Ailen Lujo, Amy Lumet, David Massengill, Richard Morris, Scott Morrison, Arash Nadershahi, Len Nahajski, Joel Nichols, Kevin O'Brien, Sandy and Stephen Perlbinder, Janet Rumble, Astrid Sabella Rosa, Paula Schaap, Corey Stein, Marvin and Yolanda Stein, Liane Thomas, Doug Thompson, Terry Tirrell, Andrea Vitalich, Jonathan Wald . . .

Caleb and Eamon

and, in all dimensions, throughout all time,

Drella